Police, and with the release of her debut novel she hangs up the gun for the pen.

Pull of the Yew Tree

Book 1: The Chronicles of Crom Abu

Pauline Toohey

Indigo Dreams Publishing

First Edition: Pull of the Yew Tree

First published in Great Britain in 2013 by:
Indigo Dreams Publishing Ltd
132 Hinckley Road
Stoney Stanton
Leics
LE9 4LN
www.indigodreams.co.uk

Pauline Toohey has asserted her right under the Copyright, Designs and Patents Act 1988 to be identified as the author of this work.

©2013 Pauline Toohey

ISBN 978-1-907401-72-5

British Library Cataloguing in Publication Data. A CIP record for this book can be obtained from the British Library.

This book is sold subject to the condition that it shall not, by way of trade or otherwise, be lent, re-sold, hired out, or otherwise circulated without the author's and publisher's prior consent in any form of binding or cover other than that in which it is published and without a similar condition including this condition being imposed on the subsequent purchaser.

Designed and typeset in Minion Pro by Indigo Dreams.

Cover design by Ronnie Goodyer at Indigo Dreams

To Jo

For your drive and patience, all my thanks.

Look in thy glass, and tell the face thou viewest
Now is the time that face should form another

Sonnet III, Shakespeare

Pull of the Yew Tree

Cast of Characters

Fitzgerald Family

Anne Fitzgerald:	*daughter of Earl Thomas* *
Donal Fitzgerald:	*cousin of Earl Thomas*
Eleanor Fitzgerald:	*daughter of Earl Thomas* *
Gerald Fitzgerald:	*eldest son of Earl Thomas* *
James Fitzgerald:	*son of Earl Thomas* *
Jarlath Fitzgerald:	*nephew of Earl Thomas and nephew of Esmond O'Toole*
Joan Fitzgerald:	*Countess of Kildare, wife of Earl Thomas* *
Maurice Fitzgerald:	*son of Earl Thomas* *
Thomas Fitzgerald:	*7th Earl of Kildare, Justiciar of Ireland* *
Tom Fitzgerald:	*son of Earl Thomas* *

O'Byrne Family

Ainnir O'Byrne:	*daughter of Hugh O'Byrne*
Bradan O'Byrne:	*son of Hugh O'Byrne*
Brigid O'Byrne:	*wife of Hugh O'Byrne*
Eamonn O'Byrne:	*eldest son of Hugh O'Byrne*
Hugh O'Byrne:	*Gaelic Chieftain of Wicklow* *

Eustace Family

Manus Eustace:	*nephew of the Baron Roland Eustace*
Roland Eustace:	*Baron of Portlester* *

Abbess:	*Abbess of Achad-Finglass*
Barnwell, Barnaby:	*nobleman of Meath* *
Baron, Robert:	*nobleman of Howth* *
Bellew, Richard:	*nobleman of Louth* *
Claire:	*daughter of Glendalough's blacksmith*
Dowdal, Robert:	*nobleman of Dublin* *
D'Anjou, Marguerite:	*wife of the Lancastrian, King Henry* *
Edward IV:	*King of England* *
Ferghal:	*blacksmith of Glendalough*
George, Duke of Clarence:	*brother of King Edward* *
Henry of Lancaster:	*deposed King of England* *
Milewater, John:	*retainer to the Duke of Gloucester* *
Muirne:	*nurse to the children of Hugh O'Byrne*
Neville, Richard:	*Earl of Warwick* *
O'Kavanagh, Lochlann:	*Gaelic boy of Wicklow*
O'Kavanagh, Maeve:	*Gaelic girl of Wicklow*
O'Toole, Esmond:	*Gaelic Chieftain of Wicklow* *
Plunkett, Alexander:	*nobleman of Meath* *
Plunkett, Edward:	*nobleman of Meath* *
Richard, Duke of Gloucester:	*brother of King Edward* *
Taaf, Lawrence:	*mayor of Drogheda* *
Tiptoft, John:	*past Lord High Treasurer of Ireland* *
Ussher, Arland:	*mayor of Dublin* *

Those marked * are recorded in history

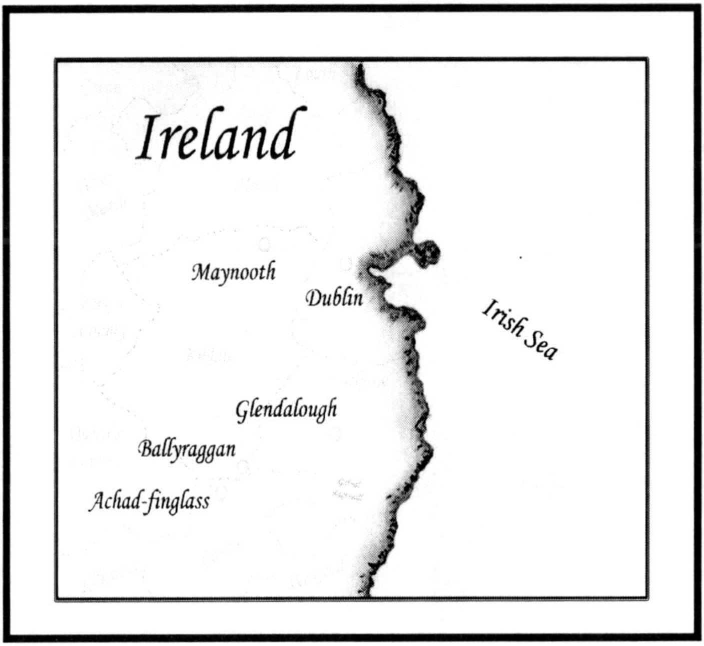
Ireland
Maynooth
Dublin
Irish Sea
Glendalough
Ballyraggan
Achad-finglass

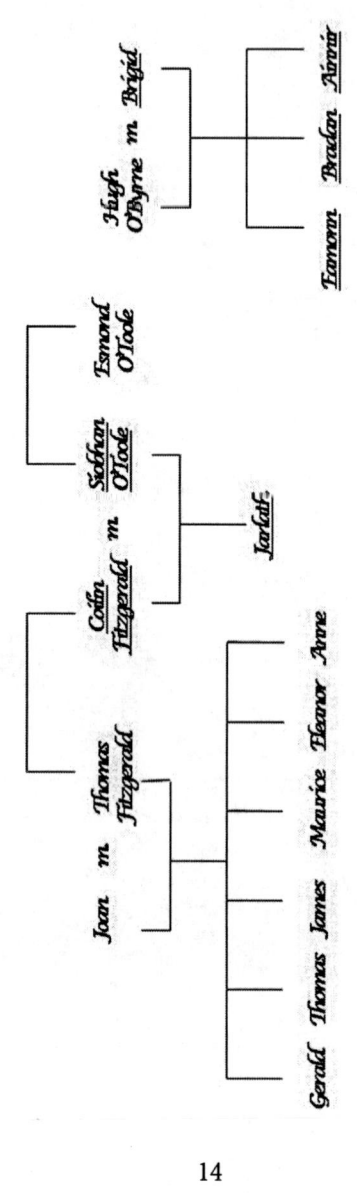

```
                                                                    Hugh
                                                                  O'Byrne  m  Brígid
                                                                    ┌─────────┼─────────┐
                                                                 Éamonn   Bradan   Aróirí

              ┌──────────────────────────┬──────────────┐
                                      Colin                Esmond
          Thomas                    Fitzgerald  m  Siobhan  O'Toole
         Fitzgerald                                O'Toole
Joan  m                                    │
                                        Iarlaf?
    ┌────────┬────────┬────────┬────────┬────────┐
 Gerald  Thomas  James  Maurice  Eleanor  Anne
```

Denotes fictitious

Part One

Prologue

County Kildare – Ireland

The nephew speaks..........

Although many years now mark the passing of time, my memory of the long ago does neither blur nor falter. For me, it is as if only yesterday. For me, on that night, no wiser words were ever uttered.

I was only five years of age, had seen too few summers for sensibility and care, and chased too many adventures for concern. I did not mean for the stable to catch alight. It was a mishap, a blunder, a regrettable slight which could have been avoided if I had thought better.

But I did not.

The tiny mewing kittens born only hours earlier to the stable cat were far more captivating than practicalities and diligence. Recollecting the name of the new mother brings much laughter for its absurdity. Arthur. Arthur was the name I granted the well-loved feline. A name obviously given at a time before I came to know her well, but a fitting name all the same for she fought other cats valiantly, like King Arthur of legend.

Excitement and gentle mewing had stolen my attention from the peril stirring. My ears did not catch the spitting sparks or the dim squeal of mice. My nose did not recognise the smoke chasing escape through splintered walls. It was the thudding hooves of panicked horses which brought me to my senses and it was then I realised my midnight adventure had plummeted into disaster.

The creeping flames shed eerie fingers of light. They climbed and withdrew, shifted and vanished. An acrid stench set my nose twitching, and coughing came in uneasy gasps.

Of a sudden, hands snatched roughly at my small body. Turned upside down my world fell askew and I bounced on my rescuer's hip as his steps took me away from the danger. Without warning, the strong calloused hands dropped me to the ground. Dust stirred like a troubled cloud. A moan escaped my mouth and a burning ache at my elbow told me just how heavily I had landed.

My ache forgotten, I looked up. What seemed hundreds of legs rushed in a squall of organised chaos. Heavy pails moved so hurriedly that much of the needed water sloshed to the ground. From a distance, I caught sight of the toppled lantern. My lantern.

To run and hide was all I could think to do. It was all I ever knew to do.

And so, I did.

From the safety of my tree, my yew tree, I turned back to the castle, and watched whirling spirals of grey rise high above the outer bailey walls. I knew that servants, villagers, men-at-arms and captains alike worked at an unholy pace. The cacophony of voices contended with the fire's crackle, and like winter sleet, flew across the night air singeing my guilt at every syllable, every curse, every yelled order.

Some hours passed and the coming morning began to

soften the black sky. Donal found me. Donal always did, no matter where I huddled. It happened time upon time, and too often I felt it an uncanny ability. Uncanny, yet not so strange to qualify him a sorcerer as he frequently claimed, for I was not so dim-witted even at that young age to believe there be truth to such an assertion, no matter how much appeal the claim begged.

Time has taught me Donal simply knew I would be in my yew tree. How could he not? It was the place to which I often fled. A place not so far I would fret overly much in the dark, yet of sufficient distance to feel removed from the great hall, from worry or pain. It was also a place to run from myself.

I did not acknowledge Donal's presence.

With a nail plucked from my pocket, I traced my initials, *JF,* crude lettering carved into the thick trunk, an inscription that remains visible to this day. I presumed Donal knew I wept. He did not yell, nor did he tease. He simply climbed and sat on a branch a little lower than my own.

'Thomas sent me to find you, Jarlath. He is worried,' he said.

His usual perfunctory tone held a measure of sympathy, and a miniscule of relief flickered within me, for it was not what I expected to hear. Tethered and dragged back to the castle, kicking and screaming to face an embarrassing inquisition was foremost on my list of predictions.

'The horses are safe. The fire is out. There's just a smouldering pile now.'

Again, I heard that semblance of sympathy. I did not respond but was glad, for the news could have been far worse, devastating even.

'And Arthur and her kittens, they're safe too. I've placed them in the kitchen's alcove,' he added.

In shame, I chewed at my lip. I had forgotten Arthur in my self-pitying escape. I remember looking down, my tear-filled eyes giving voiceless thanks. Donal could not see, I am sure of it, for the receding night still held a presence. I now wish he had. I now wish many things.

'You have to stop running. Every time something goes wrong you run.'

I found my voice. 'I do not!'

'You do,' he countered. 'You ran when your father died, you ran when Thomas was angered over the spilt milk tanks, you ran when the village lads called you a bastard's spawn and a half breed. And now, here you are, running again, all because you refuse to face life's misfortunes. As sure as the sun rises in the east, you run, Jarlath. There will come a day you must make it rise in the west. Make the impossible happen.'

My face fixed upon the drifting smoke above the castle walls as I searched for a retort, one which would not betray my ignorance, for the meaning of Donal's words was lost to me. *Sunrises and making the impossible happen?* What did it all mean? It was a question I pondered for some time. I decided a modicum of honesty seemed the best option.

'I get frightened, 'tis all, and I don't want anyone to see me cry.' What more could I say after listening to the inventory of what had passed? It was all true, every painful charge. It had always been easier to flee to my tree and avoid any sort of emotion than to stand and feel its full fury. Even happiness at times was too overwhelming, a puzzling sentiment of sorts threatening to uproot my staid existence.

'Do you not think we all get frightened? Do you not think we all cry?' Donal's voice was calm, almost rueful, not what one would expect from an older boy, one verging on manhood.

'You don't.' Quick words revealed my envy. I believed him brave and reckless, bold and daring, unlike myself. Nothing ever bothered Donal.

From the lower branch of my tree, Donal's hazel eyes looked up to me. Even in the shadows, I knew they fixed upon my own.

'Let me tell you, Jarlath, you are wrong. Truth has many faces and that is something you would do well not to forget. I do get scared and I do cry.' Donal pointed to the smoke. 'For your stupidity you may have to suffer the wrath of Thomas, but that is what being a man is all about. Face your fears and deal with them. You have to stop running, and you have to break ties with this tree.'

Donal was as persuasive as the Devil. Talking me down from the tree he took my hand, a gesture I believed not befitting my age, yet I was grateful all the same for the small offer of reassurance. I questioned Donal as to how he knew so much of the world.

'Because I am fifteen,' he replied.

As we walked back toward the castle's gatehouse Donal said with an air of nonchalance, 'That bit about me being frightened and crying, let's keep that our secret shall we?'

I took a moment to wonder whether everyone possessed their own yew tree, but gave no voice to my thinking. I nodded my answer.

And we did. We kept that secret.

But I continued to run. I continued to hide. I could tell

you how many branches that yew tree laboured during my youth, and how many wood-warblers nested in its arms each spring. It took me many a year to understand Donal's words of wisdom, and many a year to make my sun rise in the west.

Seasons have since lived and died, and sensibility and care now visit me from time to time, not as often as they should, and for that I have none to blame but myself. But that said, I have learnt some.

I am Jarlath Fitzgerald, nephew to the great Earl of Kildare, and born of both Irish nobility and Gael. How the impossible came to pass needs to be told.

Part Two

Chapter One

1470 – Wexford – Ireland

The rebels were in flight. The need for killing was done.

It was with a scowl that Thomas Fitzgerald, the 7th Earl of Kildare, watched the retreating backs of the Ormond ranks. Sitting high in the saddle, discomfort biting at every muscle, an unwelcome reminder that these forays grew more taxing with each year, Thomas lowered his sword, removed his helmet, and swiped at beads of sweat. Casting eyes to the sky, he squinted. The weather proffered a perfect day, an occasion more suited to picnics and romantic interludes, not the spilling of blood. The breeze whistling across the high cliff top from the Irish Sea amended the hot summer to a warm spring. It seemed a blissful setting. *How perverse,* he thought with little pleasure.

'Shall we give chase, my lord?' The interruption to his thoughts came from one of his harried captains.

'No.' A perfunctory order, but Thomas knew he need say no more. He was a man accustomed to obedience. Wind whipped at his long red hair painting mulish streaks across his cheeks. A raven cawed and Thomas followed its circled flight. The Earl knew his men wanted more blood, knew the sigh on the wind sang as a battle trumpet to his companions. No. He would not let it come to be.

'We have captives enough at our feet,' said Thomas. 'Let

the fleeing Ormonds skulk back to their pens and inform John Butler his raids found no victory here this day. They are naught but a bloody nuisance, for I can conjure nigh on a dozen ways to better entreat my time.'

One face with a toothless grin dared to laugh.

Thomas' regard brushed over the man with little attention.

'Impatience can be a regrettable transgression.' He put heels to his mount and moved amongst the dead.

In truth, Thomas wearied of John Butler and his southern rebels. It was arduous commission enough keeping the native Gaels at bay, maintaining a semblance of peace without Irish Lords lifting swords for their own ends. A troublesome quandary he endured, something akin to one pack of wolves lunging at his throat whilst he warily watched a second – a second that ran stride for stride at his side.

He looked to the leaders of that second pack, the Gaelic Wicklow Chieftains. The heavily bearded Hugh O'Byrne did little to disguise his glower of impatience, and, as expected, the thin-haired Esmond O'Toole, with an unsightly scar running from temple to chin pulling the corner of his eye down in a lewd wink, offered a look no less amiable. Thomas knew they too, heard the battle trumpet.

He would not give the order. The need for killing was done.

Bloodied bodies marred the green field like a macabre painting. Thomas silently cursed John Butler, the Earl of Ormond, marking his measure of courage most evident by his absence. He would give Christendom to meet that man on the field again and not proxies unworthy of his time. He turned his back on the dead and looked to the living. Thirteen rebels knelt at sword point. Their faces looked to his for a portent of what was to be their fate.

Thomas spat at the ground. 'Jesus wept.'

Unworthy seemed a bawdy joke. None were the Ormond Earl's captains, none his trained men-at-arms. These were young lads, all seen too few winters, untrained peasants and villagers, none of standing in their clan, their leathers and armour useless on the field of conflict.

Through clenched teeth and with dwindling control, Thomas began his victor's address. 'Men of Ormond, pathetic little men of Ormond, men who cannot begin to comprehend an Ireland joined in peace, your warring on these fields does naught to advance you, does naught to provide safety for your own people. It brings only death.'

Thomas suspended his words and gladdened in the impatient dance of his mount, an ally, a buoy to the remainder of his delivery. 'You are my countrymen. By place of birth, we are brothers not enemies.'

The Gaelic Chieftains looked to each other with unwelcome foresight. The O'Byrne urged his mount forward a pace. Then, sensing the alert of Thomas' captains to his movement, he stilled his anger and held tight to the reins.

'My offer to you,' Thomas continued, 'is to join my protection or forfeit your life.'

Silence. Eyes darted amongst the captors. Who would be the first to speak out? The O'Byrne signalled his order. Now was not the time to challenge the Earl's authority. There would be ample time for that later.

Yet Esmond O'Toole refused to heed the warning and

turned in almost noiseless protest, steered his mount away from the crowd, controlling his stallion's pace to a leisurely walk, a gait he could not impress upon his own sharp tongue. His scar twitched. 'Who will close their eyes tonight with Ormonds in our camp? I for one, will not.'

Thomas resisted the temptation to turn toward the stir. The O'Toole was a simmering cauldron, relentlessly bubbling, hissing steam with no respite. He would deal with the troublesome Chieftain another time.

Nods of agreement from the captured men bobbed like flotsam adrift on a wave. The lack of challenge, the lack of cursing, gave credence to Thomas' first suspicions. These men were simple villagers and children, not trained men. They held no allegiance to John Butler save for fear of ill favour. No, these men would be of no threat.

Thomas returned his sword to its sheath, averted his eyes to the sea and issued quiet orders to the two men at his side, his cousin and his nephew. 'See to the injured. You may war with me in private once we are gone from this place.'

Above, crows sounded their excitement.

Thomas moved his horse. 'And for the sake of Christ, see to the dead. Have the Ormonds bury their own.'

Donal Fitzgerald, all frown and sharp eyes, watched the retreating path of his cousin. He agreed with the Gaels, agreed thirteen more lives taken this day to be the cost required to serve a greater purpose. Nevertheless, Thomas was his Lord, his kin, and a man who earned great respect. It was not for Donal to challenge his orders.

He looked to the Ormond captives, then to Jarlath, the Earl's nephew. 'Thirteen. Does Thomas not know thirteen numbered those at the last supper? Tragedy ended that tale too.'

Jarlath grinned. 'You forget the Resurrection, Donal.'

'You have blood on your shirt. You are injured?'

'It's nothing.'

The captured were ordered to dig.

Accompanied by the O'Byrne and the O'Toole, Thomas led his men northward along the Barrow River to the Abbey of Achadfinglass in Idrone, only eight miles north of the destroyed uprising. The worn gates of the humble structure opened to the Earl with nigh a pause. Beyond the gates once stood a glorious Abbey founded by Saint Fintan. Its magnificent walls, razed to the ground six centuries earlier by the Danes, were rebuilt to resemble only a small share of their previous grandeur. Simple grey stone structures with rows of long corridors now stood in its stead.

Thomas reined in his mount before the Abbey's well. Young novices in soiled aprons, laden with wooden pails and digging tools, watched on curiously at the arriving men. Beds of leafy, green vegetables, dotted with the red and gold of summer fruits, lined the raised ground beyond. To the side, onion grass and woody sprigs of rosemary grew amongst curling vines, vines boasting an array of blossoms, a promise of a fruitful yield to come. The air was infused with the scent of herbs, a sweetness to Thomas' senses following long days in the saddle with no reprieve from grime and sweat.

The Abbess stood with hands on hips and chest pushed out. She was an intimidating sight. Despite the lack of colour in her garb, Thomas conjured a strutting peacock in his droll musing. Yet he had too often witnessed the Abbess' softer side, knew the peacock's showy plumes were mere pretence. This woman, short in stature, graciously rotund with a youthful complexion belying her aging years, was more turtledove.

'My lord, you have travelled far.' Hers was the voice of authority, not salutation.

Thomas swung from his saddle, closed the distance between them. He offered a playful grin. 'It is good to see you again, Abbess.'

Her thin lips stretched wide, and with the skirt of her homespun apron, the Abbess wiped at smudges of dirt on her pale cheeks and button nose. 'And you, Thomas. And the reason for your visit? I do hope it will be for a time.'

'Our Lord has seen fit I should once again impose upon your hospitality for short a time only.'

'I see you bring with you the O'Byrne and the O'Toole.'

'We make a fine display, something akin to your garden here. I would know what type of animal dung you use to keep harmony in such variety. I could use some.'

The Abbess' smile grew. She took Thomas by the arm, guided him away from inquisitive ears. 'I pray you bring good news. Too often bad tidings interrupt my day.'

Thomas spotted an overlooked smudge on the Abbess' forehead. His focus betrayed his find.

She flicked at her face, once, then twice, and finished with another wipe of her apron.

'Then I shall remain mute, unless you wish to hear of my children's latest escapades which brag of captured frogs and spider legs.'

'That will indeed be music to my ears.' The Abbess

stopped, looked to the Earl's eyes, wondered if his quest to bring peace to these lands still weighed heavily on his heart. His eyes gave away too much.

'And the true reason you come to my humble home? Have the Ormonds challenged you again?'

'It does not surprise you?'

'Nothing does these days.'

She looked back to the men, all patiently waiting for the private conversation to end, and noticed they indeed looked weary. 'If I am prepared to offer what you seek, will your men remain courteous?'

'I swear on my very soul.'

'And civil?' Another query with a gleam in her eyes.

'I cannot promise that of myself, for I have been labelled a wretch too often. But as for my men, I give you my word they are beyond reproach. But I would suggest you keep your distance from the overbearing, red-haired ogre behind me.'

The Abbess looked toward Thomas' muse, and gave a belated nod of welcome to Donal. 'How fares your cousin?'

'A little more time is needed for that wound to heal. It has been a twelve month since Elizabeth's passing.'

'A year is not long, Thomas.'

Thomas nodded his agreement. 'I will admit to bearing witness to some much-needed improvement. All praise to Our Lord, for Donal now speaks without a perpetual grunt, and, at the risk of appearing ungrateful to our merciful Lord, I still ask for more progress.'

'Christ carried the burden of His people.'

'Then perhaps some Blessed water from Saint Fintan's well would be of benefit. It may bring a measure of relief. And it is of course my own relief I speak of. For Donal seems insistent on my martyrdom.'

The Abbess laughed aloud. 'Then He has heard your prayers, for I have a small amount left. It was brought here from Kilmoylan last month. I will see to it after you are fed and rested. But your men look weary, Thomas. I see no need to have them tarry longer in the hot sun. Shall I begin?'

Thomas did not reply. He simply smiled, lowered his head and turned toward the men.

In a loud and demanding voice, the Abbess dictated her final instructions. 'By your promise, my lord Earl, you will receive my hospitality, and I pray to Our Lord God that all who follow you this day be resolute in their pledge of chivalry.'

'You have my word, and we are again in your debt, dear Abbess.' Thomas gave his riposte in an equally strident voice, and looked to his men with a menacing glare. Let any dare bring fear to those within these walls.

Donal rolled his eyes, for such inane theatrics had been played out before him time and again.

As the Abbess turned, giving instruction to the men and her novices, Donal's brow lifted. He caught what appeared to be a wink sent his way. He looked to Jarlath seeking witness and noted a smirk before an averting turn. He looked back toward Thomas and saw much the same.

He was right. His eyes did not fail him. For all her demeanour, the Abbess was a jester in disguise.

The steam beckoned. Thomas longed for the bath. Alone in the sparsely furnished room, he seated himself upon a thinly cushioned chair and removed his long boots. The effort caused him to pause and rest elbows on knees. He felt every one of his forty-five years and the solitude gave him opportunity to reflect on his own actions that day. So many orders, so many thrusts and parries of his sword, so much deafening noise and so much eerie silence. The vision of a frightened lad charging toward him on foot with dagger drawn came to mind – a red spreading to cover a thin doublet, eyes wide in horror comprehending his death was at hand. The lad was a boy, too young to be on the field, seen too few summers, too few birthdays. He was younger than his own son, Gerald. At fourteen years of age, his eldest child was vocal in his indignation, having been forbidden to ride with his father. Thomas knew that soon his son would join his side in battle. He could deny him no longer.

His frown altered to a smile. Gerald showed great promise; unshakable will, courage, enviable cunning – all traits of a great leader. He also possessed a tendency for self-aggrandisement.

Thomas often entertained his children with tales of the invasion of England by William, the Duke of Normandy. He spoke with great hauteur of the astonishing seventy mile journey across seas in one night to reach the shores of England. An army of one thousand longboats, seven thousand armed men, partially structured fort walls, and three thousand horses, all beached successfully at Pevensey. Gerald would intercede during these tales with boasts that he could have ferried twofold that number.

Yes, Thomas thought with pride, Gerald was almost a man, and it neared the time for him to ride at his side. But for now he was at home, safe, unlike so many on that field today. He sighed heavily. To have his children grow in a world where battle was a mere memory noted in the annals of history was a prayer he offered up every day to any Saint who would give their ear.

With a conciliatory grumble, he lifted himself from the seat and removed the remainder of his garments. Feet in first, he silently measured the tub's short girth. To lay back was going to prove an impossible feat. Thomas crammed in as best he could. A kingdom for the comforts of home. A tub large enough to stretch his weary legs and douse his body wholly in warm water would be a start. A point to remember – larger tubs as reward for the Abbess' hospitality. He would see to it when he returned home.

From behind, the chamber door swung open.

'Thomas.'

He closed his eyes to his name, disenchanted at the interruption to this small slice of peace. When finally he opened them again, he found Donal and Jarlath standing at the end of the tub with amused looks upon their faces.

'You put me in mind of a tavern whore's breasts in a too-small gown,' said Donal with no laughter to his voice.

Thomas knew to expect none. It had been too long since that sound was heard from Donal's mouth.

'Big breasts, Uncle,' added Jarlath, filling the room with the laughter that should have come.

Thomas joined in the mirth in spite of himself. 'I am sure you do not disturb me just for enjoyment. Is it to see to my bathing?' He threw a dripping cloth at the two men.

Donal was not quick enough. 'As much as I hate to disappoint you, cousin,' Donal began, wiping remnants of a well-aimed toss from his jacket, 'no, that is not why we are here. The O'Toole is ranting in the hall causing a stir. He preaches that your stayed hand is nothing short of blasphemous. I think it past time we douse the fire he sets.'

Thomas' grin died. He thought for a long moment. The O'Toole was an unrelenting impediment to his plans, a festering splinter. He wondered, with frustration, whether that man could be subjugated or controlled and he gave his reply with little pleasure. 'Then we delay our return home.'

Donal shrugged. 'You will hear no argument from me. I have no great need to be home, although I cannot speak for Jarlath. His harem may be none too pleased.' He turned and looked squarely to Jarlath. 'Enlighten your half-soaked uncle of our earlier conversation. What name does your current bed sport give you?'

Jarlath lowered his head with a slight shake. This was the third request this evening. He now regretted ever having opened his mouth. Yet he grinned. 'They call me, spectacular.' Jarlath delivered the humour well, hands on hips, shoulders straight and with a cocky beam.

'Hah!' said Thomas. 'That rouses more questions than it answers.'

Jarlath nodded with indifference. 'My harem can wait, Uncle.'

'Ah. Perhaps. But can you?' And as a challenge to providence, Thomas finished, 'Time will prove one way or the other.'

'And your plan?' asked Donal.

'We accompany the O'Byrne. A ride through the Wicklow Mountains.'

'An adventure? I'm willing,' Donal said with a dull whistle. 'It is past time we took the lad here into his mother's mountains, let him see for himself what we have spoken of for years.'

'Good,' said Thomas, satisfied. 'But for now, unless you wish to soap my back, I suggest you leave me to my peace. I'll join you shortly and see to the ranting myself.'

Thomas was left alone, the door slamming shut to the retreating voices.

'Ah, Joan,' he said aloud, thinking of his beautiful wife. 'If you were here now.'

His words trailed to thoughts. She would soothe his aches, clear his mind of heavy burdens, lap warm water over his tired body. *My Nimue,* he fondly called her – his Lady of the Lake, the enchanting Goddess and caregiver to the legendary knight, Lancelot. She had given him five children. How he longed to be home at Maynooth and savour her sweet scents, primrose on her fair skin, lavender and lilac in her hair, and feel the pinch of her tender hands kneading his aching muscles. Now with his new plans such pleasures would have to wait.

His manhood stirred pleasantly, forcing a grumble, or was it a heavy sigh? He smiled to himself, decided it best to endure a quick wash, and face the passionate conversations expected at the evening's meal, rather than endure the torturous passion now threatening to swallow him whole. He would be home soon enough and would speak to his wife of increasing their brood.

'At what occasion is harsh punishment to be served as warning, if not today?' The O'Toole shouted his ranting. 'Do we not kick a wolfhound if he ignores instruction? If not, I would be concerned that hound may learn to bite, and John Butler, the Ormond Earl, has sharp teeth.'

Thomas sat at the hall's table admiring a selection of roasted quail, baked partridge, a broth of stewed onions and gourd, and rough cuttings of cheeses rolled in garden herbs. He was vexed, undecided whether he should address the problem of hunger before the remonstrations of the O'Toole.

'He has a valid point, Thomas, delivered with a vicious voice, but nonetheless, valid.' Donal sat beside Thomas and pitched his verdict quietly as he too, eyed the food contemplating whether it was advisable at this point to best Thomas to the quail.

Thomas raised an eyebrow. 'Was it not you who ordered me from my tub to curb this man's tongue?'

'The O'Toole rants and raves. I never said his point to be wrong.'

Thomas fought the tugging lift of his lip. He was ever proud of his cousin. Donal's loyalty never swayed and he possessed sufficient gumption to remind him the opinions of the Irish were as varied as the colours in the summer skies following rain. Together they made for a seemly team and were alike in many ways; their red hair was of an identical shade, long faces rarely betraying emotion, noses misaligned – Thomas' more from failing to avoid a hefty punch than a hereditary trait – and both were given the name, Thomas.

Donal's mother was not fond of the name, and at a young age he came to be known by one more preferred. It was well she did choose this course for Thomas was a name too prevalent amongst the Fitzgeralds, a circumstance that caused hilarity and utter confusion. Now in his twenty-ninth year and widowed, Donal's grief made his counsel bitter in all circumstance. His wife had suffered overly long in the birthing chamber, and their infant son followed her path to Heaven.

Thomas remembered the weight of that grief. It sent Donal into the night and he did not return for two days. Thomas found his cousin kneeling in the Chapel with tears and shudders that refused to cease. Despite offers of comfort, Donal's was a grief that could not be shared.

But now was not the time for recalling past anguish. There was enough stirring in this hall. Thomas returned his attention to the present.

'And what would you have me do, O'Toole?' Thomas decided to address both hunger and remonstrations at the one time, and before continuing his reproof, gave time for narrow eyes to aim a sly glance of victory toward Donal whilst his eating knife speared the quail. 'Was not the death of more than twenty Irishmen enough for you on that field today? Do you think another thirteen would bring Butler to heel more readily, or have you forgotten more than four hundred dead Ormonds in Piltown eight years ago did naught for the same cause? And let us not forget the bodies we could not count, gorged by craven dogs or torn by carrion crows.'

'These uprisings will not cease until we strike hard to put an end to their festering. A swift sword is required, Kildare, a swift sword to a soft target.' The O'Toole's response encouraged shouts and whispers.

Thomas allowed the ministrations to continue for a time. His tongue may have stilled, his eyes did not. He watched the crowd, frowns and hand gestures evidence of the many opinions. His gaze wandered along the rustic table toward

Jarlath, who had turned in his seat, debating good-heartedly with his young companions, Eamonn and Bradan, the sons of Hugh O'Byrne.

Eamonn was a good lad, Thomas thought, respectful and disciplined. Bradan was just the opposite and followed in the O'Byrne's footsteps; stubborn, a mind of his own, preferring to remain indiscernibly wary of Irish Lords. Thomas silently acknowledged Jarlath had proved himself this week, had encouraged a measure of trust and friendship from these two young men, Bradan included. A plan well achieved; an achievement not expected.

'And what say you, young cubs?' Thomas brought the sounds of debate to an end. He waited for a response, watched as both the O'Byrne boys looked to their father for direction, and then returned his focus to Jarlath. Thomas smiled inwardly for he knew what loomed.

Thomas had been a constant presence in Jarlath's childhood, had raised him as his own following the passing of both parents. It was he who first taught the lad to conquer a bow during fowling, he who remedied his balance in the saddle after too many falls, and he who encouraged him to think of strategy and politics with a calm head. Jarlath's habits were as well known to Thomas as were his own. He could not help but pause for a moment and wonder at how much Jarlath was like the lad's dead father, his own brother Coilin; dark unruly hair, skin touched by the sun's pleasure, and cautiously private, a trait only a fool would interpret as compliant.

Jarlath cleared his throat. 'Your judgement, Uncle, will not be questioned by me now, nor in the future. I bend to your instruction. My heart desires peace for our lands, like yours. If you choose the road I will follow. Only a fool would do otherwise.'

'Thar Barr, Jarlath,' the Earl laughed throwing back his head, using the expression reminiscent of the unforgotten Gaelic of their lands, a use to raise the eyebrows of the Chieftains.

'Excellent, nephew, and very ... sobering.' Thomas laughed again.

Banter erupted around the room as the men returned to addressing their hunger.

Thomas leant toward Donal. 'We are strong with such offspring. I suspect Ireland has a bright future. In fact, I am sure of it.'

Donal flinched at the mention of offspring but salvaged his mood before his spirits lowered overly. 'Jarlath is certainly steadfast and good in judgement, and has become the man you are, Thomas.' It was said somewhat awkwardly, Donal no more comfortable with an exchange of sentiment than any other man.

Thomas clapped a hand upon Donal's shoulder. 'He is a credit to us both.'

There was pause.

'It may be so.' Donal shrugged. 'I fear he would follow us to the gates of Hell if we asked. He covered my back well today and those of some of your captains too. They look up to him. He holds his sword and his head well, does our Jarlath. And yes,' he added somewhat lighter in voice, 'I believe as do you, Ireland will soon be at peace, but not if you refuse to share some of that quail.'

With a snigger, Thomas passed Donal a small cutting of the bird's breast. 'Do not be fooled that his dramatic pledge was for my benefit.'

'You presume me daft?' Both men looked toward the O'Toole. 'Jarlath has taken advantage of every opportunity to test that man's patience, and he has good reason.'

'Yes, he does. That he does.' Thomas gave a nod – one slow movement.

'Do you think the O'Toole to be in need of a measure of appeasement? His hackles are still pointing to the sky.'

They both watched Esmond O'Toole's portrayal of self-importance as he continued to rage for the entertainment of those who chose to give him an ear.

'No,' answered Thomas, his voice low. 'He has enough scavenging seabirds to pacify his wayward mouth. He will find ample comfort in that flock, and in any event, it is only his own men who give his words any credence. No, for all his blustering he is of no concern. He makes far too much noise to be cunning. It is the O'Byrne we need watch. See?' Thomas nodded almost imperceptibly toward Hugh O'Byrne. 'See how he sits like a hawk, studying the commotion, measuring warring words, strengths, weaknesses? A deserving adversary, I give him due. A valuable ally and a precarious foe. A doubled sided coin.' Thomas took a mouthful of food, chewed slowly. 'Yet like most, the O'Byrne is self-serving. Perhaps self-serving enough that a sweetened bait will keep him to our way. We need these Gaels, Donal, need them as allies, not enemies.'

'And what bait do you have in mind?'

'That is something I have not yet figured.' Thomas raised his cup and swallowed deeply. 'Not yet, in any event.'

The ale flowed steadily, heated exchanges cooled, and the end of deliberations made room for merriment. The abbey was not the place for excesses usually the wont of these men, and it was to this that unsoiled tales were adequate on this occasion, the Earl of Kildare standing guarantee that the men would not overstep the mark of the Abbess' hospitality. Before too many hours passed, Thomas stood, raised his voice so all within the hall should hear.

'We shall not impose further on the hospitality of the Abbess and therefore shall depart at dawn.' Turning toward the O'Byrne, he continued. 'Your new home in Glendalough, O'Byrne, is but two days ride from here and I have a fancy to waylay my return to Maynooth and meet your lady wife and daughter. What say you?'

Hugh veiled his suspicion. The arduous ride through the forests and mountains of Wicklow would keep the Earl and his men from their own home for a lengthy period, and with that, he understood the meaning of this request. As sure as snow would fall in winter, Thomas Fitzgerald would soon rise to the position of Justiciar of Ireland, with an undertaking to bring all Gaels to compliance with English rule. Hugh was a target for that undertaking. He understood that no less than any other man in the room. But for all the warning asking to be heeded, Hugh knew Thomas' courting to be fortuitous. It served his own purpose, the opportunity Hugh had been long awaiting. To take back their lands in County Kildare!

To have Thomas distracted would serve only too well. Yes, indeed, he thought with certainty. The wily Chieftain looked forward to the game to be played out in Glendalough. A few days of hosting Kildare's men was not too great a cost for this charade. But caution would be needed.

'It would be my pleasure, Thomas, and my wife would lock me from her room if I said otherwise.'

Laughter filled the room and plans were agreed upon.

'So, you have decided on the bait?' Donal's query was almost a whisper.

'No, not as yet. Simply the place to set the trap.'

Chapter Two

Glendalough – Wicklow – Ireland

The sun sat high. Thin wisps of white cloud were the only intruders to the endless blue above. Lapwings and kestrels shared the camouflage of treetops, watching the busy meanderings of the village folk. Ferghal the smith, whistled a merry tune around his forge, matching the rhythmic sounds of incessant hammering.

Ainnir giggled quietly. She knew her maidservant worked hard to keep pace with her stride, dodging hissing geese and foraging pigs and ducking to avoid being struck by oversized bundles of lashed wood carried on high shoulders.

'Ainnir,' Muirne snapped, almost stumbling. 'I do not want to speak to the man. Not now.'

Ainnir looked to the smith. A shy grin indicated his pleasure at their approach. The whistling and hammering ceased. Steam billowed as a white-hot poker met with cold water.

'You cannot avoid Ferghal each time you venture outside the castle walls, Muirne.'

'And why not?'

'Love is a Blessing from God and should not be ignored.'

'And at your grand age you would have me believe you know of these things?'

'I am sixteen, not six.' Ainnir bit down on her bottom

lip trying to conceal her enjoyment at this game. If she was to be accused of interfering too often in the business of others, she would make sure there was good cause. 'He has seen us in any event and it would be rude not to offer our greetings.'

'It is not for you to decide who I should speak to, child.'

Child. When will Muirne think her otherwise? 'If I do not make the time –'

Muirne's mouth opened to argue.

Ainnir held one hand high. 'Your quarrelling does not become you.' The words were more a regular ode used by Muirne, lines habitually recited over the years, as expected and welcome and frequent as frost in winter. Sweet laughter escaped Ainnir's lips for Muirne threw a look as sharp as a dagger. 'And in any event, I have another purpose for our visit.' She waved a bunch of bluebells in the air before Muirne could say more.

'Claire,' Ainnir yelled toward the forge. 'I have a surprise for you.' She lifted the hem of her skirts and improved her stride.

Beside the smith's workshop, a small girl ran in circles with stick in hand drawing patterns in the dirt. Ferghal gave over a conspiratorial smile to Ainnir then moved to speak with Muirne. The maidservant's chastising frown vanished.

Ainnir found it somewhat amusing that only in the company of Ferghal did Muirne allow the role of nurse, caregiver, maidservant and protector to fall. At the playful touch of his hand to her elbow, she became the hesitant coquette, the timid flirt, the woman.

To Ainnir's mind, Ferghal was a handsome man – corded arms a sign of his trade, remarkable in height, and an eye which followed Muirne at every opportunity. He brought much trade to their village, his skill at the forge known far and wide.

He was called *Minoa* by some, reflective praise for his talent, for it was believed the people from the Minoan civilization were the first to craft the sword.

'I mould from passion,' Ferghal would say, wearing the compliment lightly. Now and again he admitted to his unique ability and confessed extraordinary attention was needed to bring precise balance to the fuller and the blade. Yet no matter his humility, each pommel bore an inscription; a penned pride giving no doubt as to the identity of the craftsman.

Ainnir's steps continued toward Claire. She knelt and handed the bunch of sweet-scented blossoms to the small girl. 'These are for you. I believe their colour to be the hue of your eyes. Are they not beautiful?'

Little Claire's face beamed, albeit hidden beneath smudges of dirt and a mop of tousled hair. Her lips parted in smile to reveal a gap between her front teeth. Her feet were shoeless and her clothing tattered, but the smile was pristine, the latter being a blessing, for not two years earlier Claire's mother had passed.

'Are they really the colour of my eyes?' Claire asked with a pretty grin.

'Yes, and they are magical too. May I tell you the story?'

Claire nodded quickly, touching her hands to the blossoms and followed with a sniff at their scent which at her tender age emerged very much like an indrawn gulp.

'Many years ago,' Ainnir began, 'a beautiful woman with the name Kathleen and eyes the glorious shade of purple, exactly like yours and just like these flowers, fell deeply in love with a monk. Kevin was the name he was known by. He lived in the caves along the shores of our lake. You know where I speak of, by the upper lake where your brothers fish?'

'And where you swim with your brothers?' Claire asked.

'Yes.' Ainnir lowered her voice. 'But do not tell Muirne for she says I am too grown to swim with Eamonn and Bradan.'

They shared a small giggle and Claire lifted fingers to her mouth, a promise she would keep Ainnir's secret.

'Alas, the monk could not return her love, for he chose to be one of God's servants. Kathleen's heart suffered greatly, and her tears and soul melted into the lake. None saw her again. But Kathleen returns each summer with the bluebells to search for her lost love, and as the summer fades and her failed search ends, so too, do the blossoms. They wither into the earth to wait out another cold winter before beginning their search yet again.'

'Truly?' Claire looked into the faces of the blossoms as if expectant of a sad Kathleen.

Ainnir laughed gently. 'Yes, truly.'

'But how can they see? Where are their eyes?'

'Ah. That is what makes them so magical. Now off you go, find a special place for them.'

Ainnir turned back to the true reason for her presence and heard Muirne bidding goodbye to Ferghal. 'We do not need to –'

'Keep walking, Ainnir,' Muirne chastised with a whisper, elbowing Ainnir toward the castle gates.

'Is something amiss?'

'Nothing. I simply do not wish that man to think I am ... well, easily won.'

'You, easily won? There is no chance of that.'

'Not one more word from you, do you hear?'

Ainnir laughed aloud and moved as instructed. The

nurse, caregiver, maidservant and protector had returned. She looked back to Ferghal, saw the disappointment in the shrug of his shoulders and offered him a cheeky smile.

'I do not understand you at times, Muirne. I cannot wait for my love to come along. I will embrace that love. It will be ungovernable and consume my heart. I will shout my happiness to the heights of our mountains and enjoy every skip of my breath. I will never, ever, avoid *his* company. If I were you –'

'And good it is then that you are not me. And who says my breath does not skip?'

'Muirne!' Ainnir stopped and turned. 'Your breath *does* skip then?'

Muirne ushered her forward again, pretending she heard not a word.

'Your silence says much. What does your foresight tell you? Is Ferghal holding your hand, twirling your hair? Are you to be together soon?'

'It is not for me to see my own future in visions. It is only for others that I can see any –' But Muirne got no further for shouts stilled her words.

'Riders!'

Twisting in his saddle, it seemed to Jarlath the mountains and vales would never end. He rode behind Thomas taking in the scent of cool, the sight of lush, the sound of silent trees. All felt as if familiar strangers. Here in County Wicklow, was the playground of his mother's childhood. Infinite greens, crooked lines of Crann Creathah trees, wandering branches of the dog rose bush, brilliant spikes of bluebell blossoms, masses of mushrooms sprouting from the rotting bases of fallen trees, and scurrying wildlife sharing chatter, warning of the intruders.

'We are here!' announced the O'Byrne.

The dense green opened to unveil an impressive stronghold standing in the distance – Castle Glendalough. Its outer lying fields boasted of a long ago settlement, with moss covered naves and crosses, fire pits and collapsed chimneys, and weathered tombstones, all speaking of the past. Village homes dotted the clearing and scents from skillets escaped thatched roofs. Rosemary wafted through the air, hinting of the day's meal. Older children herded stubborn pigs. Chickens squawked and geese hissed, men carried vats of ale to the castle's bailey. The younger boys took advantage of their reprieve from chores, the gentle thud of branches in swordplay standing in the stead of singing steel.

Further beyond stood unfinished castle walls busy with ladders and timber walkways. The narrow gaps at their height hinted at arrow slits and battlements to come. It was as the O'Byrne had said on their journey; he was rebuilding from ruins, making a secure home for his clan.

They rode beneath the gatehouse, through two stone arches, and reined in their mounts at the foot of the steps to the great hall. A variety of homecomings sat to all points of Jarlath's compass.

Hugh O'Byrne greeted his wife, Brigid, with little intimacy. Eamonn and Bradan followed behind, yet theirs seemed joyous. The O'Toole nodded to those standing at the steps then rode off toward the stables. Hugh's men enjoyed the push of the crowd. Young ones were pulled up into saddles, women wiped at tears, and the bold drew lovers into their embrace and kissed.

Thomas was his usual vocal self. 'Greetings to the beautiful wife of the O'Byrne.' His bellowing voice rang falsely, pretending an aged and cherished friendship. He dismounted and took the steps two at a time. 'It is a pleasure to make your acquaintance. I am –'

'The Earl of Kildare, I assume,' said Brigid, not unkindly.

'You assume correctly, madame.' Thomas dipped his head.

Brigid's regard quickly travelled the length of the Earl, revealing none of her thoughts. She offered a pleasant smile.

'Well then, my lord, welcome to our home.'

'I thank you.'

'See to the Earl's horse,' yelled Hugh.

A young woman ran into the open arms of Eamonn and Bradan with squeals of laughter.

'And this is our daughter, Ainnir, my lord.'

Eamonn and Bradan released hold of their sister.

She curtsied, a pretty movement. 'My lord.'

'As beautiful as your mother and a name to match,' Thomas said jovially.

From a short distance away, Jarlath stared. There were times in his life when he glimpsed something of the wonders of the Lord, but none such as now. The O'Byrne's daughter was impossibly beautiful. Her lips formed a brilliant smile and her eyes – her eyes held a vivid shade of he knew not what.

What a shame, he laughed to himself. Thomas would not appreciate any attempt to conquer that one. Perhaps if he offered to befriend the daughter, just as he was ordered to befriend the sons? Unlikely. A waste, he lamented greedily. And her eyes?

Not even the movement of his own mount jostling with the other horses could break the spell that seemed to imprison his thoughts. His stare did not falter.

'No! No! No! Do you mind?' The angry shouts in Gaelic dragged him from his daydreams.

'Whoa!' Jarlath gave a stern pull on the reins, ordering his horse away from a delicious looking barrel of apples and its owner.

'I apologise,' he said with sincerity.

'Much good that'll do!' The man spoke his rudeness in English.

'Are you asleep, Jarlath?' Donal gave a curt nod to his captain, instructions to compensate the angry merchant.

'My thoughts were elsewhere. Nothing more.'

'We are in Gael territory. Best you right that ailment.'

'Of course,' Jarlath replied with little interest. He turned his regard back to the young woman. What was the colour?

A fare fit for the welcome of an Earl adorned the tables. Venison pies with galytyne sauce, mushroom pasties, baked trout, and green salads with elderflowers were the first of many dishes to greet the guests. Hugh O'Byrne's favourite, pottage of spiced lamb, soon followed ushered in with hoots and hollers. He encouraged all to indulge. A hungry Thomas needed no more invitation.

Flickering rush lights illuminated the hall. Stories of the

uprising at Wexford and memories of long ago battles travelled the trestles. More savoury tastes replaced empty trenchers and the village minstrel entertained his audience with the lulling sounds of the cláirseach. The atmosphere was truly festive.

Jarlath's attention was fixed to the great table searching for an answer to his earlier question. Eyes did not catch. No answer came. The O'Byrne's daughter was dressed in a simple gown of grass-green satin, with orange coloured needlework at the neckline depicting an array of bog orchid blossoms. Long hair fell in loose plaits and a gold circlet, positioned elegantly at her forehead, kept stray wisps of honeyed-gold confined.

Jarlath watched on as her brothers spoke of their adventures from the past weeks. Ainnir seemed to hang rapturously on their every word, sighing at evocative recounts of the Irish Sea's roar and the endless stretches of white sands along the coast of Wexford, and then laughed at the conversations shared amongst the men as they rode through the hills of the Gabhal Raghnaill lands on their journey home. When the subject moved to the uprising and the dead, she remained awkwardly attentive, and furrows creased her brow.

It seemed more than just Jarlath noted her changed countenance. Unhappy to see their sister troubled, the brothers altered the tempo of the conversation, broke into jest and teased with stories of childish pranks played out at her expense years before. Peals of laughter flowed easily, which set a happy grin upon their mother's face. The bond between the four was unmistakable. Jarlath could not help but think such a scene was similar on many counts to that of his own home, with his uncle, his aunt, his cousins and Donal.

Of a sudden Ainnir's eyes wandered the room and came

to find his. Without any thought, his stare jumped away like a child caught with his fingers on a forbidden cake. He raised a mug to his lips with exaggerated flamboyance, pretending indifference. A quick look back found Ainnir staring his way. A small smile crept to her face. He returned the silent greeting.

His eye caught the O'Toole behind Ainnir, making his way to his seat. Esmond O'Toole wore a hooded frown. It was nothing more than a foreboding feeling, one Jarlath had learnt to ignore at his peril, and he kept his eye on the O'Toole, moved from his trestle to stand a short distance behind Thomas.

Thomas sat at the dais bantering with the O'Byrne. Their discussion of castle walls and village buildings sufficed for conversation as they ate. Thomas offered compliments at the speed in which Hugh was able to build a home from ruins.

'We Gaels are quick. Quicker than most,' said Hugh.

'You should take care, O'Byrne,' Thomas said with his mouth full. 'You are bearing the mark of an Englishman with your castle structures. Your portcullis and the battlements all sing too loudly of English persuasion.'

'English persuasion!' said the O'Toole.

Hugh ignored the comment from his side and twisted slightly in his chair, giving the O'Toole his back; an unspoken warning to curb his mouth. 'I see the benefit of strong structures to keep the enemy out and my family safe within. Although,' he paused and raised an eyebrow, 'I think I should take this opportunity to thank you, for you have reminded me to check the strength of the latch on that gate. The enemy still finds entrance albeit by invitation.' His tone was friendly even if his words were not.

'And that is surely what the Almighty would call

progress,' said Thomas.

The two men shared an unconvincing laugh.

'But you are the only O'Byrne to settle here in Glendalough. Did none of your kin wish to follow?'

The O'Byrne shook his head, swallowing deeply from his mug. 'My brother Shane, prefers Baile na Corra. His wife, Henry Mac Bhearna's daughter, has much to say in that marriage and she has become fond of the Avonberg River. I suspect Baile na Corra will be their home into their old age. But as for my brother Donal, he does not rest in one place for long. Not unlike your Donal, I see.'

Hugh gestured to the Earl's cousin, the one who shared the same name as his brother, pacing from one conversation to another, first at the doorway, then at a trestle and now at the hearth, not quick to settle too easily at any one assembly for too long a time.

'And now?' prompted Thomas, bringing the O'Byrne's focus back to their conversation.

'Now? Now my brother Donal, still wanders. He may do with Black Castle what we have done here with these walls. Rebuild, make a good home.' Hugh reached for a piece of seasoned mutton, devoured the portion and licked at each of his fingers. 'It would be a different circumstance though, Thomas, if your kin had not taken Black Castle from my clan all those years ago.' He looked squarely to Thomas. 'If memory serves me right, Kildare, that castle was given to my ancestors as a gift from yours. But that was some time ago, was it not? And things have changed.'

Hugh did not fail to note the Earl's almost imperceptible fidget, and leant back into his chair with spiteful pleasure. His suspicions were confirmed. So, Thomas thought the forced return of Black Castle dishonourable. It seemed Hugh was perhaps more aware of the workings of the Earl's mind than the Earl himself would ever permit. Such vulnerability would be to Hugh's benefit. If the great Earl of Kildare were to be so distracted he would fail to see the real enemy if such a one chose to stare him in the face. And right now ... but Hugh's thoughts were interrupted.

'Remind me, Hugh. Was that before or after your kin burnt Black Castle to a shell in rebellion ... twice?'

Hugh broke into raucous laughter, not for the reason most suspected. 'As I said, Kildare, things have greatly changed. We can now sit at the same table and share a meal. It can only be for the better I say; a small miracle of sorts. But yes, my Donal roams, just as yours does.' Hugh turned again to watch Donal Fitzgerald.

'You could be right, Hugh. That name may have its Latin roots in the word *wander*. But this may be news to your ears, his name is in fact, Thomas, as is mine, a name meaning untrusting or suspicious I believe.'

Hugh had no time to respond.

'And a name in my language to mean two, or two-faced.' Esmond O'Toole spat the words in his native Gaelic.

Thomas' hazel eyes flashed. 'Your poisonous tongue is as welcome as a Flemish blade, O'Toole. I suggest you keep it behind your teeth, lest it ask too often to be cut from its place.' He delivered the warning in perfect Gaelic.

The O'Toole straightened. 'You sit smugly at a Gael's table, Kildare.'

Hugh could almost predict the words that were to

follow. The O'Toole's tongue would run at a pace. He would tell the Earl what he could do with his analogy of a Flemish blade, and he would not limit his imagination.

'That is enough, O'Toole.' Hugh's tone was level.

'No, it is not enough!' The O'Toole's chair tipped to the ground as he rose. His arms flailed knocking ewers and cups to oblivion.

'Why are you here, Fitzgerald? Speak the truth. Is it to slither amongst us like a serpent, strike when we least expect? This stronghold,' he stretched his hands toward the roof, 'will it be the next Gael home you attempt to seize, for if that is your plan, may God –'

Thomas too, rose. 'May God what, O'Toole?'

Jarlath moved promptly to Thomas' side and placed his hand at his hip. His sword hissed at the neck of its sheath. 'Your order, Uncle?'

The O'Toole's eyes flew to Jarlath's hand. The Chieftain's chin jutted and all could see his throat working.

'Enough!' Hugh yelled.

Then utter silence.

Ingenious, this was not, Hugh cursed silently. They needed Kildare's defences to be down, needed him comfortable and trusting if any cunning was to flourish. Damn the O'Toole and his rage! Hugh's eyes darted back and forth between all parties.

Jarlath still gripped the handle of his sword and hooded eyes dared the O'Toole. Donal was on his toes as if ready to pounce. All Kildare's men put hand to hip. Murmurs began to fill the silence, low, in whispers.

Hugh waited for the opportune moment and to make a

saving mockery of the exchange, he used his Gaelic tongue. 'Yet the Welsh say my name means intelligent, so how can we lend any credence to these century old wife's tales?'

It took a few breaths before the hall erupted into laughter, one voice at a time. Thomas too.

The O'Toole, it seemed, did not share the humorous mood. He moved from the dais pushing aside men in his way, and headed out to the night.

Hugh stood slowly, giving an air of unperturbed nonchalance, and signalled for the minstrel to fill the hall with music. He grabbed for his cup and raised it to the air. 'I drink to our friends.'

Hugh drank fully of his ale. His eyes went to the door. He would speak later to the O'Toole, tell him of his stupidity, inform him once again his warring with Kildare must wait. He nodded to the Earl then turned.

'Dance. It is time for dancing,' he said in a loud voice and moved from the dais.

Thomas and his men watched the back of the O'Byrne.

'And what was that all about?' asked Donal.

'I suspect, cousin, it was to determine which of us has the largest bollocks.'

'Well then,' said Donal, with little humour, 'from where do I collect my prize?'

Jarlath interjected. 'It does pain me to bring to your attention, Donal, that you must settle for second prize. Or do you find me invisible?'

'Well, I do not find you spectacular.'

Choking with laughter, Jarlath spat his ale on the floor and wiped his mouth on his sleeve.

'As for invisible, for certes the O'Toole no longer does. And as to the size of your bollocks, believe what you want, lad.' Donal's tone turned serious. 'I trust you know what you're doing, Thomas.'

'I do. We shall remain here for a time. We need them in our pockets at all costs. But speak to our captains, have them vigilant. Jarlath, you've done well. Keep with the O'Byrne cubs. Win them over, lad. As for the O'Toole, Hugh will see to that problem, for whether he likes it or not, he knows he has need of us too, if he wants John Butler kept from his mountains.'

Donal turned back to Jarlath. 'You almost had your wish. I feared for a moment you were about to run your Gaelic kin through.'

'It still may come,' Jarlath said with little tone, then turned his mind to other things – an achievement made. Blue, he thought, rather satisfied; he had discovered her eyes were blue.

Chapter Three

After a night of merriment the day began with clarity for some, yet for others, an unforgiving fog shrouded their every move. Groans escaped from suffering heads as servants moved along the length of the hall over and around blanketed men on makeshift pallets. Breads and ewers were placed on trestles to appease appetites and quench the thirst of early risers, and more so, to provide a light sustenance for those struggling to keep the previous night's indulgences at bay.

Tiring of his private chamber's solitude, Jarlath dressed, headed down the stairs, past the groans, and out to the stables. Food would wait. Neither he nor his mount were partial to long periods of rest, so it was with no surprise Jarlath's approach was met with a toss of a head and the stomp of a hoof.

The wide eyes of a yawning stable hand peered from the corners.

'Ready my horse, boy,' ordered Jarlath.

'Yes, sir,' the boy replied with saddle and tack already in hand.

'Tell me of the better views in your lands.'

'A lake sits not two miles that way.' The boy nodded his head to the north. 'Go by the gatehouse and follow to the left. 'Tis a beautiful beast you have, sir. I will have one when I have enough coin.'

Jarlath doubted that day would ever come, but flipped the boy a coin and laughed when the lad put it between his teeth and bit down. 'Did you think it was cheese?'

'No, sir,' the boy replied awkwardly. He rushed to the front of the horse and held the reins as Jarlath mounted.

'Show me your teeth.'

The boy opened his mouth wide.

'If you continue that habit you will have none left to eat with.' He threw the boy another coin. 'Straight into your pocket, now.'

The boy gave a cheeky smile, bit at the coin and then ran into the shadows. 'Through the gatehouse and to the left.'

Jarlath rode beneath the gatehouse and turned left, keeping the horse to a slow gait as they passed busy villagers. Once clear of the crowds he gave full rein. The cool morning air slashed at his face. He kicked the horse to a gallop, covering the last stretch of even ground before reaching the beech forest.

He rode at a trot for a time, eyes taking in the world's beauty. Trees stretched to the sky. Wildflowers dotted the ground where the filtered sun danced. Birdsong filled the air. He glimpsed an unexpected thinning of trees and followed the downward slope of the terrain. The forest opened to a lake. The boy had given accurate directions. The shores seemed to stretch for miles and the still waters mirrored the surrounding trees, their reflection rigidly still as if in a painting. The blue of the sky took on a darker hue. The green appeared a grey. Not even a gnat disturbed the stillness.

Jarlath dismounted, removed his long boots then vest throwing them to the ground. He discarded his linen shirt and hose to the same pile. The air was warming and the sun began to erase the cool of the early morning, yet he was under no misconception this adventure was to be anything but cold, very cold. He hesitated, then, lifting his legs high, ran at the water before second thoughts bid him abandon the quest. A powerful leap and he plunged into the shallows. Shock stole all breath from his lungs, all feeling from his limbs. He sprang up high, eyes wide, mouth agape and an unforced holler escaped his lungs. He shook his head. Droplets flew through the air returning to the lake. He shuddered.

The depth allowed Jarlath's waist and shoulders to break free from the chill, but his hips and all the parts below, remained. His stare lowered and he laughed to himself, noting his body's reaction to the cold water.

Shrill laughter sliced the quiet. He spun toward the lake's edge. He was not alone and the eyes that met his were a familiar blue. They glistened without the aid of reflective sunlight and their owner rolled to her side, laughing with no end. His horse, his traitorous horse nuzzled her face. He may consider selling the disloyal beast to the stable hand for the return of his two coins, teeth marks and all.

'Is the water cool this morn?'

The words came from a mouth so wide with smile, it amazed Jarlath she could speak. He certainly could not. He was uncommonly mute and naked before this girl, save for the minute level of decorum offered by the almost transparent water.

Yet this girl with the blue eyes did not seem perturbed.

'Do you speak or are you a druid?' The horse nuzzled closer interrupting her words. She pushed at its snout. 'A druid of the lake perhaps, prone to bouts of silence?'

One coin for the horse will suffice, Jarlath thought to

himself. 'I am afraid you have me at a disadvantage and somewhat unsure of my next move. The cold is close to swallowing me whole, but to escape such an unfortunate circumstance ...' With open hands he gestured to the water at his hips.

Ainnir put a stop to the horse's curiosity, jumped to her feet and walked briskly toward the pile of discarded clothes. 'Oh, do you mean you are in need of this?' She lifted his vest high. 'And this?' she added quickly, holding up his shirt with her other hand.

'You would not?'

She walked with a slow purposeful stride toward the water's edge, held both pieces of clothing at arm's length, and dangled them above the lake in a teasing fashion.

'As I have said, you have me at a disadvantage.'

Ainnir's gaze wandered to his shoulders, then to his chest. He noted they rested on a scar, one not yet healed, which stretched across his heart.

Jarlath did not fail to see the awakening in her eyes, the short lapse of confidence in her composure, and was well pleased. In fact, he felt very smug. She bit at her bottom lip, and her eyes darted away from his chest and then back again. He laughed aloud. 'May I request a small measure of time to make myself presentable?'

'As you wish.' Her voice was not so playful this time.

Ainnir returned the garments to the ground and walked to the horse, petted the pushy nose, and picked wildflowers offering them with an open hand.

'It would have been kind of you to warn me of your presence,' said Jarlath.

'And miss your displeasure ... and your embarrassment?'

'*My* embarrassment?' he replied with a laugh.

Water splashed and twigs snapped. Jarlath noted Ainnir moved as he moved, her ears tracing his path, determined to keep her back to him at all times. He walked further than was necessary. She moved accordingly. He retraced his steps. So did she. He moved again, a little quicker this time. So did she.

'I know what you are doing,' she yelled in a friendly manner.

Jarlath started to dress. 'You are the O'Byrne's daughter?'

'I know my kin.'

'I am Jarlath.'

'I know that too.'

Witty. He took a few fast steps to the side. Ainnir followed the dance. He picked up some stones and threw them a distance. Ainnir swung left then right, and as he laughed aloud, she swung back again.

'And what do you find so entertaining?'

'Nothing. Nothing at all.' He picked up more stones, halved the pile into his two hands, and threw them in opposite directions.

Ainnir's feet almost left the ground. 'Good to see you are enjoying yourself at my expense,' she said.

'I believe it was you who started the game. But now that my disposition is somewhat improved, perhaps we can start again.' He was fully dressed, save for his boots. 'You may turn.'

She did. 'Thank you. And yes, I am sister of Bradan and Eamonn, and daughter of the O'Byrne.'

'And I am Jarlath Fitzgerald, nephew to the Earl of

Kildare.'

'I saw you at the banquet last night.'

He cursed silently. Had she sensed his stalking eyes trail her every move throughout the evening? He knew she caught his glance once, twice – perhaps seven times if he was to be honest. Was she teasing? He could not tell. But standing close, he could see that her eyes were indeed blue, the colour of the oceans off the western shores of Ireland, the colour captured in the waves just before they broke to white. He could not say for how long he stared, but the bite of her lip suggested it was an indecent period.

'And I saw you,' he confessed.

She lowered her head and walked along the lake's edge picking at the bluebells. 'I know that too.'

Yes, she was teasing.

'Aw-neer?'

'Ainnir,' she corrected. 'A-near.'

'A-near. I have not heard of your name before. Does it have meaning?'

'It does. A young woman with a mind and will of her own, not bothered with constraints that do not suit her.' She recited the words as if they were a commonly used chant in a prayer. 'I cannot see that my name describes me rightly.'

'Indeed! I suggest it is most appropriate.' Jarlath spoke truthfully. He admired her pluck, her confidence. Too cheeky by half, she did not shrink from conversation. In fact, she enthused. So far, she was in utter control of this one.

Her eyebrows arched. 'My name also suggests that I possess foresight.'

'And do you?'

'Oh, for certes! I knew you were going to scream as soon

as you met with the water.'

Their laughter flew across the lake and echoes returned.

Ainnir's smile relaxed, then her expression became serious. 'The scar I saw on your chest, it is not yet healed. It was received in Wexford?'

'Yes,' he replied, and offered no more than that.

'I am said to be clever with herbs, if I may prepare something for you?'

'It is not necessary.'

'But of no bother.'

'Then, if you insist.'

'I do. I will seek you out tonight.'

Her smile was radiant – Jarlath censured his wandering thoughts – and innocent. This beautiful, charming, exquisite Goddess was simply offering to be of assistance, not proposing a thinly-veiled enticement to indulge in pleasures of the flesh. She was not another notch to be tallied.

'Thank you.' He levelled eyes toward hers.

She looked no less intently to his. 'I come here often. This is my special place.'

'I can see why. The scenery is beautiful.'

Ainnir widened the curve of her lips with laughter. His eyes had not left hers and the beauty he spoke of was not limited to her mountains or the lake.

'My brother Eamonn speaks highly of you. He says you have the skill of a mighty swordsman. He also says, if not for you he may have come to be at the wrong end of an Ormond's dagger.' Ainnir kicked at the long grasses at her feet with her slippers. 'But Bradan has accused him of being poisoned with a love potion for the English. Do I owe you thanks for saving my brother or a curse for your unholy sorcery?'

'I am Irish, Ainnir, not English, and you owe me naught. Your brother and I fought together, 'tis all. He would have done the same for me, I am certain.'

'Perhaps. Yet I hear it told in myth that the English once had forked tails and breath of fire, like dragons. I did not see a tail when you left the water.'

'Perhaps,' Jarlath mimicked her uncertainty, 'you did not look well enough. Or did you?'

Her obvious confidence waned. Eyes evaded.

'I proudly bear the name of Fitzgerald, Ainnir. My father was born here in Ireland and my mother was from your mountains. Both my parents died when I was young and I have little memory of either, but I can confidently say that I do not remember any dragon tails nor breath of fire in my cradle.'

'Your mother was from my parts?'

'Yes. My father fell madly in love with a Gael woman and I am told she gave her heart in return. Laws forbade new settlers to marry Gaels, but they risked all to be together. And so, here I am, the product of their story.'

'So you are the Fitzgerald I have heard spoken of. But that means you are kin to –'

'The O'Toole? Yes, he is an uncle to me – in blood only. I know naught of my family here in your hills. My mother was disowned when she left with my father, and I too, of course, for I was tainted at birth with the same ... sin. I think my being here puts him on edge and was the reason for his outburst last night.'

'I did see you enjoyed it.'

'I saw you did not,' he answered quickly, for he did not fail to notice that the raised voices on the previous evening caused Ainnir much discomfort. 'So now that you know my story, what does that make me in your eyes? Irish or English?'

'Twirl for me. I will check for a tail one more time before I decide.'

He obeyed.

'I am as Irish as you, Ainnir, but I will admit to struggling with your Gaelic tongue. Your bard last night spoke of a tale. Diedre and ... ?'

'Diedre and Naoise.'

'Yes. Diedre and Naoise. I could follow for the most part, up until the end when Naoise was laid in the grave beside his two brothers.'

'Oh, allow me to finish the tale. I myself would not be a true Gael if I did not offer my assistance. May I?'

'Please, I would be indebted,' he said, taunting.

She smiled. 'Diedre was so overcome with the death of her love and his two heroic brothers that she fell into their grave, and died alongside their bodies. I will finish the tale in the English language so *you* may understand.'

> *'Move thou hither, 0 Naoise of my love;*
> *Close thou Ardan over to Aillean;*
> *If dead had understanding,*
> *Ye would make place for me.'*

'Ah, it is a beautiful tale, and I am grateful for your assistance, for I thought it finished something like,

> *'Teann a nall, a Naoise mo ghràidh,*
> *Druideadh Ardan ri Aillean,*
> *Na 'n robh ciall aig mairbh,*

Dhèanadh sibhs' aite dhomhsa.'

Jarlath's pronunciation of the Gael was near perfect. Ainnir picked up a boot and threw it at his teasing grin.

'You mock me, sir.'

Jarlath ducked. 'I but taught you a lesson.'

'Where did you learn to master our language?'

'I have already explained. I am Irish, and a Fitzgerald at that, and we are very proud of our education. I have been schooled in many languages, including *your* Gael.'

'And the language of mockery.'

'For which I am most proud.'

'Well I am impressed. You now have the adoration of both my brother and I, no potion nor sorcery needed for either.'

Your adoration, Jarlath mused, smiling inwardly. This young woman laughed as easily as she breathed. Never had he found such enjoyment in conversation with a woman. For too long these dialogues began and ended in a bed or in a barn, or under the shelter of a tree. He felt quite vexed to find great pleasure in the candour of the morning, no bed nor barn close by, but the simple bounty of trees – may the good Lord help him if she truly did have the skill of foresight and could also read minds.

'I should be heading back to the keep.'

Her words came so quickly that Jarlath believed for a short moment she could indeed read his mind, thought she wished to escape the trees before he could entice her beneath one.

'I will be expected at the Chapel shortly.'

Her explanation dispelled his alarm. Jarlath collected his boots and took hold of his horse's reins.

'Jump on. There's plenty of room for both of us, and besides, I think he likes you,' he said, throwing a comical frown at his horse.

'Yes, I think he does. But wait.' She returned to the edge of the lake and retrieved a small collection of books.

Jarlath mounted first, offered a helping hand and pulled Ainnir up behind him. 'You like to read?' he asked.

'I love to read. Mama always encouraged the use of books, and 'tis now a habit I cannot cease. The words are like music, like gentle rain in the summer.'

She sat stiffly behind him at first, placing her arms hesitantly around his waist.

'That is another thing we have in common then, for I too, have a love of books.' He put heels to his mount.

'Romance, love stories?'

'More myth and legend, history and warfare. But I have been known to read of romance.'

'My papa was wrong,' she said into his ear.

'About my forked tail or my fire breath?'

'Neither,' she replied. 'You Fitzgeralds do not seem to be the devils he would have me believe.'

Chapter Four

The world seemed to spin, then came to a sudden halt as Bradan hit the ground. Breath would not come easily, but the sounds of raucous laughter surely did. Bradan dared not move. He checked his body for injury. Firstly his back, then shoulders, then legs. Not too much pain. But the head, the head hurt mightily. On any other day the haze before his eyes would have convinced him a mist had settled in his mountains, but upside down, dazed and sore, he knew better. Gingerly raising himself up onto elbows, he rubbed the back of his head. Teasing laughter reached his ears again.

'Spawn of goats! Do you have no sympathy?' He winced and looked to his two companions. 'Best I see your backs before I rise, for if I get to you ...'

No pity was forthcoming, simply the view of Eamonn and Jarlath roaring with mirth.

'Let's see if either of you can do better.' Bradan slowly stood, stumbled a little before righting himself and then decided to enjoy the comforts of the soft grass a little longer. He lay back down, all the while uttering descriptive words best left for a tavern brawl.

In the absence of a quintain, a length of rope hung from a tall oak tree, a hoop of iron wrapped in wool attached to its end. The three young men had decided to fill their leisurely afternoon with competition and had erected a target.

Bradan was the first competitor. He nestled the end of a branch, like a lance, into the cradle of his armpit, and kicked his mount into a full gallop heading straight for the target. He gave a monstrous yell of victory when the end of the branch slipped straight through the centre, but neglected to let go of the weapon. The horse continued straight ahead at a great pace and Bradan catapulted into the air, landing abruptly on his behind. A small amount of humiliation on Bradan's part, some aches and perhaps a profusion of bruises that would yellow and darken over the next few days were the only wounds received. The unfortunate theatrics provided great delight for his companions.

Eamonn gave a soldierly belt to Bradan's back. He jumped from his brother's reach and retrieved the branch. 'Perhaps if you had listened when I was schooling you in horsemanship, you would not be looking up at me right now.'

'Perhaps if you were not a club-footed, pig-headed, feminine-gallant, you would not be such an ass, dear brother.'

Eamonn made a feeble sound, pretending a whimper, stealing a morsel of time to commit the impressive insults to memory. 'Well then, your second lesson begins now, little brother.'

Eamonn mounted, the branch unbalanced and awkward. He corrected his seat, repositioned his grip and kicked his mount into flight. Within seconds he neared the target. A mighty wail hit the air, 'Watch and learn, brother!'

Not even close to success, Eamonn and the horse flew past the mark. He veered his horse around sharply, galloped back to Jarlath and Bradan. 'This branch is bent,' he moaned, only to be met with equally pathetic quips.

'At least I have not been unseated,' Eamonn threw back at his brother. And then to Jarlath, 'That smug grin may disappear soon, my friend. Let's see how you perform.'

Jarlath grabbed at the branch. 'Hold fast you children and see how a man jousts with the speed and grace of a knight. Which shall I be? Lancelot or Charlemagne?'

'Two silver coins say he'll miss the mark,' Bradan said to Eamonn, knowing Jarlath heard every word.

'If you have two silver coins to wager, then you have pilfered from my purse,' Eamonn accused light-heartedly.

Bradan jeered.

Jarlath left the two brothers to their exchanges. He played the part of a knight readying for the joust well, stretching his neck left then right in a mock display of concentration. He did not miss the movement from beneath a large sally tree some distance away. A lone figure sat amongst tall grasses watching their sport.

Her face gave over a brilliant smile as if knowing his eyes met hers. He stalled his horse, allowed the mount to prance impatiently, all the while returning her smile with a masked grin. A measure of furtiveness was necessary. He dared not reveal to Ainnir's brothers the harmless dalliance that had progressed over the past two days.

Jarlath raised his hand to his chest, held his palm to the binding that held a poultice in place, her poultice. He returned his attention to the task at hand, circled his horse like the valiant soldier readying for battle, sent a smirk to his competitors, and with an ear-splitting yell, urged his mount to full speed. The ring came into view and he lunged forward. The branch pierced its mark then he quickly let it fall to the ground. His eyes again sought Ainnir's, and he raised his brow in a conceited show, laughed when he saw her clapping in applause.

'Pay up,' said Eamonn.

Bradan smirked. 'Well here's the thing, dear brother, I now have need to borrow four coins; two to fill my pocket and two for the wager.'

A loud voice bellowed from across the field. 'You have an empty purse yet again, Bradan?' Hugh O'Byrne approached on his horse. 'I dare say from the look on the faces of my sons, neither is the victor of this game.'

Esmond O'Toole followed closely with a small band of men, one guiding a grey riderless mare. The O'Toole made no attempt to hide his derision at the sight of Jarlath enjoying time with Hugh's sons. He let out a laugh, his cackle almost to the point of foolishness.

Jarlath knew not to repay insult with indulgence. 'You choke on a bone, O'Toole. Best watch what you feed on.' He gave the O'Toole no time to respond. 'Let us call it a draw, sir,' Jarlath offered to Hugh.

He risked a glance sideways and caught Ainnir scampering into the cover of the woodlands, then turned back to the O'Byrne. ''Tis best to allow young ones a taste of victory now and again lest they sulk.'

Hugh roared with real laughter and looked to Eamonn and Bradan. 'He has your measure, boys. That he does. But you could not use a real lance?'

'We have mastered the lance, Papa, and in need of a challenge,' said Bradan.

'A stick?'

'You have a new mount, Papa?' questioned Eamonn.

Hugh motioned for his men to bring the grey mare forward. 'Your sister's birthday gift. She's skittish so a firm hand may be required for an interim before Ainnir attempts her, although I am sure to receive some argument on that point.'

Bradan turned to Jarlath. 'Our sister is a splendid rider, impetuous and pert and most importantly, her behaviour irritates our father.'

Hugh nodded. 'And to dictate her ways would be akin to demanding the Irish Sea to part, I fear.'

'I'd wager the mare will be shadowing Ainnir up stairs within a day if it is her want,' said Bradan.

Eamonn cocked an eyebrow. 'And with whose coin will you cover that wager?'

Jarlath stole a quick look to the woodlands.

She was gone.

He would cover that wager with his full purse. He harboured no doubt that Ainnir could tame any beast. As to what breed of beast he considered himself, he was still debating, but saddled and tethered, he surely was. He gently rubbed the binding on his chest, the poultice of fox clote – *to stave off infection and speed the healing* were the words she had spoken only the night before. Her magic was working on him in more ways than one.

As promised, Ainnir had sought him at the stables. She carried a small leather pouch containing the poultice and linen strips. He stood alongside his mount's stall and she slipped the pouch into his hands, her fingers lingering as long as she seemed to dare and not as long as he hoped, offering whispered detail of its contents.

They had crossed paths a number of times earlier that

morning, resulting more from Jarlath's inquiries as to the whereabouts of the O'Byrne's daughter than chance. Their brief conversations were full of innuendo, unspoken invitation, each future assignation planned with the precision of a sailor's compass and the timing of a sandglass. It had pleased him hugely when he had spied her watching their joust. It made his need to best her brothers more urgent.

They seemed to play this harmless game of tryst as allies. In their few short meetings he had discovered much: the slight turn of her lip just before her mouth broke into full smile, the way her chin jutted signalling she was about to jest, the three defiant honeyed-gold curls which refused to be confined by combs. Jarlath caught his thoughts. Perhaps this dalliance was not as harmless as he first believed. He had never allowed his heart to be captured before.

Nonsense. A little flirtatious behaviour would hurt none – as long as it remained their secret.

The birthday gift began to shift and toss its head.

'Take her to the stable,' Hugh O'Byrne ordered.

'Allow me,' said Jarlath. The mare danced at his approach.

'One win does not make you champion, Jarlath,' said Bradan.

'Then on the morrow, I will have to make it two.'

The O'Toole and the O'Byrne sat astride their horses watching the backs of the three younger men.

'This friendship between your sons and the Fitzgerald,' began Esmond. 'Do you encourage it?'

'It does well for our plans.'

'I do not recognise your sons playing a game. I see bonds emerging, and saw them on our journey to Wexford.'

'You are wrong.'

'Am I? Your plans are ambitious, Hugh, and rely I fear, too much on the stupidity of Kildare. You credit him falsely. If we are to remove all risks, you should see to the end of these friendships. Your youngest wears a biddable conscience and the last thing we need is the lad sprouting untimely morals.'

'Your worry is unnecessary. Eamonn is aware of our plans.'

Esmond turned sharply in his saddle. 'Your youngest is not?'

Hugh ignored the question. 'Jarlath is your dead sister's son, and with that you yourself could have played a part in our plan. You could have brought the lad to a false trust instead of running off at the mouth. Perhaps if you had chosen such a course, it may have prevented what you now find so worrisome.'

The O'Toole frowned. 'His mother made her decision twenty years ago, turned her back on her clan and was rightly disowned for her folly. I cannot ignore that fact and will not condone any attempt at forgiveness. Surely you of all people understand?'

'I do not ask you to embrace the lad. I ask you to put our cause before your own hate.'

'My sister's union with Kildare's bastard-born brother gave too much offence. Our father warned her well enough. She made her choice.'

'And your father missed an opportunity to slither his way into the Fitzgerald camp.'

'How could a Gael condone the marriage of one of their own to these Lords and their kin?'

'It would not be such a great price to pay if it wins back our lands.'

'You speak madness,' spat the O'Toole.

Hugh did not reply. His eyes speared the distance.

'Hugh, you do not mean to tell me ...'

'I do not mean to tell you anything. Your sister is dead, man. Use your head, not your hate.'

The O'Toole laughed loudly, a callous tolling laugh, rough and filled with danger. 'Beware, Hugh. Kildare is no toy to be played with. I long to be home and to enjoy the warmth of my bed and my wife but I will stay two more nights. God forbid I should miss the entertainment.' The tweak of his scar pulled at his eye. 'Care should be taken though, O'Byrne. This well-stoked fire may scorch.'

Hugh looked to the sky then to the green of his mountains. 'Time will tell. But I am willing to play this game, for the sake of my clan.'

Chapter Five

The game of chess at the far end of the solar neared its end. The imposing window along the southern wall offered a display of diamond-shaped panels, casting late angular rays and bright colours across the board as the sun too, neared its end. Beautiful as it was, the display failed to illuminate the board sufficiently. Dusk made its presence known and servants busied themselves lighting candles, whilst the O'Byrne and his guests relaxed, enjoying fresh mugs of ale. After a full day, the men were pleased to shut all doors to the noise of the household, keeping the privacy of the solar to themselves.

Their sun-filled hours had differed greatly.

The Fitzgeralds shared the early part of their day with the O'Byrne walking the heights of the castle walls. Amongst the sounds of hammers, chisels and pulleys, they debated heatedly over outdated building methods and the virtues of newer techniques. At noon they followed Hugh to the outer fields. Bradan and Eamonn had spent much of the morning overseeing construction of the new village granary. After one short inspection Hugh declared the structure inadequate and the roofing sparse, and demanded the afternoon be spent rectifying the alleged blunders. Thomas raised an eyebrow at the O'Byrne's criticism for he thought the lads acquitted themselves admirably.

The O'Toole's day saw him keeping his distance,

spending the morning in the forest seeking game for the evening meal. He and his men returned with a large stag and three young hares. Despite the good catch, their reception was less than cordial. The cook shook her head in disgust, demanded how the men thought she could possibly have time to skin, drain, gut, clean, roast and present the meal to their table by evening. Angrily, she had the servants take the dead animals to the bleeding grounds and left in a huff.

All were glad to see the end of this day. Thomas more so to discuss news just arrived from England. He stood at the hearth beside Jarlath, watching Donal and Bradan at the chessboard.

'Four more moves, my young friend, and I believe I shall declare victory.' Donal moved his king one space. 'You will soon learn that experience is a man's best ally.'

'Experience you say?' queried Bradan with friendly sarcasm. 'Don't you mean old age?'

'Old age?' snapped Donal. 'I am no more than ten years your senior and will defeat you in more than a board game. Now hold your tongue and do your best to counter my king, boy.'

'King? Why are you all so concerned with the King and his moves? It makes no difference to me.'

'You are too daft by half, lad. Of course it will make a difference. If the Yorkists fall, the Ormonds will be sitting in your seat, feeding off your cattle and bedding your wenches.' Donal caught the casual roll of Bradan's eyes. 'More fool the man who takes this lightly. What would you say to endless nights with just you and your own hand?'

No reply came.

'Your tongue sleeps?' asked Donal.

Bradan kept his eyes down and moved his king. 'A king often steps into the protection of a pawn, and the English do it all the time.' He leant back in his chair with a satisfied grin. 'But to imagine Bradan O'Byrne with no wench at his beck and call ...'

A small curse fell from Donal's mouth. He pulled his chair closer to the table and studied the board. He did not plan for that counter move.

'Bested by the young, Donal?' asked Thomas.

Donal offered a single grunt in reply.

Thomas laughed then returned their conversation to the news. The King of England had chased his rebellious brother, George, and his cousin, the Earl of Warwick, from England's shores. Forced to flee, the Prince and Warwick took ship from Southampton. Both escaped unhurt, but twenty of their men were captured and dealt with by Sir John Tiptoft. The captives were hanged, drawn, quartered and beheaded, their bodies strung up by their legs for all to see, one end of a stake impaled into their buttocks, their heads impaled at the other.

All were enraged at this barbarism and so too, according to the missive, were the people of England.

Tiptoft was a feared and despised man. He had rightly earned the name of *The English Butcher*, and Thomas, more than any other in the room could testify to such an assertion. It was only three years earlier that Thomas and his cousin, the Earl of Desmond, were charged with treason by Tiptoft. The words *"alliance, fostering, and alterage with the King's enemies, for furnishing them with horses, harness, and arms, and supporting them against the King's subjects"* had been used in the charge.

Blatant lies and conniving deceit. The Earl of Desmond had simply offended the Queen, intimated to King Edward he married beneath himself by finding a match with Elizabeth Woodville, and unfortunately for Thomas' cousin, the Queen was not one to ignore such slights readily. Tiptoft allied himself with the Queen and plotted Desmond's downfall, content to bring down any or all Irish Lords with him. Desmond was arrested and beheaded. Thomas too, was arrested, but support from the north saw his release, and the King ordered both the withdrawal of all charges and the return of Tiptoft to England.

'No guessing your thoughts,' said Jarlath.

Thomas raised an eyebrow. 'One day the favour of the King will not shield that man, and if there is any justice in this world, I will be there to bear witness.'

'You waste your time in concern, Thomas,' said Hugh. 'The King and his brother are like Cain and Abel.'

'Edward and George are not foremost in my mind, but as you raise the subject, Warwick and George's alliance with the Lancastrians is not to be underestimated. They bargain with the devil herself.'

'Marguerite D'Anjou will fade back to France before long.'

'Fade, O'Byrne? King Louis has given them haven, even demanded his queen with child in her eighth month be on her feet to welcome them all at Amboise. That is an unwelcome portent. We may see France giving support to the rebellion at hand. A miracle is needed.'

'I am in need of one too, it seems,' said Donal as he moved his bishop to the corners, out of direct play.

'If a miracle is to be offered, I shall claim it, for I fought too hard to have all taken.' Thomas sniffed unceremoniously.

'The Ormonds will not best us, Thomas, no matter who

leads England,' said Hugh. 'You know, I once thought Warwick a clever man. To be called *The Kingmaker*, and have the attention of powerful ears, I thought his political acumen something to be admired. Now he seems but a fool. His treason, and not his good, will be remembered in history.'

'That will depend on the author. If written by a Lancastrian he will be hailed heroic. If written by a Yorkist –'

'A coward,' Donal broke in.

'I was about to say likened to Judas.'

'Do they not mean the same?' asked Donal.

Bradan moved his rook.

Donal shifted in his seat.

'No, they do not mean the same,' Thomas disagreed, 'but all depends on bias. Would not the account of Troy rendered by Menelaus be tragically different from any written by Paris or Hector, and perhaps if the Trojan horse found voice, would that account not offer yet another adaptation?'

'A talking horse, my lord?' quipped Bradan.

'A talking pile of wood,' Donal threw back.

'Either way, the Lancastrians and the Yorkists would both vie for Warwick's epitaph,' Thomas continued. 'Crusader or criminal, saint or sinner, his burial to be on consecrated ground or his body thrown to the dogs.'

And what of himself? Thomas looked from the silent O'Toole, seated in the shadows, his form barely distinguishable, and then to Donal, scratching his head. Yes, Thomas decided, the chronicles of Warwick will indeed vary greatly, and he prayed his own would not cause him anger enough to roll over in his burial place when the time came.

Bringing his thoughts back to the conversation, Thomas

said on an outward breath, 'Our aid will be expected.'

'And aid he shall receive,' said Jarlath. 'If you wish to send men, I'll be the first.'

'He will get none from my kin, mark me,' said Esmond O'Toole stepping from the shadows and into the candlelight like a devious pawn.

Donal moved his bishop back into direct play and thumped the chess piece down.

Esmond looked Donal's way for only a moment. 'I will not have the blood of an O'Toole shed for an Englishman. Let the English fight their own battles, leave us in peace.'

'You err, O'Toole,' Jarlath said smoothly. 'Did you not just hear your own kin offer his blood for the cause?'

Donal choked on a laugh. Thomas raised knuckle and thumb to his chin with deliberate tardiness. Even Hugh found himself hard pressed to conceal his surprise at that barbed gibe, for although it was not the first occasion Jarlath had given antagonism to the O'Toole, it certainly was the first that any public voice was given to their blood affiliation.

'I do not believe the Earl has any expectation of our help in that quarter, Esmond,' Hugh said with control. 'I am certain Thomas is aware that the progression of any positive relationship with we Gaels is a wretchedly slow process, like honey in winter. Or like a game of chess.'

The O'Toole looked into his cup. 'My ale now bites.' He licked at his lips. 'Yes, very unfavourable. I will leave you with your ... friends, Hugh, and join you later for the evening meal. Perhaps the drink will have sweetened by then.' He turned on his heel and left the room. The door slammed.

'Esmond does not hold the foresight that I do, Thomas.

He will come to understand what is best for his clan.'

Thomas gave a half smile. 'As you say, Hugh, it is wretchedly slow.'

Hugh sat facing the low flames, frustrated that his ale too, like the O'Toole's, was no longer palatable. He would again deal with the O'Toole, but again, later. Here in the room he busily examined the responses of each man present to the banter and arguments that flew around the room. He silently measured each man's fealty to the English throne, and to the Earl, and to the prospect of leaving the County of Kildare unprotected and vulnerable to attack if a decision to travel to England was made.

He knew Thomas to be an ardent supporter of the Yorkist cause, quick to champion King Edward. Knew too, Donal and Jarlath would worship the Devil if it was Thomas' ask.

Hugh's thoughts grew cold. For all of Kildare's want, that would never be the way of a Gael. To think he could bring Gaels to English rule was foolhardy, ridiculous in the extreme. The Blessing of Hugh's reign as Chieftain, high on the hill at Dun Caillighe Bearre, demanded he never forget the invasion of their lands, the English atrocities. No amount of years would ever lessen the depth of loss, the hate, nor the yearning for revenge. In this, Hugh believed Thomas to be remarkably ignorant, or perhaps arrogant, perhaps both.

For now, patience and caution were necessities. It was crucial that theirs appears to be an uneasy alliance. To give over a resolute surrender would encourage suspicion. To fight and oppose at every turn, as the O'Toole chose to do, would do naught but hinder their plans. Yes, the appearance of an uneasy alliance was called for. And to strengthen that misconception, Hugh had yet another scheme in mind.

He left his seat. With heavy prongs, Hugh poked at the burning logs. Although the summer neared its end, the coming autumn brought chill air with the evenings. The fire threw off a pleasant warmth.

'The Ormonds will be plotting,' said Hugh, plotting cleverly himself, and closer than the Butlers could ever dare dream. 'We must prepare for more uprisings on our own shores. John Butler will use the Yorkist King's plight as reason to head north and test us again.'

'You are right, Hugh. We will get word to MacMurrough in Wexford, have his scouts readied. I hope Butler is willing to engage me this time. It may be that forgiveness is between Butler and God, but it would be my pleasure to arrange the meeting.'

Hugh nodded a false show of agreement and decided now was the opportune time to progress his scheme further.

'If I may have a private word with you, Thomas, I have a proposition to make.'

Before further could be said, all heads turned.

'Check and Mate, old man,' yelled Bradan.

Donal cursed at his best.

Chapter Six

'Your father is awaiting you in the bailey. Do you hear me?'

Muirne's patience wore thin, and no matter how many times and in what fashion she spoke, the lass seemed indifferent to the warning.

Ainnir lay sprawled across the large bed, fingering pages of a book gifted by her mother earlier that morning – a collection of poetry.

Today was her birthday, and her response was a recitation.

'Love is a melding of sun and rain
Unexpected in its appearance, welcome at its coming,
A greatness that removes burden,
It makes heavy to light;
Burden no longer a burden.
Lacking in trials and chasms,
It knows not no
For restrictions are absent.
An illness devours those who refuse its embrace
Though weary, falter it does not,
Though hammered, break it does not.
Forged of the greatest steel, love is the strength of a man.
Blessed are they that drink of this well.'

'It is not poetry that is wanted at this time. Your father is waiting,' Muirne warned again.

Nothing.

She looked to the girl. Seventeen this day, her charge no longer a child. With this came a fleeting regret, a slight sombreness for the loss of what was. But Muirne repaired her mood and with a none-too-quiet *tisk* began sifting through a silver trinket box. She lifted a heart-shaped silver pendant edged with violet stones. Memories replaced her impatience, memories of a small girl smitten with that pendant and its fabled story. It was said to be presented to Ainnir's great-grandmother one hundred years before. A gift from a great warrior in the hilly lands of Breifne. In the retelling, the stones were the exact shade of the woman's eyes; *an ethereal violet*. The story told of sadness, for with the gift came surrender and farewell. The two were very much in love, but both were promised to another and bound to duty.

The warrior was never seen again, some say killed by the jealous new husband. Others believed the warrior too heartbroken to remain on earth. But that pendant never left the woman's neck, and the young Ainnir never tired of such a beautiful tale of love.

'Forged of the greatest steel, love is the strength of a man.'

Ainnir's words interrupted Muirne's thoughts. Shaking her head of the past, she gently swatted Ainnir's behind.

'Up, I tell you.'

'Why should love be likened to a man? Why can it not be feminine, or even lacking of sex?' Ainnir rolled lazily, her eyes focused on a spider web at a corner of the room.

Muirne followed Ainnir's line of sight. The silvery thread shuddered with the movement of a gentle breeze. 'There once was a time when your poetry would have finished with *woman,* when a female was venerated for her power to bring life into this world. That was before the Christian priests brought fear to the land, fear that if man did not give veneration solely to the one God, and also suffer for it in adoration, their souls in death would be forever exiled to the place they call Hell. Those priests say we are born with sin on our souls. A damnable sin in itself if anyone can believe your soul is so tainted.'

Ainnir's lips lifted at the compliment. 'And you, Muirne? What about your soul?'

'You wait until you are my age, and with my experiences before you judge others and their misgivings.'

'Oh, how I wish to have lived in such a time,' Ainnir said, wistfully. 'To be adored and held in esteem for simply being a woman. 'Tis a thing I can only imagine.'

Muirne was delighted that her charge enjoyed stories of legend and myth, of the old world and pagan beliefs. Ainnir opened her heart to worlds and cultures far removed from her understanding, and yearned to learn more from ways now long past. Wise enough to know these discussions were not to be repeated beyond their chamber walls, Muirne knew Ainnir ensured that only Christian teachings fell from her lips, lest she suffer needlessly for her blasphemy; blasphemy as quoted by the self-proclaimed righteous.

'Priestesses wore flowing robes of white and blue, not the coarse dark garbs of the Christian nuns and monks. But for all their lecturing of the superiority of man, Christians do forget they hold one woman higher than others – the Blessed Virgin.

They dress her in gowns of white and blue in their murals and paintings, just like priestesses of long ago.'

'And the Goddesses, were they too virgins?' Ainnir asked.

'No, they lay with Gods of their choosing.'

'The female chose?' Ainnir lifted herself from the bed. 'Why did we turn our backs on such a life?'

'Best we leave that for another day, for neither you nor I will have a heart or a head to fathom that one if we don't get you outside, and now.'

Ainnir sighed in resignation and stood, lifting her long hair as Muirne fitted the pendant. 'And what of your love, Muirne? Would there not be a tale or two to tell?'

Muirne's fingers stilled on the necklet's clasp, and her first thought was to chastise the girl before allowing herself to travel to another time past. Yes, she had her own tale, but not for the telling. She fussed with Ainnir's hair and, as always, was amazed with the fall of spun gold. She left it unbound, save for two thin braids she pulled back from Ainnir's forehead and fastened with a leather tie.

She glanced back to the pendant, fidgeted unnecessarily altering its placement. 'No tales for the telling now, young lady. You and your brothers fill my heart enough.'

Ainnir threw her arms around Muirne and squeezed tightly. 'I do love you, Muirne.'

Looking up again to that cobweb, Muirne returned the embrace, and noted the complexity of the many silvery threads, the way they clung and turned and sat at such even intervals. It was a snare of methodical patterns, one that no fly or moth could ever hope to escape. Stirrings and visions suddenly took her mind, a whirlwind of vibrant grins and despairing empty looks, fitfully supplanting each other over and again with the speed of a stinging wind. They made no sense. The quick changes, the fitful pace; she could find no meaning.

It would come. She knew sooner than later it would come. It always did. 'I know, my love. I know.'

Ainnir hitched up the hem of her gown and hastened down the steps of the tower.

'I wonder what daughterly duty he has for me now.' Her tone was one of annoyance, of spiteful expectation, expectation of the usual rebuke. 'Is it not my birthday today? A small reprieve from Papa's dour lectures would be a welcome gift.' Her pace increased as she stepped out into the daylight and steeled herself to meet what criticism awaited.

'Happy birthday, little sister.'

A group of men stood not ten paces away. So too, did a riderless grey mare. Eamonn wore a large grin, holding the reins of the gift. The mare threw its head and stomped its hoof, starting at the loud greeting.

Ainnir's mouth fell open 'She's mine? She's really mine?'

'Careful, lass. She's a little skittish. Your brothers will need to spend time with her before you attempt your own acquaintance.' Despite Hugh's warning, the mare did not shy at all.

At Ainnir's approach it dared to take a step forward and pushed its nose into her hand, sampling new scents. The white tail flicked high in the air, and the mare snorted before bobbing its head. It was as if the two were familiar friends.

'It seems she has cozened you, Papa,' Ainnir said with laughter in her voice, delighted with the horse's acceptance and its part played in proving her father utterly wrong.

Bradan gave Ainnir a knowing wink and Eamonn drew her into a warm hug.

'Jump on her now and ride like the wind,' Eamonn dared in a whisper.

'And open the gates of Hell to release Satan's wrath? I think not,' Ainnir replied, her voice equally low.

'The wrath of Hugh, you mean?' added Bradan,

'Share your conversation,' ordered Hugh.

'I only offer to test the horse, Papa,' Bradan lied then turned back to Ainnir. 'So what do you think?'

'She is the most beautiful beast I have ever seen.' Ainnir wandered to the horse's side, gently running her hand along its length to feel the racing heartbeat. On the mare's underside splotches of a slightly darker shade mottled her coat. Ainnir began with short melodic whispers and a rhythmic stroke, and gladdened at the slowing thud of its heart and the curious eyes that followed her every move.

'If I may, Ainnir.' Thomas announced. 'We too, have a gift and I hope it pleases you.'

A smiling servant stepped forward armed with a saddle of polished tan, newly-tempered and soft to the touch. Thomas explained in his usual thunderous voice, that it was a gift from all the Fitzgeralds.

'It was the best we could find in such a short time.'

Ainnir's fingers found an imprint stamped into its skirt – *Ainnir*.

'My lord, it is ... wonderful. Thank you. Thank you.'

Ainnir liked Thomas – his smile true, his time given generously. He bore no similarity to her father, or to her preconceived images of the infamous Earl of Kildare. He certainly did not appear to be the overbearing monster she had conjured in her mind. She looked to him hesitantly, then remembered it was her day, a day to ignore duty and etiquette if she so chose. And she did. She hugged him with a laugh contagious to all her audience – all save her father.

Despite orders, the birthday gift headed north, not south to the stables. Muirne lifted her hand, shaded her eyes from the bright sun, and with a concealed smirk, watched Ainnir and her new mount fly across the field. She knew there would be no waiting for Eamonn or Bradan to give time to that horse, knew that as much as Ainnir gave the appearance of listening to her father and for as long as he deemed proper, all that was said would be tossed aside and ignored.

If the O'Byrne could see his daughter now! Perhaps it was best he did not.

Muirne started for the herb garden, thought to pick scented leaves for Ainnir's bedchamber. The fitful visions came again flashing with colour, not in warning but in polite counsel, a persuasive reminder that too often silent dangers lurked in ambush. Her focus was inexplicably drawn to the stable door. Jarlath leant against the uprights, watching Ainnir's flight. He turned into the shadows and shouted for his horse.

Time fragmented. A heavy yet fleeting ache came to Muirne's forehead. She knew what her mind spoke of and could now interpret those earlier visions. No longer vague or perplexing, they were distressing, and more so for the fact that nothing could be done to alter their course. The passing of the events she saw would come to be, just as all routes in life lead to one destination.

'Help them,' she whispered to the air, a perfunctory prayer to whatever power cared to listen. It was said with hope.

'Give her strength. Give them all strength.'

Jarlath rode for a time. The landscape and terrain seemed familiar, yet he lacked certainty that this was the path he had travelled some days before. His concern tainted the songs of the birds. Trills became callous laughter, melodic harmony became righteous cackles and he shot a suspicious glare toward the treetops.

'Do you mock me?'

A short interval of silence followed. His eyebrows arched. *Surely not?* He laughed at himself for the ridiculous thoughts then stopped short his mirth as the sounds of derision again filled the air.

'So, you do then.'

It was not long before a recognisable rise came into view. He took a deep breath, moved his horse forward. The sun bounced from the lake as if a welcoming beacon. He squinted.

'You too, find this place irresistible?'

Although his sight was blinded by the sun, his hearing did not fail him. He knew it was her voice. She was no different to the forest birds. She mocked.

'Yes. It is as you say, irresistible.' Jarlath guided his horse through low rambling thickets. 'You speak as though you expected me.'

'And you have proven me right.' Seated on her birthday gift, Ainnir sent him a triumphant look. 'There is much more to my home. Come. I will show you.'

She spurred her mount forward.

Jarlath followed, suddenly stung with nervous anticipation.

As they rode, Ainnir chattered and laughed, laughed and chattered, and pointed out much of County Wicklow's splendour. Jarlath did his best to keep his eyes on Wicklow's riches, but there was one more striking than most which stole his attention, and she rode a horse with great skill.

Before long they fell upon a narrow trail accommodating only one horse at a time. They followed its winding path along the cliff face – up and across, and then around and down, passing steep drops, ducking low-hanging branches, coming eventually to a patchwork of caves and rocky recesses. Ainnir stopped at a wide inlet. Spikes of yellow and orange dotted the floor of grasses. Rambling branches hung overhead providing shade. The view from this height was stunning. Bursts of white sailed across the endless sky, crossed paths, merged, then altered shape. Beneath lay a myriad of greens brushed with a bluish trim. Feathered greys danced into the distance. The lake's shore stretched and recoiled with the rising hills. An inquisitive hawk glided high, the underside of its wingspan a dusky pink.

'I need not ask your thoughts. Your face speaks quite clearly,' said Ainnir. Both dismounted and Ainnir tethered their horses to gorse bushes. 'It is dreamy, is it not?'

'It seems there is surprise at every turn in your

mountains.'

This last was said with eyes fixed to Ainnir's.

Neither mistook the meaning.

Ainnir seated herself on the grass, busied her hands tucking skirts around her ankles. 'They are your mother's mountains too.'

Jarlath joined her on the ground. 'It was in these mountains that my parents met. I can see why they fell in love. How could you not in such a place?' Hearing his own words, he shifted slightly and veered the conversation to a less awkward path. 'You ride well.'

'I was sitting in a saddle before I first walked, or so Mama tells me. Best my papa does not discover I have ridden this day, for he believes my new mount too skittish for my proficiency ... or lack of.'

'What is it I sense about your father?' Jarlath asked, breaking a small branch from a honeysuckle bush. He inhaled its sweet scent then turned, waiting for an answer to his question.

'Where do I start?' Ainnir sighed. 'I am a daughter forbidden to have a mind of my own.'

'So he did not choose your name?'

'No, he did not.' They both laughed. 'But at times I do wish I was born a man.'

'You would make for a strange man, but a great muse for minstrels and bards.'

Ainnir punched him gently as she would do to her brothers, and Jarlath grabbed hold of his arm, feigning injury.

Jarlath's voice altered, his face took on a solemnity. 'It would be a disappointment to me if you were a man.'

An evocative pause lingered.

Ainnir cleared her throat. 'Should I correct myself and say that I wish I could do as I please, choose for myself, live without the thought of duty?'

'We men also live with restrictions and rules. It is no different for us; duty, honour, battles, conflict. There is much to my existence I would see changed if the world was a different place. Yet surely for you it is not so bad? From the little I've witnessed, your brothers offer you liberties in their presence, and I suspect your mother may do also. Perhaps time is all you need to win your father to your side. He may lighten his views eventually.'

Jarlath believed that last to be a wistful illusion. But now was not the time to speak of what he thought of her father. Perhaps that time should never come. Thomas may have been convinced an alliance was nigh, but something cautioned Jarlath, something indefinable.

'Yes, that is my challenge.' Ainnir's eyes drifted to the sky.

'Well, before we alter the course of the world,' he said, raising himself from the ground, tossing aside the honeysuckle branch, and heading toward his saddle, 'I have something for you.'

The horses lifted their ears at his approach. It took only a moment to find what he sought and he returned to Ainnir's side.

Jarlath reached for her hand and set a bracelet over her wrist. It was fashioned from sheaths of dried bog rush, and entwined to form a loop. Jarlath crafted the gift himself and was pleased at the small gasp which escaped Ainnir's lips.

'I would have preferred rubies on strands of gold

thread.'

She laughed. 'No. No. This is perfect. It is such a beautiful gift.' She stilled her laughter as Jarlath's hand hovered at the gift.

'Happy birthday,' he said with a voice soft as velvet, deep as thunder. His fingers slid upward along her wrist, to her forearm, her elbow, her shoulder. He leant into her, hesitating as blue eyes caught his. With nothing more said, he placed a gentle kiss upon her lips.

'My first kiss,' she whispered, lifting two fingers to where his lips had pressed.

There existed a sensuality to her wonder. He leant in again, touched her mouth with a little more urgency and tasted her breath.

'And that,' he said, returning her smile, 'was your second.' He lifted his hand, brushed her cheek with rough, calloused palms and pulled her toward him. 'And this, this is your third.'

Her lips moved awkwardly at first. It was indeed her first time, and with that knowledge, Jarlath was selfishly pleased. Within moments she found her way. Lips moved in perfect harmony. Her willingness gave rise to a growing need, a need Jarlath troubled to control. His mouth travelled to her chin, to her neck. He heard the sharp intake of her breath, a sound that struck his ears with a thud as if a peeling bell warning of danger. Her need was growing apace with his.

With the strength of a miracle, Jarlath pushed himself away.

Ainnir frowned. 'I do not understand. Have I done wrong?'

'No, no. Ainnir, we should stop, and now.' He stood to make more distance, a safe distance, a necessary distance.

'Why?' she asked, with an innocence he found even more alluring.

He had no words.

Ainnir too, stood. They faced each other, eyes searching, darting left to right, one trying to find an answer, the other praying for resilience.

'I do not think I can hold myself accountable for what may happen if we remain here. Let's ride and talk.'

And they did. They rode for a long time. They talked of their homes, their childhood, their kin, their hopes, their dreams. Where the path would allow, they rode side by side and at every opportunity hands joined. Jarlath gladdened at the occasions when Ainnir was the first to hold out an inviting hand, and leaning across he showed his appreciation with a lingering kiss, but all the while, determined that they should both remain mounted on their horses.

They rode to the edge of the forest where the trees opened to the village fields. Jarlath took Ainnir's hand, raised it to his lips. She smiled. She was beautiful, so beautiful.

'Did you know that you have nine types of smiles?'

'Nine?'

'Nine,' he nodded. 'I counted eight up until our first kiss.'

Bright eyes held.

'Go on ahead, lest we be found. I will follow shortly.'

'And tonight?'

He paused. 'Yes, tonight. I will find you.'

Confidence suddenly left his promise. He watched

Ainnir's back as she headed toward the castle. What folly had they started? Ainnir was not a tavern wench, ready for a roll in the hay, nor was she of experience. That Jarlath cared surprised him most. He wanted this girl, wanted her fiercely, wanted something he knew he could not have.

The fury of Thomas would fall upon him like a mangonel at a siege if he was to bed the daughter of the O'Byrne. It would endanger all their plans. And to the thought, *a Fitzgerald and an O'Byrne?* Never.

Was it like this for his mother and father? Was it these trees, these grasses, these scents and sounds that surrounded them when they fell in love? Could this place be riddled with sorcery and love potions, willing history to repeat itself? These mountains were unveiling unfamiliar ground in more ways than one.

The hall filled with chatter. As was the usual custom for the midday meal at Glendalough, basic fare lined the trestles, but on this occasion Ainnir's favourites, rissole of pork, rice pancakes and a stew of apple and cinnamon were also part of the offerings.

Hugh sat forward in conversation with Thomas and Donal, whilst Brigid sat rigid with an outward calm, hiding her impatience, none aware of the irritation stirring beneath. The three empty seats to her left were the cause. Before her mood had the chance to augment further, Eamonn and Bradan burst through the doors. Amused about something, the young men laughed, the object of their tease remaining just out of sight. But the target of their jest quickly followed behind, smoothing her ruffled hair and staring daggers at her two brothers.

Ainnir seated herself beside her mother. The two brothers eventually followed with heads lowered, but not quite low enough to conceal their smirks.

'Where have you been, Ainnir? You look flushed.'

'Bumped, Mama.'

'I beg your pardon?'

'Bumped. My thoughtful and loving brothers turned me upside down, bumped my head on the ground seventeen times and wished me a happy day.'

Ainnir turned and poked a tongue at her brothers as if a pesky little sister, not a Chieftain's daughter now a fully grown woman. Her smile suggested she thought herself clever, and with little effort she turned back to her mother with a vacant look.

'Lord, Ainnir, do not pull that face again. And as for you two boys – men, I should say,' Brigid directed the rest of her scolding further along the table, 'we will speak later. Your sister is a lady, not a child.'

The siblings were of an age to find their mother's chastising exasperating, but they allowed their mother the respect her position deserved. It was not too painful a tonic, for they loved her dearly. She was gentle and patient, and for all her coddling, she could better any of them at wit and taunts. But such occasions were private moments, and few knew of her keen sense of humour.

Nevertheless, always wanting the last word, Bradan lowered his voice to a whisper. 'Next year it will be eighteen bumps, sister.'

Servants stood behind the main table with bowls of fresh water and cloths, and with prodding from her mother, Ainnir turned and washed her hands.

'I am sorry we're late, Mama, but I've worked up an appetite.' She sniffed at the fare. 'The cook has done well, has she not?' Ainnir thought it best to find an innocuous subject lest she speak what was on her mind. *Jarlath.* She looked blindly upon the dishes spread before them, not noticing the rissoles, the pancakes, nor the mugs or the trenchers. Her head was spinning delightfully, not from the rough play of her brothers, but from a day that so far portended to be the most memorable of her life.

She searched for more conversation, anything, anything to prevent her from bursting, from screaming to all and sundry of her first kiss, a kiss she still tasted upon her lips. She was grateful for her mother's next words, for she had almost exhausted herself of all control.

'Your father tells me you are well taken with your gift.'

'Yes, she is very beautiful.'

Brigid gently squeezed Ainnir's hand and whispered, 'Just like you, my darling. I also hear you were given instructions not to ride her just yet. Is that true?'

'It is true he said that, Mama.' Ainnir cast a sly look at her mother.

'Does she ride well then?' Brigid's lips barely moved.

'Most assuredly,' Ainnir answered, and the two women shared a private laugh. 'The day is so beautiful and I thought it sinful to waste, so I rode her to the lake and then up to the cliffs. I do not know what Papa was so concerned about, for she responds dutifully to my slightest touch. Not once did she baulk at my ask. Perhaps that's what had him in a whirl; she is nothing like me.'

Thomas stood and raised a hand, demanding silence from the men in the hall. It came without difficulty for mouths were busy enjoying the foods and wine.

'Firstly, O'Byrne, if I may, allow me to offer our congratulations to your daughter on this special day. A toast to you on your birthday, Ainnir, and it is my grandest wish that your day is memorable, lass.'

Salutations echoed through the hall. Ainnir gave a shy smile.

'Now, to my men,' Thomas continued. 'It is timely we cease our imposition here at Glendalough and return to our own home. We will depart on the morrow.'

Applause and cheers came from his captains and men, all keen to return to their families. They had remained overly long, and many longed for the comforts of their own bed and women.

Ainnir dropped her eating knife. *No. Not yet. Not now.*

Again, Thomas called for quiet. 'We ride with the morning sun. The evening's birthday celebrations will be our last meal at your table, O'Byrne. The hospitality of you and your kin has been greatly appreciated.'

She heard her father reply to the Earl, the words muffled and distant. A covert glance searched for Jarlath at his usual place along the trestles. He was not there. Her heart raced. Discretion forgotten, her eyes darted to every corner of the room. She soon found what she sought.

Jarlath stood at the door and levelled his stare. She saw the warning in his regard, a warning not to say a word. How could she remain quiet? The hammering of her heart was so loud she felt certain it would betray her. Surely her mother could hear the cursing rhythm? He was leaving tomorrow. *No. Not yet. Not ever.*

Brigid laid a hand to her arm. 'Ainnir, are you not well? You have lost all colour.'

Ainnir's eyes followed Jarlath's walk to the trestles. She mustered a false smile which disappeared as quickly as it came.

'I am not sure. Just the excitement of the morning, I suspect.'

Brigid called for a ewer of water. 'Or perhaps it is your brothers' enjoyment of bumping,' she said with a frown. 'You will return to your chamber when your meal is finished. Rest may be what you need.'

Ainnir did not listen. She simply looked to Jarlath. He kept his eyes down and reached for a piece of dry cheese, then dropped it onto his trencher. The men to his side spoke words, words she could not hear, words meant for his enjoyment. Jarlath made no reply, nor did he acknowledge the utterances. The men ceased their efforts and gave him their backs. He threw the food back onto the dish and walked from the hall.

'Drink this. It will make you feel better,' said Muirne, in the bedchamber.

Ainnir took to her bed immediately after the meal and Muirne requested the kitchen to prepare a brew of basil leaves. There was no fever, nor any sign of lethargy. It was assumed by all that her ailment was caused by the warm day and excitement. Muirne knew otherwise.

She had watched the silent exchanges between Ainnir and Jarlath, dismay etched achingly across their young faces. She did not broach the subject with Ainnir, and simply sat to her side stroking her forehead with a wet cloth. No matter Ainnir's age, an ailment of the heart could be very powerful and Muirne had spent enough years with the three O'Byrne siblings to know their sorrow was felt in equal quantity to their happiness.

Her eyes wandered to the open page of Ainnir's book.

> *"It makes heavy to light;*
> *Burden no longer a burden.*
> *Lacking in trials and chasms ..."*

Muirne sighed inwardly and looked to the girl's face. Ainnir's eyes seemed to focus on the sunlight catching the dust as it spilt through the open shutters.

Muirne had suffered the same malady many years before. She too, had loved and longed for what she could not have. She was of the same age as Ainnir, and even now, remembered the pain endured by first love.

'Muirne, what do you think of love? Is it an illness with no cure?'

'Often a cure is not necessary, for the illness itself is such a wondrous gift.' Muirne reached for Ainnir's hands and clasped them gently. 'But there are times when there is no cure, and the body and spirit learn to live with the pain. It will lessen. I promise. You will see.'

Ainnir closed her eyes. Tears wound their way to her pillow.

Muirne left Ainnir to her dreams, for the tears acted quickly as a sleeping agent, and she thought an hour or two would do her charge good. In sleep she would find reprieve from the aching thoughts bound to reappear when she woke.

The garden in the bailey produced a healthy display of herbs, many used for their flavour and fragrance, and others for tonics. Muirne found herself picking coriander and rose petals, both used to remedy sleeplessness, both, she suspected, needed for the nights to come.

Her thoughts turned to memories of another garden, a smaller assembly of aromatic plants in Antrim in the north of Ireland. A place where she spent her childhood. A place where the ocean's frigid winds whipped relentlessly across cliff tops, and where giant posts of grey and red rock rose from the sea. She smiled remembering tales of Fionn McCumhaill, a warrior who fell in love with a beautiful giant. It was said this giant lived over the sea and McCumhaill built the posts, stepping stones of sorts, to carry his love back to Ireland. This was one of so many tales shared around the family table as brothers and sisters, aunts and uncles, parents and grandparents huddled together beneath their thatched roof in search of warmth, and sharing pots of hot stew.

It was there her grandmother spoke of the Tuatha De Danann people, and in time Muirne came to understand these stories were shared to prepare her for the visions that would one day haunt her thoughts without warning. There was no doubting she was a descendant of these people. Her second sight – *a mark of fortune or of burden?* – was a question she often pondered.

Welcome or not, their warning too often came to be, as did the haunting visions that came whilst in Dublin many years ago, visions that terrified her as she stood marvelling at parades and festivities. With much gaiety, the townspeople celebrated the arrival of the English Duke of York and his wife Cecily, the parents of England's current King. It was a gathering for the Christening of their infant son, George, the brother who was now the cause of much trouble across the sea. Muirne remembered the sounds of laughter and cheers, and the jostling of the crowd pressing forward to follow the progress of the entourage. It was then the ugliness came. Images of the Duke's morbidly white head and the head of another very much like his own. Eleven years later her visions were realised. The Duke and his son, Edmund, were killed in battle, their heads mounted on pikes at Micklegate Bar in England.

Worrisome images had plagued her thoughts this past week and she tried to push them aside. Although she did not fear that deathly white heads would again be mounted as warning to rebels in her lands, she did fear that the steady and predictable life of Glendalough was about to be altered, and would never again be the same.

She picked at some more rose petals – and then some more.

Ainnir woke abruptly from her short sleep, and even before eyes opened fully, her hands grabbed at her slippers. She rushed from the chamber and spent the late afternoon searching. To her despair, she could not find him.

There was not a brick, a door, an alcove nor an archway in the castle with which she was not familiar. The stables, the village, the hall, the gardens; she scoured the lot. No one knew of Jarlath's whereabouts. It was as if he did not want to be found.

The sun lowered. Dejectedly she headed back toward her chamber, and climbed the stairs of the tower. With each step, concerns mounted. Perhaps her suspicions were correct. Perhaps he did not want to be found. Perhaps he very much longed to return to Maynooth. Was there someone he missed, someone who waited for his return? She was torturing herself, she knew that. But the despairing, niggling suspicions remained. She failed to find a plausible reason for his absence. Surely his need to seek her out was no less than hers? Where was he?

Her chamber door sat slightly ajar, and she peeked inside before entering. Her mother stood to the far wall combing through the contents of a chest, discarding items to the floor. It seemed a day for fruitless searches.

'Perfect,' Brigid whispered to no one, then held a golden gown high and ran a pleasing eye over the folds. The neck was decently low and the sleeves, slim to the elbow, flared to the length of the wrist. A thread of white laced the gown's sides beneath the arm to the knee.

Ainnir stepped into the room and Brigid startled.

'I came to your chamber only to find you gone. You are feeling better then, my love?'

'Yes, somewhat.' Ainnir's voice was low, but she steeled herself and walked to her mother's side. It would be of no use to burden her mother with her forlorn mood.

'This shall be your gown tonight. Very appropriate for a young girl, I mean a young woman. Ainnir, did you hear me?'

Ainnir stood rigid, eyes focused on the gown, a sense of excitement replacing her angst. The celebration tonight! Jarlath would surely be there, for how could he not? The night would not only be her birthday celebration, but would also serve as the Earl's farewell feast.

'Yes, Mama. Of course I heard you,' she replied quickly.

Ainnir ran eager hands over the skirt folds, and as her fingers pressed, her scheming mind began to travel places not before trekked. She catalogued an inventory of risqué ideas, discarding some, embracing others, examining them all for flaws and potential. *Yes, it could be done and flaws be damned!* When was the element of risk ever repugnant to Ainnir O'Byrne? Risk was exhilarating, an almost necessary component of any enjoyable adventure. Not even the Second Coming would prevent her from conjuring time alone with Jarlath before the morning came, before the sun rose to take him away.

'Yes, Mama, it is beautiful.' A joyous voice.

Brigid took Ainnir's hand and led her to the side of the bed, invited her to sit.

'Today, Ainnir, heralds a new beginning in your life. You are a woman now, a woman with so many experiences ahead of you. Some wondrous, some exhilarating and some ... well some simply lessons and we need to think of them just as that. But, my darling, I am so proud of who you are, who you have become.' She stroked Ainnir's hair then laughed as she continued. 'You are Ainnir. Remember that. A mind and will of your own, not bothered with constraints. How I do remember the hours spent in argument with your father over your name. His preference was a more common name. If I had surrendered I may now be calling you *Jane*. But you are not. You are *my Ainnir*, my child, wilful and stubborn and cheeky, and loving and warm and heroic. Do not change, my love. Be who you are. Be the golden rose that outshines the darker hues in the garden. Aim high and well and take what is yours.'

Ainnir leapt into her mother's arms and covered her with kisses. 'I love you, Mama.'

Both held tight for a long moment then busy hands swiped at tears.

'You will be *la belle* tonight. Many heads will turn your way. You will learn what it is to be a desired woman. You know we do hold a lot more power than our men folk would have us believe, and I think tonight you will see this for yourself.'

'Mama,' Ainnir protested light-heartedly.

Brigid simply laughed. 'It will soon be time to dress for tonight's feast. I will see that Muirne attends you soon. Do not be late.'

With that, Brigid left the chamber. Ainnir felt beneath her pillow and pulled out the bracelet of dried bog rush. She placed the gift over her wrist, and whispered a pert prayer.

'May fruitless searches be a thing of the past.'

The day's beauty continued in the sights of the early evening sky. The heavens offered a portrait of horizontal strokes. Blues and yellows and greys and purples. The moon and sun vied for command. One ascending whilst the other prepared to leave. The activity in the bailey was no less a work of art, a portrait telling of many stories, many conversations and many humours.

Brigid walked with Donal, both quietly exchanging words, solemn yet unburdened looks upon their faces. Thomas and Jarlath stood with a large group, Thomas commanding much of the conversation, Jarlath alongside with his thoughts elsewhere. Hugh walked from the tower behind his sons, words of chastisement raining down upon them. Ainnir and Muirne, only a short distance behind Hugh, followed toward the hall, Ainnir almost skipping, bright with smile.

So much had occurred in the late afternoon to cause the variance of moods.

Brigid had visited the darkening Chapel, the burning cross of rushes to the side of the altar the only source of light. She had stilled, noting a shadow seated on a bench before the altar. She did not wish to interrupt the tranquillity. The shadow looked up. Brigid immediately recognised burden in the reddened eyes.

'I apologise, Donal. I did not want to disturb you in prayer.'

'No. Please. Your presence is no disturbance at all.'

Donal turned heavy eyes back to the stone cross behind the altar, a large sculpture changing beneath moving shades as flickering light danced.

Without invitation, Brigid sat to his side. 'Are your burdens too heavy to share?'

Donal released an audible breath. 'I have an empty heart which burdens me, Brigid. I miss my wife greatly and mourn my child, the infant child I never held.' His voice, although seemingly controlled, hinted at silent tears being a usual visitor to this man in prayer. 'I pray this time each day, when I can. I find the Chapel a place of solitude before vespers. Scripture says, *Blessed are they that mourn for they shall be comforted.*'

He released another small breath, one which rang similar to a laugh. 'I must admit to not finding the promised comfort, no matter how much I mourn. I ask the Lord to answer me in truth, for all I desire is absolution for their souls. Do you think my suffering is enough to allow them entry to Heaven?'

Brigid placed her hand atop his. 'Our Lord is caring and would not allow a child to suffer, or its mother. They will be in Heaven waiting for the day you are called, Donal. You need suffer no more for their passage.'

Donal lowered his head and closed his eyes.

'Donal, I too, have lost. One infant died before he learnt of the comfort of the cradle. I know the hurt you feel. But I come here and offer prayers of thanks, not prayers of pleading, for I know my babe sits well at the feet of Our Lord. I thank Him for His care. Perhaps you too, could pray in the same way.'

Donal wiped at his face and looked to Brigid with eyes speaking of gratitude. 'I feel no shame for my grief. Elizabeth is well deserving of my tears.' He turned away. 'Thomas believes my burden will ease when I take a new wife. If my heart has been taken by one love and given so wholly, how can I again hope to find the same with another?'

'Time, Donal. The Lord's greatest healer is time. Forgive me, for I do not give pretence that I knew your lady wife, but I cannot imagine she would be anything but compassionate and caring to have someone mourn her so. Do you believe Elizabeth would want you to suffer with every breath until your time comes?'

'Elizabeth.' He repeated the name. 'This is the first time since her passing that the sound of her name does not send daggers through my heart. Perhaps you are right.'

Brigid knew Donal spoke more to himself than to her.

'Brigid, I would be honoured if you would pray with me before we join the others for supper.'

Brigid bowed her head, and joined him in prayer, a prayer of thanks.

Thomas had spent his afternoon in search of Jarlath. The O'Byrne boys were out creating their own pleasure, or havoc as the Earl preferred to have it, but Jarlath was curiously missing from their company. Tomorrow they would begin the journey home. Thomas thought this last opportunity to court the O'Byrne boys should not be wasted.

Thomas found Jarlath in his chamber on the upper floor of the guest chambers. His nephew lounged on a heavily padded chair. A coarse homespun coverlet hung from its side with hues of browns and golds. Jarlath's legs rested on the window's ledge. His eyes stared out to the bailey, and such was his focus that the sound of the door's latch did not rouse him.

'A pleasant view, nephew? You are dreaming, but I also suspect you are awake.'

Thomas walked to Jarlath's side and looked out to the open, keen to note what captured his attention so. Servants tended the garden to the far side of the bailey, kitchen hands lugged barrels of apples to the kitchen, the O'Byrne's daughter strolled along the new eastern battlement, and a small group of children played tig. Nothing of import, he thought.

'Would you like to share your thoughts?'

Jarlath knew a perfunctory *no* would not be accepted, and would only encourage more curiosity. It was easier to conjure something simple to appease his uncle.

'Nothing too serious. My thoughts have wandered to home. It will be good to fall into my own bed again.'

Thomas slapped a firm hand on Jarlath's shoulder. 'There will be many a young girl in Magh Nuadhat dreaming of the same, I am sure.' Thomas often indulged in the use of the ancient Irish tongue, Magh Nuadhat being the old name for their home, Maynooth.

Jarlath had conjured the same fleeting thought of women awaiting his return home only an hour earlier. It did not soothe his ailment as he had hoped. It was true his return would be welcomed by many, but none had earned his sole attention, this foolish craving he now suffered, only his male lust. Memories of past trysts did nothing to encourage a desire to depart from Glendalough, and none cleansed his mind of cheerless thoughts.

He knew what Ainnir searched for. He had watched from his window for too long and agonised over his decision to avoid her at all costs. It was easier this way. It was his way.

'You are not out with the O'Byrne lads.'

'I thought my task already complete, Uncle. I have done as you asked. We now have them willing to fight at our side, and as ambitious as it once seemed, we now share a meal at the same table.'

'Never rest easy with these Gaels. Music and dancing are the order of the night.'

Jarlath's head snapped right. 'I planned to spend the evening in preparation for our departure.'

'Donal has already delegated that task. What?'

'Nothing. Nothing at all.'

'I was hoping to visit the stable before supper, check on their progress. Walk with me, Jarlath.'

It was not a suggestion. Jarlath lowered his legs from the ledge and followed.

'The O'Toole has left for his home. He and his men departed a few hours past, so I do not expect a war of words this eve. It will be a pleasant few hours spent with Eamonn and Bradan.'

Again, his uncle's words were not a suggestion.

Jarlath nodded. 'As you wish, but I confess I look

forward to Maynooth.'

'You do? That surprises me. I could have sworn you were enjoying yourself.'

Jarlath ignored the implied question. 'You have shown great patience with the O'Toole, Uncle. Your staid hand may come at some risk.'

'You sound too much like Donal, and I will tell you what I tell him. What is a great achievement worth if won with no risk at all?'

Bradan and Eamonn had spent their afternoon in more pleasurable pursuits.

Eamonn yelled impatiently from outside the newly built granary, 'Now, Bradan. I will wait no more.'

Inside the granary, Branagh, one of the village girls held tightly to Bradan with a pout to put a tavern whore to shame. 'Do not go, Bradan.'

He grinned. 'Put your clothes on, Branagh. I cannot test Eamonn's brotherly love further, and I fear in his rage he will burst through that door and pull me from here, clothed or not.' He kissed the girl gently and rolled from the straw, collecting his own garments. 'If the sun rises tomorrow, I will seek you out.'

With a wink he completed his dressing and left.

In the light, Eamonn stood with arms folded and a glare that could slice, but said naught.

'You have finished with Branagh's sister already, Eamonn? Do not look at me so, for I cannot help that you are quicker than I, brother.' Bradan straightened his shirt and vest. 'We should swap the two sisters next time, have them make judgement between short and sweet or long and heavenly.'

Bradan laughed at his own wit and still received no words from his brother.

'Did you see how the granary stood straight, Eamonn? Branagh insisted the earth moved for her, but I saw no shake of the uprights. Our father cannot again accuse us of shoddy craftsmanship.'

Eamonn found his tongue. 'If she told you the earth moved, I would suggest you paid for her services and she pandered to your need for adulation. But thanks to you, Papa will have our hides. It's Ainnir's birthday celebration this eve and we will be late. Late, but sated.'

They both laughed like spinsters at a wedding and ran toward the tower. Within moments they were climbing the stairs to their chambers to freshen themselves and find clean garments.

Their father crossed their path in the stairway.

'Look at you two. There is not enough time to clean yourselves up. Straighten your dress and smooth your hair. Get yourselves to the hall now.'

Turning, they retreated silently, and stepped from the tower, heading toward the doors of the hall.

Hugh was on their heels. 'And get that bloody straw and dirt from your hair, or I will have your mother at my ear all night.'

Not too far behind, Ainnir and Muirne sauntered from the tower. The younger breathed in deeply, a visible willing of strength to cleanse herself of the nerves which threatened to stab at her mettle.

On her first steps from the tower, Ainnir's eyes sought Jarlath and were immediately triumphant. But it was his back she saw through the crowd, nothing more. The swell of greetings melded to one convivial sound as she took further steps. Jarlath stood beside his uncle. He did not join the men as they stared. Not once did she see his face. Why did he not turn?

Inside the hall, Lochlann and Maeve O'Kavanagh sat with legs crossed, hidden beneath a trestle. It was late in the evening. The twins were determined to remain to the very end of the revelries and avoid their mother's searching eye.

Sticky fingers busied themselves. Fallen remnants of almond cakes and apple tarts lay scattered on the ground. Lochlann wished his sister had given him more time to pilfer a larger supply of sweets, for he could have easily carried more. But Maeve was too impatient, too keen to secure their hiding place as quickly as possible.

Now, he sat disappointed with no more to eat. He sucked his fingers one at a time, careful to cover each with a good amount of spittle, then touched the scattered crumbs lightly. With a grin which could not be mistaken for anything but success, he lifted his speckled fingers to his face and studied the captured pieces. He would have given anything for a full fruit tart covered with sugar, and what made it worse, he knew ample numbers were just out of reach on the trestle-top above. He dared not make a quick dash to replenish supplies, dared not risk being discovered, for Maeve would never forgive him.

In between feedings of crumbs, Lochlann's eyes followed sticks of fire tossed high into the air. Batons twirled, landed in the juggler's hands and then flew again. Around and around they flew.

Maeve's eyes focused elsewhere.

'She's beautiful like a princess.'
'Who?' asked Lochlann.
'Ainnir. She's like a fairytale princess.'

At eight years of age Lochlann's experience of women and beauty extended no further than his mother. Beauty was in his mother's voice, her cuddles and soft kisses; she was his true princess. But all the same, he followed his sister's gaze to Ainnir.

Ainnir's yellow gown was bright, brighter than most in the room he supposed. But she was just Ainnir, the daughter of the O'Byrne, the girl who often found time to tell stories, play games or sneak sugared delights when none were watching. They loved Ainnir. Not many people her age found time for children. She was different. She even allowed them to sneak along the unfinished castle walls with sticks, and make believe they were great knights with magical crossbows defending the keep from invaders, invaders who spoke a strange language, had plaited beards reaching to their knees and helmets shaped like large seedpods.

'Who?' he asked again.

'Ainnir, silly. Look at her. I want to be just like her when I grow up.'

Maeve's singing rose lightly as if gliding on clouds, caught in a dreamy world of love and romance, a world just opening up to this girl.

Skirts floated across the floor, the golden hue of Ainnir's gown such a brilliant sheen, no less astonishing than an afternoon sun.

'Papa says my eyes are blue just like Ainnir's.'

Lochlann turned to study his sister's eyes, see if their papa was right, but gave a simple shrug, a look of disinterest, and returned to sharing his time between searching for more crumbs and watching the fire sticks.

'Papa says my eyes are the shade of the shallow pools that dot the ocean shores in the west of our Ireland. I will visit those shores to see for myself one day.'

Maeve laughed aloud and quickly covered her mouth, stifling the rest of her outburst. Bradan O'Byrne had stumbled on the dance floor, dragging half the merry makers to the ground with him. The *Rinnce Fada* seemed to be his undoing, a dance well known to most but obviously not mastered by Bradan.

Hugh O'Byrne roared with laughter. His wife casually closed her eyes seemingly annoyed at her son's behaviour. But neither Lochlann nor Maeve missed the small smile tug at her mouth.

'What do you think that's all about?' Lochlann asked.

Maeve shrugged. 'She's a mother. She has to be bossy.'

Bradan certainly required a lot of guidance, and from a close distance, Ainnir yelled instructions, none of which improved his style or grace. Maeve tapped her feet, playing out each dance step, a legacy from hours of spinning and twirling with their father to imaginary music.

The children were not the only ones with eyes drawn to the dance floor. It was only busy servants focused on their duties who looked anywhere but at this scene. Thomas and Donal too, watched in admiration. They knew Ainnir to be a comely lass, but tonight she was beyond that. Tonight she was a vision of pure perfection.

'She is a beauty, cousin, is she not?'

'That she is.' Donal almost crooned his response.

'Hah,' Thomas slapped his cousin on the back.

Donal turned with a feigned seriousness. 'I have not given my answer, so do not begin celebrations before their time.'

Thomas gave a shrug of indifference.

Only days before, Hugh O'Byrne had offered his daughter's hand in marriage to Donal. Thomas thought it a timely and beneficial plan, just what he had hoped. It would offer a well-needed course to encourage a good relationship between the two families, and build on civilities between Irish Lords and Gaels. Thomas suspected it was also just what Donal needed – a beautiful, spirited wife to give him children, bring love and laughter back into his life. None but the three men knew of the offer, and as expected, Donal did not immediately welcome the proposition.

Thomas knew the raw memory of Donal's dead wife and child would for some time delay Donal's prospects of happiness, but he was content to plant the seed and hope the idea took root. It was of course no hindrance that the lass presented as a Goddess this evening in both looks and in spirit. Donal had not given his answer, but the look in his eye filled Thomas with optimism.

'Of course, Donal. Of course.' Thomas stood tall with an exaggerated grin of triumph and began to whistle an annoying tune. It clashed with the music in the hall.

'Give it up, cousin.'

'You should not ignore the fact that you are pig-headed, crude, vile. You could not hope to find a better match ... at your age.'

Donal would not bite.

Thomas would not give up.

'And vulgar, a little on the ugly side, and don't forget –'

'I thought I was the bait?' snapped Donal good-naturedly.

'You are, cousin,' Thomas answered. 'You are indeed.'

Jarlath stood at the opposite end of the hall, his eyes also trained on the dance floor. He had done well to avoid Ainnir for much of the evening, as well as completing the task set by his uncle. As Bradan and Eamonn busied themselves prowling the room, dancing, sometimes stumbling, and striking conversation with many of the female guests, Jarlath was left to stand on the sides and watch.

He had been resolute that his silence, his distance from Ainnir was crucial. But watching her dance with every man in the hall, he felt the unfamiliar stirrings of jealousy. It did not sit well that so many admired her in such an overt fashion. He thought it painfully unfair that she could not be his, in his arms right now.

His self-pity was dangerous. He clenched his fists. The urgency for self-preservation became overwhelming. Before he lost control, he turned his back to the dancers, marched toward the doors of the hall, and almost stumbled over two young children being pulled from beneath a trestle by their chastising mother.

Blankly, he nodded apologies and continued on his way, his stride pressing and determined. He stopped before the open door, hesitated for no longer than a breath then hastened into the darkness, alone.

One interested onlooker watched his departure with a deep sense of disappointment. But she also trusted that the night's search would not be fruitless.

Chapter Seven

A mild chill filled the air. Moonlight waved a blush across the bailey. Sentries dotted battlements, watching over the outlying village. Movement in shadows hinted at couples taking advantage of concealment. Some simply enjoyed a reprieve from the hall's noise, and wandered with little attention to any but themselves.

The tower and her bedchamber were directly ahead, yet Ainnir slowed her step and turned slightly. Her gait altered from one of innocence, to the sleek walk of a stalking cat. Toward stonewalls, toward deeper shadows. From there her hand led the way and followed the cold stone, meeting with the bailey's inner corner. She halted, leant back into the wall and held her breath.

Then more steps, low and tentative, duelled with want. Past the Chapel to the guest chambers, she pulled her saffron shawl high. The corridors were splattered with rush lights, each faintly illuminating segments of the walkways.

Stairs – quiet stone stairs – one at a time. At the top, eyes searched for movement. Moths chasing light were her only companions. All was quiet, save for the echo of laughter and merriment dancing through the air. To her left, bedchambers lined the corridor. She hastened to the fourth room, halted at its door, checked her dress, adjusted the shawl to reveal loose strands of hair, pinched her cheeks then reached for the latch.

Before entering, Ainnir silently mouthed the words she would use, and hurriedly practised their delivery again, changing the tone, changing the melody to alluring, seductive even. *Surely he would not reject her advances?*

She practised again. Her lips moved with no sound, hips swayed, head tilted then she straightened and readied herself.

The door opened with a soft creak to reveal a large chamber, dimly lit by the hearth and the soft moonlight falling through open shutters. A tapestry of blue, yellow and silver hung on the wall, and a large bed hidden beneath an ornate coverlet of masculine tones stood opposite. A figure lounged in a chair, staring out to the night sky, out to thin strips of cloud floating by the face of the moon.

Her hand did not leave the latch. She dared not move nor make a sound.

'I need no more service tonight,' the lounging figure announced with a dismissive tone. He lifted a goblet to his mouth.

Ainnir stepped further into the room, closed the door at her back and steeled herself. 'I believe the fire could do with more wood.'

Jarlath flew from his chair spilling much of his drink to the floor. He stared in disbelief for a long moment.

'Ainnir, what ... Ainnir?'

She pursed her lips, breathed in deeply then tilted her chin. 'Would you not offer your guest a drink?' Her voice was as smooth as the evening air.

Jarlath did not move.

'A drink if you please.' Her words of confidence belied her uncertainty, and the sultry tenor sang foreign to her own ears. Yet she pushed herself from the closed door, walked with an arrogant sway to the hearth, the sound of her skirts filling the room. 'I did not want our farewell to be a public affair in the morn, and thought a private goodbye would be preferable ...' She swung around, slanted a look from beneath blinking lashes, 'to us both.'

Her lips parted, an inviting gesture, and she did all she could to keep from choking on a rising ball of apprehension.

Jarlath turned away, walked to the sideboard, poured two cups and swallowed hard from his own. 'You should not be here.'

'And why ever not?'

He faced her again, but gave no reply.

'Give me a reason.' She took the proffered cup. 'You held no repugnance to my company anytime during this week, I am sure of it, so why now, Jarlath? Why?' Her voice lost much of the steadiness she had practised.

'It is not that simple,' Jarlath spat, and turned from her again, hiding his face.

The pretence of guileless wanton suddenly forgotten, the shawl fell from her shoulders, and slid away as unhindered as her charade. Her voice became insistent.

'Why do you ignore me?'

'It is not that simple.'

'So you keep saying. All I know is that today you held me in your arms and kissed me, and made me believe ... you made me believe ... but now –'

'Ainnir, we can never be. Do you not understand?'

'Because that is your want?'

He swung back with shoulders straight and a deepening

frown. 'No! I want you, damn it, and none but I could ever understand just how much.'

Echoes of laughter from the bailey below punctuated the ensuing silence. His naked honesty staggered them equally. His voice lowered, became matter-of-fact.

'I do not wish for you to make a mistake. It is unwise for you to remain here.'

'A mistake? Whether a mistake or not, it is mine to make.' She took a step forward. 'Jarlath, I cannot let you leave on the morrow with so much still to be said ... and done.'

Eyes speared eyes. A painful sigh fell from his mouth.

'You are a Chieftain's daughter, Ainnir. Your father will have designs for you, plans for you, and I, a Fitzgerald, would never be part of his consideration.'

'You are wrong.'

'You will be married to a Gael. And for reasons we both now understand, it is dangerous for you to be here with me, alone.'

'I am not my father's chattel to be traded as he sees fit. He would not do such a thing. Mama would not stand for it. She would not allow it.'

'*You* are wrong. You are beautiful. Beauty and a Chieftain's daughter will bring him great advantage in a suitable match. It is the way of our world. It was the way of my uncle, your parents and their parents before them.'

'And is this why you hide from me?'

'Yes.' His gaze moved to the hearth, to the small fingers of flame swaying left and right.

'Because you hurt?'

No answer, simply a telling sign as Jarlath ran a hand

through his hair.

'This morning in the mountains, I had never been kissed, nor had I ever offered a kiss. It was beautiful, Jarlath. The last few days have been so wondrous.'

He looked up.

Ainnir held a hand to her chest. A lone tear fell. 'My heart is thumping, all because it is you who stands here before me, the man who gave me that first kiss, and my knees are weak because your eyes see through mine. In this moment I do not care what my tomorrows will bring. All I know is that the sun will rise before too many more words are said and you will be gone.'

'Yes,' he nodded. 'I will be gone.'

'Then, we are wasting time. There is just you and me and now. We will have no regrets.'

She did not see his steps, yet before another tear fell he held her face and devoured her mouth.

Jarlath groaned. 'Ainnir, I cannot stop. It is you that must put an end to this for I am lost.'

She smiled, not lifting her lips from his mouth. 'And why would I do that? I came to you. It is I who asked for this.'

He groaned again – the sound of defeat. 'I was wrong,' he said. 'You have ten kinds of smiles.'

Time seemed an inexorable foe. Dying candles spluttered. The sky was one shade removed from black, marking the coming of the sun.

'The morning is near,' Jarlath said in a sleepy whisper. With splayed fingers he stroked her hair as Ainnir nestled into the nook of his arm.

'If I could but stop the sun so this time would not end,' Ainnir sighed. She was utterly bewitched by this man lying next to her, the warmth of his skin, the scent of his sweat and the night he had gifted her.

'Do you think we could –' she got no further.

Jarlath lifted her chin, placed a gentle seal on her lips. 'We must not torture ourselves. We know what must be.'

Ainnir looked directly to his eyes. She measured his words. Her own understanding and resignation took no time to come. He was right, of course, and she wished not to ruin these last moments.

'Can we –' and laughed as another kiss smothered her words. With muffled speech she tried yet again. 'If you let me speak you will not mind what I have to say.'

Jarlath relented.

'So may I now speak?'

'You may.' Jarlath kissed her forehead.

'Can we pretend we are Uther Pendragon and Igraine of the old Britans, and that Merlin will send us to meet in the Land Of Truths, in our dreams? If so then this will not be our last moment together. I will look forward to all my dreams for you shall be there waiting.'

Jarlath rolled so the length of their bodies faced. 'How do you come to know so much of a time long gone, and one that would have our bishops ranting accusations of blasphemy?'

'Muirne,' Ainnir laughed. 'There is much she has shown me, much she has taught me of the ways of people before our time, knowledge I dare not share with others, except you. Did you know Goddesses chose their own mates?'

'Goddess,' Jarlath murmured, sliding a thumb across her lips. 'Are you one such, come to toy with us mortals?'

Ainnir smiled. Her eyes dropped and looked to his naked chest and to the scar that had healed well. *Her healing hands*, he had earlier complimented. *Her magical fingers.* She had giggled at the praise, comprehending its true meaning.

She watched as his hand wandered and joined hers then played with the bracelet at her wrist. 'I now find myself in a world alien to me. To not have what I want is foreign, and to grieve for a loss, one not yet come,' she added hesitantly, 'is not easy.'

'Loss is second nature to me. It has travelled my way too often.'

'You are a Fitzgerald. How can it be?'

'Truth has many faces,' he answered, remembering a conversation with Donal many years before. It was a line he memorised and loved to deliver at every opportunity. 'Tell me how many wonderful stories are stored in that beautiful mind of yours. How many can you call upon to remember with fondness, time spent with your mother and your brothers?'

She thought for only a moment. 'There are too many to count.'

'I have none. I lost both parents too early. And although I bear the Fitzgerald name, all know my father was bastard-born and my mother a Gael. For this I am denied much.'

A shadow visited his face.

She hesitated thinking his words untrue. All she had witnessed this week indicated the Earl treated him like a son, no less a Fitzgerald than perhaps any of his true kin. If Jarlath doubted his worth, it was for Jarlath to fathom, and she trusted that in time he would come to see the truth. Yes, the truth has many faces, she thought.

'You have told me the Earl raised you from a very young age. Cannot memories of time spent with him replace what you feel you have missed?'

'It is not the same.'

She could not disagree, for she did not have the benefit of experience to argue such a point. It occurred to her that memories of fun with her father were limited, but she supposed the two situations too dissimilar to draw comparison.

'I for one, like your uncle well,' she said, wiping the sober tone from their conversation.

'How well?'

'Is that a streak of jealousy I detect?'

'It may be.'

'Would it be a mistake on my part to confess to finding such covetousness appealing?'

'No, for I would be no different.'

Her smile left her face at that thought. 'You will return home and I will be but a memory.'

'I cannot think of a more beautiful memory to hold.' His eyes wandered to every corner of her face. Fingers gently flicked at the curtain of hair, twirling it in place behind her ear.

Jarlath held her tight. 'Whatever course our lives will run, know that nothing can surpass this, Ainnir.'

'I do not want to say goodbye.'

'Then don't.'

Jarlath kissed Ainnir deeply and said his farewell the only way he knew.

Muirne sat in the flickering light, the lone marking on the candle an indication that little of the dark remained. Her heart weighed heavily. No clothing lay on the floor nor on the bed, proof Ainnir did not return to the chamber. Unable to sit for long in the company of her solitary worry, Muirne paced and busied herself, cleaning , folding and tending the fire.

The sky lightened too quickly.

The familiar sound of the latch on the door made her look up.

A soft smile floated across Ainnir's face. She glowed, her eyes danced and showed no signs of a late night. No words were uttered, none were necessary. Her arms fell around Muirne's shoulders and she held tight for a long moment.

Second sight was not needed to know what transpired this night.

Muirne stroked Ainnir's hair with gentle hands and understood only too well. Yes, she loved the girl and hoped, as frail as the hope was, that all would find the strength to endure what was to come.

Chapter Eight

'You are wrong, husband. This will destroy her.'

Brigid paced the floor of the solar, her eyes stinging with unshed tears.

'Did you not think to speak to me first? I am her mother. I laid in pain to bring her into this world and yet you believe it is you, you who knows what is best for Ainnir.'

The Earl of Kildare and his men had left not an hour before, and not until they were miles away did Hugh announce his news. Their daughter was to marry Donal Fitzgerald by the end of the fortnight. With all decided in Brigid's absence, there seemed no prospect of recourse.

'How could you do this?'

'He is Kildare's man. And we need this.' Hugh's bland tone failed to hide his impatience. 'A marriage to the Fitzgeralds will bring great opportunity to our clan. Do you forget Thomas is to be the Justiciar of Ireland, a trusted ally to the King of England? We must make good use of this opportunity. It is needed and it is decided.'

Brigid was not deceived. 'Do not shower me with your ill-truths, Hugh. You forget I have lived with you for too long. Our daughter is a pawn on your chessboard and you have moved her, left her out to be taken. This is just part of your scheming and cunning. I am not as dim of mind as you seem to credit me.'

Hands went to her hips. 'Ainnir is but a decoy and a bargaining coin. I cannot condone either.'

'Your thoughts on statecraft are neither needed nor welcome. The Fitzgeralds are a powerful family and their wealth will see to a good life for Ainnir.'

'You fail to comprehend. Our daughter is not impressed by wealth. It is love that fills her heart, love that fills her days. Without it she will melt like snow at the first thaw. It is not in her nature to be ruled.'

'I agree filial obedience is not one of Ainnir's strongest traits, but such lacking was not my doing.'

Brigid ignored the barbed jibe. 'She needs love.'

'We found a love of sorts in our arranged marriage, did we not?'

Brigid's lips drew tight. How could he dare to call theirs a love? He did not know the meaning of that word. She was at his beck and call, placating his every whim, bearing sons, a contract fulfilled. She put up with him, nothing more, nothing less. 'Is love what you call it?' Her words flew on an icy hiss.

Hugh's bearded face grew red. 'You have wanted for naught, are the wife to a Chieftain, and I have never given you reason to be fearful of me, Brigid, but by God I will now if –'

'Never fearful! You liar!'

Hugh stood quickly from his chair.

Brigid flinched. She saw veins at Hugh's temples, stretching like the roots of a tree. A frosty silence stilled the air, lingered for an inordinate time.

Hugh turned away. 'Will you never let that lie? I have given my apologies, enough for a life time.'

'No matter how long the Lord leaves you on this earth,

Hugh, you could never apologise enough. If you had held your temper, not pushed me down those stairs all those years ago, our child would have lived.' Her heat and confidence surprised Brigid more than it did Hugh.

'That was more than twenty years ago, and I do penance in my dreams, more than you would know.'

'I promised you then, I would never forgive you.'

Silence iced again.

Brigid straightened and turned eyes away to the wall.

'You cannot fault me as a wife. I have been dutiful, hospitable to your allies and enemies alike when it was to your benefit, and have given you sons. But I will never give you forgiveness for that deed. And now you wish to take another child from me.'

'It is not the same.'

'For whom? For you? For me?'

'Thomas Fitzgerald is pleased with the match. He too, can see the benefit from a stronger alliance with our clan. Donal will be a good husband and good provider.'

Brigid moved to the window, peered out to the mid-morning havoc as servants cleared the excesses of their now absent guests; stable needs, blankets, food barrels and empty vats. Her home would soon return to its normal pace, her home, but not the family harboured within its walls.

'And Donal, what does he say to this match?'

'Agreeable.'

'Agreeable?' A pitiful laugh blanched her words. She turned back to Hugh. 'That is not the term of endearment I hoped to hear from a man wanting to make my daughter his wife. He is still mourning his first wife and child. How can he be a good husband to Ainnir?'

'He finds it agreeable and perhaps Ainnir will find it the same.'

'You are certain or you hope?' She turned away again.

'Stare out to the world for as long as you wish. Better that than curse me 'til sunset. In any event, I will hear no more. Is that understood?'

Brigid knew those words were final. She could fight her husband forever and a day, but naught would come of her energies. Her daughter, her beautiful, precious daughter would be taken from Glendalough, forced to begin a new life with Donal Fitzgerald, a man still a stranger. Her spirit would be tethered, reined in and broken like a horse.

Or perhaps she was wrong. Brigid lifted her chin. Did she have too little faith in Ainnir, not trust her daughter to perform this duty? She tried to draw strength from these doubts. Donal Fitzgerald was indeed an honest and fair man. She had seen a private side to him in the Chapel yesterday.

And then, just as quickly, her head dropped to her hands. *Dear God! That conversation in the Chapel.* Did she unwittingly aid in this course? Donal laboured over the prospect of another marriage. She gave him words of encouragement. What had she done?

She frowned as her mind raced a fractious path to that conversation, summoning memory of his every word, seeking something, anything from which she could draw hope. Yes, his heart indeed possessed a great capacity to love, but had it healed enough to find love for her daughter? Could Donal bring to Ainnir all she could hope for, all that Brigid did not have? Ainnir would come to no harm, of that she was certain. Yet to marry an

O'Byrne to a Fitzgerald, what burden did Hugh gift their daughter?

No, she would not fight her husband further, but nor would she forgive him. His debts were too great. Hugh may have won the argument, but the women in his life would not be trodden. She would help her daughter find strength and resolve.

She slanted a look toward Hugh. 'When will you tell her?'

'This day.'

Her father's words were surely no more than a morbid jest. Ainnir looked to her mother. Pity contorted her regard. Then to Muirne seated in the corner. Those eyes remained lowered, Muirne's face bathed in despair.

Ainnir's certainty flickered to a faltering hope, and then scaled to anger. She turned back to her father, eyes wide, ready to do battle.

'I am dreaming. 'Tis a nightmare.'

Hugh gave a halting hand gesture, one Ainnir had witnessed too often. It was designed to portray impatience.

'Am I just trade to you?'

'This marriage will be good for you, for your brothers, for all the O'Byrne clan.'

'You are my father –'

'And your Chieftain.' Hugh's elbows rested on the arms of his chair. Fingers tapped on the ornately carved wood.

Ainnir shook her head. Tears welled. 'How can you do this to me? You do not even know me, for when was the last time you hugged me as a father should? When did you last sit and listen to me, really listen to what I had to say? When did you last speak of your love for your children?'

No answer came, and Ainnir almost laughed. 'You see? So how can you trade me for your profit and say it is for my good?'

Hugh was out of his chair, cheeks mottled with rage.

'That is enough. You are my daughter and you will obey!'

The echo of the shouted words filled the room like an accursed turbulent wave. Ainnir looked to her mother for aid and saw naught but a spear of hate directed at her father.

Her father responded with his own unchallengeable glare, and in the moment Brigid's disdain flickered to fear and then to dread, Ainnir knew she was a doomed soul.

'Brigid.' Hugh waved a quick hand in silent instruction.

'Come, Ainnir. We will go to the Chapel to pray.'

'No.'

'Ainnir, we must.'

'I will not.'

Brigid took Ainnir's hand.

She recoiled and screamed. 'No. Papa, you cannot do this to me. You must not.'

'Brigid,' Hugh repeated sternly.

Brigid placed an arm around Ainnir. 'Come, child.'

Tears streamed down her cheeks. 'Papa, no. Please.'

Pulled by her mother, her feet started toward the door. She twisted and turned, eyes trying to catch her father's.

'Papa. Please.'

Her pleading floated futilely out into the corridor.

Muirne stood to leave the room.

'You will continue your duty, Muirne, and accompany my daughter to Maynooth.'

Muirne bobbed her head in acknowledgement and left.

Hugh fell back into his chair. His mind chronicled Ainnir's accusing words, and his wife's declaration of a loveless marriage.

His daughter would do her duty. His wife knew her place. He was the Chieftain and his clan needed this.

He reached for a drink.

The brilliant light of the high morning sun achieved neither warmth nor cheer. The day seemed grey and abhorrent, so too, the stagnant air within the Chapel. Brigid dutifully dipped her hand into the stoup, made the sign of the cross, her eyes fixed upon the stone crucifix behind the altar. She held tightly to Ainnir's hand and guided her to a bench. They sat silently for a period, Brigid in prayer, Ainnir void of any thought.

From beneath her corded belt, Brigid pulled out a rosary of ivory.

'Here, take these.'

Ainnir's unresponsive hands lay limp. Brigid placed the beads into Ainnir's palm, and gently closed over the still fingers.

'How can he do this to me, Mama? How can *you* allow it?' Ainnir's words quivered.

Brigid took a deep breath. 'Almost one thousand years ago, my namesake, Saint Brigid, lit a small fire in her Church at *Chille-darruigh,* the Church under the oak, not far from the Fitzgeralds' stronghold.'

Brigid paused in her use of the Fitzgerald name, but saw

in the tear-filled eyes of her daughter nothing could bring more hurt than had already befallen.

'The flame was never to be extinguished. Saint Brigid made sure it remained alight for the benefit of the poor and needy, and for cold and weary travellers. It is to her memory that the cross of rushes on the wall here remains lit. It is for our poor, our needy, and travellers to our home. I have always thought you to be like this flame, Ainnir. Nothing could dim your light, your warmth, and in that I have faith Saint Brigid will not abandon you. You will endure this hardship. You will complete this duty set for you and I know with all my heart you will find your happiness. As dark as the world now seems, light will shine again. I know your strength, my love.'

Jarlath. Ainnir's thoughts turned to the man she shared her night with. She saw him so clearly in her mind, smelt his scent. She wanted desperately to return to the safe, blissful hours of this morning. Why could he not be here now, and mend this wrong?

Perhaps if she told her mother of the truth, of her heart's wishes, all would be set to right. But how? How could she tell of what they had done, what could not be undone? Oh how Jarlath's words came to ring true.

Dear Lord, she thought with panic. Had he been told? Did Jarlath now know of this abhorrent pact? Such a prospect was too agonising.

'Mama, I do not want to be with Donal. Please do not let Papa make me.'

Ainnir caught a frown, a furrow perhaps hinting at self-loathing.

'I know it seems difficult ... but you must. I have fought

your father for too many years, and fought again this morn with all my strength. I can do no more. His mind is set. I of all people should know this.'

Her mother had never given voice to the disparagement she had endured for too many years. She bore her burden stoically, with piety and grace. Yet now her words betrayed her silent suffering, and a sorrow which allowed a child to see too much of a mother's terminal pain. With that, all thoughts of speaking the truth died. All honesty was discarded to protect her mother. She loved her too much to do otherwise.

The rosary sat loosely in her hands. Ivory beads, streaked with the softer hues of yellow, were cool to her heated touch. She looked to the small cross. It was an unexpected weight. The silver was breathtakingly poignant in its craftsmanship, each carved arm of the cross delicately finishing to thin slivers. Such precise detail whilst turmoil voided all other beauty.

Up above, a trapped sparrow crazed and terrified, crashed over and again into timber and stone searching for an escape. Ainnir understood only too well the plight of the small bird. No escape was in sight. How she too wished to flee, to be gone from her fate. As if stunned, the bird sat still on a high ledge and looked at the four walls in defeat.

'When, Mama?' Ainnir asked softly.

'Soon. In the week of the Feast of the Nativity of Our Lady. You will ride to Maynooth in ten days with your brothers.'

A gentle timpani played on the floor. Brigid looked down. Ainnir's fist clenched tightly, her knuckles white.

Ivory beads bounced across the wooden boards.

Part Three

Chapter Nine

Maynooth – County Kildare

'Hunter! Here, boy!'

Eleanor's small voice struggled to travel across the open fields of Maynooth. Her breath was heavy, weighted by sobs.

'Come back, Hunter.'

The empty expanse stretched endlessly, no movement as far as the eye could see, save for the changing hue of the landscape as a gentle breeze danced through the air bending and pressing tall grasses. Her small steps slowed in surrender. *He was gone!* She dare not venture further to continue the search, for her fear was too great. The silence of the land was as frightening as the roaring dragons that visited her dreams.

How could she tell Jarf? He would never forgive her for loosing Hunter.

Palms swiped at small streams streaking her cheeks. Strands of red hair meshed with the tears, and wet curls fixed at her temples.

She turned back from where she had come. At the sight of two forms in the distance, her steps quickened to a run, and sobs kept the same pace.

'Jarf, Jarf,' she cried aloud, and stumbled as skirts caught underfoot.

Jarlath released young Maurice's hand and held

outstretched arms toward Eleanor. 'Eleanor, what is wrong?'

She threw her arms around his neck as he lifted her high. 'I am sorry, Jarf. I have lost your dog.'

Jarlath smiled. 'No, Eleanor. Hunter will not be lost. He will be chasing down a fox cub, doing what is in his nature. But he will not be lost. Now cease your tears, they are wasted. We will find him.' Jarlath turned to the young boy spinning at his side. 'What say you, Maurice? I think the three of us make a formidable army. Our mission is to retrieve Hunter. Do you think we can accomplish such a task?'

Maurice twirled in circles, his eyes spearing the clouds. No reply came. Words rarely did from the six-year-old. He hummed a sound, the buzz of a bee.

Eleanor calmed her cries. 'Maurice doesn't understand.'

'Perhaps not, but he can help us, can he not?'

'Yes,' she said with a sniff, and her eyes followed Jarlath's, scanning the fields for the wolfhound.

'Have you been practising your whistle?'

'I try, but it doesn't come out.' Eleanor pursed her lips and blew as hard as she could. Nothing. She bit down on her bottom lip and looked to Jarlath with a final sniff. 'See?'

'It is because you are such a great lady.'

Her eyes widened.

Jarlath read her excitement. 'There could be no other reason. You are the daughter of the great Earl of Kildare, after all.' He set Eleanor back on her feet and offered a sweeping bow. 'Come, my lady. Did you know that great ladies can also be great huntresses?'

'Of course. Mama has told me stories of Eleanor of *Acatain*. She has the same name as me. Did you know that, Jarf?'

'Eleanor of Aquitaine? No, I did not,' he answered with disguised amusement. 'Come on, Maurice. Let's try our lungs.'

In no time the shrill whistles of one echoed over the still air, followed by shouts of 'Hunter' from another. Maurice pranced ahead, his gait ungainly.

'Jarlath, tell me the story of Wexford.'

'Not for your ears, young lady.'

'But I like to hear how you ran down the Ormond churls.'

'That is no way to speak, Eleanor.'

'That's what Gerald says. He says the Ormonds are churls and Papa was right to kill them.'

'Then your brother should also mind his tongue, as your father may have a different telling of that story.'

'There he is! There he is!' Eleanor squealed spying Hunter in the distance.

The grey beast loped their way at a potent speed. She broke into a run to meet the dog, moving as fast as her small legs would carry her. 'Hunter. Here, boy. Here, boy.'

Eleanor's arms were spread in welcome, but Hunter passed her by, giving only a disinterested glance, doing well to avoid her small frame. He leapt straight at Jarlath. Not thwarted in the least by this favouritism, Eleanor turned and ran to the dog and her cousin, joining in the revelry. Hunter's long tail thrashed wildly and she laughed as the furry weapon pushed her to the ground.

The return of Hunter revived the day's adventure. The four followed the path along the Lyreen River, back toward Castle Maynooth, and knowing of the child's fascination with water, Jarlath insisted Maurice give him his hand. Eleanor skipped not two paces behind.

'Jarf,' she said.

'Yes, Eleanor?' Jarlath turned to give his full attention.

'I was scared. You have been so sad since you came home with Papa. I thought if I lost Hunter you would be sadder.'

Jarlath tore his eyes away, an involuntary measure of self-preservation. Eleanor's innocent words were too confronting. He stared vacantly ahead and tried to focus on other thoughts, anything but his misery. But the anguish would not dissipate, and the sounds of his stride and the drum-like grunts from Maurice floated to his ears, all as if from a distance.

Finally he spoke. 'You know too much, little cousin.'

Eleanor tugged on his sleeve. He looked down.

The girl breathed an enormous smile. 'Papa says that too.'

Only eight days earlier, Jarlath had found the impersonal farewell at Glendalough difficult. Servants and villagers spilled into the bailey to farewell the guests with boisterous *adieus* and thanks. Jarlath and Ainnir traded glances, fleeting in length to ensure none bear witness to their unspoken language. In any event, words were unnecessary, for hearts had found voice in the hours before sunrise that morning. Their lovemaking was gentle, the first time, and to Jarlath's delight, Ainnir learnt quickly and found little discomfort. She thirsted for more.

They made a pact. Neither tears nor sorrow would be the last each saw of the other, only smiles and gladness. The farewell was difficult. He led his horse away knowing Ainnir kept his heart.

But now Glendalough was a memory, a painful memory.

As horses found their place in the tracks leading from the village, Thomas and Donal had stirred their mounts to join Jarlath, both laughing and sharing a story.

'What do you think of the news, Jarlath?' Thomas had asked.

'What news?'

'Donal is to marry again. The O'Byrne has offered his daughter in marriage.'

His uncle's words did not register instantly, but as confusion gave rise to comprehension, the air grew thick and suffocating. His mind argued that those words held no truth. All was a nightmare.

No salvation came.

Donal's drab comments sounded a hateful, odious roar, and the words following from Thomas were stabs to his flesh. For a fleeting moment his mind raced along a precipice. How quick and easy it would be to take the dagger at his leg and slice through Donal, then drive a powerful punch to his uncle's mouth, the envoy of such a repulsive tale. No, it could not be true, he screamed silently.

Suddenly the darkness lifted, replaced by unbearable, gut-wrenching clarity.

Ainnir promised to Donal – and neither Jarlath nor Ainnir had known of those plans when she walked through his chamber door. He spat silent oaths at God, at all the Saints, and more so at the two men who rode beside him. No curse was vile enough.

Faint words bantered amongst the men. 'It will be suitably advantageous for the alliance. The O'Byrne would be dutifully bound, now family,' and the ribald jest, 'Not to mention to have such a beautiful lass to warm the bed.'

How had they let it come to this? He had warned Ainnir the O'Byrne would have plans. He told her so, but she would not listen. Damn her for not putting a stop to this. Damn her for coming to his bed. Damn her!

'Jarf.'

He felt another tug at his sleeve.

'Jarf, you are sad again.'

Now at a safe distance from the river, Jarlath released his hold of Maurice, and lifted Eleanor high up onto his shoulders. His eyes caught at the row of yew trees, the haven of his youth. *Distance from worries. Hide and be unseen.* He would ensure he kept his distance from Ainnir. It was all he could think to do. It was his way with such things.

Warm hands gripped under his chin, and Eleanor whispered into his ear. 'Tomorrow you will smile. Donal's *In-year* is coming.'

The words would have pained him if he did not feel so devastatingly numb. 'Ainnir, Eleanor. Her name is Ainnir.'

Chapter Ten

At the steps of Castle Maynooth's great hall, affluence and discipline were on show. Gerald, Tom and James, well-groomed, shoulders lifted, hands clasped at their backs, stood patiently beside their father awaiting the newly arrived guests from Wicklow to rein in their mounts.

Joan discreetly interrupted the pragmatic display and with little fuss ran fingers through each of her sons' hair, making last minute adjustments. Gerald tactfully shrugged off the touch.

Joan smiled, not at all perturbed by her eldest's reproach. Now fourteen, he was developing his own sense of fashion and, as Thomas often teased, soon it would be a young maid playing with his hair; a marking of independence, to which a mother did not fondly look forward.

James and Tom seemed to regard their eldest brother's rebuff with little interest, perhaps too intrigued with the arriving party. But Joan felt sure it would not be long before they too, would copy their brother's demeanour. Passing strange, she mused, that at this occasion she was spared the usual display of unconscious imitation, for her sons looked up to their eldest brother, like *Ithacans* to *Odysseus*, and shadowed him at every turn.

Her hands moved to her stomach. She wondered whether a son or daughter grew within. Another daughter would be nice, another flower to add to their garden. She looked forward to giving Thomas the news. It was only during these past few days she became certain of her condition. Her bouts of nausea had ended and now the telling swell of breasts gave further credence to her suspicions. But it was her craving for jellied eel that was a true talisman, one that bettered any diagnosis a physician could offer. There was no doubting Thomas would be elated. Tonight she would surprise him, for this morning would be too hectic for such good news, too chaotic to be celebrated as deserved.

Her two youngest children, Maurice and Eleanor, hand in hand, ran up the steps of the hall's entrance. They had waited at the castle gates for much of the morning, Eleanor eager to be the first to sight the coming of *In-Year*, as she so clumsily called Donal's betrothed.

This would be Eleanor's first wedding festival, the first she would remember in any event. Stories of princesses and warriors had been demanded throughout the entire week. She hungered for images detailing what the Gaelic Chieftain's daughter from the wild mountains of Wicklow might look like, what she would wear, her favourite colour, her favourite flower, and what games she would most likely want to play with a four-year-old girl.

Eleanor's small legs carried her as fast as they could up those steps, dragging Maurice with her. Joan smiled. No matter her age, Eleanor always did her best to care for Maurice making sure he was included in her play. And now the two stood catching their breath, watching as Donal marched forward to greet his guests.

Donal sent an unexpected bellow through the air aimed

at a nearby hand too slow to take the horses' reins. His yell caused Ainnir to flinch. Her brothers took a decisive step forward, stood protectively at her side. Their circumspect eyes were a declaration neither would be easily moved from their self-appointed role of minder.

Joan watched helplessly as Donal blundered his way through each and every particular of this welcome. His gruff orders resembled the shout of a battlefield warrior more than the agreeable husband-to-be that he was.

'She does put my mind to a fawn cornered by your hounds, my love,' Joan whispered quietly to her husband. 'And your cousin the leader of the pack.'

Thomas turned, almost imperceptibly. 'He for certes is somewhat wanting in manners this morn. The fool has less cheer than a graveyard.'

'Look how her brothers scramble to her side. I cannot blame them with Donal yelling at the top of his lungs like that. It is enough to scare Satan from the fires of Hell.'

It seemed even Maurice sensed the angst, for the lad burrowed into his father's leg.

Thomas hefted the child onto his hip. 'Donal is nervous, 'tis all,' he said, petting Maurice's head as further reprimands flew through the air at another neglectful servant. 'Clumsy and oaf-like, I grant you. But only nervous.'

Joan rubbed at Maurice's palm, an action that often calmed the boy. 'Please! That man does not know how to be nervous, and of all the days to learn.' She did not know whether to be sympathetic or amused.

Donal guided Ainnir up the steps and Thomas was the first to offer welcome – the first pleasant welcome, in any event.

'Ainnir, welcome. We are pleased to have you in our home. I do hope your journey was agreeable.'

Ainnir's eyes lowered, her face paled. 'My lord,' she said offering the expected curtsey. 'It was agreeable.'

Thomas' teasing eyes darted to Donal far too often for Joan's liking. She arched her brow amiably and hoped her husband read the silent warning.

He did. His own brow arched in reply. 'May I introduce you to my wife, the Lady Joan?'

Joan stepped forward and clasped Ainnir's hands. 'Welcome, Ainnir. My husband has spoken of your beauty, and I see he does not exaggerate.'

Joan waited for the dancing smile, the exuberant spirit and the quick-witted confidence, spoken of by Thomas in that same conversation days earlier.

A frightened and confused young woman peered back.

'My lady, I thank you,' Ainnir offered in a faint polite manner, and again added a short curtsey.

Eleanor danced with excitement, hopping from one leg to another. None had bothered to introduce the daughter of the Earl to the daughter of the O'Byrne, and Eleanor followed on Donal's heels, tugging at his shirt, shouting his name, only to be swatted like a firefly at each tug.

The crowd shifted and merged, started to sway forward. Ainnir's eyes stayed low, seemingly following the movement of Eleanor skirting around the swell of people come to give welcome to the Wicklow Chieftain's daughter.

Suddenly the blue eyes looked up, and Ainnir took on the look of a ghost.

'Ainnir, you have paled. What is it?' asked Bradan in a

quiet voice.

Joan read his lips, and with no answer offered, both she and Bradan felt compelled to follow Ainnir's rigid gaze. Joan could not be sure her line of sight was the same as Bradan's, or the same as Ainnir's for that matter, but through the throng she spied Jarlath standing in the shadows of the inner castle wall. He looked half-wild, his countenance almost as foreboding as the shadows he melded into, something she had noted with unease too often over the past week. Bradan was quick to shuffle his place in the crowd, closing the distance between himself and Ainnir.

Something was amiss.

Joan could not catch his next words. They fell soundlessly from lips she could no longer see.

'I am fine,' she heard Ainnir say unconvincingly.

Bradan grabbed at his sister's elbow and Joan was glad he did for he seemed to save his sister from a slight stumble.

Curious murmurs grew from the onlookers.

Joan looked up again. Jarlath was gone. Was perhaps the relationship between Jarlath and the sons of the O'Byrne less cordial, less affable than her husband had hoped? She doused any concern. Now that Thomas had found another way to cement bonds with the Gaels, it mattered not.

Joan moved forward to take charge. She thought it best to remove Ainnir from the scrutiny of prying eyes with little fuss and as soon as possible. 'Donal, may I suggest that I show Ainnir to her chambers whilst you see to the men of her escort?'

'Thank you, Joan. That is most gracious of you.' Donal turned to Ainnir, his tone now settled and most signs of discomfort vanished. 'I will leave you in good hands, Ainnir.'

Ainnir nodded all the while her young ghost eyes remained low. Eamonn and Bradan began to follow their sister toward the great hall.

'You have done your job well, lads,' said Thomas, lowering Maurice to the ground and taking his hand. 'You have brought your sister to her new home safely. My wife will see to her comfort whilst you tend to your own needs.'

Joan sent the two young men a placating look of sympathy. She suspected her own sons would be no less protective of Eleanor in similar circumstances. Perhaps that was the menace she sensed – an abundance of brotherly love. Nevertheless, only Eamonn seemed aware of the liberal sentiment, for Bradan's face turned hard, hard like a cold griddle.

'My sister will have further need of us yet.'

'It may be so, but her happiness is of concern to us all.'

'I hope you are right ... my lord,' said Bradan, drily adding the address of respect that should have come earlier.

Eleanor had given up on her efforts to meet the Gaelic Princess, and patted her father's side with an impatient hand.

'Papa,' she said with all the sadness of a child parted from its favourite toy.

Thomas gestured to Tom and James to take Maurice then picked up the small girl with little effort.

'See to your horses, Eamonn.' He did not bother to address Bradan. 'It seems your journey was not as pleasant as expected.'

Thomas turned on his heel. Joan followed, guiding Ainnir up the stairs. She fought the temptation to look back.

Yes, something was amiss.

Chapter Eleven

The supper ended. The moon sat high in the night sky. The solitude of the bedchamber was a welcome reprieve.

Thomas motioned to Joan's servants, a wordless order to leave the bedchamber, and waited to hear the door close.

'Here, give that to me, love.' Before the gilt-edged mirror, Thomas reached for the comb and continued with the chore left unfinished, taking care with snags and tangles. Joan's thick hair, blessed with the colour of night and the sheen of a raven's wing, bounced and floated with each ministration. He breathed in deeply, catching the alluring scent of her lavender.

'It required the cunning of a fox to escape the hall tonight and I doubt not that some of our guests will be quieter on the morrow. They do not know when they've had their fill.'

'And Donal will suffer the most I fear.' Joan laughed. 'Even the dogs were on edge this evening, worried they would be the next to wear his wrath.'

'Well, his sore head will make him even more unbearable.'

'You were right when you insisted it was but nerves ailing him. It cannot be easy, Thomas, for it is only a year since Elizabeth's passing.' She sighed. 'He still misses her greatly.'

'Yes, but I truly believe this marriage will be his tonic.'

Thomas bent, placed a gentle kiss on Joan's bare neck,

and Joan recognised that small sign for what it was. She had been married to Thomas for too long not to know he had need of her embrace this night; the immediate dismissal of servants, combing her hair, the lingering kiss on her neck. It pleased her well for she wished to give him her news, and she reached her hand to his face, let it touch lightly for a short moment before he broke the kiss.

'Yes, in that we do agree,' she said. 'Ainnir seems a sweet girl, yet it cannot be easy for her either, thrust into a world too long labelled her kin's enemy. 'Tis no minor feat for a young woman to bear on her own. When I asked her what she would miss of her home, she spoke of her mountains and flowers and painted a most wondrous image. And when I asked what she looked forward to here, she gave no answer. She is frightened and confused. I confess she bears no similarity to the spirited girl you described.'

'Perhaps the real Ainnir baulked at Donal's blustering, took flight and was replaced by a previously unknown twin. Does that sound a more probable tale?'

Joan's eyes caught Thomas' in the mirror. She pursed her lips then released them to a smile. 'I have offered to keep her company on the morrow. We have much to discuss of the wedding preparations, and perhaps talk of cloth and ribbons and festivities will ease her trepidation.'

'Whisper those words if you wish to keep Eleanor distant from your plans. She was Ainnir's very shadow this night.'

'Jarlath's absence indeed lent Ainnir to be her target. Where was he? I did not see him at all. In fact he has been missing from our table too often this past week.'

'The last I saw him was late afternoon, slung across his horse, and the O'Byrne boys were looking no less dishevelled. I believe they held their own welcome party in the village.'

'But I thought ...' Joan began, ready to speak of the awkward greetings on the steps of the hall.

'You thought what?'

She decided tonight was not for burdening Thomas with inconsequential concerns. 'It does not matter.'

'If you say so, and if tonight we wake to sounds similar to stars crashing to earth, we should rest easy knowing it's just the lads snoring. They will sleep well.'

'Stars crashing to earth? Is that book still plaguing your mind?'

'That is one way of stating the obvious. Did you notice?'

'How could I not? Last eve you mumbled and squirmed in your chair for hours and you barely spent more than a moment on each page, flicking back and forth. I found it quite amusing.'

Joan laughed at memories of last night in their library, her husband's solitary struggle with the pages of his most recent read. It was not the first time he had attempted that book, for it sat like a gilded Pyx on the library shelves for as long as she could remember. It may have been his tenth or eleventh or sixtieth try. She had lost count. So comical was his every attempt, they had come to be a well-anticipated form of entertainment.

The book contained a treatise of ancient astrology, analysing the theories of Ptolemy and Hipparchus, and *stars crashing to earth*. She believed her scholarly husband had finally met his literary nemesis. She herself had thrown her hands up in surrender when he first quoted from the text, trying to expand on some of the rationale. Thomas would not concede defeat. He wrestled with its contents as if trying to break a belligerent horse. Unfortunately that horse still bucked. It refused to accept the saddle.

Thomas chuckled. 'The mathematics used to explain the travelling path of stars and the moon set my mind spiralling, no less than Donal's aimless blabbering today. I can only hope the next reading will be less painful, just as I hope Donal's next meeting with Ainnir will be.'

'Well, whilst you read your book and laugh at our cousin's misgivings, I will worry about Jarlath. He has been distant these past days. Something is plaguing his thoughts.'

'Yes, I have noticed it too, but he will not share his concerns with me. That may be a task for you, love. Perhaps not on the morrow, though. Your time with Ainnir will give both Donal and Jarlath occasion to remedy their heads.'

Thomas ceased stroking her hair, sat down onto their bed and released a tired sigh.

'On the following day then. Yes, Donal should ride with Ainnir, show her the sights of our home. She mentioned she enjoys to ride. I will tell Donal in passing.'

'In passing, dear wife? Do you not mean you will issue an order?'

Joan turned on her stool, looked to her handsome husband as he pulled off his long boots. A sly grin, barely noticeable, spread across his face. His beard once red, now appeared a mottled yellow. His long hair, still the bright colour of his youth, found the beginnings of lighter hues. Yet it seemed time altered naught else. She was lucky indeed. She found Thomas as attractive this day as when they first met, those years long ago when legs were supple, skin soft to the touch, and speed and grace not a chore but an unappreciated simplicity. He was still a man of confidence, straight and tall, a man at ease in his own body. Never had she known a man who carried his own bearing with such poise.

'You look at me, wife, with eyes of a wanton. Oh, I make no complaint, am pleased to have a woman of loose morals in my bedchamber.'

Joan stood, feigning outrage. 'A woman of loose morals in our bedchamber, husband?'

'You are a chameleon, my love; a perfect wife beyond those doors and a perfect wanton on this side. I am indeed a fortunate man.'

Joan slid toward the side of the bed, tossed her hair across her shoulder and plucked at the lacings of her nightdress.

'A chameleon you say? What colour would you now want me to take?' Her nightdress slid effortlessly to the floor.

'That colour will do me fine,' Thomas drawled.

Joan playfully pushed her husband onto his back, and climbed upon the bed. He stroked her thighs, ran his hands along her waist and pulled at her hair, bringing her face to his.

'Come, my Nimue, I have a desire to fill you with another life.'

Joan laughed, a loving merry laugh.

'What do you find so amusing?' he asked somewhat confused. He was answered with a brilliant smile.

Thomas was quick to comprehend. He grabbed Joan's arms and rolled her onto her back with speed. She found herself staring up into his eyes.

'Are you trying to tell me something, wife?'

'Indeed, I am.' She raised her hand to his face, touched his lips softly with each of her fingers.

His eyes lit with happiness and a loving regard that wandered, covering every part of her face. He quickly rolled from her, pulling their coverlet up over his shoulders.

'Well my job is done then, and glad of it I am, for I am weary after this day and in great need of sleep. Good night. Sleep well.'

'Oh no you don't. Get back here,' she scolded.

Thomas roared with laughter and pulled her back, kissing her deeply. 'Remind me in the morning to have our ponds checked for a plentiful supply of eel. I would not have my wife-with-child go hungry.'

Chapter Twelve

From a bolt of the most magnificent blue velvet, Joan draped a length across Ainnir's shoulder. Her focus danced back and forth between the cloth and Ainnir's eyes, and she marvelled that both were of an identical hue.

'This shade is exquisite and so befitting a young bride. Even if such a blue was not appropriate, I believe God would forgive us for its use.'

Joan let the velvet fall as Ainnir's gaze fell too, staring into an unseen void. As much as the hues were alike, the textures differed; the velvet, soft and plush, and the young woman's regard, absent and austere.

'Muirne, what do you think?' Joan hoped another voice would encourage Ainnir's interest.

'I agree, my lady. 'Tis befitting.' Muirne sat meekly to the side, her interest in the planning of the gown seemingly no more enthusiastic than Ainnir's.

No ally. What ailed these two women?

The seamstress entered the room, armed with her tools of thread and cottons and pins. Many pins. She rattled as she walked.

'Ah,' exclaimed Joan. 'Mary is excellent in her craft and will have a gown fit for a princess ready for your special day. It is a shame your mother cannot be with us for the occasion, Ainnir.'

Still no response.

'Our men allow their politics to overpower matters of the heart too often. I expect it was in this, your father decided the wedding to be rushed.'

Mary moved with lengths of string in hand, measuring height, width, length and more. 'I have a pale blue satin which will make for a pretty pair of slippers, my lady.'

'Splendid! And perhaps you could stitch rabbits to the neckline and both sleeves. They will make for remarkable adornments if only they would sit still for the ceremony, unless, Mary, you think their whiskers will tickle too much.'

'Rabbits, my lady?' Ainnir questioned.

'So you return to us. Where have you been?'

Ainnir looked to the giggling seamstress. 'I am sorry, I did not mean to be rude, I was but –'

'No, my dear,' Joan interrupted. 'I did not think you rude, but am happy to have you return from your daydreams, wherever they may have been.'

A small bundle of noise burst through the door. 'Mama, are you and *In-year* ready?'

Eleanor took to serving as guide, as a duck takes to a pond. 'This is Mama and Papa's private library, and I can come here whenever I like.'

The large door opened to a room well-lit by angled streams of sunlight. Ainnir's eyes squinted, adjusting to the exquisite brightness. She could not help but think this was the Heaven of her imagination; shafts of light spearing down from the sky, welcoming the dearly departed to everlasting life. But here, shafts of light set chairs, stools and tabletops aglow.

The scent of age filled the air. Along the full length of the southern wall, shelves boasted of countless books with bindings of brown and black, and her mind danced at the world of words and tales she imagined chronicled on their pages.

Her steps took her toward that wall, and Eleanor followed, full of prattle, but Ainnir did not hear any of the child's audible wanderings.

Her hands reached out to stroke the worn spines, *Ismene and Ismenias*, *Amadis de Gaula*, *Romance of the Three Kingdoms*, *Aengus Óg*, *The Book of Fermoy*, *De Musica Mensurabili Positio*.

She turned to Joan. 'May I?' Her voice gentle, unsure whether such a collection was forbidden to any but its owner.

Joan nodded.

Ainnir reached for *Collections of Dante Alighieri*, pulled it from its place and opened the cover fingering yellowed pages, eyes scanning every line, every word.

> *"Know'st thou not at the fall of the leaf*
> *How the heart feels a languid grief*
> *Laid on it for a covering,*
> *And how sleep seems a goodly thing*
> *In Autumn at the fall of the leaf?"*

Eleanor giggled at the quiet. Ainnir suddenly realised her thoughts, yet again, had wandered far from her companions. She returned the book to its place of rest.

'Please excuse me, I do love stories so.'

'This one is my favourite, *In-year*.' Eleanor ran to the shelves, climbed onto a stool and reached high. 'The Pooka, the fairy goblin that eats crops and scares chickens so much they cannot lay eggs. Would you read it to me?'

'Not now, Eleanor,' Joan interjected. 'Perhaps another time.'

Joan gave her daughter a fervent smile, turned to Ainnir with a look no different.

'You remind me of my husband when it is just he and I in this room. He too, can become lost to me. He travels to faraway places. I do not know where he goes and I am sure there are places that would make me worry with fear, delight with enthusiasm, and turn green with envy. But his eyes dance, as yours just did. This is your home now, Ainnir, and nothing would please Thomas more than to have his love of books shared. You are always welcome in this room, my dear.'

'Thank you.' Ainnir ran hands down the length of her gown.

'Look here, *In-year.*'

'*A-near*,' Joan corrected, with a slow voice.

'*In-A-year.*'

Not concerned with the repeat stumble, Eleanor grabbed hold of Ainnir's hands and bade her sit at a small cushioned chair pulled up to a large table. Without invitation the little girl climbed onto Ainnir's lap, and from the top of the rose-red table grabbed at a gold candelabra.

'A man was going to chop off Papa's head, and to say sorry the King gave him this.'

Such innocent words from a child. Ainnir had heard of the Earl's escape from the henchman's axe, had overheard her father's men speak of the subject with humour. But as for Eleanor's words, to be again young, naïve, blameless and unlearned of adult ways, Ainnir would give anything. To be once again on the shores of her lake, or teasing Muirne, winking at Ferghal, picking flowers for little Claire, or playing with the O'Kavanagh children. To have the powers of Merlin to turn back time. To change things. But what would she change? The night the Fitzgeralds rode into Glendalough, the day at the lake, the moment she walked into Jarlath's bedchamber, the day her father told her she was to be used for trade?

The last. Only the last. *For how could I regret what has come to pass with Jarlath?*

She drew a heavy breath, willing those thoughts away and leant into the little girl on her lap.

'The holder is quite beautiful.' She rubbed it roughly with the sleeve of her gown. 'See how it shines? Look carefully and you will see your reflection.'

A distorted image stared back bearing little similarity to a human face.

Eleanor shrugged. 'It doesn't do much, it just holds a candle, and my brother James, he's nine, he says it would make a good weapon because it's heavy. Papa caught him playing with it one day and was angry. He growled like a lion.'

With that Eleanor set the ornament aside, its interest forgotten.

Eleanor jumped from Ainnir's lap and climbed onto a moss-green quilted chair with wide inviting arms. A matching footstool sat to the side with a fringe of beaded tassels.

'This is where Papa sits and tells me stories. Sometimes I make him tell me so many, that I fall asleep.'

'You and Ainnir may return here tomorrow, Eleanor. Now we must speak to the cook and see if all is in readiness for the evening meal. Let's see what sugared delights hide in the kitchen pots.'

These last few words were barely out before Eleanor's feet touched the floor.

Ainnir stole another glance at the books. She hoped this room would become a place of peace and refuge. She sorely needed one.

Eleanor skipped ahead, down the steps to the great hall. The slap of her rhythmic steps found competition as they ventured closer to the rising chatter. She jumped from the second to the last step, and her gait erupted from a skip to a pressing run.

'Jarf,' she yelled.

Jarlath was slumped in his chair like a rag doll tossed into a box. His eyes shut, he hoped that the thudding in his head would disperse. He could not eat nor drink. His stomach could bear little more than air.

The previous day's surfeit of ale was intended to numb the ache tearing at his heart, help him find oblivion. It failed and only caused further pain. His head and his heart now suffered equally from something like blows from a battleaxe.

He heard the approach of Eleanor, an event rarely conducted quietly, and frowned heavily to make a barrier against the impending explosion.

Eleanor launched herself high and landed, knee first.

'Oorrh!' He grabbed the little girl, lifting her quickly from his afflicted lap. Three pains now.

'Hello, Eleanor.'

'Where have you been today, Jarf, and yesterday?'

She left no time for an answer. Small fingers forced his eyelids open. 'Keep them open.' She laughed, as eyelids threatened to close again. 'I have been very busy with *In-year*. Why are your eyes so big and puffy?'

Jarlath ignored the innocent remark and looked to the centre of the hall. Joan and Ainnir walked side by side, toward the hearth, toward him.

He stood quickly, the fastest movement he made all day. 'That is wonderful, Eleanor, but right now I am busy. I have something of great import to attend.'

His eyes held Ainnir's for a moment, a dangerous moment. Her mouth fell agape. Her eyes welled. He could not deal with this.

Distance. He needed distance and headed for the door.

He heard his name called but refused to look back. The call came to him again. With a pace swift and unbroken, he left the room.

'Jarlath,' Joan called again. She shook her head. 'What ails that man?'

Ainnir raised a knuckle to her lips and sniffed.

'Ainnir?' Joan took a deep breath. *Dear Lord, no. Let me be wrong.*

Chapter Thirteen

'Good morning!'

Eamonn's voice boomed through the door like thunder on a blustery winter's night. Both women jumped having no creaking latch or telling rhythmic steps to warn of his approach.

Muirne pitched an innocuous frown. 'Did you leave your manners in the mountains? You know better than to burst into a lady's room unannounced.'

'She is my sister, Muirne. I see no harm.' With a beaming smile, he added, 'And what does it matter anyway? I have seen every type of female undergarment known to man.'

Eamonn ducked Muirne's whipping hand. Too many years under her care taught him from where, when and at what speed her open palm would fly.

'You are incorrigible, lad.'

'She is not a married woman yet, Muirne, and even then,' he paused, holding sway over Ainnir's silent eyes, 'she will always be my little sister.'

He had little time to finish his last words before Ainnir was in his arms with a hold to force all air from his lungs, and one to stir biddable concern. She held on too long. He gently tore her rigid frame from his, and looked down to see flowing tears. With that he pulled her back into his embrace, gave over his arms for as long as she was in need.

The sound of the closing door marked Muirne's discreet departure. They were alone, left with the sounds of sniffs and sobs, and faint echoes of castle life floating up from the courtyard through the open shutters.

'It is not easy for you is it, Ainnir?'

'I am sorry, Eamonn, I did not wish to burden you.'

'Burden all you like. Come, sit.' He guided her to the side of the bed. 'Speak. It is sometimes healing to give voice to your worries.'

Her words burst like a torrent. 'Everything, absolutely everything has been taken from my control. I am caught in a storm, at the whim of whipping winds and pouring rain. There is nothing that comes of my own accord. Nothing. I want to go home, home to our mountains. I want to be gone from here.' Her sobs caught and muffled as she pressed into his shoulder.

Eamonn held tight again. Why was she so obstinate, so abhorred by this match? Why could Ainnir not summon courage enough, as was her duty as the Chieftain's daughter? Even arrogance would be better than this defeated attitude. Ill-health was a certainty if she continued along this path of misery.

Yet to bring the needed change, he was not willing to replicate his father's harsh demeanour, chastise and debase his sister for her behaviour. As much as he failed to comprehend her reluctance, a small part of him silently offered pity, for she was ignorant of her role in their father's scheme.

Eamonn had argued with his father over the risks in his decision not to share plans with all their kin. 'Bradan and Ainnir should know.' His words fell on ears of stone just as he anticipated, just as they did on all occasions. He was now to bear the secret alone, watch on as his sister blindly walked into a web of deceit. All he could do was offer comfort in the time remaining, maybe encourage the return of her spirit.

'Papa's idea of duty has crept up on us all. I do not believe any of us saw this one coming.'

'Least of all, I,' she spat.

'Donal is not a bad man. Can you not rouse the valour I know that you possess?'

'It is not that, for I know you are right. Donal is a good man. Even Mama used those same words. I came to this place prepared to dislike him, even hate him if need be, but I cannot. He is not deserving of that. Yet he is not my choice, Eamonn. He is our father's choice. I want to marry for love, real vibrant love, to whomever I chose, and not for duty.'

It caught Eamonn by no surprise that Ainnir now referred to their father formally and not as *Papa*. The usual term of endearment grew less deserving as time passed.

'Lower your expectations, Ainnir, and you will not be disappointed.'

'What do you mean?'

'You ask for too much. You aim too high. Oh, do not get me wrong, for that is what we all find so charming about you.' He smiled. 'But now, here at Maynooth, this is real life, not the romantic stories in your books. Focus on the wonderful things to come from this match and rejoice in them, not grieve for what cannot be.' He hesitated for a moment. 'I was not going to share my suspicions, but to tell you of this news may help, show you we all have duty and honour calling. I believe our father has made a pact with the O'Toole for the hand of his daughter.'

Ainnir looked to him quickly. 'You?'

'Yes. Oh, I am not certain. He has not said a thing as yet,

but I believe by the time your marriage comes to be, the plans for mine will be well underway.'

'Oh, Eamonn, I am sorry. Our father has done this to you too, and here I am burdening you with my worries.'

'Do not fret for me, Ainnir. I will accept this path if it comes to be. It is my duty. And Fiona O'Toole is indeed a comely lass. I do not think it a burden.'

'But it is not of your choosing.'

He shrugged. 'Do not grieve for what cannot be. Look to the prospects your marriage will bring and all will be set to rights. Think of your new life as an adventure. You will want for naught, and Donal is admirable and deserving of you. All will be well if you would only accept this fate.'

She left his side, walked to the window lifting the backs of her hands to wipe away errant tears, and looked out to the streaming sun and the whirlwind of activity in the courtyard. The world below ran at the same pace as it did yesterday, and the day before that. Rain or sunshine, wind or snow, life would continue. People altered to suit. To survive, they adapted.

It seemed Jarlath found his way to survive. His way was to avoid her, ignore her, be blind to her existence. She suspected he simply erased from his mind what occurred at Glendalough. Perhaps her brother spoke wise words. Perhaps it was time she learnt from Jarlath. Perhaps she should cease conjecture for it only served to nurture shadowed eyes and a grieving heart. She could not change Jarlath. She could not change her father, her betrothal, or her life to come. She could change naught but her attitude. *Lower your expectations.*

'You may be right, Eamonn. No matter where my heart wishes to fly, I cannot see a way to alter things.'

Down below, leading her mare, Donal rode into the courtyard on a frisky black horse. Young Maurice sat before him in the saddle, snuggled safely into Donal's arm. The child smiled without end despite the horse's restlessness, his eyes trained solely upon the horse's mane. Maurice unequivocally trusted the man. Ainnir saw that in the illuminated face, and Joan explained only days before it was with Donal and no other that the child would sit atop a horse. Not even Thomas could win over that honour. Maurice must have sensed a side to Donal she was yet to come to know.

Her betrothed threw the reins to a servant, dismounted and lifted Maurice to the ground. The child's smile disappeared and he clung to Donal's leg with both hands. Donal lovingly petted Maurice's head in reassurance. How tender, she acknowledged. How caring.

Yes, it would be a difficult task to forget Jarlath, but it was one she must accomplish if she was to retain her sanity. And her mama was right; Donal was a good man.

Eamonn joined her at the window. 'Well, as I see it, you have two choices. You can sit here in this room forever and a day, have cobwebs cover you, or you can decide today is to be a good day. I suspect a picnic is planned.'

'A picnic?' she breathed with reluctant resignation, then lifted her chin and sniffed back the tears.

Donal passed the care of Maurice to a nurse. The child seemed to wave his hand in a gesture of parting, or did he? Donal lifted his own hand in a similar fashion.

'A picnic might be enjoyable.' She forced the words from her mouth. The healing must begin.

Eyes looked to the sky. The summer had ended but

refused to abate. The blue was void of cloud, the air void of chill. She drew on the tenacity of the sun's warmth for strength. Yes, her brother was right. Too many hours had been wasted with an empty heart and confused stirrings. Today would be different. Today, right now, she would give herself permission to escape, to find enjoyment in her day. It was time to rediscover the jovial Ainnir left behind at Glendalough.

She looked down into the courtyard again. Donal was smiling.

They galloped west along the path of the Lyreen River. The rolling fields gave them a good distance to set a speed, to set the sounds of thudding hooves and whipping winds above all else. Ainnir's horse kept stride for stride with Donal's, and seemed to enjoy the contest, perhaps sensing that both she and her rider were being assessed, making no error to have either of them found wanting.

They slowed the horses to a trot.

'Your brothers tell me you are an excellent rider. I see they do not exaggerate.'

'They are overly wont to praise me, sir.'

'Donal. Please call me Donal. A husband and wife should not be so formal.' He gave a curious smile and watched a small amount of colour flush her cheeks.

Donal pointed to the beech forest in the distance. 'Over there is our deer park. It is good for hunting and keeps our tables adequately filled. Permission from the Earl is required to hunt here, else offenders be prosecuted for trespass.'

'Trespass? Why should a man need permission to roam

mountains and hills when his need is only to fill the bellies of his family?'

Donal laughed. 'The forests are bountiful with deer and other game, but they do not exist in endless supply. Thomas does not prevent a man from slaking the hunger of his family, he simply seeks to ensure game is not killed before they breed and fatten their own hides.'

'It sounds very much like the history of my Wicklow kin,' she said with a hint of wit on her tongue. 'The Danes and the English raided and plundered our lands for hundreds of years, forcing us to dwell in the mountains, to take cover in the wild forests and vales, where we could breed and fatten our hides as you so eloquently put it, simply awaiting the next onslaught of hunters.'

'I prefer the taste of venison to Gael, Ainnir.' Donal smiled, amused at the pluck of this young woman. It was good to hear her banter, and see her somewhat at ease. He sent a silent prayer of thanks to the Saints above, for his own countenance was also improved. He looked back to the day of her arrival with naught but mortification, his cousin taking every opportunity to salt his wound. Yet he knew they both handled a difficult occasion in the only way they were able; she quiet and coy, he a bumbling fool. That was two days ago, and today saw a marked progress. He would do all within his power to see it continue that way.

'Are you always so quarrelsome?'

'My father would say it was so, if he was here.'

Donal pulled on the reins, circling to look directly to her eyes. He gave his full regard allowing no mistake to be made that what he was about to say was both credible and sincere. 'But he is not here, so it matters naught what he thinks of your spirit. I, for one, like it very much.'

He studied her face, searching for an unvoiced response, a reaction. He found a glimmer of appreciation. With that small sign of progress, he was pleased. 'Come, there is more I wish you to see.'

They rode further. Lines of ageless oak trees lead to a round tower stretching to the skies. Beside a pair of spindly hawthorn bushes, they reined in their mounts and Ainnir dismounted, looking up to the full height of the structure. Her eyes darted north to south and east to west like a bee in search of pollen.

'Your thoughts are in Glendalough, not Kildare?'

'The tower is like my home. That window on the second level could be my bedchamber and the one above could be Mama's. To the left would be the hall and next to it, the Chapel and guest chambers.'

Donal dismounted and tethered the horses to a squat gorse bush peeping from beneath the hawthorn branches. 'Before you once stood a magnificent monastery destroyed two centuries ago and the tower is the only portion that remains. So, yes, it is like your home in more ways than one.'

Donal thought to correct Ainnir's words, the use of *her home* when referring to Glendalough, yet decided to still his tongue. He would be patient, would do all to help her adjust; let her come to see all would be well in time.

'See the intricate stone carving along the doorway? Bishop Conlaeth established a very prosperous school of metalwork and masonry here, and this archway stood in honour of its notoriety. It is said that when you run your hands over the carvings of the clouds, you can feel the chill of winter and smell the coming of rain.'

Ainnir touched the carving.

Donal grinned. Joan had shared with him Ainnir's awe in the Earl's library and her obvious love of books and tales – and that was just before Joan gave him the order to ride with Ainnir this day – so it was no surprise that at the mention of legend and myth, this girl's interest piqued.

'And?' he finally asked.

'I smell peonies and the sun is warm.'

'You jest?'

'I jest,' she answered with her own smile.

'Saint Brigid was the one who brought Conlaeth to this area.'

'Saint Brigid? This is the site of the Church Under The Oak, is it not?'

'It is,' he nodded. 'Saint Brigid also founded a large monastery here – one side for the women, and the other for the men, and right this moment you are in danger of contravening monastic laws.'

Ainnir looked confused, and Donal whispered with a glint in his eye. 'You are standing in the men's chambers.'

'Then I am trespassing. Should I have sought permission from the Earl?' Ainnir laughed.

So too, did Donal.

It felt good; a reluctant spring finally summoning courage, calling for winter to end.

Donal spread a woollen cloth over the ground and followed with cheeses and breads and a trencher. Ainnir joined him, tucking her skirts around her ankles and took the wine skin he offered.

'Ainnir, I would know your thoughts, about us, our wedding. It is your father's wish, but I would know of yours. Do you welcome the day?' Donal was somewhat surprised at his own feeling of apprehension, not sure he truly wanted an answer.

Ainnir took a long gulp from the skin, then handed it back. 'I accept it.' Her voice low, her eyes guarded.

'Accept it or welcome it?'

She aimlessly picked at the grass. 'I accept it.'

'I too, accept it.' He paused, and saw her eyes shift. 'But I now also welcome our joining.'

He laid back, grabbed at a piece of cheese and ate.

'Ainnir, I am twelve years your senior, have seen more winters than you, and, God willing, there will be many more to come. I have endured great loss. My wife died a twelve month afore, giving birth to my dead son. That is a grief I will take to my grave. But Thomas is right; it is time I take another wife. I want children, a long line of happy, spirited red-haired children, blessed with the looks of their mother rather than their father,' he added with a gentle laugh. 'But I will be a good father and I would have you know I am not a man you should fear.'

He joined her in picking from the blades of grass for a time. 'We have been matched for our kin and I am not sure what the future holds for our two families. Our marriage may go some way to bring peace. And,' he inhaled deeply, 'well, you are indeed a beautiful lass – quarrelsome, but very beautiful.'

He studied her face, again searching for a response. None came, just magnificent blue eyes that darted back and forth.

'You are quiet. You have been so since you arrived. Very

unlike the vibrant young woman I saw at Glendalough.'

'I am sorry. Everything is simply daunting. I mean no disrespect.'

'None taken. Speak your mind.'

She hesitated and lifted a hand to her neck.

'Your pendant. What is it?'

'An Ouroboros. Muirne insisted I wear it.'

'It is beautiful. And its meaning?'

'It is a serpent with its tail in its mouth. A continuous circle. Muirne says it portrays the inevitable cycle of life. She hopes I can draw strength from its power.'

Ainnir looked down, and twirled the pendant in her fingers. 'I was given no choice in this marriage.' Her voice was gentle. 'As you say, it was my father's decision and I now find myself removed from the mountains I have known as home all my life. I do not remember a time when Mama was not by my side. Glendalough's castle is as big as your stables. My bedchamber here could host a king's coronation. Where one candle was sufficient in my home, here there are twenty. Within it I feel so ... so insignificant. And, I find that you are but a stranger to me. I do not mean to say that I have not been made welcome. Quite the contrary. Everyone has been so wonderful. It is just that I feel ... alone. Yes, alone.'

'Alone? I truly understand. There have been times when I have felt alone although surrounded by crowds. But as for our walls, Ainnir, the Fitzgeralds hold many strongholds and manors. None as grand or the size of Maynooth. Perhaps one day we will make one of those our home. But with time, the vastness of Maynooth and your loneliness will recede, and, I am beginning to find great pleasure in your company, so I do not think you will be alone too often. If I fail in this endeavour, I am sure Eleanor will gladly be your companion.'

'Yes,' Ainnir said with a smile. 'I believe I have grown a new shadow.'

'Ainnir, I am not an ogre.'

'Mama told me you were indeed a true gentleman, and I should not worry or be nervous, but I cannot still my apprehension, not yet.'

'In time?'

'Yes, perhaps.' Her answer was not convincing.

'I have missed laughter, have missed smiling. Thank you, Ainnir.'

Donal gently touched her hand for a short moment. 'All will be well. I assure you.'

The picnic completed, they returned to the castle at a gallop, slowing only to traverse the cobbled bridge beneath the castle's main gate. Ainnir looked up at the magnificent gatehouse and saw the Fitzgerald crest. Scrolls of floral vines surrounded a warrior's shield and a helm, and above that, a monkey.

'You have a monkey on the Fitzgerald crest?'

'That monkey saved the first Earl of Kildare when he was still an infant.'

She looked to Donal with sceptical eyes, and he laughed.

'It is true, I tell you. One hundred and fifty years ago, a fire caught at Woodstock Castle and our family's pet monkey saved the babe.'

They both burst with laughter, he for the unbelieving look upon her face, and she for the incredulous story, still not too sure whether he mocked her.

Her heart softened. How had she not noticed earlier that

Donal's eyes were a rich hazel, his face pleasant, long like a horse but finished with a chiselled jaw, and his voice strong and protective? Her own laugh continued a little longer than his, remembering his voice on the day of her arrival, gruff and ferocious. It now sounded so different. She was pleased her perception of some things had altered.

They continued toward the inner bailey, the echoes of their shared laughter trailing behind, and she gently touched the Ouroboros with silent thanks.

From behind a wagon laden with baskets of carrots and crates of cabbages, Jarlath watched their return. The gay laughter penetrated his soul and pierced his heart as would a sword's thrust. He saw no sadness, no sorrow, none to mirror his own.

Should he be glad that Ainnir did not suffer as he did? Should he envy her tolerance? How was he to share in Donal's happiness, their happiness? Should this insoluble anger be gone, vanished? Was it all ludicrous?

But his family's acceptance of Ainnir came at a great cost. Her happiness, her laughter, her marriage, all came at a great cost – to him.

It brought isolation and misery.

The anger was unconquerable.

To Hell with both of them.

Chapter Fourteen

The noise drew Donal's curiosity. The roosters were yet to welcome the day and the tired clashing of steel sang of a full day's practice. Donal followed the clamour to the training field in the outer bailey, and found twenty men toiling ceaselessly and, from the dark face and determined gait, it appeared that Jarlath's mood was as sharp as his sword.

Men dressed in chain mail and helmets tried themselves, harried and stretched beyond endurance, all to the roaring instructions of Jarlath.

'Again,' Jarlath ordered, and tapped his boot with the broad side of his sword to ready his opponent. The sword swung left then right, the men performing set routines.

Donal was both intrigued and disturbed by Jarlath's fervour. Rarely were the men dragged from their pallets at such an hour for basic drills, and he did not recall Thomas giving the order.

These recent dark tempers, this need for distance, they were not like Jarlath.

'Again,' Jarlath repeated to the men.

The swords grew heavy. The rhythm slowed. One man stopped to rest.

'More,' Jarlath called, wielding his own sword high.

Days earlier, Donal had voiced his concern to Thomas

only to discover the Earl too, worried. They tried to fathom the motive for the lad's changed behaviour, but were still at a loss.

In the minutes Donal stood watching, four men conceded defeat. Jarlath struck and drove as if crazed by demons. There was little if any defence in his moves. Attack and drive only, none with clever or well-crafted accomplishment, the movement of one Hell bent on violence.

'Lift your sword.' Donal swung himself over the railings, landing smoothly on the straw covered ground. 'You have our men up before the birds, Jarlath. Is there reason for such insanity?'

'None but the need for improvement,' Jarlath answered.

Donal's sword hissed as he pulled it free. 'Mind if I join you?'

He clicked his fingers and pointed at one of the men. A helmet flew through the air. He caught and donned the headpiece in one fluid movement.

'You need to alter your drills. When the attack comes from overhead, and your body takes the brunt forcing you down,' Donal explained, bending his knees deeply, 'do not remain on the defensive, it keeps you still and an easy target. Turn it to your advantage with haste. Thrust upwards like so, straight into ribs and plunge deep. Use your knees to take the initial blow and recover speedily.'

Donal nodded to Jarlath, readying him to begin.

Swords tapped helmets.

Jarlath widened his stance and bent his knees. Donal's attack came first, a succession of quick thrusts to his side, each blocked easily, then a fluster of faster blows, from left, right, then left again.

'Good.' He stepped back, taking note of Jarlath's too-wide stance, and threw a hard blow to his side. He then spun around in a full circle, bringing his sword down hard.

Jarlath stumbled to his knees, and remained in a defensive pose, suffering two more shuddering blows.

'You did not listen. Do not remain still whilst my blade is on the downturn. You should have propelled your body upwards, using the strength in your bent knees. You should have taken me when you had your chance.'

The other soldiers stopped their swordplay, turned their attention to the two Fitzgerald men.

Jarlath righted himself. Donal did not miss the clench of his jaw.

He tapped at Jarlath's leg with his blade. 'Correct your stance.'

Both men shuffled their feet to begin again. Eyes moved up and down, looking for an open opportunity.

Donal thrust forward, but was blocked too easily.

Jarlath was fast and struck hard, left then right, moving forward with strength and agility. The clashing swords rang through the air louder than bells. Jarlath lifted his sword striking down and spinning with a final blow from the right, sending Donal to the ground.

Donal would have been pleased with the lad's skill, had he not noticed the menacing look in those dark eyes, for that last blow possessed the ferocity of one used only on the battlefield.

He came to his feet.

The two men circled again. Stalking movements, with eyes more focused, more intent. Jarlath attacked first, two quick forward thrusts and a heavy blow to the left. Donal predicted the move and was quick to proffer an easy block. He followed with a low slice to the leg knowing Jarlath could do nothing but defend that last. He wasted no time and switched hands, attacking with his left, confusing his opponent, and dealt a decisive blow to Jarlath's upturned sword.

He ran at Jarlath, quickly pushed him to the ground and followed down, thrusting the hilt of his sword at Jarlath's neck.

'The blade is not the only weapon in my hand.' Donal's breath came hard and fast. Hostile eyes met his. 'What is wrong with you, Jarlath?'

No answer came.

'Whatever ails you, be rid of it. I am not your enemy.'

Donal stood and regarded the prone body with sheer frustration. He caught a glimpse of what he believed was regret, but could not be sure. He did not wish to remain to find out.

'I am expected elsewhere. As I said, lift your sword.'

With that, he returned his sword to its sheath, stormed back toward the courtyard. He had come seeking answers, but left more baffled than before. Whatever the source of Jarlath's anger, Donal prayed a solution would present itself.

He hoped to God it would come soon.

Chapter Fifteen

Manus Eustace possessed genuine charm. He could capture the ladies' attention with one benevolent grin, and this day was to be no different.

As he walked through the hall, his brash regard measured all that was on offer. To his right, *hair the shade of moonlight, pretty nose, a little squat*. To his left, *endless lashes, sweet smile, a little old*. In the corner, *red hair, poised, lips with promise*. Ten paces ahead, *honey-gold hair, eyes a heavenly blue, pretending no interest*. That could change. This could be an enjoyable stay.

'Mayhem has arrived at Maynooth.' Thomas bellowed a warm welcome.

Manus lifted a hand in protest. 'My reputation unfairly precedes me, my lord.'

'Unfairly? You jest, Manus. When my daughter is of age my doors will be closed to you.'

'Am I that predictable?'

'Too.' Thomas signalled to a servant for drinks. 'Come. Sit. I had hoped to see your uncle ride in with you. Roland was forestalled?'

Manus sat into a chair and adjusted his jacket. 'Yes. Dublin and Arland Ussher keep him busy.'

'Ussher? That man is the most unsightly in all of Ireland

and possesses a temperament to match. What trouble does he stir?'

'The usual complaints. Coin and you.'

A lively laugh fell from Thomas' mouth.

'It may please you to hear that Ussher will not bear the title Mayor of Dublin for much longer. He will step down, along with this.' Manus handed Thomas a sealed letter. 'My uncle asked that I deliver this to you directly.'

Thomas ripped at the seal, looked over the missive then nodded. 'I am to be appointed Justiciar next week at Naas. Naas. The Meeting Place of Kings. Hah! So, it is scheduled. I can only imagine the profanities from Ussher's mouth at that quirk of fate. Roland will join us for this? I would have him as my chancellor.'

'Nothing will stop the Baron, my lord. His exact words were, *I look forward to celebrating the joining of the Great Lord of Kildare and this elemental mistress.*'

'Your uncle credits me with excessive fidelity?'

Manus had heard it said that unlike most men, Thomas rarely strayed from his wife's bed. 'So it seems.'

They shared a short laugh.

'I bring more news.' Manus' tone altered. 'The Earl of Warwick and Prince George have returned to England. The King's ships patrolled the seas off France, but storms swept the Channel and the blockade scattered.' He took a proffered cup. 'Warwick and George took their chance and now race to Devon where thousands of Lancastrians and malcontents rally to their standards. The King is in England's north, Thomas. He is in need of our help.'

'You are a two-sided coin this day, Manus. First news of

good and now this. And Roland? What are his thoughts?'

'As are yours, my lord, if I am to read your face correctly. I have offered to stand in his stead, lead the way to England and fight as we must.'

Their discussion progressed no further.

'Manus, you scoundrel,' yelled Donal, joining the men by the hearth. 'When did you ride in?'

'Just now, my friend, but had I known you were here to greet me I may have remained in Dublin.'

'I see your manners have not improved.'

'Did you truly expect such a miracle?'

'Not before I see a hot desert wind sweep through the castle in winter.'

The men clasped arms.

'I see there is great improvement in you, Donal. You speak without a grumble.'

'You have just arrived, Manus. Give it time,' said Thomas.

'My cousin is a comical man.' Donal pulled up a chair and sat alongside the two men.

'Would it have anything to do with the vows we are to celebrate this week?' Manus asked.

'It may. Speaking of weddings, how is your lovely Meg?'

'I have not seen my bed for three months. Our lives are consistent, if nothing else. But when do I get to meet the cause of your change?'

Donal nodded to the centre of the hall.

Honey-gold hair, eyes a heavenly blue, pretending no interest. Manus laughed to himself then let out a whistle. 'So that's the O'Byrne daughter? No wonder he kept her hidden in the mountains.'

'Put your tongue back in your mouth before I cut it off,' Donal warned casually.

Donal gave a quick kick with his foot, Manus threw up his hands with a curse, his chair flying out from under him.

Thomas spluttered his laughter. So too, did other guests in the hall.

Manus picked himself up off the floor. 'I suppose I deserved that and will keep my mouth in check from here on. It is obvious your green streak has a tinge of red.'

Thomas gave another roar of laughter.

'Off limits, stripling,' Donal warned again.

'I ensure the nests I feather are empty, Donal.' Manus brushed himself off and collected his chair. 'Is that Jarlath by the stairs? What happened to his face? Ten rounds with a boxer?'

'One round is how I hear it told,' answered Thomas. 'A tavern brawl last night, one he caused, I believe.'

'It is not the first this week,' added Donal. 'The O'Byrne lads saved his hide two nights ago. We can assume they were not as quick last night. There is something troubling him, Manus. Both Thomas and I have tried to speak to him. He avoids me like the plague and Thomas has had little more luck.'

'He is an enigma,' said Thomas.

Head lowered, sombre-faced, a darkness covered Jarlath. Manus could not decide if he saw anger or grief. Perhaps both.

'Could he do with an adventure, Thomas?'

'Jarlath?'

'Why not? I can think of no other I would want by my side. Except for you of course, my lord,' Manus added with an elegant flourish of his hand.

Thomas smiled a thin smile, one that vanished too quickly. 'His manner of late worries me.' He said nothing more for a time. *Could Manus be right? Could a journey to England be what my nephew needs?*

'Jarlath!' Thomas shouted.

Jarlath manoeuvred his way through the hall, avoiding men gathered in games of card and dice.

Donal looked to his companions with a perplexing frown. 'What have I missed?'

Manus served Donal a brief summary of his news from England.

'It must be his decision,' Thomas said quietly, as Jarlath approached. 'I will not make it an order.'

'Jarlath, it is good to see you again.' Manus stood. The greeting included a warm embrace.

'You too, Manus. It has been a while.'

Manus noted that the usual camaraderie in Jarlath's welcome was absent, and he did not bother to disguise his curiosity. 'Too long I fear. If you had my company last night, I'm sure you would not look so ugly this day. Were you too slow, he too fast, or perhaps it was a she? Have you broken yet another fiery heart?'

'Wrong on all counts, Manus. Too drunk.'

Manus laughed. 'Come hear the news I bring.'

At Thomas' signal, a number of their men joined them. Thomas gave a précis of the news from England, bolstered by his opinions and an inventory of possibilities. He did not neglect the risks then finished with, 'We can be sure a battle is brewing, for the Lancastrians will challenge the King in earnest. He is in need of our support.'

'I will go to England.' Jarlath dared the Earl to refuse his offer.

Manus looked back and forth between the two men. They appeared like two bulls measuring and studying each other before the charge.

'You are sure?' said Thomas.

'Yes.'

'So, it is decided.' Thomas turned. 'Manus freshen yourself, lad. You have been in the saddle and your stench suggests you've been sleeping amongst turnip shavings.'

Laughter came from some, but not all. It was absent from three sets if lips – the three Fitzgerald men.

'We shall meet again after the noon meal in the solar for counsel. We have plans to discuss. Donal, roust our captains. I want them present.'

Jarlath and Manus left the company and marched through the crowd, heading toward the door.

'Thomas is right. You do stink, my friend.'

'You Fitzgeralds are all the same – all asses. But I have missed you. She is a beauty. He's a lucky man.'

'Who?'

'Donal.' Manus nodded in the direction of the beautiful woman with honey-gold hair and heavenly blue eyes. She stood in the middle of the hall looking their way, and this time, the eyes held obvious interest.

Heavenly blue looked directly at Jarlath, yet the attention was not returned, Jarlath's eyes remaining fixed upon their avenue of exit.

Manus did not miss a thing.

'Yes, he is,' said Jarlath.

'And you?'
'Me? Lucky?
'Yes, you.'
Jarlath did not reply immediately.
Manus expected none.
'I am off to try my luck with a bow and arrow. I will meet you later for counsel.'

Oh, dear friend. I fear you are need of more than counsel.

Chapter Sixteen

Gerald crept cautiously, catlike, his steps slow and deliberate. His footfall would not have disturbed a babe from sleep. A green fern-like bush concealed his form, the earthy colours of his clothing giving even more camouflage.

His prey stood on spindly legs, head bent, grazing on lush foliage. As if sensing the intruders the young stag looked up, nostrils flared, ears tweaked. But the warning came too late. The arrow pierced its side with a thud. The animal flinched almost imperceptibly then fell to the earth.

'Hoorah!' yelled Gerald's accomplice. 'You got him! You got him!' Running to the dead stag, Tom congratulated his brother. 'Papa will be impressed, and won't cook be pleased.'

The boys stood over the dead animal, examining its body with smug arrogance. The arrow pierced the skin behind its shoulder, entered straight through its lung. *A necessity to a successful hunt*, their father always lectured, *so the animal did not overly suffer, nor take flight scaring others in its herd to flee before another arrow could be nocked and loosened.*

'He didn't know what hit him,' Gerald said proudly. 'Here, Tom, you grab his legs and we'll haul him back to the horses.'

'Look, Ainnir. Look at him. Is he not a beauty? And you can tell everyone Gerald hunted him down.'

'He certainly is, Tom. I am indeed impressed. Gerald has a fine aim, but you did well too. It requires a good deal of self-control to be so still and quiet when your prey is close.'

Tom's chest visibly rose along with his smile.

The boys swung the stag across Tom's horse. The mount shifted, startled by the scent of blood. Tom and Gerald made a merry dance, avoiding the strong hind of the animal as it circled one way then the other. Tom grabbed the reins and spoke in a calm tone whilst Gerald tied the carcass to the saddle.

'It should be right now, Tom. Hop up and see if it holds.'

Gerald was magnanimous in nature when it came to his brothers and sister. He allowed Tom the honour of towing the dead stag, knowing to carry their catch through the castle grounds for all to see, would please him.

'What do you think, Ainnir?' Gerald asked, hands on hips, chin high in the air.

'It is a fine catch.'

Gerald offered her an engaging smile, a jaunty unnerving smile, one to raise her brow. He may be magnanimous to his siblings, but his manner with others was all too different. He lacked little in any degree of self-importance, was fleetingly impudent, owner of a honeyed tongue and swaggered like a man five years his elder.

She was taken aback by his flippant, flirtatious ways, yet found Gerald's manner to be almost comical.

Gerald seemed to ignore the raised brow. 'Yes, he is indeed a fine catch. You should take care, Ainnir, lest you find yourself the prey and I the hunter.'

Laughter came. 'You are incorrigible, Gerald. What

would your father say if he could hear you?'

'What's incorrigible?' queried Tom.

'Nothing good,' explained Ainnir.

'I think it is good,' said Gerald.

'I have seen enough for one day.' Ainnir threw Gerald a plea for an end to his unwelcome innuendos. 'Our lengthy absence may give cause for worry. You would want neither your father nor Donal to have concerns, would you?'

'Ouch,' Gerald said with a conciliatory smirk. 'Another day then?'

They moved on. Tom rode beside Ainnir, chatting wildly with childish enthusiasm and boasting of his knowledge of hunting in manly fashion.

'Always approach from downwind ... winter is a difficult season to hunt, for the snapping of frozen bracken on the ground alerts the deer to the hunter's approach ... horned deer is less palatable if felled during the rutting season.'

Gerald interrupted the chatter, bringing his horse to Ainnir's side. 'Papa received word this morning from Dublin. He is to be appointed Justiciar of Ireland next week. I am to travel to Naas with him for the ceremony and his first parliament.'

'Am I to accompany Papa too?'

'You're too young, Tom.' Gerald dealt the wound quickly and without thought, then added as balm, 'Mama will have need of you. One of us needs to remain and watch over the castle.'

'That is indeed quite an honour, Gerald. You must ensure you keep your tongue still. Do you think that's possible?' Ainnir asked.

Gerald's regard rounded with a look of incredulity. 'I

would neither disgrace my father nor the Fitzgerald name.' His voice rose to bells of indignation, and just as quickly, melted to a thick honey. 'Yet does it matter what I say when my thoughts are to the contrary?'

'Was that incorrigible?' Tom asked.

'Yes, Tom,' Ainnir replied with a laugh. 'It is exactly that, and precocious, and irredeemable and arrogant.'

'Oh, I know that one. I know arrogant.' Tom's attention stole elsewhere. 'Jarlath,' he yelled.

On the muddy banks of a slow trickling creek, Jarlath squatted cleaning a set of arrows.

'What do you think of our catch?' Tom's toothy grin altered. 'What happened to your eye?'

'To your first question, I am impressed, and to your second, I ducked when I should have dodged.'

'And how did your opponent fair?' asked Gerald.

'That I cannot tell you, for I did not see him coming, nor did I see him go.'

Gerald and Tom chuckled.

Ainnir did not.

Her breath shortened as she waited for Jarlath's eyes to meet hers. As much as she believed she had resigned herself to her fate, accepted the inevitability of a new life, now with Jarlath so close, so arrantly cornered, she felt as if an unwilling yet excited hunter, a nervous poacher with an arrow nocked and aimed. Too many tormenting hours, spent confused and seeking to understand why Jarlath offered naught but distance and silence, ate away her days. And here and now, in the forest with no escape, he was her captive. Nerves be damned! His release would come at the cost of his speech, a currency he seemed to value above all else.

'Any luck today, Jarlath?' she asked, with an unconvincing ring to her voice.

'None.' He kept his gaze low. 'None for some time.'

The sarcasm cracked, no less succinct than a tree hit by lightning.

'That is not the way I hear it told. You are venerated far and wide for your hunting skills. Your aim is beyond reproach. You fell your quarry before they even know they have become a target. And then of course, with the blink of an eye you turn your back and with no more thought for the injured beast, you move to find more prey.'

Jarlath refused to reply, picked up another arrow, shook it through water.

'Some would gloat at such manly prowess.' Ainnir dared a retort.

It was then he lifted his gaze. His stare shot flames; she was now charred. Her legs flinched at the unexpected recognition of misery, and her horse danced, responding to her awkward shift in the saddle.

'You'd best be on your way before the slain beast rises from the dead.'

Jarlath's words sizzled like pork on a griddle, and Ainnir felt hit by the spitting fat.

The boys laughed unaware of the heat in the exchanges, and turned their horses to head back to the castle leaving in their wake wishes of good luck. Ainnir followed, shaken, unable to say further. It seemed Jarlath had again bested his prey.

They had not travelled far.

'Gerald, go on ahead. I wish to speak with Jarlath for a

moment. We have not spoken since my arrival here for my brothers have selfishly kept him to themselves. Would you mind? I am sure he will see to my return.'

The two boys made no argument. They were keen to head back to the castle and boast of their catch.

Everything inside Ainnir screamed this was wrong, but a lurching hurt turned her deaf to the heeding. Through the trees she could see Jarlath standing by the creek. He did not turn at the sound of her return.

'We should speak, Jarlath,' she said calmly.

'And what should we speak of?' His tone was no different.

She sat for a long moment watching his back. Her horse stomped impatiently and she swung from the saddle. 'Of us. Of Donal.'

'There is nothing to say.'

'Nothing?' Her question flew on a laugh. 'There is plenty.'

'There is nothing to say for all has been decided.' With a tone now bitter, Jarlath turned his head slightly as he spoke, but would only give her his back. 'Glendalough is but a memory, and Maynooth and Donal, your future. I do remember saying your father would have plans. 'Tis unfortunate I did not know the details at the time.'

'Do you blame me?'

'No.'

'Do you hate me?'

'No. You should leave, Ainnir. And now.'

'Why do you give me naught but silence?'

'Let things be.'

'Answer me.'

'I said let things be. Go and be married. Go and be happy.'

'Was I just another whore to you?'

Jarlath spun around, one fluid movement. His jaw tightened. His eyes narrowed.

'My silence? Silence was all I could think to give anyone, Ainnir, when told of your betrothal. And silence is all I have left. Would you like to know how it felt? We were no more than a quarter mile from your castle walls, Thomas to my right and Donal to my left. Would you like me to tell you of the hate I bore for my uncle in that minute, how my hand ached to clutch my dagger, and how I wished Donal dead and did not care how it came to him? Would you like to know what birds sang in the trees, the angle of the shadows from the high branches, what flowers blossomed in the grasses around me? If you ask, I will answer, for that is how despicably memorable that moment is. And still now, I can think of naught else but silence to give you, or give anyone else. There is only hate and guilt thriving within me, and best I not give voice to either.'

His pain fell with every word. He felt just as she did. She saw that, now. His hurt cut to the equal of her own.

Ainnir took one hesitant step forward.

'It was the stinging song of the curlew at my window, and it was the white blossoms of the wood sorrel blooming in the garden below, when my father told me the news. It was loathing that churned my entire being like none I have ever felt. And I told him so. But there has been no guilt, no regret, Jarlath. I cannot tell you of the angle of shadows, for the sun disappeared too quickly for me that day. And it was just before noon when I was told, so my tears flowed whilst you bore your hate. That is how memorable that moment is to me.'

She paused, eyes blinking heavily. Her voice became a whisper. 'Yet it is not silence I wish to give you. I suffer too. No less than you. Do you not see?'

Jarlath's throat worked hard. 'My silence is my way of coping, Ainnir. Please leave, now.'

'Coping? You speak of coping?'

'For the love of Christ will you stop?' he hissed between clenched teeth. 'Ainnir, we are not the perfect people who live in your poetry. We cannot write the ending to this story.'

'I will not stop. Do you truly think you are the only one pained? My nights are the colour of black. I dare not sleep, too afraid of the dreams that come, dreams of you. And when I can no longer fight, I wake in terror. And it is empty darkness in my grasp, not what I long for.'

She took another hesitant step forward, and her words came on sobs. 'I know not what to do. I long to yell it is you I want, but I cannot. How can I when I am promised to your kin?'

'Enough!'

Desperate anguish mottled Jarlath's face. His words followed as if a plea. 'I am forced to sit mutely, watch as you marry another. Do you not think I am nauseated when I see you with him, when I imagine you in his bed at the end of this week?'

'Don't, please,' she whispered, shaking her head.

'My silence is the only thing I have to keep me from utter insanity.'

'You touched me, Jarlath. And I touched you in the

same way.'

They stood for a time, neither having more to say, neither able to tear eyes away, the gentle trickle of the creek the only sound.

Jarlath closed the distance between them with such speed she gasped. She had no time to fear anything, no time to take another breath. His mouth was on hers, fast and vicious. He was not gentle and she did not protest. He lifted her from where she stood, placed her onto the damp ground and held her face. He claimed her lips again and again and his hands moved frantically.

The sound of her gown ripping set her body alight. She welcomed his unrestrained advance. Her own hands tried to keep pace with his. He lifted her skirts, plundered quickly.

She heard nothing but her own voice – her pleas, her moans, his name. Then an echoing roar spliced the forest air.

Jarlath shuddered, strained his neck high, grit his teeth.

Neither moved for a time.

The creek flowed again.

Ainnir breathed heavily and looked to the treetops above. Nothing moved. The ambling branches stared like shocked witnesses.

What had they done?

It was not the thought of Donal that brought the stirring of regret. This man, this coupling on the forest floor, it was not the Jarlath she knew. He was as if a stranger. It was not how it should have been. It was not what she wanted to happen. She had all but made her peace, resigned herself to her path. Now, here in his arms, having given over her body, where was her Jarlath?

This was not lovemaking. This was not his heart in need of hers. It was merely his need to take, to possess, to brand. So many questions demanded to be asked. Only one found voice.

'What will become of us?'

'Nothing, Ainnir. This was a mistake. I am sorry, this will not happen again.' Jarlath moved from her body and gave her his back.

'Jarlath?' Painful confusion flooded the use of his name. 'Jarlath, where are you, for it is not the Jarlath I know, now standing before me?'

Jarlath shook his head. 'This cannot happen again. You will marry Donal. Dress yourself. You should leave before we are found.'

He made no offer to help her from the ground, collected his arrows and mounted his horse. 'Move quickly. I will follow at a distance until you are free of this forest.'

Anger enough exploded to still Ainnir's threatening tears. 'I did not come here with words as a ruse to have you take me, Jarlath, if that is what you suspect. All I bargained for was your voice, a reprieve from your silence. Do not humiliate me now with your arrant self-loathing, for it is I, lying here on the ground with my skirts high like a wanton. It is I who should call this a mistake. You should not have that privilege before me.'

Ainnir raised herself from the ground, prodded and pulled at her garments with shaking fingers, then gathered the reins of her horse.

'That was not my intent.'

She heard no apology in his tone. 'You once told me you felt second to much in your life. Well I thank you for the lesson, for you now have brought that pleasure to me.'

'You have no understanding of how that feels.'

'I do now, Jarlath. You and my father have taught me well.'

With that she swung herself into the saddle and pushed her horse to speed.

Ainnir did know what it was like. She knew only too well, and may God help her, for her heart did not find enmity as it should. She prayed for hate to come, an endless stream to banish her feelings for Jarlath, but riding away, after being used and discarded, it did not come.

The noon meal ended, a freshly attired Manus lounged in the large cushioned chair at the solar's table, sharing news from England with the Earl's captains. Voices alternated between rankled and jovial, for Manus possessed the unholy skill of aptly delivering the direst news with humour. If the lack of coin in his purse ever presented a difficulty, he could always become a travelling bard. Not a hall in all of Ireland would refuse his presence.

Gerald too, was present, chuffed and full of self-importance to be included in the deliberations of counsel. His eyes travelled from man to man, watching for openings to laugh or frown, openings to growl or throw a hand gesture to the air; the intentional imitation appeared more comical than not.

Jarlath paced along the windows looking out to the sky, not noticing the moving clouds nor birds spiriting their way across the blue. His steps were full of anxiety, keen for Thomas to join the gathering and begin discussions of his journey to England – a hooded falcon, perched and tethered, aware of the sounds heralding flight.

The undercurrents of his mind differed little. Not much time had passed since he returned from the forest. He had not found the occasion to think rationally or reflect on what occurred. Nor had he washed. Her scent still haunted him, plagued his every movement like a nettle. Although he was the nephew of the Earl of Kildare and grandson to a Gaelic Chieftain, at this moment he had never felt more sure that he came from the gutter.

Thomas burst through the doors, took stock of those present.

'You are late, my lord. We have been waiting,' Jarlath said.

Thomas arched an eyebrow. 'My apologies, dear nephew.'

Manus looked at Jarlath, his tone less indicting. 'You're in a mood. Would a girl be the source?'

Jarlath tossed Manus a warning frown; he was not willing to partake in a round of jests.

'Now that my nephew has caught everyone's attention, we shall begin. We all know the consequences of a defeated Yorkist throne. If the Lancastrians prevail, they will divide our lands. Reward will fall to the Butlers. Kildare will no longer be Fitzgerald land. Such an evil is to be avoided at all costs. I have not fought and bled for years to have it all taken.'

Thomas looked to each man in that room. Not one set of eyes looked elsewhere – studious faces, loyal, eager and ready to pounce on his order. He breathed in deeply, his nostrils flaring.

'I have not fought and bled for years to have our

achievements taken from us so easily,' he repeated. 'Yet I possess no dim-witted dreams that this path will be simple. Manus has brought news. Baron Portlester will send arms to England, if we choose to join him. I cannot see we have any other choice.'

He looked to Jarlath. 'You will lead the men. My captains, I have faith in my nephew, and I suspect there is none amongst you who thinks anything to the contrary.'

Fists of approval slammed the table in chorus. One rigid bob of his head served as Jarlath's thanks.

'Manus will journey with you from here and will meet with the Baron's men at the port of Dublin.'

'I should also accompany the men,' Donal announced unexpectedly.

Jarlath's back tightened. His eyes fell to the table.

'No,' was Thomas' quick reply. 'What I have not shared with you as yet, is that word from Hugh O'Byrne has arrived. It appears Butler is again restless. Scouts report that arms and provisions are being prepared.'

Murmurings grew. The men shared their thoughts, shared concerns for their own lands and families.

Jarlath remained mute. He did not trust himself to open his mouth again. Fury seemed to taint every word, every thought.

Jarlath noted Thomas staring, studying his face with the focus of an artist. What could his uncle see? A traitor? A Judas?

The study ceased and Thomas' eyes returned to the room. 'Butler will expect our attention to be elsewhere for a time. Donal, you are needed here. As much as I wish to give adequate support to King Edward, our families and villagers and all of Kildare may have need of us.'

Donal nodded his assent, and gave no further argument.

'And you will have a new wife by that day,' Manus said to Donal. 'I know of no man who would want to be dragged from the marital bed so soon after the vows. Well, perhaps one.'

As laughter filled the room, Jarlath felt Manus turn eyes his way. *Another artist? Does self-hate possess a stench?* Jarlath moved quietly around the room in an attempt to avoid the obtrusive stare.

'And our route to England?' he asked too quickly.

'As I said, Portlester's men will meet you in Dublin and a ship will be readied for your departure to Bristol. From there you will ride to London and our contact will seek you out. Her name is Marguerite.'

The men voiced their amusement.

'Yes, as ironic as it may be that one sharing the same name as the Lancastrian Queen should be of help to us, it is to be the way.'

'Do we know the attributes of this Marguerite, my lord?' asked Manus. 'I would like notice in advance if I am to fight your nephew for her ... favours.'

More laughter filled the air.

Thomas gave over a serious look to both Jarlath and Manus. 'I expect you will send news to us when you arrive in Bristol, lads. Your families here will be eager for word. Do I make myself clear? Your preparations begin today for you leave the day after the wedding.'

'Would it not be wise to leave earlier?' Jarlath suggested.

'Never rush to a bloody war,' answered Thomas. 'Gerald, you will inspect the armoury – twice. Leave nothing to chance. Then, my son, I wish you to be at my side, in Naas. One day it will be *your* future all of Ireland will look to.'

While Jarlath held his tongue, Gerald's lips completed a lazy dance in his failing attempt to remain as sombre-faced as the other men. A beaming, pride-filled smile won out.

'We have five days before we depart. As to the murmurings of the Ormonds, I hope to receive more information either in the next few days or at Naas. I do not think more need be said at this point. They are my instructions. See they are done.'

The men remained for a time, discussing their preparations. Thomas called Jarlath away, requested a private word.

'I do not understand your sudden fervour for battle, Jarlath, and you give no thought to staying, though trouble is brewing close to your home.'

Thomas walked to the windows. Jarlath dutifully yet reluctantly followed, and they stood for a moment, sharing the view.

'I fear what will come to pass in England may be more than what you bargain for, lad, but if it is this journey you need to be rid of your ghosts, take it, be sure to leave them there. Most importantly, return to me, Jarlath, healed or not, return to me safely. You are like a son and it is perhaps past time I remind you.'

'I will return. I promise you that, Uncle,' and only Jarlath knew how repugnant that thought to be.

Chapter Seventeen

It seemed to Jarlath the morning mass ran overly long, like a winter's frost failing to move into spring. The emotions he suffered in the forest renewed themselves; self-loathing begat pity, pity begat hate, hate begat anger, anger begat regret. And longing was now added and utterly consuming. He felt enslaved by emotions.

Ainnir sat alongside Joan, her head bowed as she prayed, reverent and still, except for the slight turn of her head and the vacant eyes slanted his way. It was as if she knew he ogled, sensed she was hostage to his watch. She looked tired, so tired, yet resplendent in a glorious shade of pink. It was a colour he had not yet seen on her skin. The sun's morning rays streamed through the high windows of Saint Mary's Chapel and touched her braided tresses.

What she prayed for he could only imagine; absolution, forgiveness, patience and hope. Nothing less than he prayed for.

Following yesterday's tryst, he had conceded defeat. He was lost. His heart was hers. Yet all the while the voice of reason screamed, demanding his heart be unshackled from this woman. Impossible! He knew that now, knew it futile to fight his heart. Knew too, in this, he betrayed them all – Donal, Thomas and Joan.

He betrayed them all.

> *'Deus meus,*
> *cum sis omnipotens,*
> *infinite misericors et fidelis,*
> *spero Te mihi daturum,*
> *ob merita Iesu Christi.'*

Pardon for my sins. It was an appropriate prayer of contrition. The Grace of the Lord abandoned his soul, and Eternal Damnation would meet him at the end of his road. Salvation was a forgotten dream. No matter how hard he sought to convince himself Ainnir was but a memory, his will failed him. Even at night, in those hours when his mind wandered unleashed, dreams were filled with lapping laughter and the bluest of eyes, hovering just out of reach.

> *'In nomine Patris*
> *et Filii*
> *et Spiritus Sancti.'*

'Amen,' filled the Chapel as all raised their hands to dutifully make the sign of the cross.

People began to leave their seats. Jarlath caught the familiar fragrance of her skin, lavender and rosewater. He looked up to the marble crucifix standing beneath the chancel arch. *Eaque detestor, quia peccando*, the priest had prayed during the mass; *I detest all my sins.*

'All but one,' he whispered to himself. 'All but one.'

England could not come soon enough.

The mass now complete, pace and gaiety filled the late morning.

Along the potted roads of Maynooth, plumes of dust and spitting stones flew in tempo with turning wheels and clopping hooves. Merchants and peddlers, distant travellers and local villagers, all came to enjoy the market outside the castle walls. Colourful, makeshift canopies – some stripped, some solid – lined the impromptu walkways, providing shelter for traders. Wooden lengths hastily nailed together afforded stages for bards and loudmouthed-peddlers, and a raised platform with trestles and benches and buxom serving-women, sufficed as an open-air tavern.

Thomas delayed meeting Jarlath and Manus at the roofless tavern, choosing to spend time with his family before he lost himself in an afternoon of carousing. Gerald, Tom and James settled into a competition of archery, and with Donal for company, Thomas stood behind each boy in turn offering fatherly advice.

'Loosen your grip on the hemp, James.' Thomas bent low, and with hands on knees spoke quietly into James' ear. 'That's it, son, just pull back gently. Steady. Steady. Aim.'

James released the arrow. It flew true and thudded into the sack not thirty paces away, albeit slightly off centre.

'Well done, lad,' Thomas said, ruffling James' hair.

'Not as good as Gerald,' James complained lightly. 'But I am getting better.'

Three arrow heads sat plum in the centre of Gerald's target.

'I'll make it four,' Gerald stated with confidence. He nocked another arrow, took aim, and released. 'Four!'

'Move over, Gerald,' Donal grunted good-naturedly. 'I'll split those arrows of yours with my eyes closed.'

'Are you sure you want to do this, Donal?' asked Thomas. 'If memory serves me right, the last time you offered a challenge in archery you spent the night walking two laps barefooted in the snow around our stables.'

'Perhaps we could up the stakes,' suggested Gerald, cocky and bold. 'Three laps of the stables. Keep your boots on if you must, but not your hose.'

'Hah! And you will abide by this wager when I beat you?'

'If you beat me, Donal, but yes.'

'Agreed.'

The women wandered closer to the archery field.

Eleanor squealed. 'Mama, look. Puppets! Puppets! Please, may we go?'

'I will take Eleanor, my lady.' Ainnir's words lacked any hint of enthusiasm.

'You are pale, Ainnir. Are you not well?'

'No, my lady. Just a little tired.'

Joan was not convinced. She watched the young woman for a moment. Eyes would not meet hers.

'Thank you, Ainnir. I did promise to join my sons before the archery ends. I will meet you once it is done. Now behave, Eleanor.' She laughed, watching her daughter run ahead before the words were out.

A quiet Ainnir followed the child's path.

Joan turned her attention to her sons – three sons, not four. Maurice would have been by her side if his curiosity with water had not earlier led him to the pond in the castle courtyard. A distracted nurse had burst into a dither, fishing the spluttering child from beneath the water lilies and he was quickly taken off to his room to be dried.

But now, her dry sons seemed to enjoy the attention their father bestowed. Thomas may be the Earl of Kildare, yet he never shirked his responsibilities as father, shared his time equally amongst them all and as often as he was able. Even during meetings of importance, if a word of comfort or a knee and a cuddle were required, the affairs of state were adjourned momentarily. For such understanding she loved him all the more.

Looking at the backs of her archers, she could not help but muse on the obvious; the three seemed forged of varying moulds.

Gerald, with his showmanship, conducted himself in a fashion many assumed to be arrogance, a trait which often caused Joan to inwardly cringe. Yet she knew his haughtiness hid a growing man whose heart was desirous to do good, to help the weak and needy, to follow in her husband's footsteps.

Tom, applauding both brothers' efforts with their bows, was their warrior, forever setting wrongs to rights, protector of all and slave to none – with the exception of perhaps his elder brother – and honest to a fault. May God help any who tried to bully or best an unfortunate, for they would have Tom and his judgement to answer to.

And James, listening attentively to instruction, was a gentle soul, perhaps the most likely of her brood to take holy orders. Always the peacemaker, he was content to be second, or go without for others, quick to find good in any lacking situation.

Joan's thoughts shifted to their youngest child as laughter from the puppetry show came to her ears – their

Eleanor, their sweet, energetic, honest, caring, little flower, the girl whose tongue stumbled over the pronunciation of Ainnir's name, no matter how she tried. A queen she would be, if she could but find a King who would allow her to run barefoot from dawn to dusk, leave her hair unbound to fly with the wind, and make every decision in the realm without question.

They were well blessed with this brood. Very blessed. Even with the quiet Maurice who at times believed himself a fish. And the child yet to be born would likely bring another depth to this gaggle of personas. And God willing, she prayed silently as her fingers splayed across her stomach, the babe would deliver safe and well.

Cheers and guffaws returned her thoughts to the archery. She beamed with pride as her boys followed all instructions given by their father. They nocked arrows, missed targets, hit some, missed some more, and nocked again. They seemed reluctant to end their time.

The competition dragged. Her sons gave little focus to her presence.

From beside the archery grounds, the hint of sweet and alien fragrances wafted through the air, their aromas enticing. Believing she had indeed given an agreeable amount of time to the three boys, Joan decided to wander; a short walk to steal the luxury of a few moments alone. Even in the midst of a large crowd, she could always discover a morsel of private contemplation, a moment lacking any responsibility.

Jugglers tossed twirling batons high. Men jeered at a game of strength lifting heavy logs above their heads. A blind man armed with a gnarled walking stick narrated a frightening tale of sea-monsters and sinking ships to open-mouthed onlookers. Children chased a small man dressed as a mouse – or was it a fox? He was a purple creature in any event with whiskers as long as her arms.

Lining the first trestle were rows of sandalwood boxes with samplings of exotic spices, small satchels of red silks filled with lavender seeds, and earthen pots with jasmine-laced creams. Ribbons hung from wooden rods. Bolts of cloth, every colour of the rainbow, sat in uniform piles from ground to roof.

'This cloth is sure to catch my lady's eye?' A small rotund man smiled warmly and pulled out a length of lemon velvet to wave before his prospective customer. His jowls twitched. 'It is certainly a colour for you, my lady.'

'Oh no, I do not think –'

'He is right, my love,' Thomas interrupted from behind.

'Lemon is not for a woman of my age, Thomas.'

'You are a woman of eighteen to me,' he whispered. 'We'll take this one,' Thomas continued, now addressing the merchant, 'and perhaps the orange, and the blue, and ... the red, yes the red. New gowns for my Countess should be the order of the day. Make it a double order, add some laces. And pick some ribbons. I will never hear the end of it if my pockets hold no surprises for my daughter.'

The merchant's eyes widened and he rushed to gather the order before the Earl could change his mind.

'How did our boys do at the archery?' Joan asked.

'Tom learnt to lift his aim, James will have sore hands for the next few days, and our eldest is expected at the stables tonight to run naked around the buildings – three times.'

Joan turned to Thomas, not at all sure she heard correctly.

'Do not fret, wife. We will make certain no women witness the event. 'Tis just a wager made between the men, of which our eldest was the loser. Gerald needs to learn to keep his tongue in check, and that a debt owed is a debt to be paid.'

'I will never understand the male mind, Thomas.'

'And that is the way we like it to be.' Thomas ordered the merchant to deliver the items to the castle then guiding Joan away, placed her hand in the nook of his arm. They wandered a time.

Villagers bobbed for apples in a vat of cold water. White and orange feathers floated above a cockfight. Jesters rolled and tumbled, circled and flipped, and melded into the crowd with the sounds of jingling bells following their trail. Thomas' eyes remained speared to the sky.

'Tell me your thoughts, Thomas. Your silence says your mind is elsewhere.'

'Jarlath.'

She squeezed his arm. 'I thought as much.'

'This fervour of his to fight at every turn and his manic need to travel to England, it is worrying. Not even the threat of trouble stirring here at home gives him pause to remain. It is not like him. And whatever the source, I fear it will blind him to risk.'

'I too, worry.' She could guess the source of Jarlath's woes, but would never give voice to her suspicion. 'Is there something we can do?'

'Wait, pray?'

More bells jingled, close and far.

Their wanderings returned them to their family.

The puppeteer held his audience spellbound. Eleanor

bounced on Ainnir's knee, clapping with delight. The handsome knight, a simple wooden stick with straw for hair, a small twig for a lance and a red silk bag for a cape, finally kissed his love, an equally skinny stick with a coarse woollen veil tied with yellow thread, and scraps of blue velvet for a rather threadbare gown.

Joan spotted Manus and the O'Byrne boys seated at the tavern with drinks in their hands, and Jarlath, turned in his seat, his back to his companions, watching the crowd at the puppet show. He looked solemn, preoccupied. His brow wore the tired frown of one cursed with a warring conscience. Joan sighed. It was not the kiss of the handsome knight and the maiden, which held her nephew's attention. What if Thomas was right? What if Jarlath's private anguish made him blind to danger?

James' gentle tug at the folds of her gown interrupted her troublesome thoughts. 'Mama, did Papa tell you how well we did at the archery?'

'He did indeed, James. He said you equipped yourself admirably.'

'And did he tell you Gerald is to –'

'James,' scolded Thomas. 'There are conversations to be kept between men and men only, and that, my son, is one of them.'

'Sorry, Papa.'

'Mama,' broke in Gerald. 'I am to join the men with Donal and Papa.'

'Mama, Mama, it is finished,' Eleanor squawked. 'Can we buy some cakes now, please, please, please?'

'Mama, may I go with the men?' pleaded Tom.

Joan was inundated, yet as always, she competently fielded each child.

'Eleanor, yes.' She patted her daughter on the head. 'Tom, no,' and before he could brook an argument, she added, 'Your time will come soon enough. Gerald, you may join your father, as long as you convince Jarlath to join me for a walk. I am sure he could spare a few moments. And James, before you ask, yes, there will be cakes for you too.'

Joan pulled Jarlath close, linking her arm with his. 'I have great need of your company for a short time, Jarlath.'

'I thought it may have been Eleanor's wish.'

Joan laughed.

'No. Just mine. We have not had time to talk of late. In fact, I do not believe we have conversed overly much since your return from Glendalough. Perhaps we can take this opportunity to rectify such a slight. It would please me.'

There was silence for some time as they strolled. The blind man's tales now spoke of dragons and gargoyles and fire breath. No more apples floated in the vat.

'So, how do you fare?' she asked.

'I fare well. Possibly a handsome bit more than you have over the past few weeks, but as always, you glow when with child.' Jarlath smiled a generous smile, and patted the hand that held his arm tightly.

'I do feel well now. It does not take long for my body to adjust. But you? You have been somewhat unseen. Are you avoiding our company?'

'No.'

'You seem distant.'

'Distant? Do I?'

'Yes.'

'I am fine.'

'Truly?'

'Truly.'

No amount of short answers would have her think he was indeed fine. The telling shadows under his eyes, the permanent furrow of his brow, and the morbidly low tone lacking its usual energy were evidence enough to charge this man with the offence of deceit.

They spied a limping jester taking shade beneath the branches of a sprawling beech tree, and Joan took time to acknowledge and return the greetings of villagers enjoying the sun and the festivities before she continued her interrogation.

'Donal has changed too, do you not think? I believe this marriage will be good for him. He has suffered enough with the loss of Elizabeth, and I think he is already quite taken with Ainnir. His smile and laughter I have missed for too long. It pleases me greatly to see their return. He does not deserve more heartache.'

'Yes, he is a good man.'

'Ainnir is lovely, is she not?'

'I have not –'

'She is a pure beauty, both of face and of spirit. Yet I suspect she arrived here full of apprehension. It must have been difficult. Leaving the ones you love brings great sorrow. I can only imagine you will depart for England with a heavy heart not too dissimilar. But of course your path will be different, for you will return home, safely. Promise me that, Jarlath.'

'Yes, Aunt Joan. I promise.' The pledge sounded empty.

'I will pray for you. It is a great sacrifice you make. It is also a great sacrifice Ainnir makes to appease her father's wishes. I think she is doing her best to reconcile herself to her path, and we should do all within our power to help, do you not agree?' Joan gave him no time to reply. 'Did you hear of my sons' catch in the forest yesterday? Gerald and Tom took Ainnir out for the morning and returned with a stag. Oh, but of course you know. They told me they had spoken to you at the creek, and that Ainnir remained with you for a time. Ainnir's smile, it is a rarity is it not? One to easily capture a heart.'

Jarlath's silence convicted the man. The revelation brought Joan no pleasure. It was time to speak straight.

'I was sitting in our library last night with Thomas. Eleanor, not surprisingly, coerced her father into the telling of one last tale before she went off to bed. You know how those pleading eyes can convince Thomas of anything. I would think that child could talk her father into jumping from a cliff if she so set her mind.'

Joan felt Jarlath pull away. She held tighter to his arm.

'Thomas chose a favourite of mine, a sad tale, one which never fails to set a sigh upon my lips. Do you know of the story of Tristan and Iseult?'

'I do.'

'It is such a beautiful story, an unconquerable, limitless love, a selfish love that brought so much sorrow to so many people.'

Jarlath looked from their course, turned his head as far from Joan's as physically possible. Her steps stopped suddenly, and she drew Jarlath's eyes back to hers.

Pain. Desperate pain contorted every inch of his face to that of an oil-smeared looking glass.

'Aunt Joan, I –'

'No, let me finish, Jarlath. I do not know what I would have done if Thomas and I could not be together. If I were Iseult and he, my Tristan, I do not –' she broke off. 'But we are not people of legends and tales. We are Thomas and Joan Fitzgerald. I have the Lord Our God to thank for that, and I do, every day of my life.'

She held his hands, firmly, yet gently, and her eyes would not let his gaze escape hers.

'Listen to me,' she laughed, 'going on about myself, and holding your hands in the middle of this crowd. Perhaps I should take my leave, lest my husband think you and I were playing him for a fool.'

'He would not!' Jarlath sounded surprised.

'No he would not. He would not think that of you, nor would Donal.' She paused, the pause of a tolerant teacher. 'I worry your heavy heart will trail you during your time in England and bring peril to your every move. Be rid of your grief, Jarlath. Be rid of such an anchor for it will only bring unwise counsel. I want you to return to us, safe and unharmed. I love you like a son. You do know that?'

She peered lovingly into his eyes and saw hot tears threaten. She touched his face gently then walked away to leave him with his thoughts – and hers.

Jarlath's dread hurt mightily. How had she come to know?

The voice of reason, he thought implausibly, was female.

Chapter Eighteen

'My coin is on Bradan,' Jarlath slurred, and cursed as wine sloshed to the floor of the great hall in his failed attempt to rise from the chair.

'Don't be daft. Manus will best him before you can pull a coin from your purse.' Thomas' pronunciation was no more controlled, but all the same he laughed at Jarlath. He called for their cups to be refilled and stood from his seat, succeeding in the task unlike his companion.

'Make way, make way,' he yelled, moving to the trestle. 'Now, you both know the rules, an elbow lifted is a disqualification and your second hand is not to leave your cup. Are we all in agreement?'

Neither combatant was given a chance to reply. Cheers from the drunken crowd urged the arm wrestle to begin. And so it did.

Bradan bore a grimace and uttered a grunt.

Manus simply smiled, raised his cup to his mouth and took a long, deep swallow. Then with a resounding thud, the back of Bradan's hand hit the table. The sport was over all too quickly. Shouts of applause and jeering spliced the air. Bradan jumped from his stool, sent his own cup flying across the trestle.

He cursed with much colour, more at the loss of his drink rather than the loss of the competition. With a sigh, he flopped into an empty chair, joining Jarlath by the hearth.

'We should not have returned to the castle, my friend. That flaxen haired vixen at the market was craving my attention. Instead, I return with you, and for what? Humiliation at the loss of an arm wrestle! I tell you, it would not have been humiliation suffered at the hands of that buxom girl. It would have been pleasure and grat –' he hiccoughed, 'gratification.'

'Do you remember her name?' asked Jarlath with a dead smirk.

'Of course I do. I am nothing if not a gentleman. It was, um, Kathleen, Jane, no Moira, no Mary, yes it was Mary, a seamstress. I have a hankering for a Mary with prickly needles. What say you, Jarlath? There will be music and dancing and wenches for the picking for a few more hours yet. Will you join me?'

No answer came.

'It may be just what you need, my friend.'

All drunkenness was gone from Bradan's voice. He spoke clearly, compassionately, and for a moment Jarlath thought he heard the sound of pity. He looked to Bradan's face. Pity stared back, but he refused to believe what Bradan's regard hinted. Surely too much wine played trickery with his imagination?

'I for one will lead the charge.' Manus tripped, his boot catching at the leg of Jarlath's chair, but corrected his balance before it was too late. 'And I say we go now.'

'Where are we off to?' broke in Eamonn.

'A-wenching.' Bradan raised the tone to a boisterous cacophony, one that played like a badly tuned orchestra.

'A-wenching?' repeated Eamonn.

'A-wenching,' they all chorused.

'Do not even think about it.' Thomas noted Gerald's eyes widen in anticipation. 'In what world do you think your mother would forgive me for allowing you to join this lot of drunken swine with their romps in the hay this night? I know, I know, son.' Thomas raised his hand to prevent a deluge of protests. 'I would have no objection to you sailing off into the night and finding your joy, but for your mother's wrath.'

Thomas laughed. 'Let it be, for just this night.'

Gerald folded his arms across his chest indignantly, ready to bellow his own annoyance, but was ignored as shouts from the drunken swine came louder and louder again.

'I object to the charge of swine,' said Eamonn.

'I object to the charge of drunken,' said Manus.

Bradan stood quickly. 'And I object to ... both.'

'And tell me this, you sods,' said Thomas, 'am I wrong?'

They all collapsed with laughter – all except Jarlath and Gerald.

'Do not be too quick to part with your heart,' Jarlath said, watching Gerald's disappointment.

'It is not my heart I wish to part with.' Gerald walked from their company in defeat.

Raucous sounds from the other men rang out. Jarlath remained in his seat.

'You dally for what?' asked Thomas.

Jarlath shrugged.

'There are no ears to overhear a private conversation now, Jarlath. Perhaps it is time for you to speak of what is on your mind. We both know it has been festering too long.'

Jarlath leant forward in his chair, stared at the glowing

embers. A fire-worn log split in two. Sparks burst into the air then seemed to vanish.

'This world is now foul. The sun is cold, the rain is hot. Have you ever felt like nothing mattered anymore? Have you ever felt that even your sleep is an enemy, no longer a reprieve from the torment of your day?'

'Where do these thoughts come from?'

Jarlath sniggered, wondering if he had already said too much. He held up his cup. 'Perhaps from this. Don't listen to me, Uncle. I am as they say, in my cups.'

'Jarlath, perhaps England is not the place for you now.'

'It has to be, for I cannot remain here.' His words came in a vicious whisper.

'Why, lad? What wrong have we done?'

'I am sorry. You do not deserve my moods. It is no one's fault but my own. I should have known better.'

'Jarlath, you must tell me. What has happened to cause fault with anyone?'

'Nothing. Nothing.' Jarlath stood from his seat, hoping the sadness would simply fall from his lap. But he knew better. It clung like a vine. It clung and wound and crept and choked. 'I think I have kept you too long, and my friends will be worried for my whereabouts.'

Thomas gave a sympathetic smile from beneath worried eyes. 'Then on your way young man before the years catch you, and nights of opportunity such as these become mere memories. You only have a few more days here. Go. Enjoy. I pray it brings solace from whatever tortures you.'

Jarlath smirked, a pathetic laugh spilling from his mouth. None could come close to understanding how he felt at this moment. His heart was crushed, broken by guilt, longing, want, anguish, and now to have the pain more amplified as he looked again to his uncle. It was unbearable. Thomas, his father's brother, the man who raised him, the man who loved him as a son. He was disgusted with himself for his sins – his past, present and future sins.

It was late and for Ainnir the night dragged woefully. The sounds of music and merriment from the village drifted through the unshuttered windows of her bedchamber like smells from a skillet, hinting at tales shared around small campfires, and minstrels speaking in chord of love and romance and fanciful trysts. How could such happiness fill the air, when Jarlath would soon leave Ireland, off to a world of uncertainty and danger?

They all worried – Joan, Thomas and Donal. And none but Ainnir knew the reasons for his torment, for his anguish. She was the reason he was leaving and it stole her very breath. If she could change all, she would have done so. But the opportunity had long since vanished. And now, with the worst set in motion, she was desperate to set things right, not have him leave with so much anger still between them. But Jarlath made it impossible, hiding behind the hectic pace of preparations, avoiding her at every turn. She knew he would give naught but his usual silence, but it mattered not. She possessed a despairing need to speak kind words, wish him well, a safe journey, have him know she bore him no hate, for how would she ever survive if harm was to befall him and nothing reconciled.

She looked to the corner of the room where Muirne sat nodding in her chair, eyes heavy, fighting sleep.

Then looked to the needlework on her lap, crushed in a taut hand, knuckles white with strain. What if harm was to befall him? She shuddered. Yes, she needed to speak kind words.

'Just kind words,' she whispered, and repeated the phrase over and again like torture to a prisoner, one who would admit black was white if dealt enough pain. 'Just kind words.'

Rowdy noise in the courtyard stole her attention. From her window she saw her brothers riding away, and then Jarlath, walking to the stables.

'I must go,' was all she muttered, the needlework tumbling to the floor as she gathered her woollen cloak.

Muirne shifted at the noise, sat upright, eyes blinking. 'Where to at this hour, child?'

'Out.'

Now fully awake, Muirne jumped from her chair, and moved to the window to find the source of Ainnir's haste.

'Ainnir, no.'

'I must, Muirne. Do not try stop me.'

'Ainnir, you do not know where he is headed.'

'I simply must.' With that, the door closed.

'Gerald!' Ainnir startled at his approach up the stairs. She scoured her mind quickly, searched for conversation trying desperately not to reveal her urgency to be gone from the castle. 'You are retiring early?'

'Not by choice. Your brothers and the men are off to the village, but apparently I am too young for ...' he paused awkwardly, 'for more ale. Anyone would think I still need the services of a nurse.'

He did not stop to elaborate further, continuing with his railings as if she was not even present, and climbed further up the stairs, each step creating more distance.

More ale, she thought. 'Thank you, Gerald', she said in a whisper never intended to reach his ears.

Jarlath was off to the village to continue the day's merriment. He would not be too difficult to find, she knew his horse, knew his saddle, and she ran at a frenzied pace down toward the hall.

Her hair was cherry red, thick and luscious, yet blemished by the heavy odour of ale and sweat. Her familiar hands wandered across his face, inviting and tempting. Her legs were a shade of heavenly white, long and soft to the touch, an allure to any Saint let alone a mere mortal who had already sold his soul to the Devil. She perched seductively on a crate in the corner of the barn as he knelt before her. Gown hitched up, she leant back and licked her lips.

'I missed you whilst you were away, and hoped you would seek me out earlier than this, Jarlath. But I knew you would come tonight. I knew when I caught your eye at the market.'

'Did you? Well I did not,' he slurred. 'Perhaps you are a soothsayer. Tell me what else you see. I would give the world to know.' His hands glided roughly over her knees, trailed down to the gentle curve at her ankle.

'Your future? Shall I speak of this night's future or –' she drew a sharp breath as his tongue rolled over her shoulder, 'do you yearn to known what is beyond the sunrise?'

Her voice came deep and sultry, a tonic to his ailment, a siren to loosen the binding on his heart – and his garments.

'Let's start with now, shall we? Help me forget my yesterdays.' He moved awkwardly toward her mouth, hands at this belt, and rocking slightly he tried to right himself.

He heard a giggle muffle in her throat, and her tone altered to officious. 'Well right this moment, my love, we are to receive a guest.'

He followed her gaze to the open door. Hell's Gates! Would that woman's ghost ever cease its taunting? He shook his head to obliterate the vision, but it refused to erase.

Ainnir's eyes looked past Jarlath. She could not wrench her stare from the naked leg, nor could she dim the blow of the words she had just heard, words said with that lazy languor, that smoky voice she knew well; *forget my yesterdays.*

What could she say? What words were appropriate? What on earth was she to do now? Speak. Speak! But speech became almost a forgotten skill. 'I ... I followed you from ... from the castle. I followed you ... I thought ...' her voice quivered and faltered entirely. She tasted tears on her lip.

'God, no,' Jarlath said in a whisper.

Ainnir stepped backward.

'I thought ... thought you were alone, and –'

'No,' he said again, loud enough for the voice of regret and utter loathing to ring as clearly as vesper bells. Jarlath raised himself from the ground and stepped forward.

Ainnir shook her head, rigid small movements, terrified, willing him to stay where he was. She did not want him anywhere near her.

One shaking hand came up. 'I can only apologise for the

interruption. I had no right to come.' She turned quickly, and threw the door open with such force it swung back and slammed in her wake.

She bit down on her fist, imprisoning a scream, and ran as fast as she could, stumbling as her feet caught in the hem of her skirts.

'Ainnir, stop!'

Jarlath's words came from behind, somewhere from behind, maybe close, maybe afar. Pain blotted too much.

'Ainnir, stop.'

The words yelled at her again. She felt her body jerk like a rag doll. Jarlath had hold of her wrist.

'Why have you come?' Jarlath demanded.

'Why have I come? What does it matter why I have come? What does anything matter anymore?' She shrugged off his hold, and turned rushing toward her waiting horse.

'No.' He grabbed her again. 'Why did you come?'

The horse shied at Jarlath's shout, backed away tossing its head high. It pranced sideways then bumped the hind of Jarlath's horse. Both mounts sniggered and stomped.

Ainnir grabbed at the reins. She could not look to Jarlath. Painful confusion kept her eyes to the ground where they were safe, protected from torturous images. Her head shook slowly, disbelief and refusal melding into one. With no thought, words spilled from her lips, practised words that now made no sense.

'To speak kind words, just kind words.'

'Lies!'

She flinched, felt the jump of her body.

'Why did I come?' She turned, gave Jarlath look for look

and began to shake.

Jarlath blurred behind a wall of tears, but she saw through the haze, and saw in his face a ferocious need. *Dear God, no – let me wake from this nightmare.* It was impossible now, she could no longer tether those words, words she had fought over and again; she could no longer pretend. His heart willed them from her lips, as the moon willed tides from the shore.

'I came because I love you. Are you now happy?' The emotion came like a roaring waterfall.

'Oh, God. Ainnir!' His despair saturated each word. 'How do we make this stop?'

What words could mend their naked agony? The two lives they both fought in vain to keep apart were colliding and erupting, here and now. Nothing else mattered, just that one question, and the painful absence of an answer.

Ainnir caught movement from behind Jarlath and looked to the swirl of cherry red peering from the doorway.

Jarlath turned too.

Ainnir watched that woman, not knowing for how long she stared.

'How do we make this stop?' she echoed his words. 'I think you just did.'

'You were not meant to see that. I would never –'

'Do not. Please!'

'You do not understand,' he said with the heat of a forge.

'You are right, I do not. I do not understand you. I do not understand myself.'

'I came here to find a way to forget you.'

'Forget your yesterdays? Is that what you mean? Perhaps

it is time we both forget.'

Jarlath lifted his chin like a belligerent child. 'You will soon have a warm bed to forget me, yet you curse me for finding mine.'

'Your silence is more appealing, Jarlath.'

She turned, swung into the saddle and kicked hard.

Her mount galloped with frenzy, attuned to her harried thoughts. The dark night and its shadows fitted well, offering an endless void to lose her churning anger. What had happened? Why was her world spinning so violently?

She screamed into the air, spurred her horse faster and faster, willing the speed to wash away the ache. The castle gates loomed ahead, encasing her new home. This was no place of comfort. There would be nowhere to hide, no solace. Why could she not be at Glendalough now?

She rode at a pace alerting the servants to her arrival, and as she rounded the inner castle wall dogs scampered for cover. A stable hand, laden with sacks, was not quick enough to veer from the peril. Ainnir pulled the reins in tight. Her horse shied and turned too quickly. She heard a loud snap, felt herself thrown into the air, tumbling through the night, then a blinding thud as she hit the ground.

Chapter Nineteen

Shouts stole Eleanor from sleep. The hazy twilight between slumber and wakefulness banished her dreams. Her mind tried to make sense of the commotion. None came. It was not the usual laughter or muffled conversations she came to expect during the many late night revelries. There were new sounds, drenched in worry and alarm.

She crept from her bed, dragging her coverlet behind.

None noticed the small frame moving along the corridor toward the stairs to the great hall. All were too busy scampering amidst the fluttering candlelight to notice the young girl in her nightgown, hair thoroughly tousled, a small rag doll tucked beneath her arm and a square of blue following her steps.

Now behind her, the shouts lessened to a mumble. In the great hall, solemn faces at the hearth uttered not a word. The fire intermittently threw its disruptive crackle into the silence as if marking time.

Eleanor stepped over a prone Hunter and climbed onto Gerald's lap. It felt a refuge. His steady heartbeat offered comfort from the grave expressions. She curled under his arm, warily eyeing the others. What was so wrong?

Her brother stirred, stretched his legs and brushed warm fingers across her forehead. No words accompanied the touch, and she dared not ask.

She watched Jarlath, his head low, eyes dark, mouth downturned. She thought to unwind from Gerald's lap, climb up to Jarlath and nestle in. Perhaps such companionship would bring him cheer, for he often said she brightened his day. But his dark eyes spoke of a foreboding torment. He did not look like the Jarlath she knew and as much as she longed to offer comfort, her inner voice told her to keep her distance.

She waited. Too much tension, too much worry. She wanted to be gone from this room. Eleanor climbed from Gerald's lap. Hunter's tail shifted. His eyes, like hers, had been darting back and forth regarding the tangible gloom, no less bewildered. Her movement seemed an invitation to escape, and the wolfhound followed her small frame up the stairway, back to the bedchambers.

Muted voices became clear. She crouched against the wall to listen, unseen.

'They could not save the horse.' It was Donal's voice.

'Best we do not tell Ainnir such news tonight.' Her Mama. 'The gash to her head is only slight. She needs good rest, and to know of her horse's fate will only cause more upset.'

Her father spoke. 'What took her to be out at such an hour on her own?'

Her mother answered and Eleanor detected a hesitance. 'Oh, Thomas. You, yourself, told me she is impulsive. If memory serves me well, *delightfully reckless* was the phrase you used. Best you both head downstairs and relieve our worried guests. Her brothers will be eager for word.'

None noticed the small body huddled along the wall, feet tucked under her nightgown, and arms around Hunter. Her upturned eyes looked to the commotion of servants moving to and from Ainnir's room. Her eyes filled with small pools of unshed tears. Her bottom lip quivered knowing how sad Ainnir would be when told of her horse's fate.

Eleanor remembered how miserable she herself felt when her own puppy died a few months past. A small bundle of brown unsteady legs and silky, floppy ears, trampled by horses in the courtyard. Her mother had sat with her through the night with words of comfort and hands gently stroking her forehead, as tears and sobs flowed with her grief. Ainnir would be just as sad, for she knew she dearly loved the horse.

Eleanor quietly moved from her place, careful not to be seen. She opened the door to Ainnir's bedchamber and tiptoed inside with Hunter not far behind. Ainnir lay beneath her coverlet, eyes hooded, but still watching the flickering candles. Eleanor climbed up onto the bed and snuggled in beneath the coverings, cuddling into the warm body.

Muirne moved to the side of the bed.

'Eleanor, you should not –'

'It's alright Muirne. I'll look after *In-year*.'

Eleanor leant in close to Ainnir, gently stroking her forehead with soft whispered words. 'Everything will be better in the morning, Ainnir. You will see. I will stay with you while you go to sleep.'

Eleanor's eyes closed. So too, did Hunter's.

Muirne dozed fitfully and when roused checked on her charge. As the birds declared the coming of day she woke again, the squirming bodies beneath the coverlet indicating more than animals were ready to rise. Muirne moved to the side of the bed and saw Ainnir had woken. The small body beside her tossed and stretched in her own deliverance from sleep.

Swollen eyes and a pale face looked up.

'Did I dream it all, Muirne?' Ainnir's eyes were full of futile hope.

Muirne shook her head and ran a gentle hand across Ainnir's forehead.

Ainnir closed her eyes again, spilling fresh tears onto the pillow.

Eleanor stirred with a yawn, sat up high in the bed as Ainnir rolled her face into the sheets.

'She will be sad for a while, Muirne, won't she?'

'Yes, Eleanor, she will, for a while.'

'I'll fetch some books. That will cheer her.'

With that, Eleanor left the bed with all the energy of a young child replete from sleep and ran to complete her errand.

Banter during the noonday meal was rife with ribald jests, all concerning last night's celebrations, in particular those which continued beyond the castle walls. Manus humorously defended the light-hearted allegations and parried with a host of his own bawdy remarks. Beside him, Jarlath failed to be baited, toying distractedly with a bowl of cabbage and almond soup.

'You are unable to eat,' noted Manus. No reply came. 'Nor speak it seems.'

'We need to saddle our horses,' Jarlath said blankly, proving Manus only partly wrong.

'We do?'

'We do.'

'And where are we off to?'

'North. Our preparations for England are not yet complete.'

'They're not?'

'No.'

'And we are to head north?'

'Yes.'

'Where north? And what are we yet to prepare?'

Jarlath pushed his trencher away. 'You ask too many questions, Manus.'

Manus thought to lecture Jarlath on the wealth of Maynooth and its neighbouring towns – their smiths, glovers, tanners, carpenters, seamstresses and masons, its flourishing waterways, fertile soils, bountiful crops and endless fish supplies, the skins, wool, milk and meat from well-fed herds, the apothecaries, taverns, brothels, even the endless number of Churches and Chapels. There certainly was no need to travel excessive miles. All their needs could be met close by.

Instead, he found himself in the saddle galloping north, hooves throwing clods of soil and autumn leaves through the air. Jarlath set a blistering pace. Manus had no choice but to keep up. Every stride of his horse, every bounce, every jolt brought a throb to his ailing head, for his own night of revelry had ceased with the rise of the sun.

'I hear that Ainnir was injured last night.' Despite the predicated discomfort, Manus raised his voice to be heard above the pounding hooves. He could guess at the source of Jarlath's mood, but would permit his friend a confession in his own good time.

Both men ducked their heads to avoid a low branch.

'I am sure she will live.'

'Good news for Donal then.'

Jarlath made no reply. Manus expected none.

With Maynooth a distance behind, they finally sought beds at a well-fitted inn. Spacious and homely, it sufficed as billeting during the unnecessary journey.

Manus allowed Jarlath his quiet contemplation and reluctantly settled for the companionship of silence as they browsed workshops and stables, purchasing little. Whatever raced through his friend's mind, Manus doubted not, it would remain there, locked away and festering. But he also knew that Jarlath could not hide forever, not even from himself.

They would return to Maynooth late on the morrow, before the wedding of Donal to the O'Byrne's daughter. Their presence would be expected.

Chapter Twenty

In the private courtyard behind the tower frightened fish disturbed the waters of the pond, scurrying to seek refuge in dark corners away from the sun.

In her reflection, Ainnir saw a picture of which many spoke; honey-gold tresses, a heart-shaped face, and almond-shaped eyes holding a shade of blue, just like her mother's.

And what profit did it all bestow? What pleasantries, what dreams were granted? What wondrous dues came from the face that stared back? Naught, she acknowledged with resignation. Naught but duty, responsibility and obligation.

It was all so burdensome, like a cloak of gold – striking yet an insufferable weight. Zeus, the pagan God from myth and legend, was known for wearing a heavy cloak of gold. She remembered that fact from a long ago story. Yet Zeus possessed unequalled strength and she was a mere mortal. Her trial was near impossible.

She dangled her fingers in the cool water. A pattern of rings and shifting lines distorted her reflection. Ripples tore lips from mouth, and eyes from face, all beauty gone. The pond was very much like her life – serene one moment, disfigured the next.

A lone fish, intrigued and braver than the rest, slowly made its way from the cover to the surface, toward light and uncertainty. Hesitant at first it nibbled her fingertips. She smiled when it darted away then circled back, no longer apprehensive, now confident her fingers were of no threat. She could take a lesson from this brave fish.

She was to be married on the morrow and had hidden too often in the dark corners of her own pond, hoping the world and its demands would vanish. And in seeking refuge, what had been achieved? Nothing but sadness and despair.

Why could she not have let things be? Why did she have to force everything to her way?

'It's all my fault.' It was she who attended Jarlath's bedchamber at Glendalough, she who had returned to him in the deer park, and she who had sought him in the village.

But the truth of the matter was that Jarlath wanted to forget her and she would become Donal's wife, bear his children, make this place her home. That would be her path.

So be it. If she was to be imprisoned in her new life like this small fish, she would no longer hide in the dark corners. She would seek strength from the sun's warmth. Yes, so be it and God grant her strength.

She moved from the pond and strolled across a carpet of grass. Floral borders flourished on both sides, and beyond the borders, the intricately trimmed bushes stood preened, in marked contrast to the wild overgrowth of her mountains. Peonies and violets speckled the ground and the long stems of monkshood with their blue petals stretched toward the sun. Taller trees created corners for covert rendezvous, shady picnics, or children's games. And quoits, she added belatedly to her thoughts, spying the pile of discarded horseshoes and an iron spike.

She walked toward the rear wall and examined a multitude of herbs, some she had never seen before. She was not aware of company.

Donal joined her. 'That is arnica, for use on bruises and wounds. Over there is centuary which does much the same. Gentian,' he continued, pointing to stems of purple blossoms, 'was named after the Illyrian King Gent, and used to heal his soldiers in battle, but we now use it as a bitter flavouring. And this one is houseleek, once believed to ward evil spirits from homes. Charlemagne so believed in its properties he ordered the growth of this herb on all rooftops, but here at Maynooth we mix it with small portions of vinegar, and find it does well to keep foul smells at bay. And the stems of the monkshood over there are used to keep rodents from the kitchens. Its petals hold a poison so the gardener keeps it well away from the other herbs.'

'I thought I knew so much about herbs and medicines, thought myself to be wise when it came to remedies and poultices, but this ... you have your very own apothecary.'

'Time spent toiling in a garden can be as valuable as time spent in the fields.'

'And your blossoms, I have never seen such a variety sitting happily side by side.'

'Yet no matter what our gardener does, he cannot keep the bluebells at bay. They have a mind and a will of their own and show themselves when and wherever they please. Legend has it, it is the nymph Kathleen who appears each –' Donal stopped abruptly and looked to her wide eyes. 'Have I said something wrong?'

'You know of that story, of Kathleen and the monk?'

'Yes, of course. And your expression tells me you do too.

She blooms here in search of her lost love.' Donal continued the story, exact in all detail, just as Ainnir remembered it.

'That is a story Mama told often when I was younger. Did you know there is another version of the tale?' They walked on slowly. 'Some say the monk pushed Kathleen to her death, pushed her from the cliff into the deep waters of the lake, all because she would not defer to his refusal.'

'Yes, I have heard it told that way too. It is well then that sentimentalists like you and I can alter a tale of tragedy to something more romantic when the opportunity presents itself. Who does not enjoy a happy ending?'

'My brothers,' she answered good-heartedly. 'They would tease me mercilessly at each telling, demanding the morbid version. They were more wont to enjoy stories with blood and death.'

'Typical boys, then,' Donal laughed. 'Your brothers will be departing after the morrow.'

'Yes. Yes they will.'

'Does it distress you?'

'It does.' Ainnir touched her neck, pleased Muirne had insisted she again wear the Ouroboros this day. 'But that is something I cannot change. I am to be grateful our father has allowed them to be here for this long.'

'Even a blind man can see you love your brothers well, Ainnir, and they return your love no less. My wish is that their impending departure will not bring you despondency on a day meant only for happiness.'

Muirne had often told Ainnir, when troubling thoughts plagued, answers and solutions were always within reach if only she would open her mind to see. Well, her mind was as clear as a cloudless sky this day, as perceptive as birds before a coming storm. Zeus, a fish, romantic bluebells!

'No, Donal. It will not. Tomorrow will be a wonderful day.'

He gave an appreciative smile, took Ainnir's hand and raised it to his lips.

Footsteps on the stone pathway interrupted their private moment.

Donal laughed again. 'And now, here come your antagonists. Their timing is impeccable and only confirms your accusations of their aversion to romance.' He nodded a welcome to the intruders.

'Bradan. Eamonn. I will leave you with your sister.' Donal turned on his heel and left.

'You have a smile on your face today.' Eamonn invited Ainnir to place a hand in the nook of his right arm.

'I can see beyond that smile, Eamonn.' Bradan offered his left arm.

'You are daft, Bradan. I believe our sister has found peace with this arrangement and is looking forward to tomorrow's celebration. Am I right, Ainnir, for there is a hue of rose to your cheeks, or it is simply a blush from the kiss I saw Donal place on your hand?'

Bradan answered for Ainnir. 'It is you who is daft, Eamonn. It was not five days ago we rode to these walls, ready to deliver our quivering sister to the lions. Not even that bump on her head could have changed her mood so quickly.'

'Christ, Bradan, but you can be a foolish ass at times. Are you looking to wipe the smile from Ainnir's face? If so you're making an easy task of it.'

'Is it that my brothers suddenly believe me struck with an affliction of deafness, or have I truly become invisible? You talk about me as though I were as far away as the moon. Still your worry, both of you. I will be fine. I now consider myself to have the might of Zeus.'

'Zeus?' Eamonn arched an eyebrow.

'Yes, Zeus the God who carried a heavy load. And a fish.'

'A fish? What has a fish to do with your current mood?'

Ainnir giggled. 'You could not begin to understand, Eamonn.'

'By fish, do you mean with fins and gills, and a mouth that puckers?' Eamonn grabbed at Ainnir's face, pinching her lips to bring her mouth to a pout.

Ainnir tried to answer. 'Yes, that is exactly right.' Her words came out mumbled.

The three laughed and continued their stroll.

Bradan leant into Ainnir and whispered, 'You may be able to fool our pig-headed brother, but you cannot fool me, Ainnir.' He planted a soft kiss on her forehead and gave a playful squeeze to her hand. 'Fish or no fish.'

Chapter Twenty-One

'Mama, I want a wedding bun.'

'I have told you more times than I can count, Eleanor, it is not yet time.'

'But, Mama, I want one.'

'Oh, that wonderful feeling of want, my dearest.'

Eleanor rewarded her mother with a stern look of frustration, a sure sign that the gale of a tantrum was about to be unleashed. Joan was too skilled, and sought to cut off the outburst before it be given the light of day.

'See how excited you feel right now, how your anticipation tickles your belly, all for the wonderful feeling of that want? Well, little one, if you get what you ask for, you will no longer have that excitement or those tickles.'

Eleanor altered her expression to intolerance. 'I just want a wedding bun, Mama.'

'Your mother asked you to be patient, Eleanor.'

Eleanor could bend one parent to her will, but never two. With that she turned toward the trestle only to admire from a teasing distance the pile of out-of-reach bread buns.

One hundred buns stacked high, drizzled with honey and sprinkled with a sifted mixture of sugar and flour. Sugared figs pressed into every crevasse and large strawberries made a base of vivid red.

Eleanor's eyes darted to the many guests who passed to admire their cook's creation. Forlorn eyes worked hard, hoping one would slip a small slice her way. She would wait for as long as such a miracle took.

Thomas and Joan smiled at their daughter's obvious scheming.

'I cannot blame her, Joan, for I too well understanding that *want* can be excruciating.' Thomas gave his wife a very public display of affection. From behind, he wrapped his arms gently around her waist and placed a kiss on her neck.

'Hold your hands still, Thomas. Your growing babe is awake and moving. Can you feel her move?'

'Her? You are certain of that, wife?'

'Yes, I am, husband.'

'Another Eleanor then? Could our home cope with another?' They both laughed.

Joan leant back into his embrace.

Thomas looked from their young daughter to the centre of the hall, to the groom and his new bride. 'Do you think that is *want* we see in our cousin's face?'

Donal stood, speaking animatedly with Richard Lang, Bishop of Kildare, who presided over the wedding mass. Ainnir was at his side, just as Donal had ensured for much of the evening. His face could not conceal the happiness this marriage was to bring. Eyes were bright. Lips stretched in full smile.

Hours before, Ainnir had walked into Saint Mary's Chapel swathed in a gown of luminous blue, its skirts trailing generously behind. Sleeves were fitted to the elbow then flounced loosely falling to the length of the floor. Her steps, in satin slippers embroidered with tiny pearls, peeped from beneath a layer of pleated white silk. A coronet of glittering silver chain, dotted with small turquoise stones, crowned her hair, and her great-grandmother's heart-shaped pendant sat well in the low square-cut neck of the gown. She was indeed a beautiful sight – and the rabbits were spared.

Donal's eyes rarely left her face. He was generous with his time, selected foods and drinks for his new bride, and whispered words of understanding when Ainnir seemed inundated with well wishes from people who were strangers until this day.

'In Donal's? Undoubtedly, my love,' said Joan, patting Thomas' hand. 'I saw that same look in your eyes on our wedding day.'

'I do not think we can compare the two days, Joan, for we both know your wedding gown was a little larger at the waist. Do you forget Gerald was with us on that day, somewhere right about where my hands are now?'

Joan scanned the faces close by, hoping none overheard their conversation. 'I think you may have had a little too much wine, Thomas. Your tongue is wagging like a hound's tail. Maybe you should busy yourself. Donal will not welcome the public celebration of their bedding. You may need to create a diversion.'

'I have already made plans. As soon as Eleanor has had her mouthful of sweets,' he said then whispered his scheme.

Joan's eyes flew wide. 'Oh, I do not think that is wise, my love.'

'It will work well. I promise.' Thomas simply smiled, then moved away through the crowded hall.

'Dear Lord, no.' Joan sighed.

Jarlath sat alongside Manus at a trestle in the great hall, deep in discussions about the coming weeks, their journey to England, and their plans once they made it ashore. For much of the day they had avoided the conversations of festive foods, wedding gowns, and, to the torment of Jarlath, the prospect of further Fitzgeralds to come. Tonight they did not join their companions in raucous celebration.

Tonight, final stocktaking and last-minute planning were needed. The two men were more eager to discuss and debate statecraft and politics. Manus more so to ensure nothing was left to chance, and for Jarlath, it was a much needed distraction.

The wedding mass forced Jarlath to look to Ainnir for the first time since their night in the village. He thought he was prepared but she rivalled the beauty of an autumn sunset. He thought the Lord could not make him suffer more, yet the sting to his heart and the constriction of his breath were beyond endurance. With the mass finished, he found escape. There was no longer the need to look to the bride. He kept his distance and counted down the interminable hours, now grateful the end of the night was near.

'Jarlath.' Thomas interrupted the men. 'Take Ainnir to the dance floor.'

'Does the bride not have enough dance partners?'

'This is your part in the charade.'

'Charade?'

'Just do as I ask. Take the lass to the dance floor and move your steps discreetly toward the door. Joan will be there to lead her away.'

Understanding dawned. Jarlath looked to Thomas with

disguised dread.

'Could it not be someone else?' he asked.

'No.'

Jarlath stood only a few steps back from the private conversation. Nodding an apology for his interruption, he offered Ainnir his hand.

She declined. What on earth possessed Jarlath to approach and solicit a dance? She only yielded when she noticed an unexpected look of insistence upon her new husband's face. Ainnir knew immediately there was a scheme in play, one of which she was as yet, ignorant.

They took to the centre of the floor and moved to the same steps as their fellow dancers. Neither locked eyes. Both looked about the room and forged smiles; a difficult task.

'I apologise for my part in the distraction. It was not my doing.'

'I do not understand.'

'You don't? Thomas has ordered me to steer you slowly toward the door. From there Joan will steal you into the shadows of the walls, and then your husband will take you from the hall. A ruse, if you would, so your guests do not follow you to your wedding chamber.'

Bland and lifeless. Jarlath delivered the explanation without expression. It sounded a trivial colloquy. Contrary to its sound, Ainnir felt the presence of a chill. She understood. *How perverse!* How could Jarlath be the one to begin her progress to the wedding bed? This was torture, an abomination, and to hear the words, *your husband* from his lips. Surely he too, felt the same abhorrent bile rising in his throat?

Ainnir risked a look to Jarlath's face and for the shortest of moments, he returned her stare. She was right. The ice in his eyes spoke all.

He spun her around moving their steps toward the door.

She hated every touch of her slippers to the floor.

Jarlath pulled her to his body, turned her left and then right, as was the dance. His touch burned. A thin layer of moisture covered her palms.

'You are leaving on the morrow?' asked Ainnir.

'Yes.'

'I do hope God keeps you safe.'

'Thank you.' Jarlath cleared his throat, an involuntary sound. 'Although I do not deserve your prayers, I would not want to leave here thinking you held nothing but hate for me.'

'Hate? There is no hate, Jarlath.'

Ainnir stared bleakly to the far corner of the hall, fighting the desire to look upon Jarlath's face again. The distance to the door shortened with every step, with every beat of the music.

Why now? The day was almost done. She knew Jarlath had kept himself from her presence and was grateful. But now, here at his touch, his words, his pain, her resolve began to topple.

Why did he have to do this to her, to them both?

More steps. The doors closed in. Too close.

She could see Joan waiting expectantly. She would leave him soon.

And with that thought, her battle for self-control was lost. She surrendered. No binding could stop the words, words that should have been buried and left to decay. She took a deep breath and forced a small curve to her lips.

'If duty bid me otherwise, would you be with me, would you have wished to take me as your wife?' The words were out, and she did not regret one.

'With all my heart.' Not one miniscule of time stolen for thought, no pondering or self-questioning. 'With all my heart,' he repeated and turned toward her for the last movement of the dance.

Neither pair of eyes caught. Both knew it to be too dangerous. Their regard fixed upon the sea of guests, past revellers clapping the end of the dance, encouraging more from the minstrels. The rapid beating of two hearts dimmed all other sounds in the hall.

They knew their dance had ended.

'Then I shall think only of you.'

Ainnir's hand left his, her face lowered gathering all the strength she could muster to summon the smile she knew to be expected. A sharp intake of breath kept her tears at bay and as planned, she walked directly into the shadows of the walls.

Jarlath returned to the trestle, sat down alongside Manus and hung his head low.

'Surely nothing could be that worrisome?' asked Manus.

Jarlath lifted his mug and hurled it at the wall.

'So, my friend, I appear to have been wrong.'

Along the banks of the Lyreen River the night shadows of the yew trees entwined with eerie calm. The moon's glow danced on the slow moving waters, and the creatures of the dark sent their sounds into the air. A brooding figure leant submissively, his back against a trunk, his eyes fixed high to the tower behind the castle wall. Candlelight brightened each of the bedchamber windows. His gaze rested with one.

Then I shall think only of you. The words scratched and clawed at Jarlath's skin.

The candlelight flickered and died. He turned, reached high and ran fingers over carvings of initials in the trunk – **JF**.

The morning sun would rise in the east. He could not change that. No matter the haunting words from years gone by, words which sang through the leaves of the trees, there were simply some things he could not alter. The miles between Maynooth and England could not come soon enough.

Jarlath mounted his horse and rode leaving that now darkened bedchamber behind him.

Part Four

Chapter Twenty-Two

Naas – County Kildare

Waiting for the ceremony to begin, Thomas and Gerald moved amongst the throng of men in the meeting hall at Naas. Despite the day's significance, Thomas was none too pleased.

Roland entered the hall and headed their way. 'Is the news true, Thomas?'

Thomas motioned Roland and Gerald to the far side of the room, below the portraits of Ireland's past Lord Lieutenants: Thomas Stanley, John Talbot, Henry of Monmouth and Edward Sutton.

'Yes,' Thomas spat his reply. 'I was dealt the news as we mounted to leave Maynooth, so forgive my mood.' He turned his back to the line of painted faces looking down upon him in censure. 'How could I have been so bloody blind? The O'Byrne could give Judas a lesson or two in deceit.'

'So they will not stop at Saggart?'

'You need ask?'

Only yesterday, the O'Byrne and the O'Toole mounted raids upon the town of Saggart, taking control of the sole entry to Wicklow from Dublin and The Pale. Thomas had seethed; seethed more at his own stupidity than the Gael's actions. How did he not see the marriage to be a ruse, a conniving means of distraction? And many stood here today to publicly witness his damnable idiocy.

'Best we set things to rights. Your plans?'

'To see to their demise.' The muscles along Thomas' jaw twitched, and his hands locked behind his back. 'If it were not for this occasion, I would now be in the saddle. But my vengeance must wait. As to how I shall see to their ruin, I have not yet decided but I will not commit the same mistake.'

'Is there need to head off Jarlath and Manus, call them back before they set sail?'

'No.' Thomas met his gaze. 'I do not know the Gael's future plans as yet.'

'You have ample support in this room?'

'From some, yes,' Thomas said looking around the room. He could almost smell the spite and ridicule from those he considered adversaries. 'And I may call on it before all is finished. Is there more known from England?'

'None. I fear the worst. Manus was too keen to see his first big battle. He does not comprehend the magnitude of what brews on those shores, and is yet to come to know the colour of blood when it runs like a river.'

'Jarlath too, and they will do naught but lead each other into the thick of things. How did our kin inherit such damnable stubbornness and Hell bent pride?'

They shared a tentative laugh, Thomas' first for the day.

'Papa,' interrupted Gerald. 'Who is that gentleman in the corner looking to us as if we have the plague?'

Thomas turned, following his son's line of sight. To the casual eye the muse appeared a web of misaligned angles. Bushy brow, hooded eyes hung over a large nose – a nose more a hooked ridge – and taut pale lips pasted across an unnaturally square jaw.

'The Lord's generosity was lacking on the occasion that one was designed. That, my son, is Arland Ussher.'

'I thought the man to be one of Eleanor's Pooka fairies.'

Thomas snickered. 'He may just be. He'd certainly stop the village chickens laying their eggs.' The humour quickly left Thomas' voice. 'He is of no consequence to us, bears no love for the Fitzgeralds. He thinks only in extremes, murder in enormous numbers to exact the Gaels, although my anger today tends to agree with such a scheme. He is the mayor of Dublin and today steps down from that position. And, he was also a supporter of John Tiptoft.'

Gerald's shoulders stiffened. 'I could spit from this distance if you would allow me, and with deadly accuracy.'

'Ah, you are your father's son then, lad,' chimed in Roland.

'Think no more of the man. We have business to attend. What say you, Roland? Shall we get this celebration underway?'

'Of course, then we must speak further of my daughter and Gerald. Alice is now eleven. It is not too many years before she will be of age.'

Gerald rolled his eyes with no attempt to hide his irritation.

Thomas fought a smirk. He would address his son's indelicate qualities another time.

Hoots and hollers followed the declaration of Thomas to the position of Ireland's Justiciar, and the ceremonial sword was passed into his hands. Roland was also appointed a commission, that of Ireland's Chancellor. Then with no time to waste, business began.

Richard Bellew was the first to speak. 'It is to Saggart we need look, Kildare, and the trouble the Wicklow Chieftains stir.'

'Raid!' called one man. 'It is only for the Lord to show His Mercy.'

'Their next move will be into our lands,' yelled another.

Barnaby Barnwell of Meath stood. 'I am not averse to the shedding of blood, my lords. But it is trade on which the clans of Wicklow rely heavily. We can hurt them more on that front.'

'Yes,' agreed Robert Dowdal of Louth. 'And it is here our first penalty should be aimed. They are herdsmen, not farmers, and to cut off crop supplies should bring them to their knees. Starve them into submission, I say.'

'More. 'Tis not enough,' suggested one.

'Yes, blood,' said another.

'A few lives will not stop the brutes,' complained another voice.

Arland Ussher stood, his bushy brow knitting, his nostrils flaring. 'Is it Saggart you believe the Gaels will stop at? Are you so simple as to not see their plans? They want all noblemen gone.'

Sounds of accord and disagreement jostled.

'And what contingency plan do you have, my lords,' Ussher continued, 'when your Wicklow friends do not abide by the laws imposed here today? Oh, I do beg your pardon, for they are no longer your friends, are they?'

The room quietened.

'Ah, Sir Ussher,' Thomas said politely. 'Dublin's previous mayor. I remember you as a supporter to Sir John Tiptoft.'

'Your memory serves you well, my lord of Kildare.'

Thomas' face remained impassive. 'Does it therefore follow that a beheading be your preference? Perhaps many beheadings?'

'Such a punishment has its uses.'

Explosive words flew through the air, chairs tipped and the memory of the beheaded Earl of Desmond, Thomas' cousin, echoed with a chorus of rage. Men threw curses across the room. Gerald stood, arms flailing like a threatened rooster. Thomas believed his son readying himself to fling some well-aimed spittle.

Yet Thomas remained fixed in his position. He called for silence. It came, but not quickly, and it was with unnatural control that he continued. 'The people of Dublin are surely indebted for your past service to their city, Ussher, given no doubt with unerring devotion during your employ this past year. But, it is just as I say, past. Thomas Walton is now Dublin's Mayor and you no longer have business here.'

Agreement came in the form of jeers amongst the men.

Thomas raised a single hand, again requesting silence. 'I suggest you take your leave immediately, lest you risk my name to be changed to *The Butcher of Ireland*.'

Ussher feigned interest in the many rings adorning his fingers. 'Business or none, you fail to answer my question. What will you do to those who have recently outsmarted the great Earl of Kildare?' He leisurely looked to the Earl. 'Would you offer them another Fitzgerald in marriage?'

'I may offer the head of a past mayor on a stick.'

More chairs shuffled noisily.

Ussher titled his chin nonchalantly and gave a slow and

deliberate flicker of his eyes. 'I prefer my head attached to my neck, my lord, but before I take my leave allow me to extend my congratulations on your appointment. May your success reward you accordingly.' Taut lips threw a cackle to the air as Ussher left the hall.

The cursing returned, and Thomas allowed anger to exhaust. Roland physically restrained Gerald, insisting he give Ussher's words no more thought.

Edward Plunkett steered the conversation back to the room. 'My lord, as much as I am reluctant to broach Ussher's question, if the O'Toole or the O'Byrne scorn our warnings, what is your plan?'

'To the comfort of our people and the terror of our enemies, we raise our swords. And may Purgatory be Ussher's resting place and John Tiptoft his bedmate, and may the Wicklow Gaels soon gallop into the flames of Hell.'

The room laughed.

Business continued.

Business finished.

Thomas turned his mind to the Wicklow Gaels.

Chapter Twenty-Three

Castle Maynooth – Ireland

For years, winds blowing northward from Saint George's Channel ferried ships carrying messages along the course of the Irish Sea. One such message now sat in the hands of the Earl.

With the afternoon light streaming into the solar, Joan listened as Thomas read from the pages, the words as welcome as the arrival of the message itself.

The past weeks lent themselves to departures and returns, farewells and homecomings, enough to rival the spinning of a weathercock. The absence of her loved ones haunted her every hour. By day, she comforted her children. By night, she prayed. All too often Thomas and his men rode out to quell the increasing raids along their eastern borders, and of course, her nephew, her son at heart, Jarlath, was more than one hundred and fifty miles away. A farewell had, and a homecoming longed for.

Today her lips stretched in smile. All were safe – for now.

'Ah, Joan, this is indeed good news,' said Thomas then continued with the letter:

'Manus has invented a new shade of green, unintentionally developed in the swells of the Irish

Sea, and I will tell you, although he does not wish it to be known, he did hang his head frequently over the port side to impart unpleasantries. He also made close acquaintance with a barber, so aching was a tooth. It took three of us to hold him down to have the tooth pulled. So it goes without saying Manus is not enjoying his time here in Bristol.'

The men landed on English shores unharmed, and the war they sought and the Yorkists they were to fight alongside, were nowhere to be found.

'The King was chased from the realm, and the Lancastrians now hold tentative control. Much of England believes the King's exile will be short-lived, that he will return and battle will then begin. We are in no threat of harm. Please assure Aunt Joan of this fact, and of course, Eleanor. It is only the Lords loyal to the Yorkists who are sought for punishment, and surprisingly, townsfolk have no fear of voicing their support for either York or Lancaster. Be at ease, we will use cunning and remain as travellers without loyalties. I know this letter will be received well and allay your concerns. We may not have found our battle as yet, but once Manus regains colour, we will journey to London and wait for its arrival, and from there I will send further word.'

Joan and Thomas debated the possible age of the message, and settled on it being no more than four weeks. That being, Jarlath was more than likely now in London.

'I take more from this letter than the simple meaning of the words, my love.' Joan squeezed Thomas' arm. 'I am relieved beyond belief he is safe, but Jarlath speaks with humour. I hear nothing acrimonious about his spirit.'

'A true blessing. Now we hold our breath at his arrant need for battle.'

Quick footsteps padded in the corridor.

'Papa!' Eleanor burst through the door, her eyes full of unshed tears. 'Tom said a letter arrived from England.'

'Yes, Eleanor. Jarlath is fine. Come here and I will read you his words.'

Eleanor climbed onto Thomas' lap and nestled in, smoothed her gown over her legs, wiped at her eyes with the back of her hands and gave one last sniff. 'I did not want the King to chop off his head.'

'Eleanor, that will not happen.' Joan knew from where her daughter's fear stemmed – the execution of Thomas' cousin at the hands of *The Butcher of England,* and that candle holder. She would ensure its removal from the library before the night was over, but for now, there was a little girl in need of much reassurance.

She moved to their side, her hand gently wiped Eleanor's forehead. Her eyes met her husband's. He gave a quick wink and looked down to their daughter.

'Do I still have my head?'

Eleanor looked up and nodded.

'Well there you have it. All the proof you need. The King has made special promise all Fitzgeralds will keep their heads. It is like a sacred oath to God. It cannot be broken. Jarlath is safe. You should not worry yourself so.'

Joan hoped her daughter would never have cause to take her father to task for his words.

Chapter Twenty-Four

Glendalough – Wicklow

Late autumn winds swirled across the bailey of Castle Glendalough, stirring dust and leaves not yet sodden by the weeping sky. Within the shelter of the hall, the hearth glowed brightly and banter echoed the length of the room. Servants placed trenchers of meagre foods along the trestles to appease the returning men.

The embargo on trade, imposed by the Lords at Naas, achieved its aim. Essential foods were scarce and the people of Wicklow suffered. In response and from the concealment of their mountains, the O'Byrne and the O'Toole led troops of raiders almost daily, relentlessly attacking the bordering towns of County Kildare at the northern most point, pilfering valuable food sources.

In the aftermath of the last raid, Hugh found it almost impossible to address his men. Raucous celebration and sharp voices were high in volume, the previous night's success surpassing any previous incursion.

Before too long a semblance of quiet settled. Hugh stood leaning over a trestle studying a large map. Tallow wax sent an unpleasant smell through the room, no more abhorrent than the stench of sweat and grime accumulated after three days in the saddle.

'For the next month, we will continue our presence in the north. Each day Kildare sends growing numbers to patrol the villages. We will keep his focus there and when the time is right, we will send large numbers to the south, here, near Ballyraggan.'

His fingers slid from the northern towns already attacked, to the southern towns, their victims to come. 'Here, we will begin forging into Kildare's lands. Here, we begin to take back what is ours.'

His men cheered.

Movement at the doorway caught Bradan's eye. He stood, leaving the hall, his departure not noticed by any.

'Mama,' he called.

Brigid walked into the solar under the weight of an armful of ledgers. She turned and squinted in the dim light, dropped the books onto a table.

'Ah, Bradan, come, sit with me. It is a sad day when a mother does forget the sound of her child's voice.'

Bradan placed a polite kiss on his mother's cheek and sat.

'It is good you are home, my son.'

Bradan studied his mother. Permanent lines appeared at the corners of her eyes. A crisscross of etchings lined her hands where once elegant fingers stretched with grace. When did this happen? Did the shift from youthful and vibrant to accepting and old curse overnight?

'Is it my voice you speak of or Ainnir's?'

'Ah, you and Ainnir, both of you, always the sentient ones.' Brigid sighed. 'It is Ainnir, you are right. We have received no word from Maynooth, and in the absence of words the imagination wanders. Such is the burden of a mother. And of course my concern for my two sons weighs just as heavily.' She reached for his hand. 'For they are also of my body and of late have been absent from their home too often.'

'You heard Papa then, in the hall?'

Brigid nodded. 'My heart is burdened with so much fear for the three of you, and all I can do is fill my time with prayer.'

'Do you also pray for wise counsel for Papa?'

'Yes, I do,' she answered without hesitation. 'Every morning. Every night. God listens, I am sure, but too often I dislike His reply.' She gave a weak smile.

'Mama, I have not spoken yet of Ainnir and Maynooth, but it was like watching a moth caught in a web. She was so fearful, so lost. I could see the fight in her that others could not, and she surrendered only when all hope vanished. It is unforgiveable what father did. She should not have been forced to make that marriage.'

'Many thought you to be the hellion of my three children,' she said with a laugh. 'Yet I knew better, knew you were wont to find birds with broken wings and nurse them to health, albeit swinging a sword to punish the perpetrator.' She paused, gave over a beautiful smile steeped in pride. 'You do not need to remind me of what your father did to your sister, for I was no less grieved. Her pain became my pain, and I will bear it until my dying days.'

Bradan nodded his understanding. 'Even now, he makes decisions without any thought to our own wishes. We are but chess pieces. First Ainnir, now Eamonn is to be married to the O'Toole's daughter, and I am sure I will be given some objectionable order soon. Do you think there will come a time he would consider our wants first?'

'Your father is unbending.' Brigid's lips tightened, a mirror to Bradan's thoughts. 'But do not fret for Eamonn, for he will be fine, I am sure of it. Fiona O'Toole is a good lass and I have seen the way they look to each other. Not that your father would have noticed the same, nor cared. But Eamonn is different. He is accepting of duty. He goes to this marriage believing it to be an honour. Whether it is because he was the first born, I do not know. Whatever reason, he follows your father as a sheep does a shepherd. You should not fault him for that, Bradan. It is his way.'

'Ainnir was used, Mama.'

'Yes. Yes, she was.' Brigid lowered her face. 'The Earl believed your father honest and loyal. That was the Earl's mistake. Your father did not share his plans with you for he knows your heart dominates your mind. As for me, I was no different, told nothing until it was too late.'

'For all his scheming, Papa could have achieved his purpose without hurting Ainnir. She would now be the happiest woman in Ireland if he had just opened his eyes.'

'What do you mean?'

'Mama, did you not notice Ainnir before she was told she was to marry Donal?'

Brigid smiled. 'The happiest I have ever seen her. Those are the memories I call upon when my worries anchor me too deeply.'

'Did you not also notice Jarlath?'

Her smile disappeared. 'No, I did not.'

Chapter Twenty-Five

October 1470 – London – England

Jarlath and Manus wandered the chill streets of London wishing they had travelled with heavier coats. The English autumn was proving unusually cold, and Londoners left the crooked streets before time for the shelter of their homes. The alcoves and lanes luring them to the bordellos of Southwark were uncommonly quiet. No rouge-painted faces with bawdy invitations paced the alleys in search of client or victim. No lice-ridden cutpurses sat in wait in shadows. Even the dogs stalled their daily meanderings.

Today offered an even more profound quiet. The two friends assumed the recent political change added to the townsfolk's need to stay indoors. The Earl of Warwick now held the city, and in the wake of celebrations, his men emptied the prisons, releasing political prisoners, those loyal to both the Lancastrian King and to Warwick. And in the unlocking of those dank cells, thieves, bandits, murderers and the like also fell to the streets. Only the daring ventured outside.

Bored and thirsty, Jarlath and Manus found a somewhat welcome door at *The White Hart*. The seedy tavern was sanctuary enough. Here, only men drowning in a surfeit of ale, with punchy fists, were of any concern.

They took seats amongst the small number of guests and

listened to the barroom banter. Opinion was divided over whether the Yorkist King drowned in rough seas or whether he had made it to exile in Burgundy. Flemish merchants, craftsmen and villagers, Yorkist and Lancastrian supporters alike debated the subject, none overly celebrating either option.

Such was the tenuous hold on the throne, and such was the concern of Londoners as to who held England's interests paramount. If the Lancastrians and Warwick held power, Marguerite D'Anjou would again reign over England alongside her inept husband. If Edward still lived, his queen, Elizabeth Woodville and her greedy family would suck England dry. It seemed the people of England could not decide which well-groomed, powder-faced harlot it preferred.

'Are you lads looking for a good time?' A woman with a mop of tousled flaxen hair and large breasts snuggled next to Manus like a cat.

'And what is on offer?' Manus played along, keen for a distraction from the day's boredom.

'Isabelle. They call me Isabelle, and that, sir, depends on your purse there.' She purred her reply and ran a short fingernail down the length of his thigh.

It seemed boredom was about to be a thing of the past.

'You are Irish lads. I haven't entertained an Irishman for a time.' Her laugh was wide – too wide. Yellow teeth stole attention from the endearing curves and eyelashes so long they curled at their ends. 'And would your friend like a playmate too, or shall we have ourselves a party for three?'

Jarlath smiled. 'He's all yours.'

'She's gone, Jarlath.' Manus pitched his matter-of-fact announcement at his friend, and at the same time threw an arm around Isabelle offering her a sip from his mug – perhaps an encouragement to close her objectionable mouth.

He looked back across the table. 'Don't give me that blank look. You know what I mean.'

'I must confess, I do not.'

'I have known you too long. She is gone. Here and now in the bawdy streets of London, you will find no better opportunity to put that memory where it belongs – in the past.'

Jarlath looked perplexed.

'Ainnir, you lovelorn fool,' Manus accused.

Jarlath could do naught but hang his head, a silent confession. He knew it futile to deny the allegation, pointless to even try. And for some strange reason, so far from his home, so far from the girl with those enticing blue eyes, a bizarre sense of relief flowed with the admission, like fast river waters flushing away silt and scum and debris.

'It took no time for me to see your brooding for what it truly was,' Manus continued. 'At every turn you couldn't wait to be gone from her presence, your eyes struggled to meet Donal's, and you caused fight after fight for no good reason, many of which you were poorly outnumbered. I am not daft, Jarlath.'

'Nor subtle,' Jarlath responded with a low voice.

'No. Nor subtle, my friend.' Manus shrugged with a rueful smile. 'For a time I thought it best not to mention your unfortunate situation, but here we are in England looking for a fight, and find none to appease us. I am bored.'

Isabelle elbowed Manus playfully. 'Is your friend lovesick?'

'Dreadfully,' he answered before turning back to Jarlath. 'It baffles me why I was the only one to see it. Your pitiful pouting almost had its own scent.'

Jarlath emptied his mug in one deep swallow. 'Was I so pathetic?'

Manus took a swig from his, and nodded as he swallowed. 'For the life of me, I cannot think how it all began. Would you care to enlighten me?'

'No,' answered Jarlath quite coolly. 'Not today in any event. Enough has been said, perhaps too much.'

'As you wish,' Manus ceded. A conspiratorial smirk followed. 'Isabelle, perhaps another friend at this table might be welcome after all.'

'Of course,' said Isabelle with a curious tone, and she raised a hand.

A swirl of skirts and the smell of lavender mixed with cheap ale wafted across their trestle as a young red-haired woman slid across the bench toward Jarlath.

'How do you do, lads? Marguerite is my name.'

Manus pitched Jarlath a knowing look. 'Marguerite is it? Are you the French daisy or the French born English Queen?'

'That is up to you. I can also be known by another name if you would prefer, but I do so like Marguerite, and you will too.' She cooed her words with a conniving pout and hooded eyes. Jarlath was impressed. This woman played her part well. 'You have news?'

Her voice lowered. 'Stay at your current lodgings. We will find you when it is time.'

'More waiting. Will it ever cease?' Jarlath did not aim the question at any one person.

Marguerite lifted her chin. 'The rightful King will return soon.'

'How can you be sure?' asked Manus.

Marguerite smiled her belief. 'The Duke of Gloucester's man awaits word. Once given he will summon you.'

'You know more than you let on.' Jarlath returned the smile. 'So which of Gloucester's men shall we expect to hear from?'

'You ask too many questions, Irishman. Enjoy a few more drinks for now. And if what you see pleases you,' she added with a sultry grin, 'we can continue our conversation above stairs. My price for you will be reasonable, for I did not expect such a handsome Irishman to grace my presence.'

'A discount for services then,' Jarlath laughed putting an arm around her shoulder for good measure.

The tavern door flew open. New guests in large numbers spilled into the small room. Manus cocked his head in the direction of a feisty voice with a cheap English accent. Both men listened intently.

'We will have celebration enough at Tower Hill on the morrow. Today was but a taste, and we can be doubly pleased he will suffer another night of fear,' yelled one of the newcomers.

'Let's drink to that,' said an equally loud companion, raising his mug in mock salute. 'I have waited too many years for the henchman to bring his axe down upon that one. Here's to the Butcher of England being butchered. Hah!'

Applause from all corners of the tavern joined in with the chorus of celebration.

Jarlath's face betrayed his sudden pleasure, for if they heard correctly, the man responsible for the beheading of the Earl of Desmond three years ago, was to be beheaded himself on the morrow.

'It seems the Lord has a keen sense of humour,' declared Manus. 'If naught else happens on this journey, my friend, the morrow will bring us more than we could have hoped. It would be sinful of us not to witness such an event in history. Our families would want a blow for blow account.'

Isabelle laughed.

'Ah, this is news to you?' chimed in Marguerite. 'Tiptoft was to be executed today.'

Isabelle asked the noisy crowd, 'Why is the man not dead?'

'He waited at the Temple Bar to be escorted to Tower Hill by the Sheriffs,' came one voice.

'So packed were the streets, his guards could not make their way,' said another.

'He now sits in Fleet Prison and will be executed on the morrow.'

Jarlath and Manus shared a confused look.

'He was captured by the Lancastrians before he could flee with King Edward, *mon cheri.*' Marguerite's fingers travelled along Jarlath's open shirt.

Jarlath bit back a smug smile. From the mouth of a tavern whore the allusion to culture held little attraction. Yet he felt a familiar stirring at her touch, perhaps an enhancement to the contagious mood now swallowing all English and Irish alike at this most welcome report.

Marguerite's hand travelled lower. 'It does please you, like most of England, I see.'

'*Oui ma petite*, it does please all of Ireland.' Jarlath curled his finger beneath her chin. It was indeed a day to celebrate in as many ways as the body could discover. Marguerite had pleasant features, and eyes that promised adventure, and perhaps Manus was right. 'And that, my love, calls for another drink.'

The two whores looked at the men with pleading eyes.

Manus was too accustomed to the rules. The sooner the women appeased their customers, the sooner more could be lured.

'What say you, Jarlath, one more drink and then these ladies might be kind enough to help two lonely men celebrate in a more gratuitous manner?'

'Why not,' Jarlath answered, lifting his mug to drain the last mouthful. 'And here's to tomorrow, and to the end of my yesterdays.'

No one but Jarlath knew how much the words soured his ale, but he refused to wallow, and sweetened the moment by ordering another drink.

'And here's to tonights,' added Manus, nibbling at the creamy shoulder seated to his side.

Marguerite's look darkened suddenly. Her eyes travelled beyond Jarlath's shoulder.

'Marguerite, my love, I have been searching for you,' came a booming voice in broken brogue, undoubtedly common to the unwashed seamen of the shipping ports. A toothless smile and a dry stench gave credence to the suspicion.

'Wait your turn, sailor,' was all Jarlath said, no malice or challenge. But brightness sprung to his eyes, hinting at a fervent desire for madness to erupt.

'Not again, Jarlath.' Manus' plea was meagre if not blithe.

Jarlath gave it little credit.

'Irishmen then, is it?' said the sailor with accusation in his voice. He grabbed Marguerite by the wrist, all the while keeping eyes on Jarlath. 'What brings barbarians to the shores of England?'

Jarlath sensed their cover and possibly that of Marguerite was in danger.

The sailor took a step forward. 'I asked you a question, Irishman.'

Fists were readied.

Necessity demanded a diversion.

'You heard me, swine, wait your turn,' Jarlath bit back.

Marguerite stood between the men. If she caused a brawl, the tavern owner would take a stick to her at the end of the night.

'No, please, I am sure that we can work this out, gentlemen.' Her small voice was utterly wasted.

'Swine?' roared the sailor, and before he could finish his incriminations, Jarlath's fist flew hard and fast, knocked what was perhaps the last remaining tooth from the now bloodied mouth. Jarlath jumped forward, pushed Marguerite from harm's way, and more fists were exchanged. The sailor connected one squarely on Jarlath's jaw, sending him stumbling back a pace. Other guests joined in, and with a bellowing laugh, Manus was on his feet, throwing a punch at the closest head.

He yelled to Jarlath, 'This sport of yours, my friend. It is becoming a bad habit. Perhaps we could take up the harp next week, or something more musical than breaking heads.'

For the moment, breaking heads would have to suffice.

A new day arrived. Any man loyal to the Earl of Kildare would have sold their soul to the Devil for the view at Tower Hill, and so too, it seemed, would most of England. The men of Ireland pressed with the large crowd, all vying for position. The platform stood high enough for all to see. It seemed anticipation and excitement simply encouraged bodies to shift forward.

Dark stains around the block stood as a morbid reminder that the royal henchman had done little else this week. The Lancastrians did not pardon or forgive the Yorkists too readily.

At the sight of a lone figure, clothed in a coarse homespun garment, the crowd hushed and made path for the bleak procession, keen nothing should delay the inevitable. A monk walked in step behind Tiptoft, shouting prayers in Latin for the soul of the sinful one before him.

Wasted words, Jarlath thought, but noted, for a man walking to his death, Tiptoft showed no sign of cowardice or panic. He held his head high, eyes fixed to the Heavens as if in search of the journey he was about to embark upon. The only sign of unease was the tight grip on the cross in his hand.

Tiptoft paused at the bottom step. Eyes wavered on his executioner, to the dark hood and the deadly blade resting lightly against the faceless man's shoulder. The crowd began jeering, their voices free to delight in this imminent death.

Looking out to the crowd, the condemned Tiptoft slowly shuffled his feet until he stood before the block. He removed a shawl from his shoulders, bared his neck fully, and whispered unheard words to the henchman. He knelt, lowered his body. It was his lack of terror which stilled the crowd, and no time was wasted. The henchman brought down the axe in one deathly swing.

Jarlath heard a mixture of jubilant cheers, vile sobs, and retching. He felt a hand on his shoulder.

'It is done. Now we celebrate.'

Chapter Twenty-Six

Maynooth – Ireland

It was of no surprise to find his young wife in the library. So engrossed in her book, she failed to hear his approach and from the doorway Donal took a leisurely moment to stare, admire her peaceful presence. Serenely beautiful this day, as every day, she wore her favourite gown made of a plain green woollen cloth with loose fitting sleeves which gathered at the elbow. Her plaited hair lay across her shoulder and hung gracefully on her lap. She seemed more at ease in simplistic comforts. Yet to appease his sense of benevolence, she wore the silver bracelet he had given her only yesterday. A gift for no marked occasion; a gift of thanks for bringing laughter and a semblance of love back into his life.

He marvelled often that such a Holy Chalice, once thought to be unobtainable was again in his hands. It was not the all-consuming love he and Elizabeth had shared. Nonetheless, Ainnir was a cure. She was a tonic to a fever he thought would never lose its heat, and his heart now beat to the rhythm of a song, not the rattle of a boat floundering near the shore.

It had been difficult for Ainnir. He knew that now, and understood more than he would ever allow Ainnir to know. The frightened despairing young woman who arrived at his home three months earlier had now summoned the courage of a mighty battle commander. He had been prepared to be patient, yet to his surprise tolerance was not needed. She seemed to accept her path with grace though it was not of her choosing. He thought it possible that his new wife had been created by Vulcan, smith to the pagan gods, and forged from the strongest of irons.

Donal still witnessed her thoughts stray to another place, but as time passed this happened less frequently. His mind was more often taken back to the young, spirited woman on the dance floor at Glendalough, celebrating her birthday, swirling and twirling to music, her laughter filling the air, and that pleased him well. Even in their bedchamber, although fearful at first, she now welcomed him with gentleness and each time he embraced his wife, the ghosts of the past seemed to lessen their presence.

She did not speak of her family, yet he saw her pain. Every time messengers approached the castle walls her anticipation was palpable, so fraught was her want for news.

None came.

She fought well to have such disappointments not dent her mettle. Donal found he often became the one to deliver the hammer-blows to her courage.

It was he who, with tenderness, delivered the true reason behind her father's offer of her hand in marriage, the ruse, the deception. It was he who spoke of the raids, the burning of villages and the senseless loss of lives. He concealed his rage for the O'Byrne as best he could. He found little pleasure in his wife's dismay.

Thomas and Donal rode to quell the mayhem, and on each and every occasion the Wicklow Gaels were absent. Constantly finding deserted encampments was insufferably frustrating and Thomas cursed to no end.

Donal's disappointment, to the contrary, suffered a guilty sense of relief.

In truth, the alternative would result in bloodshed and death for one or more of Ainnir's family, whether blood kin or kin by marriage. Despite greatly desiring to wring the neck of the O'Byrne, the sadness that would inevitably follow was something Donal did not wish for his wife. It was bitter-sweet and something he must bear alone although he suspected similar contradictions found a place in the mind of Thomas, for all at Maynooth had come to love the lass well.

However, there was a duty to be done and the O'Byrne had earned his position as enemy.

Ainnir wished Donal God's speed at each departure and never asked for details on his return. She would say that it was gift enough that he returned whole and unharmed and without dire news of her kin.

They also gave thanks that the Ormonds had not antagonised the Earl with their own insurgence from the south, and it soon became obvious the O'Byrne planted false suspicions. The scheme worked for a time, for the Earl kept a portion of his men prepared and at the ready in Maynooth, whilst the rest, in smaller numbers, dealt with the Gaels in the north of Kildare.

It gladdened and pleasantly surprised Donal that he missed his wife during his absences. He had not thought such a yearning would again visit his life, and he was happy to be wrong. He missed her recital of poetry, the tone of her voice, the soft touch of her hands soothing his tired muscles, her scent of spring and summer blossoms and her warm body.

A smile curled on his face with these thoughts whilst

another, not too dissimilar to his own, began to show upon his wife's lips.

'How long do you plan to stand there, husband, and stare?' Ainnir asked the question without moving eyes from the pages of her book.

'Forever, if you would allow me.' Donal pulled up a chair and sat directly in front of her, resting hands on her knees.

'And what is it that has taken you from my company this day?' He saw the almost imperceptible pause in her breath, the ever-present expectation of bad tidings, followed quickly by the gentle release of air at the understanding that bad news was not to be delivered at his visit.

'Geoffrey Chaucer's story of Blanche of Lancaster, *The Book of The Duchess.*'

'And?'

'And her husband must have loved his wife well to have mourned her for so long, and to have commissioned Chaucer to scribe a poem to her memory. May I?'

Without waiting for a reply ...

'I, wretch, whom death has made naked of all bliss that ever was, who am become most miserable of all men, who hate my days and my nights
My life, my pleasures are loathsome to me for all welfare and I are at odds. Death itself is my enemy; though I would die, it will not so.'

Donal's face dropped.

Ainnir shifted in her seat. 'Donal, I am sorry. I did not wish to bring unwelcome memories of Elizabeth or grief.'

'No,' he said convincingly, giving over a conciliatory

smile. He knew it contained a measure of compassion, a meaning wasted upon Ainnir, for the things he had come to know that were best left unsaid. 'Any memory of Elizabeth is no longer sorrowful. I loved her dearly and have no regrets.'

He took hold of Ainnir's hand and raised it to his lips. 'You are my wife now. God has been generous. And it does no good longing for what has passed and what cannot be again.'

He searched her face intently. She blinked over and again, her eyes darting. She seemed to gather herself and pressed her fingers gently into his hand with a wan smile. He knew where her thoughts travelled in that short moment.

Eager to steer their conversation to less sombre lands, he added with cheer, 'If Blanche were alive today, I wonder what her thoughts would be of her children, for both the Lancastrians and Yorkists are of her direct bloodline?'

'How can a family fragment so?' Her brow furrowed and with one swift movement Donal lifted Ainnir from her seat, nestled her comfortably onto his lap.

'The Duchess and I have taken you to thoughts of your kin, I see.'

She nodded.

'The day will come soon, Ainnir, when your father and I will meet again, and it will not be to share a mug of ale. For your sake, it is not a day I look forward to.'

'And on that day I shall come to know how Blanche of Lancaster would feel.'

'Well, dear Blanche,' he said standing, lifting her high. 'Until then, we should push all worry from our mind. There are still a few hours before the evening meal. Would my lady wife like to accompany me for a walk in the garden?'

'Donal!' James burst through the door and pulled up sharply, only to be bumped squarely in the back by a non-attentive Eleanor hot on his heels. Both faces broke into cheeky grins, silently commenting on such a private embrace.

'Yes, James? Eleanor?' Donal bit back laughter. 'Is there something either of you wish to say?'

'What are you doing?'

'That would be none of your concern, James,' answered Donal, enjoying the warm breath at his neck as Ainnir tried woefully to stifle her own laughter. Donal was none too surprised by James's inquisitiveness, being the boy who had innocently inquired only a few days earlier when Ainnir would give him sons.

'Again I ask, is there something you wish to say?'

'Papa has received news from England.'

All looks of merriment vanished. The book tumbled to the floor, and all thoughts of the Duchess of Lancaster were left in their wake.

'Read for yourself, cousin.' Thomas handed the letter to Donal.

The Earl's face remained impassive, yet a twinkle danced at the corner of his eye. Ainnir took tentative hope from that. It had been more than four weeks since Jarlath's first letter.

Donal scanned the pages. Joan's stance shifted anxiously. Ainnir held her breath.

'He is well then,' Donal said without lifting his eyes from the page.

Joan choked back a sob. Ainnir lowered herself into the nearest chair. Donal reached for her hand.

She forced a smile. Ainnir had waited too long for news of Jarlath's safety. Her prayers were all for his protection and safe return; repetitive, imploring prayers offered to the Blessed Virgin to bring him back to Ireland. She dared insert a particular detail into each and every entreaty – *return Jarlath to the shores of Ireland, but not to Maynooth.* It was necessary, in the event the Holy Mother paid close attention to her every utterance.

Her resilience came at the cost of his absence. She remembered only too well, Muirne's warnings to be wary of what she wished for. She would make no mistake, leave nothing to chance. She had even ventured a similar wager with Satan, prepared to suffer in wretchedness for the remainder of her life if such a sacrifice was the expected due.

It suddenly grew unbearable waiting for the remainder of the news, news that would tell whether her prayers in whole were to be answered.

'Tell us of the news, my love,' Joan asked before Ainnir blurted the same request.

'It is good, Joan, very good. Our nephew is alive and well. Our men remain in London and believe King Edward is soon to return to their shores.'

'They are still in danger then?'

'Yes.' Thomas walked to the window. 'And still Hell bent on battle.'

Ainnir closed her eyes readying to offer another prayer and wondered what other spiritual body she could implore.

The prayer did not come, for Donal let forth a mighty laugh.

'Share what is so funny, Donal. I could do with some light banter,' said Joan.

'I think the pleasure should be left to the Earl of Kildare.' He raised eyes to Thomas.

'John Tiptoft was beheaded at Tower Hill,' announced Thomas with delight.

Joan gasped. 'Beheaded?'

Thomas smiled. 'He was arrested before he could escape England with the King. And would you believe the righteous swine asked the henchman to cut with the blade three times to emulate the Holy Trinity?'

'Dear Lord,' Joan walked to the window and stood beside Thomas.

'His last wish was denied. Only one cut of the blade. Pity.'

'I must admit I do not celebrate the morbid detail, but I will join you in thanks. I shall never forget the months you were imprisoned by that man.'

Ainnir made a sound similar to a growling cough.

Joan turned. 'Ainnir, you have lost all colour. Are you ill?'

'No. I mean, yes. I think I'm about to be –' she caught her last words, fought to hold at bay the rising nausea, and lifted her hand to her mouth.

'Come.' Joan helped Ainnir to the door.

Donal rose.

'I will tend her, Donal.' And they were gone.

Thomas laughed. 'Your wife has a weak stomach for beheadings.'

'So it seems.'

'Joan will ensure she is fine. In any event, your wife has unwittingly played ally. I have further news, news not to be voiced in her presence. My scouts tell me her kin is preparing to march south. Gather our captains, Donal, for we have urgent need to talk.'

'This is the first occasion we have received warning of their movement before time.'

Thomas nodded. 'We may meet the O'Byrne, face to face.'

'Yes.' And Donal said no more than that.

The hours robbed Donal of sleep. The night aged, candles burnt low, too low. He envied the fire in the hearth its somnolence. Rousing himself, he added kindling to encourage small sparks and flames, and banked them with narrow cuts of wood. The onset of winter chilled his feet and he was quick to return to the warmth of the bed.

Donal watched his sleeping wife, her soft lashes masking eyes which almost closed. He had long noticed her face in sleep. Watchful waiting eyes, behind eyelids that refused to shut fully. He had thought her eyes to be sentries, guarding their lady. This night she had fallen asleep with thoughts of worry, for he had spoken of the outcome of the evening meeting with Thomas.

The Wicklow Chieftains were preparing for heavy raids into the south of County Kildare.

Their few hours together before she slept were quiet, and filled with troubled thoughts. They made love, a coupling in which he knew she found little enjoyment this night, save from ensuring his physical needs were met.

Now lying on his back, hands clasped behind his head, his own eyes grew heavy and he began to find sleep.

Abrupt noises in the corridor brought his eyes open again. Servants moved hurriedly and shouts from men running up the stairway filled the air. Before he could roll from their bed, a loud thud came to the door.

Ainnir woke. 'What is it?' she asked sleepily.

'It is time, love. I must ride.'

'No,' she protested.

He fell into her arms and kissed her deeply.

'My dream told me you were to go this night. I fought to close a book in my hands, but it would not shut. The story demanded to be read.'

'Then wait until I am returned and we shall write the next chapter, together.' His hands swept away an errant lock of hair, and his eyes savoured every corner of her face, memorising every inch, every curve, every line.

'If I could stop you, I would.'

'It gladdens my heart to think you will pine for me.'

'Then God speed, and return to me as you are now.'

Donal kissed her again. 'Keep yourself well,' he said, and moved the coverlet bringing his hand to her stomach, 'and my child.'

Her eyes opened wider. 'You know?'

Donal nodded. 'I suspected as much.'

'I did not want to tell you, not until –'

He lifted a finger to her lips. 'When I return, you will be wrapped in soft fleece. We will argue over names for my red-haired child. 'Tis time we argued over a trifle, wife. I think you would look radiant with cheeks flaring.'

They shared a nervous smile. Donal took her hand, and placed a long kiss on her palm.

He left without looking back.

'Papa, our mounts are ready in the bailey,' Gerald said to his father.

Joan looked to Gerald and placed a hand upon his arm.

'Joan.'

She heard the voice of her husband, but did not turn.

'Joan. He will be safe. I give you my word, love.'

'Mama, do not stop me,' Gerald pleaded.

'No, son. I will not stop you.' She lifted her hand to his face. 'You are a man, Gerald. It is now your duty to ride with your father. Promise you will come home to me.'

'Mama, I could not bear to suffer your wrath if I did not.' Gerald smiled.

Joan raised her hand further, fussing with his hair, for no reason other than to give a mother's loving touch before he departed.

Thomas placed a kiss on her forehead. 'Keep the fires burning. We will not be long.'

They rode onward through the night for twenty-four miles, resting only briefly. Thomas believed the Gaels were west of the Slaney River, heading toward Ballyraggan. If his scouts were correct, they would head them off in the forest area bordering Wicklow and Kildare. Every minute counted.

The morning's faint winter sun, hidden by ill-boding clouds, did naught to bring warmth. Snow replaced drizzling rain. Light flakes swirled through the air buoyed by a dank breeze.

Ahead, smoke rose above the height of woodland trees.

Distant screams climbed and petered.

'Christ, do not let us be too late.' Thomas roared the war cry of the Fitzgeralds, 'Crom Abu!'

He drew his sword, kicked his mount. His men took no more than a breath to follow his lead.

In the clearing, buildings were alight. Flames devoured flames. Sparks danced into the sky. Dogs scattered and mothers cradling infants ran to the cover of trees. The warning yell of *Kildare* was shouted from the dense green, but the Gaels were not quick enough to retreat.

Thomas focused on a burning torch carried by an unhorsed soldier. His sword swept down and severed the arm. A vile shriek cracked across the clearing. The torch fell to the ground, its flame dying in the sodden earth.

The sound of loosed arrows flew through the air. Screams of agony followed. Thomas veered his horse and rode frantically at a bowman on foot. His sword sliced through flesh and ribs and a gasp of strangled pain sputtered and gurgled from the dying man's mouth.

Two soldiers armed with poleaxe and sword, circled his son. Gerald pulled hard on the reins, digging his heels deep into the horse's flanks. Hooves beat down on one of his attackers. The horse squealed its excitement.

Gerald turned and swung his sword to the rear, deflecting the flying poleaxe from the second assailant.

Quick legs had his attacker to his other side. He struck again and missed.

Gerald circled the horse. Another swing and the poleaxe missed yet again. The Gael was quick, and before Gerald could bring his sword down the poleaxe swung again and sliced the mount's neck. Blood spurted. The horse tossed its head. Legs crumpled. Gerald crashed to the ground.

The Gael jumped clear of the flailing hooves, found his footing, held his bloodied poleaxe high and scampered toward Gerald.

Thomas kicked his mount and roared.

Donal must have seen the same danger. Of a sudden he was strides ahead, kicking his horse and jeering with sword held high. An arrow swept past Thomas' ear. He felt a searing burn.

More arrows came.

And then a thud.

An arrow hit Donal, piercing the flesh of his armpit between breastplate and faulds.

Thomas roared again.

Donal moved the sword to his other hand and brought it down. The chain mail of Gerald's attacker could not save the man. The head fell from the neck.

The yell of *retreat* echoed across the air. The raiders' mounts pounded the earth.

Thomas looked up to see the O'Toole staring down from a small rise in the woodland. The order of *retreat* screamed from the O'Toole's mouth again. Even from such a distance, Thomas could see the Chieftain's scar twitch and redden.

A lone horseman rode to the same mound. Bradan O'Byrne. His face, although covered with filth and sweat, could not hide the torment in his eyes. Within seconds they were gone.

'My lord, your orders?' shouted one of Thomas' captains.

'Chase the bastards down!' Thomas turned to another of his captains. 'Keep enough men to douse the fires.'

Thomas gave no more thought to those orders. He was off his horse helping his cousin from the saddle.

'It is but a scratch, Thomas,' Donal hissed, his face contorting in pain.

'And I am Jesus Christ.'

Donal slumped to the ground. 'The arrow has pierced deep. Pull it free.'

'Donal!' Gerald fell to the ground beside him.

'It is alright, lad. Your father, like Merlin, is about to make the arrow disappear.'

Donal grabbed at Gerald's knife, pulled it from its sheath and placed the handle between his teeth. He bit down hard then nodded.

'Hold him down, son. That's it. On the count of three. Are you ready?'

Without even beginning the count, Thomas pulled the arrow free. A harrowing yell and ragged breaths followed quickly.

'Who schooled you in numbers?' Donal threw his head back.

'Put your hand here, Gerald,' said Thomas. 'Hold fast to stop the bleeding. Got it?'

Gerald nodded.

'Grab the man a drink,' Thomas yelled.

Within moments a skin was held to Donal's lips. He drank deeply.

Thomas regarded Donal with troubled eyes. The arrow came free, but he suspected it had embedded into bone. A wound that deep was vulnerable to infection if marrow had spilled into the blood stream. They needed to move him and find help now. The distance back to Maynooth was too great, their pace would be slow and Donal would suffer.

'Two hours ride. Can you manage it?'

'How many is two?' Donal answered between pained breaths.

'Good.' Thomas interpreted Donal's humour as an answer of *yes*. He turned to the sounds of his returning men. His captain shook his head, a sign he knew meant the Gaels had escaped.

Molten fire flowed through his veins.

'This is not the circumstance in which I hoped to enjoy your company again, Thomas.'

'Nor I, Abbess.'

Thomas watched the rotund woman fuss about Donal. Blood was quick to seep from the freshly bandaged wound. She pulled the bedding up high to cover the dark red.

'Donal rests comfortably now. The henbane and hysseop will see he remains so, but he floats in and out of consciousness too quickly. We will bathe him with a pitcher of Saint Fintan's water to reduce the fever.' She rested the back of her hand to Donal's forehead. Creases grew on her brow.

'Do you remember, Thomas, the time we forced Donal to sip Saint Fintan's water? You told him it would heal his grieving heart and bad moods. He was none too keen as I recall.'

'I do, and I believe his cursing fell short for your benefit. The Lord knows Donal never held his tongue in my presence.'

'He is a Fitzgerald then,' she said with a rueful smile. 'But more than the herbs, Thomas, I do not –'

'Thank you,' Thomas finished. 'You look tired. You need rest.'

'I will have all the rest I need when the Lord calls me home.' The Abbess rolled up her sleeves and tended to the bloodied cloths. 'Until then, whilst I still have able hands and mind, there is much to be done. Some prayers may help. Visit our Chapel. I will stay with Donal until you return.'

All was in darkness, save for two small spluttering candles lit by the quiet novices who had led him to the Chapel. Thomas' body ached. He was bone-weary and eschewed the wooden bench, summoning the strength to kneel on the cold floor before the altar, hopeful that his suffering would give him more of an ear with the Lord.

Thomas had sat with Donal through the night. His condition did not bode well. Thomas knew that. Fever racked his body too quickly, but Thomas would not give up hope, never, no matter how frail it appeared. Donal could not leave them now. There was still too much to be done. Too many uprisings to quell, too many laws to proclaim, too many Gaels to win over. And children. Donal still had children to come, God willing. He wanted Donal to experience the joys of fatherhood. He wanted Ainnir to give Donal so many sons and daughters that his knees and arms would be filled, just as his own had been.

Thomas lowered his head, resting his forehead on clasped hands. Donal saved his son. Fourteen or more hours earlier on that clearing, Donal had saved Gerald's life. In turning his back to danger, he now lay fighting for his own life. Thomas shuddered at what may have come to be. Donal may not have reached Gerald in time.

Thomas gave Jarlath a thought, offering a prayer that he be safe from harm. His two mainstays, the strongest stars in his firmament, filled his minutes with grievous worry. One fever ridden, infection spreading through his body, the other – he did not know – somewhere in the battle-ridden lands of England, perhaps now in combat. God could be not so cruel as to have both men struck down. Surely not?

There was never a time Donal did not risk life nor limb for Thomas, his children, and for Jarlath too. Thomas gave a morose laugh, a sound which echoed along the empty walls. He remembered back to fifteen years ago, to Donal and his usual bravado, once again putting himself in danger for his kin.

A young Jarlath caused trouble whilst on a midnight adventure. His knocked lantern set fire to the stables. Flames licked high at the walls and the heat fought any sensible man back. But not Donal.

A new litter of kittens mewed in the stable's loft, left deserted by their fleeing mother. That cat, what was her name? It would not come to Thomas readily, but it was a name which had brought much hilarity.

Donal knew how Jarlath loved those kittens, and, dousing himself in water, had thrown a blanket over his head, and ran into the heat. He had never told Jarlath of this heroic deed. Donal wanted no thanks for such an act of selfless bravery – or stupidity, as Thomas had cursed afterwards.

If Donal survived this battle, he would ensure he told the story to Jarlath in full. One way or another, Thomas would make sure Jarlath knew.

'Papa.' Gerald's footsteps were soft. 'How is Donal?'

'The Abbess has done as much as she can, son. Now our prayers are needed.'

'We would not be here if it were not for me. If I had only–'

'Do not say that, Gerald. Donal would do nothing differently if he had his chance over again.'

Gerald lowered his head. 'Is there something I can do?'

Thomas understood his son's guilt but he could not deal with that now. Neither could he deal with the hatred he bore for the O'Toole, nor his desire for revenge. All would have to wait. 'Pray with me, pray the herbs and Saint Fintan's water –' Thomas stopped.

'Papa, what is it?'

The Abbess had said Donal would be bathed in Saint Fintan's water. *Saint Fintan's water!* The water Donal drank during their last stay at the Abbey, to speed the healing of his heart. Yet it was not the Holy Water which remedied his ailment. It was not the Holy Water which mended his grieving heart.

'Gerald. There is something you can do. Ride. Ride like the devil is at your back and bring Ainnir here to Donal.'

Ainnir remembered Donal speaking of the Abbey at Achad-finglass. He talked much of the stoic aged walls and the echoes that travelled the length of the corridors.

Footsteps could be heard coming from the next county, he had laughed, *if the building had only been built that length.*

He spoke of the scents, *not fragrant nor womanly, but sterile, cleansing, perhaps earthy or manly*. Ainnir remembered he had not been able to settle on one description. But here in the sickroom, amongst the fetid smells of bodily waste, none of the descriptions rang true. There were no echoes in the corridors, nor were there distant footsteps, only the laboured breathing of her husband.

She had ridden at speed with Edward Burnell, the Earl's physician, an escort of men-at-arms, and an exhausted Gerald who had squashed all argument that he remain at Maynooth. The fear that haunted her journey did not abate at the sight of her husband. His cheeks were hollowed, his pallor, grey. His fingers curled listlessly, clawing at sweat-soaked sheets as the fever soared.

The Abbess detailed to Edward Burnell the herbs and lotions she had administered, and was given a nod of approval. Burnell bled Donal at the ankle, announcing he was none too pleased at the colour of the blood, confirming what all knew – that infection ravaged his body. The fever grew at an alarming pace. He ordered honey be given as often as possible to give the body energy to fight. It was done more so for the benefit of Ainnir, for to Thomas he spoke only of fetching a priest.

Ainnir gave her own orders, asking the Abbess to prepare a poultice of fox clote for the wound, and a brew of laurel berries for the fever. The Abbess believed none would help Donal now. He was in God's hands. But Ainnir's need to believe that her husband would mend was great.

Ordering a pallet be moved into the chamber, Ainnir refused to leave the room, insisting Donal was in need of her. It was true for in his fretful hours, Donal seemed to settle more easily when his wife held his hand, and whispered words of encouragement.

Yet Ainnir was not certain Donal knew of her presence.

When hallucinations took his mind, gravelly words from his dry lips seemed to speak to Elizabeth. It did not distress her overly for when she answered *yes, I am here, my love*, his ragged breathing calmed. It was the only thing that mattered.

She chose to bathe him herself, using soaked cloths to take the heat from his body and cleanse his skin of sweat and waste, whilst the novices brought fresh sheets and silently removed those soiled. She held cups of wine mixed with herbs to his mouth. She fed him berries and spoonfuls of honey when he was lucid enough to swallow, and spoke of names for their child and of plans for a nursery.

She had dozed, still seated, holding his hand. She drifted into frantic dreams, none of which made sense, but all spoke of fear, worry and alarm. She heard her husband's voice calling, but could not reconcile his words with the dream. Her name came again and her eyes fluttered open to see Donal looking to her.

'Donal?'

'You should not have come.' His voice was weak.

'You are my husband, of course I should be here.' Ainnir managed a meagre smile.

'The babe?'

'You sound like Muirne. She was none too happy I travelled either.'

'You should have listened to her.' His droopy exhausted eyes stayed fixed to hers.

He was with her. She was certain. No longer in a torrid hallucination, he was talking to his wife, his living wife, not Elizabeth.

'I was keen to have our first argument, and you did not return home when you had promised.' She lifted his cold hand to her cheek.

'Ah, yes – our first argument. And the book, the chapter.'

'We will write it together.' She held back tears, watched as Donal bravely fought sleep beckon his return.

'Ainnir, listen. My body is weak, and I fear –' He grimaced in pain.

Ainnir lifted a cup to his mouth urging him to swallow deeply.

'Jarlath,' Donal continued, 'bring him home.'

She jerked suddenly, tipping much of the fluid onto the bed. 'What did you say?' She scarcely heard her own words.

'Bring him home. My child will need a father. You have my blessing.'

Her eyes flew wide and Donal became a blur. 'You knew?'

'Only when it was too late. Had I known –'

'You knew?' she repeated.

His revelation froze time.

'You have my blessing,' Donal repeated. 'Tell him it is time for the sun to rise in the west. He will understand. Jarlath can help you write the chapter.'

'Oh, Donal!' Tears fell like autumn rain. 'I did not want it to be –' but she got no further.

He slipped back into fitful slumber. His eyelids twitched. Her body fell onto his. She sobbed like never before.

The door of the quiet library opened.

'Eat this. No arguments.'

Thomas looked to the bowl of broth and coarse bread. 'There are not too many people in this world who can tell me what to do, but my daughter and you, dear Abbess, are the first to come to mind.'

'Two females, Thomas? Do you not find that interesting?'

'Chilling.' They shared a tired smile. 'We are about to lose him.'

'Yes, I fear we are.'

'I find myself questioning everything that has come to pass. Donal is to celebrate his thirtieth birthday next month. Have I repaid his loyalty, or did I use him, just take him for granted?'

'Tell me your memories of your childhood, Thomas, the happy wonderful times that sit prominently in your mind.'

He looked to the Abbess with an inquisitive eye then obeyed.

'My father, John, died when I was ten. My mother raised me at our home in Kildrought, Cill Droichid, not far from Maynooth. Father brought Maynooth to its current grandeur, but did not live to see it filled with children. It was my Aunt Joanna and her husband Donal MacCarthy who were most influential to me in those years. He was known as the Prince of Desmond, and a Prince in every way was that man.'

Thomas played with the broth, swirling the bread through the liquid.

'Passing strange, I am to tell you of a great man by the name of Donal. He was as a father to me. Even at a young age I joined meetings of counsel. He encouraged me to listen intently and make my own decisions, for it would come to pass, he told me, that I would one day be a great leader in Kildare.' Thomas paused and dwelled momentarily on that proven prophecy.

'He taught me that a strong mind is greater than a sword, and that my people should be respected with the care I would give my own kin. Oh, he had a fearsome temper. One I learnt to avoid at all costs, but he was a great man and stood in my father's stead well.'

'If I did not know better, I would think I was listening to Donal speak of his life with you.' The Abbess shuffled a pile of papers at the table and lit another candle. 'Do you not think Donal would speak of you in such glowing terms?'

'You are a wise woman, Abbess, too wise I fear. However you have had me talk so long the broth is now cold.'

'Eat it,' she ordered.

She did not know how, but sleep had taken her again, much like it had her husband. Ainnir's dreams were now different. No longer was *she* in his arms. It was Elizabeth. His smile was so blissful, like none she had ever seen upon his face. How she knew it to be Elizabeth, she could not fathom. Yet without doubt, she knew.

Together Donal and Elizabeth thanked her, thanked Ainnir and called her *caretaker*. They did not call her by name. The two held hands and exchanged longing looks, looks of a wondrous and mighty love.

She walked at their side along a crooked path of loose stones. Their footsteps should have brought scrapes and crunches, but no sound came. And when Ainnir looked down to wonder at their silent steps, the path blurred into a lush meadow of flowers. Yellows and pinks dotted the green. Wind whistled and taunted the blossoms. The scent of lavender played through the air. She looked left and right and with each turn they wandered through a different place. Sometimes at the shores of her lake with small waves lapping at her feet, another time in the garden at Maynooth beside the pond, and then in the deer park surrounded by towering trees, blinking as sunlight filtered through the canopy of leaves.

A warm breeze touched her cheeks and in that soft caress, she knew Donal and Elizabeth's love to be real. It felt pure, eternal. This was Donal's one true love, his only love.

Elizabeth carried a large book, its binding worn and faded. The wind ruffled the pages, but the cover would not open. No matter how forceful the gusts of wind, the pages remained shut. The telling was complete.

Ainnir woke with a start. Her head rested on Donal's covered leg and her hands clasped his wrists. His previous words came to her again, for they had been forgotten in her dreams.

He had known. He had known about Jarlath. How and why did he bear such knowledge in secret? Not once did he lead her to suspect. Not once did he damn her, accuse her, curse her.

God forgive her for all she wrought. How had he borne that burden? Perhaps to helplessly witness his physical agony was her punishment, punishment for the heart she had not given, and punishment for the heart she gave.

She looked up. Donal rested well, no fidgeting, no rasping breath, and the weight in her heart lessened somewhat at that thought, for periods of peace did not come often. It was a good sign. Was the fever breaking?

Suddenly, alarm filled her whole being and she moved

quickly to his face. No sweat fell from his forehead and a once heated temple was now cold, so cold.

'No,' she heard herself say.

'No,' she said again kissing his cheek.

'Sorry,' fell from her mouth over and again, until the words became an incoherent scream.

Chapter Twenty-Seven

Dawn brought a murky light to the earth as Bradan reached the castle gates of Glendalough. The sound of his galloping horse alerted servants in the hall. All had risen early to stoke fires and see to warm foods for the morning breaking of fast.

'Son!' Hugh descended the stairs two at a time, adjusting his dress. 'Thanks be to the Lord, for we thought you had fallen into the hands of Kildare's men. The others returned days ago and I only returned from the north yesterday. Come. Come by the hearth. Tell me what delayed you. What of the mission?'

Bradan's mantle billowed like raven wings and his boots fell with a dull thud. His mood was less than affable.

'Our mission? We burnt, we plundered, we thieved. We did all you asked of us. And now, your daughter is a widow.'

'You say what?'

'I said your daughter now wears the colour black.' Bradan removed his gloves and threw them to the floor.

'Donal is dead? You are sure?'

'Kildare knew of our plans. I saw Donal take an arrow. They gave chase. I turned my horse south and found refuge along the border of Carlow. I waited all this time for word. They took him to the Abbey at Achad-finglass. Ainnir was summoned. She cared for him unto his death. Is there more you wish to know?'

'Donal is dead?'

'And my sister, distraught.'

'We all have our burdens to bear.'

'And she, more than most.'

'Death comes to us all.'

'Your hearing fails you, I am sure. The man you chose for Ainnir, the man who was to father your grandchildren has been killed at your hands. Oh, the O'Toole was more than pleased to share your blame. His last words as we fled were filled with laughter. He relished the thought of such a trophy kill. But it is your daughter's grief you have caused, yet again. Ainnir – your daughter!'

'You need not remind me of her name.'

'Do I not? Her grief, her loss, her despair, it is all on your hands.'

'How dare you?'

'Oh, how I dare! All blame falls at your feet. When is this madness to stop? Mama keeps from your bed, and –'

'That, Bradan, is enough.'

'No. You have sent my sister from these walls to a life of misery. What great scheme do you have in mind for me? Do you wish to lose me as well?'

'Where does this anger come from? You have never questioned me before. You know all I do is for our clan, the O'Byrne clan, and you are one yourself.'

'This feud, this endless fighting, Gael versus Irish, native versus settler. To what point? By my reckoning it is our fathers, hundreds of years now gone, who have reason to hate the English invaders. Not us. When do we forgive? When do we begin to forget what we were never part of?'

Eyes clashed. Hugh was the first to look away. His head lowered.

'After I sent Ainnir to Maynooth, I had the marriage between your brother and the O'Toole's daughter secured. I thought both were for the best, and yes, both were to achieve a purpose, one so great that personal sacrifice was necessary. That is my duty, Bradan, as Chieftain no personal sacrifice can be too great.'

Hugh walked some steps toward the windows, and slipped a backward glance to Bradan. 'But your mother came to me, with as much anger as you have in you now, and she made me promise you would not be used for bargain, made me promise you would be free to choose a marriage of love, not advantage. It was all I could do to make peace with her. She spoke of birds with broken wings or some like tale. I now see her meaning.'

Bradan released an audible breath, more a sound of sympathy. 'In Ainnir's marriage, you were too busy planning and conniving to see her heart was given before her birthday. You gave her to the wrong Fitzgerald.'

Hugh's chin lifted. Confusion creased his forehead then the lines vanished. 'Jarlath? But how? I would not have cared either way. Why did she not say?'

'Would such a plea have been heard?'

Hugh gave no direct answer. 'Jarlath?' he asked again.

'None of us saw it, not even Mama, and that breaks her heart.'

'You have spoken of this with your mother then?'

'Before our last raid.' Bradan saw he had punished his father enough. Hugh looked grey, perhaps allowing himself to feel exhaustion for the first time.

'I am chilled to the bone. If I have your leave, I will –'

'Of course, son. Of course.'

Bradan thought to leave, but hesitated. 'One more thing, Papa. Your daughter is with child.'

Hugh watched his son's back, then caught his wife's still form, standing to the corner of the hall. He had not heard her entry.

A vacant hollow look met his. There was no hatred, no loathing. No smile, no blinking, no fidgeting – nothing. Just an empty sightless stare. But tears, there were so many tears running unchecked, splashing to the collar of her night gown. He thought he recognised a fleeting glimpse of forgiveness or pity, or perhaps it was simply a niggling sense that both were warranted.

Brigid followed their son with quiet unhurried footsteps.

Hugh turned to the hearth, now bright with blazing wood. He stood perilously close to the flames and spared no concern for the hazard. The fervent heat burned him less than the silent tears of his wife.

Why do they not understand? How can they not know I do all for the clan?

Then with unease he quietly cursed. 'Ainnir, what have I done to you, lass?'

One week later, in the grounds of the friary near Cill-Dara, in the shade of the oak trees, Donal was laid to rest alongside his first wife. Richard Lang, Bishop of Kildare, celebrated the mass.

Ainnir heard the distant chant of prayers, said in Latin, and looked up to the Bishop. She had met this man on two occasions, here and at her wedding to Donal. Both times her heart weighed heavily with unbearable burden. She never wanted to meet this man again.

Chapter Twenty-Eight

April 1471 – Gladmore Heath – England

The rightful King of England returned. It was no small blessing that his wife, the Queen, gave birth to a son whilst in sanctuary; an heir to the throne, proof to the people of England the Yorkist King had both right and God on his side. It mattered not that the Lancastrian King already had a son, one able to sit a horse and fight.

Prince George was forgiven, crawling to his brother like a repentant dog with a tail between its legs. The King embraced the Lord's words to *turn the other cheek*. His English subjects thought their sovereign muddled of mind, no less than Henry of Lancaster, for most men would have struck their brother down where he stood, and many of the Yorkist nobles wished King Edward had done just that.

Yet bountiful with forgiveness in one hand, with the other King Edward chased Richard Neville, the Earl of Warwick all over England, baiting him into either bloody confrontation or surrender. With George once again riding under the York standard of the white rose, and Marguerite D'Anjou still on the shores of France, Warwick was left to stand alone against England's greatest battle commander.

The King led his army to Barnet, keen to bring battle to Warwick on the following morn. Scouts alerted Warwick to the Yorkist King's proximity, and the Earl stilled his army's movement and made ready for the inevitable.

And now, on the darkened field of Gladmore Heath, some twelve miles north of London, Jarlath sat quietly in the eerie calm that always came before a storm, for tomorrow they would do battle.

Under the cover of night, Yorkist canons strategically blasted at Warwick's troops from a distance well away from the main portion of the King's army. The army, more than ten thousand men, progressed forward with stealth in a daring manoeuvre and set up camp within striking range of Warwick's men.

Crouched beneath twinkling stars and a dome of endless ink-black, they positioned themselves in the usual battle formation of three divisions; vanguard, centre and rearward. No camp fires were lit, lest they be seen and their ploy discovered. The men remained sober and waited for the morning, whilst canon fire in reply from the Warwick camp flew harmlessly overhead.

Manus' men and the men of Kildare were to fight with the vanguard under the command of Richard of Gloucester, the King's youngest brother. Soft moonlight allowed Jarlath to see Gloucester's tent nearby, the standard of the white boar erected high, fluttering with the movement of the night air. To his sides, hands checked and double checked equipment. Whetstones hissed along blades. Sand and vinegar worked at scrubbing rust from coat mail. To busy the mind men quoted from scripture, confirming to all they were fighting for the right side.

'Scripture says that rebellion is the sin of witchcraft,' said one, 'and it is the rebellious sinners we will meet with the rising sun.'

Another dutifully listed a string of events from which King Edward miraculously survived. 'Like a phoenix from the ashes,' he explained.

'Or Christ and His rise from the dead,' yet another hastened to add, his analogy so daring, it received glances of rebuke from some who thought it blasphemous.

'It is Easter Eve,' he reminded his critics sourly as if none could deny the similarities. A resurrection was imminent.

Another said, 'They are but a flock of sheep with wolves amongst them. They will be too concerned watching the soldier to their side to worry about our oncoming attack.'

All laughed in agreement, debating the political and private history of each of the battle commanders they were to face on the morn.

The Earl of Oxford and the Duke of Exeter were long time enemies, yet on occasion, had fought side by side against Warwick. The Marquis of Montagu was Warwick's brother, however, he had often given support for the cousin he loved well, King Edward. It was indeed an interesting quandary and none doubted that the various contingencies would keep their enemies sleepless and tossing on their pallets this night.

Yet none ventured to speak of the wolf amongst their own flock: George, the Duke of Clarence. How many times had he changed his colours? He could teach a chameleon a thing or two. Worries were given no time to prove, for rumour spread that the King gave orders George was to remain at his side for the duration of the battle. Rumours also spread that the Prince spat oaths at this insult, curses which tent walls could not keep private. But he was given no choice. The Yorkist wolf was to be tethered.

Whispers of *Gloucester* interrupted the chatter. All eyes turned to a group of men walking through their encampment. Jarlath saw garments in the colours of York, blue and murrey, and recognised the face of a man he had met in London – John Milewater.

Milewater looked Jarlath's way and then said quiet words to the companions at his side. A young man, not quite Jarlath's age, smaller in height, hair of a similar dark sheen and with the presence of a great lord, walked his way. Surprise almost bested Jarlath.

He knelt deeply. 'Your Grace.'

'We are battle comrades this eve, Irishman. Rise,' said Richard of Gloucester, the King's brother. 'You are the Earl of Kildare's son?'

'No, Your Grace. I am his nephew, Jarlath Fitzgerald. His son remains in Ireland, fighting uprisings on our soil. And this is Manus Eustace, nephew to the Baron of Portlester, and of course,' Jarlath gestured to his awestruck men, 'these are our men-at-arms, all at your service, Your Grace.'

Gloucester smiled. 'Most men would choose to steal conversation with the King's brother for their own gain, not bring notice to the men under his command.'

Jarlath kept his face low.

'His Grace, the King of England, is grateful for your support. And so am I,' the Duke added with humour. 'You and your men fight by my side on the morrow, and I suspect we will face the Duke of Exeter. But know we fight for the rightful King of England. Make sure your men get their sleep as best they can with this canon fire threatening to curse our rest, for we will have a busy day and it starts before sunrise. I expect to see us all alive and well, ready for celebrations at sunset, and to give thanks to Our Lord. That is a command from His Grace, the King.'

'Your Grace,' both Jarlath and Manus said in unison.

As the Duke of Gloucester left their presence the candid smile and nod from John Milewater said much. Jarlath understood the unexpected favour shown by the King's brother was Milewater's doing; a small token of esteem.

Only a week earlier, in the upstairs room of a tavern in London's south, John Milewater and his men had met with Jarlath and Manus and detailed orders for their part in the coming battle. A no-nonsense man, his liking for the Irish contingent was apparent. The Duke of Gloucester's man covered all dues for drink and foods enjoyed during their meeting. He stayed for a period longer than expected and shared conversation of a more personal nature; tales of family and childhood hilarities, irrelevant to the cause of the meeting at hand. Even their covert contact, Marguerite, was bestowed a measure of attention and celebrated the large purse awarded for work well done. But business needed to be attended, and the excited Marguerite used every known ruse to entice the men away from their company; expenses again covered by Milewater. And she succeeded with some.

Jarlath returned Milewater's nod, then settled down under the stars to begin the long wait.

Thoughts of home brought an involuntary touch to a leather purse tied at his waist, a movement noticed by Manus.

'You have not spoken much of your news, Jarlath. Those letters reached you months ago, and you have shared little of your thoughts. Donal was friend to me, also. Perhaps tonight of all nights you should unburden your mind. Talk. What harm can there be when I may not be in this earthly world much longer?'

Jarlath thought for a moment then uttered, 'I should have been there.'

It was a phrase he had repeated over and again, ever since he received the letter. Even in offering prayers for Donal's soul and in the silent moments used to rouse memories, those accusing words bit at his thoughts with sting and venom.

'An impossibility. You were here in England.'

Jarlath shook his head. 'Donal would be alive if I had not been so Hell bent on escaping my home. Never was there a time we were not side by side looking to each other. His death came because of my selfishness.'

'Again, I say – an impossibility. It was your duty to be here.'

Jarlath gave no acknowledgement. 'It brings a burning guilt as hot as white fire.'

'You did what you had to do. Thomas and my uncle wanted us here in their stead.'

'No!' Jarlath spat. He refused to be absolved so easily. 'Thomas did not want me here. He warned me against it, but I was caught up in my own self-preservation. I baulked at his caution. I wanted to be far from Maynooth, as far away as possible. If I had only ...' Jarlath's words trailed off, his arguments banished to the silent corners of his mind.

He loved Donal, loved him as a brother, and in the first reading of Thomas's letter Jarlath's hundredth bout of self-loathing had hit hard, perhaps his thousandth. His thoughts had stumbled to the shameful hate he bore, the harm he wished for Donal on their ride from Glendalough, and the heated swordfight on the training field, and every other detestable thought that followed thereafter.

He questioned himself repeatedly. Did he somehow ask the Lord for Donal to be gone? He knew his heart had taken control of his mind. Had it somewhere in the darkest hours betrayed him so foully?

'It was not you who shot that arrow, Jarlath. You do yourself great disservice by taking the blame. Donal would not want you to feel the way you do right now.'

'How do you know what I feel?'

Manus gave half a smile. 'You have never been good at trickery, my friend. But,' he sighed, 'I wonder what my Meg is doing now.'

Jarlath slanted a questioning look. 'You rarely speak of your wife.'

'Because I do not find enjoyment in non-stimulating conversation. Life is too short.'

Jarlath waited for a moment, intrigued as to where this conversation was likely to lead. 'Nothing has changed then?'

'If God would grant me the chance over again to capture love and happiness in my marriage and its bed, I would gladly sell my very soul. I very much lack the appetite to do what a man should do with his wife, and have no doubt that the idea is no more palatable for Meg. I wish it were not so. You are here because you needed escape. Have you stopped to think that my reason could be the same?'

Jarlath shook his head.

'It is not often I speak of my frustrations. Perhaps I do now because I see someone dear to me, looking at the opportunity to quench his thirst from the waters of love, yet he baulks for no good reason. Oh yes,' he said quickly seeing Jarlath move to argue, 'you may want to correct my use of, *no good reason*, but it is just that. Your feelings of guilt are not valid. You cannot change the path God has made for Donal. Neither of us would have wished it so, but it has come to be.'

'I should have been there.'

Manus leant in close. 'Jarlath, do not turn from the chance of happiness. It may be God's wish you remain here on His earth for many years yet and that is a damnably long time to be miserable. I will say no more.'

'I doubt that.'

'It is time we get what rest we can. Light will be with us soon.'

Jarlath found what warmth he could with no fires to ward off the chill. He looked to the stars, gave only a moment or two to think of the morrow and contemplated the promise he made to both Joan and Thomas; he would return home safely.

The star *Alderamin* showed itself. It was a rare occasion indeed to see this star. Yet this night it flashed with thousands of others in the sombre palette. From that point Jarlath found the constellation *Cepheus*, the *King of Aethiopia*. Thomas had favoured discussion of Ptolemy's study of the stars and Jarlath warmly remembered many summer nights lying on the cool grasses of the village clearing staring upwards; his scholarly lessons for the day conducted by night.

He wondered if Joan or Thomas now gazed up to the same night sky. He wondered if *she* did too. Would Ainnir also be looking upward?

There were two letters in his purse, one from Thomas with news of Donal's death, the other from Ainnir.

So often had he read her letter, every syllable, every deletion, every smudge, every word seemed carved into his memory. Each line said so much yet refused to say all. Despite the darkness, he pulled Ainnir's letter from its place, believing the simple touch of the page made her voice sing in his mind.

> *"My heart struggles with the decision to write you, the reasons too varied to venture here, yet ink and paper have won out. I know your uncle also writes at this time to inform you of Donal's death. It has brought great sadness to all here at Maynooth. But I know, by means that none could ever begin to understand, Donal now rests in peace with Elizabeth. It is the following lines over which I tried to resist this communication, yet my heart pesters me greatly, advises that these are words owned by you, not I. In Donal's last moments he asked that I bring you home, gave us, gave you and I, his blessing. He knew of much, said he came to comprehend only when it was too late, too late for us all. His heart obviously held great love to have such Saintly forgiveness. Donal also asked that I tell you these last words. Although I do not comprehend their meaning, he assured me you would understand. He said it is time for you to make the sun rise in the west. I pray I was right in sending this letter. Know that none share in the knowledge of these words. They may therefore be buried with the movement of time, if that is your wish, or be cherished for your comfort."*

His fingers rubbed at the pages. Donal had known, yet he forgave, and offered his blessing. It was incomprehensible; how could a man have such generosity. Yet the instant he asked himself, Jarlath knew the answer, for such was the greatness of the man.

Ainnir gave no intimation to her own thoughts in the penned words. It gave a factual account only, an account that raised too many questions. Was she so full of guilt that any thought of a future with him would be as accepting a gift from Satan? Were her careful words simply a hesitance, unsure how he would receive her unvoiced plea? Could either of them ever reconcile Donal's death to a path allowing them to be together?

Manus' words flew through his head. Could his friend be right?

Suddenly Jarlath knew without contradiction he had to give himself reason to survive on the morrow, to fight with all the will and strength he could muster, if for nothing else, but to find those answers.

Manus stirred. 'You have read her letter again? Does that mean I will have a friend by my side, Hell bent on surviving?'

'Yes,' Jarlath answered, and gave no more than that. No longer did the prospect of death lack meaning.

He looked up again to the stars and knew instinctively that their light shone down upon the woman who filled his thoughts.

Chapter Twenty-Nine

Maynooth – Ireland

'Come from the window, Ainnir. The night's chill is not good for you.'

Ainnir smiled. Joan was right. Despite the warning, the view was too alluring. The constellation *Cepheus* was more vibrant than usual this night. *Alderamin* shone with a lustre she had not before witnessed, the minor stars tracing the crown and the arms of the astral King as if sketched on a page by an artist. Ainnir could not help but sense a magic in their brilliance. Perhaps they spoke words, their twinkling a message.

The servants busied themselves closing shutters and stoking the hearth. Ainnir felt a movement inside and looked down to the skirts of her gown. Black, the colour of mourning, hid her bulging form, hid the red-haired child who moved and wriggled inside, the child Donal had yearned for. Black, the colour she donned without protest as penance for her sinful longings, a hair shirt tearing at her very soul. No, the stars held no message.

'Here, come take Anne,' said Joan.

Blissful and belly replete with milk, Joan's infant daughter fought to keep her eyes open, content to return to sleep as was her wont for the most part of each day. Ainnir carried the swaddled baby to a chair close to the warmth of the library's fire, and watched the amusing pouts the little one made.

'It will not be long before you'll be holding your son, Ainnir.'

'A son?'

'I have had too many babes of my own not to see the signs.'

'A son,' Ainnir repeated, in a hushed and reverent tone.

'Papa says Anne is as beautiful as me.' Eleanor climbed onto the arm of Ainnir's chair, nestling in to watch her baby sister. She giggled when a gentle cooing sound came from tiny red lips.

'Oh, I can only agree with your papa, Eleanor.' She reached for Eleanor's feet dangling close to her growing body. Even to sit as she did now had become difficult.

'Mind your feet, Eleanor, they press my side. Ohhh!'

'Eleanor. Hop down from there,' Joan scolded.

'I do not believe it is Eleanor's feet, Joan. Something is wrong.'

Only one hour into the pains, the overwhelming need to push the babe free from her body possessed Ainnir's whole being. The worried conversations amongst the other women in the room were drowned by her screams.

'Look to me, girl.' Muirne said with such demand that all sets of eyes obeyed. 'Ignore what your body tells you, Ainnir. Hold and breathe and journey with the pain, do not allow it control. This babe needs longer within your womb to be strong. It is not its time, lass. Do not push.'

Ainnir's linen chemise was soaked with sweat, her eyes

wild with panic. When the pain took over, her fear was unmistakable, but to everyone's surprise, with that fear came the will to win. At every need to push, she breathed in and out at an exhaustingly slow pace, and as the pains subsided, all the women gave words of congratulation.

'You are winning the fight, Ainnir,' one told her.

'Your babe is listening to you already, heeding your chastisement. What a dutiful child this one will be,' said another.

'He will stay within your womb for as long as you keep this control,' said yet another.

Ainnir could not tell from whom the pieces of encouragement were voiced, yet she knew the last to be from Joan, a voice sure the fighting babe was a son.

The pains continued. Candles burnt low. Expressions dimmed. All knew it did not bode well. This babe was coming before its time.

Ainnir's courage could not be questioned. 'Be damned to Hell whatever plans You have for me,' she hissed, through gritted teeth. 'You will not take my child, You who call yourself God?'

She bargained with the Devil, something she knew was becoming too much a habit. But if he helped this babe survive she would gladly surrender her soul, even wrap it in a cloth of gold with a ribbon of silver. She did not think it too great a sacrifice for her soul was damned in any event, and the detestable Satan would only be rewarded goods already damaged.

She asked Saint Brigid to bring the Lord's forgiveness for her wrath and desperation. She could not ask the Lord directly, for all signs indicated that He had ceased listening. Saint

Brigid would help. Her mother always told her so. And how she wished her mother was here now.

'Dear Lord,' she heard as the surge of pains began to grow again. The midwife raised the soaked shift higher and reached between her thighs.

The pain stopped. Its sudden halt was surreal, dreamlike.

Ainnir's breathing returned to a heavy, but controlled and receding pant, and she felt Muirne's arm touch lightly around her shoulders. No one in the room spoke. She looked down to see the midwife holding a tiny child, so tiny it would have laid comfortably in her two hands. Its skin was blue. Tufts of thick black hair clumped in balls. No crying sounds, no mewing sounds came to celebrate new life.

'Call for the priest,' the midwife ordered quietly

Ainnir did not feel her mouth open, but knew wails and screams came raging from her lungs. She leant forward, arms and hands flailing to grab her child, her dead child.

Muirne held tight, pinned her to the pile of pillows at her back. Joan moved quickly to the other side of the bed, taking up the same fight.

The screams still came, now muffled, distant to Ainnir's ears as if from outside the room.

The midwife carried the lifeless infant to the table, and turned to see the spurt of blood from Ainnir's thighs clotting at the floor.

Ainnir felt darkness clawing. All energy was gone. She could not fight the two women who pinned her down. All will had been taken with the dead child.

My babe, she heard her mind whisper in utter

desolation.

The room blurred.

No more battles, were the last words that rang through her mind. A plea or an acknowledgment, she did not know. Her entire body slackened. She could fight no more.

Eyes closed, darkness stole her away.

No more battles.

Chapter Thirty

Gladmore Heath – England

Jarlath and Manus stood side by side, blanketed by fog as thick as soup. The banners of the white rose of York, and Gloucester's standard of the white boar fell limp laden by the damp air. It was past four in the morning. The sun had not yet lightened the earth and the only sounds to be heard were the nervous clinks of swords and the faint whispers of prayers polished with *If God wills it.*

'May God be with us this day, my friend.'

'He is, Manus,' replied Jarlath.

Eyes focused ahead, seeing nothing but a floating grey sea. It was as if a scene from a dream, a nightmare. Terror lurked in that fog, in that darkness, unseen in ambush.

Trumpets blared their monotone. The vanguard began at a slow, cautious run. The breath of soldiers was like a line of chimneys in London's winter; a short line, for none could see more than ten strides ahead.

Their pace hastened, urged on by the roar of the Duke of Gloucester. Weapons waved high.

The wall of grey would soon unfurl. The enemy led by the Duke of Exeter waited beyond.

They raced further. Further still. No enemy was met.

Archers fired a torrential rain of arrows into the air, but

no screams came and no arrow fire answered. Their footsteps lost the easy comfort of hardened ground, and now duelled with squelchy sodden earth. The land slopped downward. Still no enemy appeared.

To the left, mist-dampened echoes of combat and the muffled thuds of steel. Ahead, nothing. Where was the vanguard's enemy? Where was Exeter?'

With sounds to the left intensifying, rising in volume and urgency, it became all too plain a terrible blunder had been made. In their approach on the previous night, the battle formations had been misaligned. The three Yorkist divisions failed to position themselves opposite the three Lancastrian divisions; a ruinous move which now had the Lancastrian's leftwing, which was to meet Gloucester, fighting hand to hand combat with the Yorkist centre. Gloucester had to make a quick decision.

The men wasted little time before quick hand gestures passed the Duke's decision along the lines. The vanguard turned left and moved at an ungodly pace. It was a bold move, for this course took them through a mud-filled ravine, forcing the entire division to climb a steep slope to meet the enemy.

If the Lancastrian leftwing learned of their approach, they would surely swing, trap the Yorkists in the gripping mud and turn the ground into a slaughterhouse. There would be no means of escape. All would be butchered where they stood.

Boots filled with mud. Muscles and spirits tired even before the vanguard's first clash of steel came to be. They pushed on. Up and up they climbed. Closer to the noise, closer to the clashes.

Gloucester's risk paid off.

They met with the high, dry ground, and the surprise attack to Exeter's left brought an advantage not expected. The vanguard pushed well into the Lancastrian ranks. Battle sounds roared. Spears, battleaxes, poleaxes became the devisers of terror and torture. Death came to many.

Jarlath exchanged a pelting of vicious blows with a filth splattered Lancastrian. He forced his adversary back, and lack of balance brought his foe to the ground. Jarlath raised his sword. The man died.

He rounded to his left just in time to fend a strong blow, took two steps backward blocking further strikes then stabbed quickly in a forward move. His blade found soft flesh beneath his enemy's jaw. He took his short dagger from its sheath, buried it into belly, finishing the duel.

No time. A warning scream came from the right. Jarlath lifted his sword high. He swung. A head flew to the ground.

He turned in search of another opponent, mindlessly stepped over bodies ripped from throat to stomach. A horse thrashed wildly on its back, eyes wide, snorting, screaming, two front legs missing. Jarlath speared the neck with one fast thrust and released the animal from agony.

Fresh bellows sounded in the distance. Lancastrian reserves were sent to the aid of Exeter.

Gloucester's line fell back for a time like a tide pulled out to sea. Only with sheer grit did the Yorkists come to restore control, hold their line, but no more than that.

Jarlath surged forward, seeing one of his own men-at-arms outnumbered. He tripped momentarily, but regained his balance giving only quick regard to the body, the headless corpse, its head resting only inches away, turned, facing the earth as if unwilling to watch the terror this day wrought.

He reached his comrade in time, and threw a sure slice with his blade. His gaze did not need to follow the body of his victim; he knew its face also turned to the earth.

Five kills, ten kills, twenty-five. Thirty, sixty, one hundred, twice that number. What man could count? The fighting continued for an interminable two hours and they were not yet finished.

It was savage, unrelenting. The sun rose. Crows cawed. Swords clashed. Men screamed. Arrows hissed a deathly rain. Battle lore, finesse, balance and timing were all now mythical notions. Exhaustion lent itself to brutish survival. The putrid smell of death and bodily waste was consuming. Stomachs retched, and retched again.

Jarlath was not accustomed to praying for his life, but this was not like an uprising on the shores of Ireland. This was not a few slices with a blade, a trickle of sweat, and a triumphant ride home. This was a mindless bloodbath. Any sane man would believe they were all to die here in this God-forsaken fog. It concealed a nightmare, a world gone mad. But Jarlath could not afford the thought processes of a reasonable man. He was wielding his blood-covered sword to stay alive, thrashing with God-like strength. If nothing else was to be achieved here this day, he was going to live to take passage on the next ship bound for Ireland.

Where was Manus? He had not known the whereabouts of his friend for the last hour though most of his men remained close, as close as possible. It was an order he had given before the battle began, but in the moments when eyes were free to look, he could not find Manus. He knew his men-at-arms used his armour as their compass, their own north star. Jarlath too, wisely held to another north star. He looked for Gloucester's banner of the white boar. If he could see that flag, he knew he followed his battle commander, for there was no hope of hearing yelled orders above this mayhem.

He had moved too far. He could not find it through the fog.

'The white boar?' he yelled to the air.

'This way. This way,' came the reply.

And there it was, thirty paces to his right. Gloucester's knights kept the York line impressively solid, moving forward step by step. The muddy mire, now long behind them, no longer threatened. The roared chants of 'York' and 'Gloucester' pushed forward.

'Jarlath.'

'I thought you gone.'

'You thought wrong,' barked Manus. 'I'm not going anywhere. Are you alright?'

'As can be,' Jarlath answered.

'Good. Let's show these swine spawn what an Irishman can do.'

Swords swung. Swords clashed. Swords sliced. Swords fell.

Jarlath's throat burned. He fought to bring air into his lungs.

'Stop and catch your breath, Fitzgerald.' John Milewater ordered a water carrier to Jarlath's side.

'Drink deeply and give yourself a moment. Without breath your arms and legs will be of no use.'

Jarlath took the advice, knew Milewater to be right.

Sweat poured into his eyes, stinging, blurring his vision, but he dare not remove his helm. He grabbed at the offered skin, drank as best he could and poured the remainder over his face. He looked to the surrounding battle, knew from the screams and clashing weapons hidden in the fog, that the battle was hard and long.

The frantic pace of his breath began to recede. His throat still burned, and he knew it to be a hurt requiring more than a week to heal. Yet the morsel of time he afforded himself gave some measure of repair.

He watched Milewater return to the fighting and swing his sword high at two of Exeter's men. One skulked to Milewater's left, the other to his right. Both taunted as if waiting to launch an offensive attack. Neither took that step, both simply jabbed with their swords. Their eyes darted quickly to what rushed at Milewater's rear.

Jarlath's eyes caught the same movement. He roared a warning. It was too late. A battle axe came down on Milewater's skull with all the power of a man fresh to the battlefield and sliced though his helm. Blood spurted. Milewater dropped to his knees, hand limp, sword fallen already surrendered to the ground.

Jarlath did not have time to witness the body slump further, for he heard a bellow at his side. He turned just in time to block an imposing blow aimed at his head. A second blow came just as quickly. He staggered back. He felt no fear, only a bizarre elation as death threatened its coming. A third blow forced him to his knees, but in the panic, a memory sailed through his mind. He allowed his low and dangerous position to remain no more than a quarter of a breath then sprang upwards with all the power of his shoulders behind his sword, thrusting into guts and ribs. The eyes of his adversary darkened and widened. They harboured death. His victim fell forward. Jarlath took back his sword and pushed the dying man off.

His first thought was to give thanks to Donal and his training, and with that a strange sensation, a rush of energy travelled the length and breadth of his entire being. He knew instinctively that Donal was with him. He knew without any uncertainty, no harm would befall him this day. He knew now he was safe. Donal was here to make certain his chance to make the sun rise in the west would come.

'God be damned this day,' he cursed wildly. 'You will not have me!'

Sweat in his gauntlet lessened his grip, and fingers cramped with overuse, but from a throat that struggled to utter a solitary sound only moments before, a roar erupted. 'For York, for York,' he screamed over and again, only to hear others take up the same chant and press forward.

A sword hissed through the air and he felt a slicing heat as it ripped through his vambrace. Blood trickled down to his left wrist, a mixture of sweat and blood pooling in his palm. If he could ignore the searing pain, his right arm could still swipe and thrust. And he did.

The mist began to lift, and the line of the vanguard continued forward. Their pace grew to a brisk run, and the Lancastrians no longer stood to battle with swords or axes. No more arrows rained from the air.

The gold and white colours of the King of England's standard appeared. All knew at once, York had beaten the Lancastrians. Shouts of triumph, exhausted triumph filled the air more heavily than the fog had done, and Jarlath allowed his knees to give way. Many of the victorious fell to the earth, minds and souls spent. Their prone figures lay alongside the maimed and the dead, their curled lips the only features to differentiate the delivered from the deceased.

Jarlath had never felt so exhausted. His body and mind craved for a month of sleep, but the physician tending to his wound had other ideas until the stitching was complete and clean bandages applied.

'So, my friend,' said Manus, leaning over the makeshift pallet watching the skilled handy work of the physician. 'We found our battle, and now have wounds aplenty to prove only that we must work on our defensive skills.'

'Do you ever give up on jests, Manus?'

'You have spent enough months with me now to know the answer to that. But I fear that arm of yours is a greater trophy than I can produce. A vivid memento from elbow to wrist will follow you for all your days.'

'And glad it is I will have days to brag,' Jarlath quipped. His voice then fell vacant. 'Thomas was right. We could never have imagined this.'

Manus simply nodded his agreement. He may have been the jester, played the fool often, but this day brought horror that would never leave his thoughts. Deep scratches to legs and arms, a bloodied nose and a shoulder wrenched from its socket were amongst his short list of injuries, but it was wounds to the mind, wounds suffered by all there that day, unseen lacerations that would never heal. Whatever youth had been left to these two young men was surrendered on that field. There was no glory in the battle, no majestic triumph. It was naught but pure evil.

This was to be their crusade, their Holy war. The two words did not sit together comfortably for how any such atrocity could be branded *Holy* was now beyond comprehension.

'Men will speak of this day for many years to come, and none will truly comprehend its magnitude. Whatever we face in the future will pale into significance.'

'How many men did we lose?'

'Twenty-nine,' was Manus' quick answer, spoken with a reverent voice, a voice already in prayer. 'They are saying the Earl of Warwick was captured, but killed before he was brought before the King. His body was defiled, too many dagger wounds for counting, and the King and Gloucester are mighty livid. Clarence too.'

'Clarence remained true to the King?'

'So it seems,' Manus chuckled.

'And Warwick's death? Was it our men?'

'No.' Manus shook his head. 'No, we need not fear that.'

'Good.'

'So where to from here now our job is done?'

Manus watched Jarlath's eyes fall to nowhere, with unsaid thoughts. 'Home then. I like your thinking. And I trust that as a friend you would fill our time aboard ship with stories of Glendalough and Ainnir. That should bring some distraction to the queasiness I will no doubt endure.'

'Will you speak to me of your wife Meg?'

Manus smirked.

Part Five

Chapter Thirty-One

Maynooth – Ireland

Filthy and unkempt, he was not immediately recognised. The towering gatehouse with the Fitzgerald crest and the monkey which caused more querulous conversation than a dancing bear at a market place, seemed to trumpet a welcome. It was good to be home.

Servants paced through the courtyard going about their business, giving short attention to the new arrival, until one noticed it was the wolfhound, Hunter, greeting the riders with thunderous barks. As the troop progressed to the inner bailey, bellows of welcome sprang from every direction. The Earl's nephew was home.

The noise floated through open doorways and echoed along the walls of the great hall. Joan gave no thought to the basket of flowers she carried, dropping all to the floor and rushing outside. She stopped at the top of the steps, savouring what her eyes found. With a sprint enviable to a woman half her age, she ran to Jarlath's arms and embraced him like never before, squeezed tighter and tighter to convince herself he was real, not a figment of her imagination, one to vanish with a blink.

'You are home.' She sniffed and laughed all at once. 'We did not expect you within the week. But you are here. You are home.'

'Jarf!'

The familiar squeal heralded the imminent whirlwind that was about to hit in the form of a small girl with tousled red hair streaming behind. Eleanor jumped into Jarlath's arms and clung with all the strength she could muster. 'You are not to go away for so long again,' she said sternly, all the while burying tears of happiness in his shirt.

'Never again, I promise.' He placed a gentle kiss on her temple, allowing the little girl to find comfort in his shoulder for as long as she needed.

Remembering the last occasion Eleanor's tears soaked his shirt he added, 'I have some news for you. I met with Eleanor of *Acatain's* grandson.' He applied Eleanor's slippery pronunciation of the now French-owned lands, and it was for simplicity he chose to give the lineal relationship between the legendary Queen of both England and France, to the Duke of Gloucester in such meagre terms, rather than trudge through the meandering mire of three hundred years of Plantagenet rule. It would only confuse the girl.

'And I can see you have looked after Hunter well. He looks very happy to see me.'

Her eyes came out to do battle. 'Her name is Eleanor of Aquitaine, and Hunter missed you no less than I did.'

God help the man Eleanor took as husband, Jarlath laughed to himself, for it would require a Saint to keep this girl content. He knew her words were a reprimand, and the petulant frown, chastisement for his absurd notion Hunter did not spend one less day pining than she.

'I missed you, Eleanor.' He took her into another hug.

Thomas followed quickly on the heels of the shouting. Jarlath placed Eleanor back on the ground. Both men stood silently for a long moment, eyes levelled.

Thomas closed the space between them and held his nephew with great fervour, with great love. No amount of manly pride could prevent the emotion that flowed. Even the servants, gathered to witness the homecoming, found they too raised the backs of hands to wipe moisture from their cheeks.

'You're home, lad,' Thomas whispered. 'You are home.'

As the strength of the embrace petered to claps on shoulders, Thomas stood back, releasing a heavy sigh. He looked Jarlath up and down with an appraising nod.

'Yes, you have come home to us. But your stench is rife.' They both laughed. 'The evening meal is to be served soon. A bath will be readied for you. Wash and rest for as long as you need, then join us in the hall. Then we shall talk.'

Jarlath nodded hesitantly, knowing the difficult conversation that lay ahead. Eyes darted, searching unsuccessfully for Ainnir as Joan led him toward the stairway to the chambers. Eleanor clung to his leg, not yet willing to let go lest he disappear again.

Hunter was by no means different. The wolfhound was not about to entertain any further time apart from his master. The dog followed at first then took the lead, confident Jarlath was trudging a familiar path.

The meal was plentiful. The castle's finest hippocras flowed without restraint. Jarlath had little appetite. He toyed with the cheeses, fruits and minced tarts. Gerald, Tom and James pestered him continually, demanding stories of adventure, triumph and blood. Thomas, attuned to Jarlath's mood and with a quiet

Maurice clinging to his side, fended off his insistent sons as best he could. Anne, at six months of age, was introduced to Jarlath, and Eleanor took great pride detailing all the comical accounts of her baby sister, including the day the infant emptied her belly over Gerald's lap. Gerald seemed to find no humour in the retelling.

Jarlath was edgy, his jaw taut. He turned to Joan. 'And Ainnir, how does she fare? Does she still grieve Donal so? Cannot she join our table?'

Joan smiled awkwardly and sighed. 'You look weary. Finish what is in front of you and we will retire to the library and speak.'

Jarlath pushed his trencher away, a gesture suggesting he had finished.

Joan was not fooled.

Joan stooped at the hearth.

'You should not be left with such a chore, Aunt Joan. Here, let me.'

'I ordered the servants to leave us in peace. Besides, although I am the mother of six, I am not yet a crone. I think there is a small measure of life left in me yet.'

'I did not mean to suggest otherwise.'

'I know,' she laughed. 'But you, it has been only a twelve month and I can see much change. Life's experiences alter our features more so than the passing years. There is a maturity, a certain understanding, new to your countenance.'

There was indeed a change, she thought with sorrow, not convinced that the alteration was for the better. 'And me, do you see the changes in me? Anne's coming has ensured the seams of my gowns be let out an inch or two, and my hair is starting to take on the look of midwinter with the first loosening of snowflakes.'

Jarlath smiled. 'And it becomes you well.'

'A drink?' she asked as he rose from the floor and wiped dust from his knees.

'Thank you, but no.'

The flames took hold. Herbs sprinkled into the hearth gave a pleasant scent.

Joan noticed Jarlath's regard dart impatiently from corner to corner with no real intent.

'We can dance around the subject of Ainnir like gypsies at a campfire, but I see that is not your wish. Come.' She invited him to join her on the settle.

'I have not seen her in the hall, and none mention her name. I imagine it is her grief that keeps her away.'

'In a way, yes,' Joan began. 'Ainnir grieved Donal's death, Jarlath, grieved privately and with composure beyond her years. But what you do not know is that she carried a babe through all that grieving.'

Jarlath took on the look of a menacing cloud ready to burst its hold on misery, and it was the compassion of a mother that compelled her to reach out. But he recoiled.

'The babe died before it was born. It came before its time and drew no breath.'

There was more to Ainnir's story, but it was not her place to tell Jarlath the babe was his. The thick black hair of the infant could give no better proof. None but she and Muirne shared that knowledge, their comprehension confided only in the meeting of eyes in the birthing chamber, and neither woman ever dared to speak the words aloud. They were words best kept to silence.

With sudden alarm Joan comprehended the path of Jarlath's thoughts. Her hand flew to her heart. 'Oh Dear Lord, you think she is ... no, Jarlath, no. She is well. Ainnir is well.'

His misery transformed into confusion.

She nodded. 'Ainnir is alive.'

Jarlath stood from the settle and let out a loud breath that ended on a note ringing similar to a laugh. He ran hands through his hair and leant heavily on the carved Italian mantelpiece.

'I am sorry, Jarlath. I had no idea my words would bring you to believe she –'

'No, Aunt Joan, it was my foolish thoughts which steered me astray. I am genuinely relieved she is well. Genuinely relieved,' he repeated with a choked tone.

'She pleaded to return to her home. Thomas and I could see she needed her mother and her mountains if she was ever to heal. Ainnir has been gone three months now.'

Jarlath returned to the settle. 'Aunt Joan, hear me out for what I am about to say may at first seem incomprehensible, perverse, maddening even.'

He took hold of Joan's hand. 'I have loved Ainnir since the day I first laid eyes upon her. It was as if a gift from God and I know she felt the same. We both held our tongues when we should have spoken, but Thomas arranged her betrothal to Donal, and from that point I felt I could do naught. If I had only spoken ... but I did not.'

He paused for a moment, took a deep breath.

'I know you saw my pain. I did all I could to deny my heart, for Donal's sake, for Ainnir's sake, for you, for Thomas. And for that, I could not remain here. I still love her. After all that has come to pass, I want her. I know it sounds reckless and perhaps malicious with Donal now gone –'

'You are right.' Joan's voice was soft. 'It does sound reckless, and yes, I saw your pain. I also saw Ainnir's. I do not know if you did right by keeping your silence, but I know your reasons were pure. And this may surprise you, for I truly believe if Donal was able to grace us with his words right now, in this room, he would bestow his blessing. He loved you dearly, Jarlath. In fact I suspect there was a time he knew of Ainnir's thoughts, knew you were a great part of them. Oh that was long after you left for England, but too often I saw an understanding mingled with empathy, and not once did he show envy or jealousy.'

'But how? How did he come to know?'

'We may never understand. But now Donal is with his greatest love, Elizabeth. He is at peace, watching over us all. You should never doubt he would want you to rejoice in the same love he and Elizabeth shared if that is your will, whether it be with Ainnir or another.'

'You knew I would tell you of these things?'

Joan simply smiled. 'I have told you before, Jarlath, you are like a true son to me, and your eyes are a mirror to your soul. It was also your mother's way, God rest her beautiful spirit. She could never hide her true feelings either. With Ainnir, I do not know what reception you will receive. She has suffered much. Her healing may not have begun. But you have my blessing. And now,' she said with a casual smirk, 'we must gain your uncle's.'

'I will be in need of more than luck in that quarter.'

'Give him more credit, Jarlath. You may be surprised.'

'I trust your word, but –'

The library door opened.

'So it is to the library you have both retired.' Thomas closed the door behind him, moved to the hearth.

'Come sit, my love.' Joan gestured to a chair. 'Jarlath has news to share.'

Thomas' eyes narrowed. 'I smell trouble. Should I have a drink in my hand?'

'Let me,' said Joan. 'You will need one too, Jarlath.'

'And what is this news I suspect you are hesitant to share?'

'Uncle, I ... I do not know how to begin.'

Thomas lifted his chin.

Joan placed a mug in his hand. 'Drink, love.'

He did. 'Then don't think. Just speak.'

Jarlath hesitated at first then followed Thomas' advice. 'I want to ask for Ainnir's hand in marriage.'

Thomas choked on his drink, spluttered much of it to the floor. 'You are what?' he barked when finally able to take a breath.

Joan made no comment. Her eyes stayed with Thomas.

'Pray tell me, from where this plan of yours is hatched, Jarlath, for to me it seems –' but he got no further with his sarcasm.

Joan lifted a hand, a call for silence. 'Hear him out, Thomas.' She placed a gentle kiss upon her husband's lips. 'I am weary and look forward to the comfort of our bed. There is much for you both to talk of and I think it best I leave you to do just that. I expect you will be here for hours to come. I will have servants bank the hearth and bring food and plenty of ale. You will find more occasion to splutter a ewer full over the floor.'

'There is more?'

Joan touched his cheek. 'Much more.'

She returned to Jarlath's side, planted a kiss on his forehead, bidding him a good night. 'Remember, I love you both.'

With that she left the room, leaving in her wake tangible silence.

And she was right. There was much more.

Jarlath gave an emotive narration of a full year's events. He spoke openly and honestly, spoke of as much as was decent without bringing disgrace to Ainnir.

Thomas was no fool, nor was he one to sit in judgement prematurely. He listened intently to the secrets of Glendalough, the lake, the night of Ainnir's birthday, the ride home through the mountains to Maynooth, the fierce sword training in the abysmal early hours, Jarlath's guilt and tears, his longing, his heart wrenching fight with Satan at every turn, Gladmore Heath and Donal's saving presence during that battle.

Thomas marvelled with compassion how all of life's emotions had visited this young man in such a short span of time. He could almost feel the sympathetic nods of the books lining the shelves, parallel stories sitting in audience to this emotional outpouring, all with complacent understanding.

Each man unashamedly took their turn shedding tears.

Jarlath finished his plea with the reverent retelling of Ainnir's letter, of the words written and the words he imagined were not.

Then it was Thomas's turn to talk. There was no

bitterness or scolding. He spoke of Arthur, the cat of long ago, suddenly remembering its name and how Donal had rescued the kittens from the fire fifteen years before. He spoke of the uprising near Ballyraggan. The mountain of prayers said at the Abbey. The times he and Donal spoke privately of the pride they felt for the man Jarlath had become. And his belief, his agreement with Jarlath's conviction, that Donal was indeed present on that battlefield. It was always Donal's way, to protect his kin no matter the obstacles.

'Not even Saint Peter's key of gold would have kept Donal locked behind Heaven's gate that day,' Thomas claimed with humour.

And he believed every word.

The humour vanished.

'Why did you not tell us?' Although such a question was rather predictable, it was delivered more a rueful curse. Yet before Jarlath could take a breath, Thomas raised his hand, an instruction no reply was required.

'Life is,' Thomas paused, grappling for the right word, 'an interesting journey.' He lowered his head with a tired laugh, knowing he had failed miserably. 'The heart follows no defined road, honours no rules of battle lore, nor does it give fair warning to its course. Love is as controllable as the seeds of grasses blown high and far, and they, as the good Lord wills it, take root in some of the most unexpected of fields. Love is a gift given by God, and there is too little of it in our world, Jarlath.'

Eventually they shared the quiet, taking stock of all that had been spoken.

Unshuttered windows framed the night sky, ink-blue giving way to steel grey. The morning was on its way.

'Have you given thought to what happens from here? It is well and good to want these things, but Ainnir is the daughter of our enemy. I cannot see the O'Byrne welcoming you. And then what of Ainnir herself? She has suffered greatly, Jarlath. This may all be too much for her. Your offer perhaps comes at great risk.'

Jarlath simply grinned. 'I recall only too well an occasion when a very wise man said to me, *what is a great achievement worth if won with no risk at all.*'

'And I assume by the smirk marring your face, I was that wise man?'

'You were indeed.'

'In your chamber at Glendalough?'

'Yes, it was.'

'Good to see my aging years do not addle my memory.' Thomas took a deep breath and lowered his head. He could only guess at the trials that lay ahead for his nephew, wondered if he would prevail. He knew Jarlath would make his dream come to fruition, make the sun rise in the north, south, west, or whatever the words Donal had used.

'The manor house between Castledermot and Kilkea Castle is yours, Jarlath. Consider it an early wedding gift if the lass will have you. It will be an ideal location for a new start, a new home for you, your wife and children to come.'

'Thank you, Uncle. Thank you for everything.'

A farewell party stood at the steps of the great hall. Thomas wore a solemn face.

'I would feel more at ease if you would allow my men to

accompany you to the Wicklow border.'

Jarlath climbed into the saddle. 'I am both a Fitzgerald and a Gael. It will serve me well.'

Jarlath and Thomas shared a nervous laugh, but both men were happy to include mirth and well wishes in the farewell.

'Are you travelling directly to Glendalough?' asked Joan.

'I have one stop on my way,' Jarlath answered.

'I thought as much.' Joan's expression altered to a conspiratorial smile. She called to Eleanor.

Thomas lifted his young daughter high so she could reach Jarlath. Eleanor handed him a small posy of wildflowers picked early this morning, droplets of dew still cupped within their folds.

'These were some of Elizabeth's favourite blossoms,' Joan said. 'God speed, nephew, and may His love grant you all your goodly wishes.'

'I will visit you and *Ainnir*, Jarf.'

Jarlath smiled at Eleanor's slow and correct pronunciation of *Ainnir*. He noticed too, *Jarf* was still his bestowed title. It pleased him. As much as many things needed to change, some certainly did not.

'Then I look forward to seeing you again soon, little cousin.' Jarlath placed a kiss on her forehead before Thomas moved from the horse.

Nothing more needed to be said. He turned and headed toward the castle gates.

Reaching the grounds of the friary near Cill-Dara, Jarlath reined in his mount in the shade of the oak trees. He remained in the saddle with his thoughts for a time.

The faint summer breeze wrapped his shoulders as if a welcoming embrace and he gladdened at his decision to make this one stop. Before too much time passed he swung from the saddle leaving the horse to roam and feast upon yellow blossoms.

He found Elizabeth's burial place and dropped the posy – the petals now a little wilted – to the earth.

'Joan and Eleanor thought you might like these, Elizabeth. We all miss you dearly.'

Donal's burial place lay to the left.

Jarlath sat down on the warm grass, sat still and quiet for a time, perhaps an hour, perhaps more. Time was difficult to gauge. He was not waiting for a sign, not lingering for answers. He simply wanted to enjoy this time alone with the memory of Donal. It was much of what they did together in any event, for simple companionship spent in unshared conversation was an enjoyable past time they often treasured. Words were not always necessary. *A waste of energy,* Donal would crow, more so when Jarlath voiced an unwelcome opinion. He smiled at the memory.

But the calm and simplicity of this day's silence began to falter. A yearning for sound, for Donal's voice became a hunger. And Jarlath sensed that Donal sat alongside elbowing impatiently to prompt him to speak his mind.

'Alright!' Jarlath cried suddenly, startling the surrounding world.

'It hurts. It hurts mightily. Everything that has come to pass ... it all hurts.' He hung his head, picked at blades of grass at his feet. A trail of wetness found its way down his face.

'I should have been there for you. If not for my selfish ways, life would be different for us all. I am so sorry, Donal. I am sorry for all that came to be and it is better that all those secrets, all those lies, are no longer hidden. I didn't know how to deal with things. It was anger that took control of every foolish step. I know it to be no excuse, but it was my way of things, my stupid ignorant way. You were like a brother. I loved you. I still do!'

Silence followed for a time. His voice softened.

'I just thought you should know, and if I came here today I could be sure you would hear me.'

Jarlath gave a gentle laugh, and followed with a telling sniff.

'Keep your ridicule to yourself, old man, for I can hear your scorn. You were with me at Gladmore Heath so why would you not hear me wherever I may be? I know. I know.'

More silence.

'I guess I am simply wanting to be sure I truly do have your forgiveness and now your blessing for what I am about to do.'

The morning sun climbed high in the sky and its warmth brushed his neck. Blossoms stretched. The sounds of bees filled the air. His horse wandered to his side and nudged his shoulder.

The horse was right. It was time.

Jarlath stood and looked down to the two graves. The lines of each, so consummately replicated, spoke to all who had ears to hear of how content these two must be.

Yes, it was time.

'Thank you,' were the final departing words.

Yet Jarlath could not be sure from whose lips the words were uttered.

Chapter Thirty-Two

Glendalough – Wicklow

The summer was at its best – a cocky braggart. Yet if the skies had bestowed either sleeting hail, biting winds, or scorching sun, it would matter little, for Jarlath's resolve was unyielding. He was on a mission.

Unchallenged, his journey to Glendalough was uneventful. He doubted not that armed men followed covertly, watching his every move. Only foolhardy or desperate travellers rode these paths alone – or as it seemed this day, the staunchly determined – and the Gaels possessed ghostly powers of moving imperceptibly throughout their domain, unseen, unheard, unheeded.

Servants hurried from harm's way as he galloped into Castle Glendalough's bailey. He pulled his mount to a stop, threw the reins to a willing hand and gave orders to water and feed the animal immediately, for he was not willing to tarry longer than necessary.

'Is it absurdly brave or reckless of you to ride to my walls, Jarlath Fitzgerald?' The O'Byrne flung his condescending greeting to the air as he walked from the top of the steps.

The sight of the O'Byrne caused Jarlath to harness any retort. Shadowed eyes and slouched shoulders accompanied the Chieftain's words; he carried the unmistakable poise of a downtrodden man.

Sympathy of any measure had little time to surface; the sounds of horses moving at speed grew closer, proving his earlier suspicion. Jarlath took in the arrival of five men-at-arms, deciding their well-kept distance signified no immediate menace.

His regard returned to the chieftain. 'Mark my presence here what you will, but I will be heard this day whether it is to your liking or not.'

Jarlath gave Hugh no pause for mistake. Whether here and now, for all his servants and men to hear, or whether in private, Jarlath would find his audience.

With reluctance, Hugh seemed to allow Jarlath that small victory and led him to the solar.

Tired lines formed web-like patterns at his forehead, and vacant eyes struggled to give over an air of authority. He waved quick hands at servants, a silent order to have drinks brought at once.

'Sit,' Hugh instructed as he took his place in his own chair.

'No.'

'I said sit, Fitzgerald.'

'I have no need to take rest. I do not plan to tarry. I am here to ask your daughter for her hand in marriage.'

Hugh spat a muffled laugh. 'Your intent therefore is to seek permission for my daughter's hand?'

'No.' His face grew serious. 'I do not seek your permission. I am here to ask Ainnir directly. Where is she?'

'Are you Fitzgeralds so arrogant? Ainnir is my kin, not yours. I therefore suggest you depart now. Follow my wishes and I will guarantee you safe passage to the ends of my lands. Dare to defy me at your own peril.'

No life erupted from those vacant eyes, despite the plainspoken words. Jarlath's first thought was to scorn the measure of trust he would place on the O'Byrne's guarantee, but his purpose here was not to cross sharpened tongues on that point.

'Did you not hear my words? I seek neither your permission nor your blessing. My issue will be delivered to Ainnir's hearing, and from my tongue, and she may answer as she sees fit.'

'You go too far, Fitzgerald. This is not your home and it is to a Chieftain that you speak. You are the enemy of my people. My daughter is newly widowed, still grieves her dead child and right now her place is here in her home, with her family.'

'Jarlath?'

A soft voice came from the open door.

'Madame.' Jarlath turned to give polite greeting to Brigid.

He refused to trouble this woman who he believed to be both gracious and foreboding all at once, and summoned a slim smile to negate the terse mood. His short stay at Glendalough, a twelve month past, instilled the notion Brigid could teach Job a thing or two about patience, and in no less measure, forgiveness to the Lord. Yet it took no more than a fleeting glance of the widening blue eyes to recognise an ally had just entered the room.

'How long have you been standing there, wife?'

Brigid stared at her husband. 'Time enough, Hugh. Ample time to know God has not yet deserted my daughter, and long enough to know you still do not see the error of your ways.'

She turned back to Jarlath, almost without movement.

'My daughter is at the lake if you wish to speak to her, Jarlath. I cannot express how happy I am you have come. You have been in my prayers, day and night.'

'Thank you,' Jarlath nodded. 'All I ask is to speak to Ainnir. You have my word I will abide by her decision.'

Brigid's lips curled tenderly. 'Ainnir has shared much with me these past months.'

Her smile told Jarlath just how much.

'Your presence here is welcome. You have my blessing, and that of my husband. Reluctantly or not, you will have it.'

Jarlath fought back a mischievous grin. That was a threat none in the room could mistake.

Standing from his chair, Hugh raised his voice. 'Know your place, Brigid.'

She gave her husband no credit, no acknowledgement.

'Do you know where the lake is, Jarlath? I would gladly lead if needs be.'

'I know my way, madame. Again I thank you,' he answered and caught the slight inclination of Brigid's head, a gesture implying now was the time to make his exit.

He gave a smile of gratitude, wasted no more time and turned for the door. But before he could take his leave, he felt the gentle touch of her hand to his.

'No matter the words my daughter speaks, know you are her remedy, and I can see in your eyes, she too, is yours.'

The door closed behind him, and he heard the telling sound of the latch. The O'Byrne's wife had readied her arena, the battleground for the mêlée that she would undoubtedly win.

He knew the path well. Jarlath urged his horse up and around rises, through thickets, over felled trees and carpets of bluebells. He gave little notice to the scurrying movement of wildlife as hooves played a rhythm on the earth.

A familiar expanse of blue appeared. Birdsong drowned his approach.

Her eyes, those blue eyes, wandered the far reaches of the lake and to the cliffs beyond. He could only hasten to guess Ainnir's thoughts, and wondered if he walked with her somewhere in her daydreams. She was seated amongst the grasses, her feet tucked beneath her legs, no books by her side, no horse tethered nearby. She wore a simple gown of green wool over a cream kirtle and skin slippers. Her hair fell unbound, tousled by the slight breeze that whispered silent words from the lake.

He dismounted and stood for a time watching her stillness. His memories had not betrayed. Her beauty was God-given.

As though she heard his thoughts, Ainnir turned.

'Jarlath?' she whispered as a question, scrambling to her feet. He heard a fragment of excitement. 'You are not a ghost?'

'No.' He smiled at the thought. 'I am not a ghost.'

Her hand flew to her neck as if to quell a jolting breath, then eyes returned to the lake, her back as straight as a tree. 'It seems only yesterday I laughed as you dived into these cold waters. Do you remember reciting the ending to the tale of *Diedre and Naoise?*

'In your Gaelic.'

'Yes, in my Gaelic.' She turned back, looked to his face, swiped at an errant tear. 'You are alive. I prayed everyday you would return to Ireland, safe and well. I am pleased, so very pleased for you.'

Jarlath sensed a hesitation, a confusion and took an uncertain step forward. 'Ainnir –'

'Does my father know of your presence?'

'Yes, and he is none too pleased. I left him to the rage of your mother and I suspect by now he may be cowering in a corner like a flogged animal.'

He caught a small smile. But that was not enough. He wanted her embrace, he wanted to hear her lips swear her love over and again.

'I have come for you.'

'Why?' she asked.

'Why? Should there be need to ask? I want you. I want you to be mine.'

Ainnir dropped her head. Her regard remained low, away from his.

'Ainnir, look at me.'

She refused. 'Jarlath, there is so much –'

'Ainnir, I want you to be my wife.'

'Your wife?'

'My wife, yes.'

At those words she came undone. Her body shuddered and great sobs fell. Jarlath moved quickly to her side, but she held up a halting hand.

'Am I so loathsome?' he said with a nervous laugh.

'What you ask, Jarlath, cannot be.'

'If you need reassurance –'

'No. Hear me out, please. Nothing can ever be remedied. Too much wrong has come to be. I was broken the day you left these mountains and everything that followed brought only more heartache, and now ...' she shook her head, 'now I could never be the wife you want. I am not the girl you remember. I bargained with the Devil for your safety. I promised my soul, and I suspect he has kept me to my promise.'

'You are wrong.'

She looked up, misery altering to steely determination.

'Do you think you could ever forget I lay night after night with another man, my husband, your kin? Could you forgive me all my words of spite when I did not understand your pain? Could you? And lest we forget, our families bear unbendable hatred for each other, a hatred that may never die. And what about the visions, the visions, Jarlath, images which plague my thoughts every day, of you and ... you and that woman in that barn. They will not cease.'

Jarlath shifted uncomfortably, suddenly suspicious. 'Your words are practiced.'

Her eyes fell away. 'Perhaps,' she admitted.

'Your letter, your words, I thought this is what you wanted.'

Ainnir moved to walk away.

Jarlath caught her arm.

'I can forget all if I have you by my side.'

She looked down at his grip. He released his hold.

'I know you grieve. I know how you cared for Donal both in your marriage and in the days before his death. I would never deny you that for it was right and honourable. I know too, you lost a babe.'

Ainnir's eyes flew wide, her mouth fell agape. 'No!'

Tears and more tears claimed every inch of her face.

'Speak to me of your grief so I may understand. Can you not trust I will help? We can be tonic for each other.'

'No!' Ainnir slid to her knees.

Jarlath followed quickly, lifted her limp frame, stood her back on her feet and wiped at wisps of hair caught at her cheeks. Her pleading eyes clawed at his, locked and shackled, they begged.

Suddenly, understanding came.

He froze.

Time shattered.

He could feel the tightening of his chest, an unbearable pressure.

'It was my child?'

Ainnir gave no audible response, her tears fumed like rain. They were answer enough.

'Oh God,' he whispered. 'You carried my child?'

'Forgive me, forgive me,' Ainnir sobbed, repeating those words over and again until they were no longer coherent. 'I did not mean for you to know. I never wanted you to know.'

'Christ Almighty,' he cursed.

This woman he loved beyond all comprehension, this woman denied to him had carried and given birth to his child, his dead child. When was his ship to find fair weather? When was his ocean to calm? Hellfire! What had they done to deserve all this pain?

He embraced her tightly, kissed her forehead, pressed heart to heart.

'No. I am glad I know, for do you now not see? We are given the chance once taken. We can have more children. I want you to be the mother of my sons and daughters. Thomas has granted a manor house in the south of Kildare so we need never return to Maynooth. And your letter, Ainnir, your words from Donal's lips, it is what he wanted. You must understand that. Do you not see?'

'I see it all, but *you* do not see how wretched I am. There are only memories now, and I cannot swear happiness to those distant thoughts. And I would not wish you to be saddled with such misery, my misery. I could never bring you joy, for there is none left to me. I became a blackened void at the death of our babe and endure an agony I cannot give voice to, an agony I will never be free from.'

Jarlath felt as though he held a blazing fire, feisty and flaming, determined to burn itself out to ash. These last were not practiced words. She truly believed all to be lost, utterly forsaken.

'What is there left?' she whispered.

'Left?' He remembered Brigid's voice. He was her remedy, no matter what Ainnir said. 'We begin anew.'

He felt the shake of her head against his chest. Stubborn! There had to be a way to quash her obstinacy. He was her remedy and she was his. Those words persisted.

His mind raced to plan. And then ... yes, perhaps there was a way. He made an inventory, a battle plan. It was plausible. Achievable. Risky. But what else could he do? He almost laughed pitiably – *what is a great achievement worth if won at no risk?* Yes, perhaps there was a way. But first, one more plea.

He rested his forehead on hers, held her face in his hands and looked intently to her eyes. 'Am I never to bring you around to my way of thinking?'

She returned his look, no less intently. 'No. You will not.'

He dropped his regard. She could say what she liked. He would not let it come to that. He had survived a bloody battle, sailed the Irish Sea, risked honesty and raw emotion with Joan and Thomas, sought reassurance at the burial site of Donal, rode through danger in these mountains to arrive at this place and unabashedly abused her father. Moreover, he remembered that sinking feeling when he thought her dead. He relived that moment when he could not breathe. He needed no more to convince himself that he would not be beaten.

Jarlath began to think like a battle commander for he knew he now stood on his own private Gladmore Heath. He took strength at knowing no great victory was won at the first thrust of a sword, and here and now, at the shore of the lake, this was his first strike. He listed all the weapons needed for this fight: sensitivity, pretence of acceptance, the keen-sightedness to discern the need for retreat, yet most of all, patience, an unholy abundance of patience.

It could be done. His plan had merit. It would work.

He released his hold, took two steps backward.

'If that is your final word, then I must go.' The melancholy was not contrived.

She gave him a smile so pained, he inwardly cringed.

'But you will give me one thing, Ainnir. I heard you out just as you asked. Now, you will hear me out before I leave.' He walked to his mount and swung into the saddle. 'I once said to you, whatever course our lives will run, know that nothing can surpass this, you and I, here and now. Do you remember? Words said as you lay in my arms. That is a memory, a memory to bring us through whatever we are to face together. And Donal's words, *to make the sun rise in the west,* that was his way of telling me to make the impossible happen. I go now to do just that. I will never give you up, Ainnir, never. The impossible will happen.'

Jarlath threw one more look of determination and drew on unearthly reserves of control to not grab Ainnir by the waist and steal off with her.

'Find your memory and know you can trust in it.' He put heels to his horse, did not look back.

Behind lay the first part of his plan, the pretence of acceptance and the wise retreat. And now, the wait. Jarlath prayed like he had never prayed before that his strategy would indeed make the sun rise in the west.

Ainnir watched Jarlath's back. The vision disappeared before the sounds of the horse's gait. She turned, looked out over the lake. The birds no longer sang. The water was so still it mirrored the trees and mountains. Not even a ripple. *A ripple* – her thoughts stalled.

That fish. That fish in the pond at Maynooth, the brave fish that refused to hide in the shadows.

She swung around on her toes and ran toward the Castle.

The ride from Maynooth to Cill-Dara, then to Glendalough, and now back through the Wicklow Mountains, was harried. His mount endured the journey, but now laboured through lack of rest.

Jarlath reined in, not wanting to push his horse further, and not wanting to be further away from Ainnir. Perhaps both he and his horse could do with a rest, breathe in the fresh summer air and take stock of all that had happened.

His horse snorted, wandered away grazing, swinging his tail up high along his back bringing a well-needed breeze to his lathered coat. Jarlath allowed his own legs to wander. Neither his body nor his mind would still.

As he kicked through the grasses and looked to the treetops and to the leaves moving without sound, he felt himself smile. Did she truly make a pact with the Devil? Surely she knew any bargain struck with such a creature was not binding?

Donal taught him that exact lesson long ago, when bullies had plagued him. *Do what it takes to escape their clutches,* he would say, *even if it rankles. Lie, concede, pamper, bow then dig the boots in so hard that they see stars. Never forget your guile, lad.*

The smile vanished.

She bore his child.

Knowing they had created a life, albeit one taken to Heaven before its time, brought a sense of hope. A bond existed, a bond that could not be broken. How could she not believe they belonged together? They would have many children, would fill their manor house with laughter and love. The gardens would overflow with her favourite herbs and flowers. The library would house books from every land. Whatever she wanted, she would only need ask once. He could not bear to think such a life would not come to be.

Jarlath turned to the sound of thudding hooves. His horse shifted anxiously. Ten or more armed men barrelled down a hill. One low whistle and his steed was by his side. Jarlath pulled a sword from the sheath tied to his saddle. He held it low, an unambiguous warning. If a fight was what this band of men sought, they would not be disappointed.

'Put that away, Fitzgerald. There will be no need,' the O'Byrne's voice rang out.

'You guaranteed my journey from your lands,' Jarlath replied, not yet willing to release the weapon, not daring to trust the O'Byrne.

'I did. You tarried too long.'

There was no malice in the tone and Jarlath returned the sword to its sheath, but kept his hand close to the hilt.

'I am departing as you requested and stop to rest my horse before it fails me. I know these lands are yours but I will be gone before long.' Jarlath looked to the other men, found Bradan and Eamonn. Their eyes met. Nothing was said.

The ensuing silence confused Jarlath. He could not imagine the O'Byrne had raised so many for a farewell. He waited, allowing the Gaels to explain their presence in their own good time.

Hugh dismounted, signalled his men to stay at a distance. Jarlath's horse stomped at the approach. Hugh raised a hand to its neck, firm strokes settling the animal.

'You are to make a new home for yourself in the south of Kildare. Is it true?'

'I am.'

'You left without what you came for.'

'People are not possessions. I cannot take what she is not willing to give.'

'She suffers much, Jarlath. Whether you care to believe my concern or not, I think we can agree Ainnir suffers greatly.' Hugh paused for a moment. 'And I did not rejoice in the death of Donal, for the pain it brought my daughter.'

Jarlath knew that such a confession did not come easily to this man. He nodded his understanding.

'You are a Fitzgerald, and by the mere presence of that blood in your veins, you and I will most likely be enemies for a long time. But you are also a Gael. You may be nothing like your O'Toole uncle, and it is perhaps a Godsend you are not, but the true spirit of a Gael is obvious in your courage for all who have eyes to see. Maybe a miracle will be conceived on this very land one day soon. Maybe you will play a role in bringing peace. It is something I have often longed for, and it is before you now I am forced to stand if I am to have any with my wife.'

A sound similar to a muffled laugh escaped Hugh's lips. 'You do not know what it is to placate a Gael woman. Our Lord did not gift man enough wisdom. But there is a son of mine too, who also stands firm with Brigid, and a formidable army they make together. Although it goes against my nature I am forced to compromise. My bones weary, so too, my heart. I want peace with my wife and my son, and am willing to pay what I must.'

Hugh turned to one of his sons.

'Bradan.' He said nothing more, and walked back to his horse.

Bradan urged his mount forward a step, turned in his saddle and helped the pillion figure slide from the rear of the horse.

She walked slowly at first, looking to the retreating form of Hugh then hastened her gait.

Ainnir smiled, timidly. Her lips then curled to the brightness of a summer sun and she raised her wrist.

'I did as you said. I found my memory and I trusted in

its strength.' Her sleeve fell away to reveal her bracelet of entwined bog rush. His gift to her. 'I have found trust. Can you forgive me?'

He reached for her wrist and planted a light kiss to her palm. 'You kept it?'

Ainnir nodded.

No more words.

He kissed her deeply. Jarlath saw only Ainnir, and cared not a whit for their audience.

The men made audible their appreciation for the display. Full-hearted laughter filled the air before a grievous cough broke through.

Ainnir and Jarlath turned to the O'Byrne.

'Papa, thank you.' Ainnir's quiet voice hinted at a past regret that never had to be.

'You have not called me Papa for too long, child,' he said with an answering smile, and swung up into his saddle. He trained his eyes on Jarlath.

'My daughter is not an olive branch, Fitzgerald. She is not chattel in a bargain to be struck this day. But know this, I am no O'Toole, there is no disowning to be had either.' His steely glance moved quickly to Ainnir, changing in that small movement to a look of love.

Hugh kicked his horse to begin the journey back to Glendalough. Bradan waited a moment. He gave Jarlath a curt nod and a shining smile, proclaiming that everything was now set to right. Nothing could hide his pleasure. He galloped away to catch the men.

'And now?' Ainnir asked.

'And now, I take you home.'

With that, he kissed Ainnir as deeply and for as long as he dared, until his mount disturbed their embrace with a nudge. Passing strange, his horse was too often giving him the *hurry up*, keen to have this love progress as quickly as he did himself.

Part Six

Chapter Thirty-Three

Manor Kilkea – County Kildare

Marared knew only of the solitary life of Manor Kilkea. Long silent corridors, empty rooms, grandiose grounds, immaculately groomed gardens, and the large pond – more a swimming hole – with eels, eels that bite.

A magnificent property owned by the Earl of Kildare, its use seemed limited to the infrequent stays of guests or kin to the Fitzgerald family. Nonetheless, Marared and her fellow servants prided themselves in their attention to detail, and ensured the home and its grounds received the same care expected if royalty itself was in residence.

Yet this day brought credence to the foretelling of a prophecy. Marared's mother, blessed with the gift of foresight, assured all that love and new life were soon to arrive at the steps of their home.

It was in a song carried on the chords of the north winds, her mother told her, and Marared knew without doubt, it would come to be. Her mother was wise beyond understanding.

The beginning of the prophecy arrived in the form of a laden cart, two horsemen, and a dog almost the size of the nags that hauled the cart. The dog's deep barks dragged servants from their chores, and sent ducks to the pond, and chickens into coops.

One of the horsemen spoke to Mrs. Mulhearn the head

housekeeper, and delivered an unexpected letter. Her scream – of joy or horror, none could tell – preceded orders flung into the air, one after the other and her urgency stirred the servants to move as swiftly as the frightened ducks and chickens.

The messenger tarried outside and stared beyond Marared's shoulder. She followed his line of sight and saw her sister smiling with badly-disguised invitation.

Marared sent an elbow to her sister's ribs, yet she could not berate the younger sibling overly much, for this visitor to their home was indeed a pleasant change of face if not on the upside of handsome.

The second horseman, an unfortunate looking gent with a grin boasting few teeth, focused his attention Marared's way. His look sang of optimism. Marared rolled her eyes to the sky, and allowed an arrogant *tisk* to fall from her mouth.

No teeth – no conversation. She had standards.

She swung her attention back to the first horseman. The handsome man busied himself, building on her pert sister's silent invitation. Of more interest to Marared was the message he delivered to Mrs. Mulhearn, and the contents of the cart. Interrupting their step-free dance, she made short work of her request for detailed information.

He indulged. His telling meandered across the lines of truth and marched into extreme embellishment. Nonetheless, she learnt that they were about to receive a warrior as handsome and valiant as the fabled Achilles, and a Gaelic Princess as beautiful as the legendary Helen of Troy.

Marared's excitement boiled. She left her sister to her game and the second horseman to count his losses.

Chosen to be responsible for the yet-to-arrive new

mistress, Marared found herself in the upstairs bedchambers unpacking coffers and serving treats to the wolfhound, Hunter.

The second part of the prophecy came to be as hues of red and purple greeted the evening sky. A tired and saddle-worn *Achilles* and *Helen* rode up the winding track and through the small entrance gates of the manor. Noting their weary state, Mrs. Mulhearn hastened a perfunctory welcome and hustled the two indoors.

Marared's eyes followed her new mistress. She looked beautiful. Tired, but beautiful. Although of a similar age and height, she and her mistress could not have differed more in colouring if they tried. Not that any of that mattered of course, for short and squat, lanky and hunched, Marared would be pleased to be of service to any new mistress on the condition they were affable.

'You may call me Ainnir.'

Marared was more than pleased.

Ainnir did not know how weary her body was until she laid back in the tub, water lapping high over her shoulders. She held her breath, immersed low, feeling her hair glide. As she came up for air, hands began to knead her scalp and the calming scents of lavender and clove blended with the rising steam. An involuntary moan of pleasure floated from her mouth. She kept her eyes closed, enjoying the relaxing touch.

'You have the most beautiful honey-coloured hair, Ainnir.'

'Thank you, Marared. It is the same shade as my mama's. We have the same skin colouring too and our eyes also share the same hue.'

The kneading hands stilled. Ainnir knew without doubt that inquisitive eyes peered impatiently over her face. She looked up. A quizzical frown and contemplative eyes meet her gaze, before the kneading began again in earnest.

'I can indeed see why my lord cannot take his eyes from you.' Marared giggled at her boldness. 'I should apologise for such impudence, but none here failed to notice that love of a magical quality walked through our doors this evening, and it is grateful we are to have you both here.'

'Is it that obvious?' Ainnir replied with her own giggle. She knew in that short conversation that they would become good companions. 'Your name is Welsh, is it not?

'Yes. But I am known as Marared for no other reason than my mother liked the name. The English version is Margaret, and some fall back to that use. I refuse to answer their call until my rightful name is used.'

Ainnir smiled at this young woman. To find one such as Marared in her new home was all she could hope for. She could not remember a time when Muirne was not by her side, as nurse, as comfort, confidante, servant or companion. She would miss, Muirne.

She would miss her mother.

Two weddings and her mother would never lovingly witness either. But naught could dampen her spirit or excitement this evening. She had chosen the path of her heart. Regrets would never flourish.

Ainnir stepped from the tub to the waiting cloth. Exhausted, she was grateful for the attention to her drying and dressing. A dusky pink nightgown with wide shoulders and sparkling beading lay on the bed. Ainnir recognised it to be one of Joan's.

'I pulled it from your coffer. I hope you are pleased,' said Marared.

The garment seemed more appropriate for a night of dalliance, but Ainnir nodded her approval. No matter the clothing, she longed to embrace sleep.

Marared brushed Ainnir's hair with long, rhythmic strokes and all the while chattered, scarcely taking a breath.

Ainnir found no annoyance, for it prevented a need for her own contribution. But her ears pricked at the mention of the lambs delivered this past spring, the blossoms in the Church, and talk of Marared's favourite story, *Diedre and Naoise*.

Ainnir responded, haphazardly relating that her father's favourite dish was pottage of spiced lamb and that the last time she enjoyed the dish was the day she first laid eyes on Jarlath. She also announced bluebells would be an appropriate blossom in the Church for she had felt like a bluebell herself this past year longing for the return of her true love, and boasted also of Jarlath's ability to recite the story of *Diedre and Naoise* in perfect Gaelic.

Marared held the brush midair. 'So that is where your mind has been. Every one of your points involves your husband-to-be.'

Ainnir laughed. 'I should apologise.'

'No. You should never apologise for love. 'Tis a wondrous thing.'

'I think we are going to become good friends, Marared.'

'I think so too.'

A yellow ribbon secured the end of Ainnir's braid. Her

dressing almost complete, Marared dabbed a spot of oil at Ainnir's wrists and neck, and cheekily dabbed low at her neckline.

Ainnir sniffed. 'A summer garden. My bed will appreciate this beautiful scent, if not this nightgown.'

'Well, all is done.' Marared turned down the coverlet and bid her new mistress a good night.

Before the door closed, Marared poked her head back through the narrow opening.

'There are no other guests on this floor, so there will be no sounds to disturb your sleep this night. I know our new master will also have a good sleep. His bedchamber is at the far end of this corridor. Goodnight.'

With that she was gone, the rest of the prophecy left to complete itself.

Jarlath's eyes wandered the four corners of his bedchamber. Soft linen towels created an illusion of a sweet pudding; layers of white, cream and pink. A laver of fresh water rested on a rustic bench, yellow petals caught at the edges. Tapestries decorated two walls. Fresh cuts of wood filled the hearth, unnecessary in the warm summer night, but of amenable appeal all the same. Candles shed dancing light. A ewer of ale sat upon a sideboard beside a bowl of fruits. Sprigs of rosemary lined a squat bench, ready for the morning ritual of cleansing, and familiar garments draped across three coffers.

Indeed, the servants had conducted themselves admirably. Most notably for decency's sake, Ainnir's bedchamber was at the far end of the corridor, almost as far away as the moon.

The warm night air spilled in through the open shutters and carried sounds of night animals. Jarlath wondered how he was to settle and find sleep after such an eventful day. He felt as if in a dream, and baulked at the childish prank of pinching himself to see if in fact he slept. If it was a dream, leave it be, for it was marvellous.

He settled onto the bed, pushing aside the coverlet. He could not sleep. His want would not deliver such a prospect so easily.

In the darkness, he did what was usual to be rid of such restlessness. He laughed, for his release did not help in the slightest.

Foremost on his list of priorities for the morrow would be to seek the local priest. Surely being the new master of Manor Kilkea and nephew to the Earl of Kildare would ensure a wedding could take place before too many more nights took their toll?

His dream-like thoughts wandered to the myriad of emotions experienced in the span of one day, and rested on memories of the O'Byrne's words. It was true. The Fitzgeralds and the O'Byrnes were likely to be enemies for much of their lives, so how were he and Ainnir to traverse through such difficulties? Would peace come? He would pray for such a miracle, for Ainnir's sake.

He laughed at Hugh's suggestion that God did not gift man enough wisdom to placate a Gael woman. Jarlath would do his best or die trying, and would find pleasure in all.

The candles burnt low. Heavy eyes began to find solace. He heard the restless groan of Hunter stretching on the floor, and Jarlath's last thoughts drifted to the gowns, books and the well-loved wolfhound delivered before their arrival. Aunt Joan. Clever, Aunt Joan. He smiled and pushed the thoughts aside. *Leave all thoughts for the morrow.* Let sleep take him now.

He felt more than heard the intrusion, and opened one lazy eye.

'I could not sleep.'

An ethereal figure stood to the side of his bed.

'And pray tell me, dear angel, do you believe you will be granted sleep in this room?' He dared not move. One slight stir might vanish the vision.

'I would be disappointed if that were so.' Ainnir pulled at the yellow ribbon, shaking out her long tresses. The thin chemise did little to hide her body. Sweat from the warm night trapped the gown to places that drew his eyes.

Jarlath grabbed her wrist and pulled her to his side. The scent of a summer garden wafted through the air.

She wore his bracelet. His fingers played with the dried rush. This gift would remain a symbol of so much for all their time. He decided a bracelet of rubies and gold threads would be readied for their wedding, but he doubted Ainnir would prefer anything to this simple, precious adornment.

His hands wandered. His fingers splayed through her hair, gently flicking back the long strands curtaining her face. His touch explored from chin to forehead with a stroke as tender as the flutter of butterfly wings.

Neither said a word. Eyes locked for a boundless time. He had given thought to their first time together, here in their new home. Would it be thwarted, be hindered by memories, regrets and unspoken grief?

He worried for naught. The beguiling honesty in Ainnir's eyes and that mesmerising smile could not reassure him more.

As though reading his very thoughts, she began. 'I am here because I do not want us to spend another minute apart. I want to be yours and you mine in every way this earth can offer. I love you.'

He felt his heart race at her words. His throat convulsed, swallowing heavily as if devouring every sound, every breath, every second. 'I feel as if a gift has just been bestowed upon me.'

'Then unwrap your gift.'

His hands shimmied downward and grabbed the delicate laces at the neckline of her nightgown. With one fast movement, the garment fell from throat to thigh. His gift now unwrapped, he was glad that he had found his release earlier, for if not, the control he now wanted would be like grasping feathers in a wind.

Jarlath brought Ainnir to heights both thought impossible. She found her delicious completion, her cries of release muffled as lips ate hungrily and tongues played.

Jarlath followed quickly, taken beyond return by ankles tightening at the back of his legs.

Their bodies collapsed.

Words were not said for some time as both absorbed what had come to be this night. Ghosts and regrets were laid to rest. Nothing, nothing would ever again build a wall to separate these two.

The hours flew by, exhaustion interlaced with soft exploring touches and weary voices fighting the beckoning slumber.

Ainnir traced the familiar scar across Jarlath's chest, and found another, still red and vivid running from wrist to elbow.

'This scar is from England?'

'Yes.'

'You will tell me about England, one day?'

'Yes, one day.' He would be more than amenable to share everything with this woman in his arms. His hands followed the curve of her breasts, her waist and her hips. Thoughts focused on the obvious changes to her body.

'And one day I will share with you my story, our story,' she offered.

No sorrow fell upon those words. It was simply confirmation there was still much to say, but none that would alter what the course of this night had begun.

Jarlath smiled and kissed her gently in thanks.

'I am reluctant to be the one to raise the subject, but will you have need to return to your room before we are found together? I for one don't care what the world thinks.'

Ainnir laughed. 'I suspect Marared is standing guard at the bottom of the stairs right now, fully armoured ready to battle anyone who tries to venture our way, and she will do the same, night after night, for as long as needs be. Until we are wed.' She kissed him on the lips.

'We have an ally in Marared? That is good. Her name is Margaret in English, is it not?' Jarlath asked knowing the answer.

'Yes, but do not call her by any other name than Marared, if you wish to be heard.'

'A stubborn one then? She suits you well.' He lifted an arm as if to fend a blow.

Ainnir giggled. 'Yes, stubborn and lovely. I like her well

already.'

'And her name is Marguerite in the French language,' he said matter-of-factly. 'It does not surprise me that a woman with that name is our ally. We have nothing to fear then.'

He saw confusion in her eyes. 'A story from England, my love. One for another day. But so the nights are not full of sentry duty for your Marared, on the morrow I will seek the priest. We will be wed the moment all can be arranged. Does that please you?'

'Yes, it pleases me well.' Ainnir snuggled in tightly.

They lay with legs and arms entangled, words gone, beaten by the tiredness of body and mind.

The night sky began to transform to one shade removed from the deepest and darkest of blues. The croaks and clicks from the night animals ceased. It was that hushed moment before the first of the birds sang welcome to the new day.

'Jarlath,' whispered Ainnir with a faint muffle.

'Hmm,' was all the reply he gave.

'The sun begins to rise. It rises in the west.'

Jarlath opened one eye, slowly, groggily, and looked down to the tired face clinging to his body. Even in utter exhaustion, her arms gripped tightly, not willing to sever their touch. He placed a gentle kiss on her forehead, and followed her into sleep.

Author's Note

Pull of the Yew Tree is a work of fiction. Many of the characters, events and places are chronicled in the pages of history. Many are not. Thomas Fitzgerald was indeed the 7th Earl of Kildare, and the Geraldines wielded power from the fortified walls of Castle Maynooth. Hugh O'Byrne was the head of a Wicklow clan, yet the minimal information known of this man presented an opportunity to construct a family and design its dynamics with little restriction, along with his home, Castle Glendalough. Although this location was a monastic settlement, with the help of Hugh I repaired broken walls to create a magnificent home for the O'Byrnes. The Abbey of Achad-finglass was destroyed six hundred years before the period of this tale, yet I restored its walls to house the affable Abbess. The Yorkists certainly misaligned their three battle divisions during preparations at Gladmore Heath, and the Battle of Barnet is a well-studied piece of Britain's War of the Roses. But as to whether the Duke of Gloucester met an Irishman named Jarlath Fitzgerald – well let me simply state there are many instances where my pen wandered from the conventions of an historical writer, and blended fiction with fact to bring this tale to life. Where practicable, I remained close to fact. Where accounts differed, I made a choice. Where none existed, I created. Nonetheless, whether factual or otherwise, many of my characters will return in the next instalment of *The Chronicles of Crom Abu*.

COMING SOON

Melting of the Mettle

Book 2: The Chronicles of Crom Abu

by

Pauline Toohey

Rows of exquisite tapestries sheathed Maynooth's hall stealing much of the grey-blue stone. Images of epic battles, golden fields before harvest, an Italian winter's countryside, French terraced gardens, unicorns feasting on engorged bluebells, and to the end of the hall a recently hung piece depicting what appeared to be undernourished angels caught in thundering clouds. If his wife insisted on expanding their collection, Ireland's looms would weep with exhaustion.

Thomas Fitzgerald, the 7th Earl of Kildare, sat at the dais tapping fingers distractedly. He studied that last piece again. *Angels or slaves?* A closer inspection would be required, a task best left to an occasion when his home held less distraction.

The trestles and benches below spared no room. His

guests ate and chatted, gorged and purged, scoffed and ranted and little else. With their brocades and laces, the women granted a picture no less an event in thread than his walls. And to the men, Thomas gave over the discriminating attention usually afforded a game of chess. Men of power, men of affluence and men wanting both.

He wondered for a long moment which of the flesh and blood game pieces were sincere in their joy at this occasion and which were parasitic.

Knights, Pawns and Bishops, he branded the minions.

Knights for their loyalty, Pawns their expendability, and Bishops their cunning. Thomas favoured not the Bishops and their facades of righteousness, their trinkets of gold and tongues as sharp as a Flemish blade. Pretenders all of them.

His fingers no longer tapped. They thumped...

The story continues ...

For more details contact Indigo Dreams Publishing
www.indigodreams.co.uk